BARBARA CARTLAND

Three Complete Novels of
Marquises and Their Ladies

Ola and the Sea Wolf

Looking for Love

The Call of the Highlands

WINGS BOOKS
NEW YORK • AVENEL, NEW JERSEY

This 1995 edition is published by Wings Books,
distributed by Random House Value Publishing, Inc.,
40 Engelhard Avenue, Avenel, New Jersey 07001,
by arrangement with the author.

Random House
New York • Toronto • London • Sydney • Auckland

Printed and bound in the United States of America

Library of Congress Cataloging-in-Publication Data
Cartland, Barbara, 1902–
    Three complete novels of marquises and their ladies / Barbara
Cartland.
      p.   cm.
    Contents: Ola and the sea wolf — Looking for love — The call of
the highlands.
    ISBN 0-517-14678-9
    1. Man-woman relationships—Great Britain—Fiction.   2. Nobility
—Great Britain—Fiction.   3. Historical fiction, English.   4. Love
stories, English.   I. Title.
PR6005.A765A6   1995
823′.912—dc20
          95-21906
          CIP

8   7   6   5   4   3   2   1

CONTENTS

OLA AND THE SEA WOLF

Author's Note

The English exploring Europe in the Eighteenth Century travelled at considerable risk not only to their purses but to their lives, and it was not much better in the Nineteenth Century.

William Beckford, going to Venice, was warned: "Your route is sure to be very perilous . . . there lurk the most savage *banditti* in Europe."

The winding coast road to Italy at the foot of the Ligurian Alps was known to be beset by bandits, and the country roads in Germany were extremely dangerous.

Spain and Greece were even more perilous. In the Nineteenth Century the *Pallikares* were legendary mercenaries from the Albanian mountains. They were handsome and breathed fire and adventure, and the ladies of King Otto's Court found them very romantic. Travellers described them differently, if they lived to tell the tale!

CHAPTER ONE

---※---

1831

*I*t was very quiet in the bar-room of The Three Bells, which was unusual.

Being close to the Harbour at Dover, it was usually filled with seamen and those repairing and victualling the ships.

But the thick fog outside seemed to penetrate even into the low-beamed room, and only the crackling of the logs in the open fireplace seemed to relieve the gloom.

The Landlord of The Three Bells found it difficult not to keep watching the door and hoping it would open. Then his eyes would go to his only customer, who was sitting in front of the log fire with his long legs outstretched.

He had not moved for some time, when he reached out to pour another glass from the bottle which stood beside him.

This made the Landlord anxious, not that the gentleman might be overindulging but because the bottle from which he was drinking, being of the best French Cognac, was the only one in the Inn.

It had been brought across the Channel by a seaman from whom he had bought it cheaply, considering its worth, and it was of a quality that was seldom demanded by the clientele of The Three Bells.

He looked at the gentleman and wondered who he was.

There was no doubt that he was of some social standing, and he had an authoritative air about him which had made the Proprietor greet him effusively on his arrival.

He supposed, for the gentleman was uncommunicative, that he owned one of the yachts in the Harbour and that it had been rendered immobile along with all the other shipping since the fog had closed in.

The gentleman raised the glass to his lips and as he did so the outside door was pushed open and someone came into the room.

To the Proprietor's surprise it was a woman, or rather, as he saw at a glance, a lady.

She was wearing a cloak trimmed with expensive fur but there was a tear in the fabric, and her hands, which were holding a leather case, were trembling.

For a moment she just stood looking round her as if she was a little dazed. Then as the Proprietor found his voice, saying respectfully: "Good-evening, Ma'am!" she turned to look at him and he saw that her very large eyes were wide and frightened.

"There . . . has been . . . an accident," she said a little incoherently.

"An accident, Ma'am?"

"Outside . . . at least . . . a little way down the . . . road. I saw . . . your . . . lights."

"I'll send some'un to help, Ma'am," the Proprietor said, "an' if ye'll come an' sit down by the fire, my man'll report to ye when he's found out what's a-happening."

As he spoke he turned and walked to a door which opened onto the back of the Inn.

"Joe! Are ye there?"

"Aye, Guv'," a voice replied.

"Then nip outside an' see if you can give a hand. There's a lady here says as how there's been a accident."

"Oi'll do that."

The Proprietor came from behind the bar to follow the lady, who was moving slowly, almost as if she was afraid of falling, towards the fireplace.

He pulled out an arm-chair for her which was opposite the one occupied by the gentleman, and as she sat down he said:

"I'm sure, Ma'am, ye'd like a drink after what must have been a nasty experience."

"It is very . . . foggy."

"Yes, I knows, Ma'am, it's been like this all day. Now, what can I get ye? We've got just about everything ye might fancy."

"Would it be . . . possible to have a . . . cup of tea?"

The Proprietor hesitated.

He was thinking that the tea that his wife drank, which was coarse and strong, would hardly be to the liking of anyone so elegant and delicate as the lady appeared to be.

Then, without moving, the gentleman on the other side of the fireplace remarked:

"If you have been in an accident, you had best have a glass of brandy. What I have here is quite drinkable."

The lady looked at him and after a moment's hesitation replied:

"That is very . . . kind of you . . . Sir . . . but I would . . . prefer tea or coffee."

"In this sort of place I would not recommend either!" the gentleman replied in a contemptuous voice.

As if she felt he was being unnecessarily rude to the Proprietor, the lady said quickly:

"Perhaps a glass of . . . Madeira would be easier . . . but only a half a glass, if you please."

"I'll get it for ye immediate!" the Proprietor replied.

Pleased that the choice had been settled, he went behind the bar.

The lady was conscious that the gentleman opposite her was regarding her through half-closed eyes.

She thought he seemed a disagreeable type of person, and because she felt a little embarrassed she set the leather case she carried down on the floor at her feet and occupied herself in taking off her gloves.

The Proprietor returned with the Madeira in a small glass.

"This be a good quality, Ma'am," he said, "and I hope ye enjoys it."

"I am sure I shall," the lady replied, "and thank you very much."

She took the glass from him and said in a tone that was urgent:

"Can you tell me when there will be a ship . . . leaving for . . . France?"

"That's a question I can't answer, Ma'am," the Proprietor replied. "Nothing's moved out o' the Harbour all day. In fact, I were a-saying a short while ago that 'tis the worst fog I've known for twenty years or more!"

"There must be . . . one, perhaps very early . . . tomorrow morning?"

Now there was no doubt of the urgency in her tone.

The Proprietor shook his head.

"Depends on th' wind, Ma'am. If the wind gets up in th' night, then the *Britannia* should reach here from Calais an' make the return journey sometime in th' afternoon."

The lady gave a little cry of horror.

"Not until the afternoon? But surely there will be a ship leaving in the morning?"

"They be stuck t'other side of th' Channel," the Proprietor replied.

"B-but I must leave . . . I have to leave as . . . early as possible."

The Proprietor did not reply and she said almost frantically:

"Perhaps there would be a fishing-vessel that would take me? I believe they go out at dawn?"

"Not when th' weather's like this, Ma'am. An' anyway they fishes along th' shore."

The information he had given the lady obviously agitated her.

He could see an expression on her face that was almost one of desperation, and she was twisting her long fingers together almost as if they were like a problem which she had to solve.

"I'll tell ye what I'll do, Ma'am," the Proprietor said, as if in an effort to comfort her. "When Joe gets back t' tell ye about th' accident, I'll send him down to th' Quay to ask th' Harbour-Master if he can think of a way to help ye."

The lady's eyes seemed to brighten.

"Would you really do that? It is very kind of you. Please tell Joe I shall be pleased to reward him for his services."

"Thank ye, Ma'am. He should be back here soon. I wonder what's a-keeping him."

As he spoke, he walked away to open the outer door. As he did so, the fog seemed to swirl into the room like a grey cloud.

The door shut behind him and the lady sat back in her chair and shut her eyes.

She felt as if she must faint from the horror of it all. Then a voice at the other side of the fireplace said sharply:

"Drink your Madeira!"

It was too much of an effort to reply, and she felt a darkness like the fog creeping over her, and despite the fire she suddenly felt very cold.

Then somebody put a hand behind her head, there was a glass held to her lips, and almost despite herself she swallowed.

She felt a fiery liquid coursing down her throat and into her body, and almost instantly the darkness faded and it was easier to breathe.

"Another sip of brandy," the voice said sharply.

Although she wanted to protest, she obeyed because for the moment she was not capable of arguing.

The second sip was even more effective than the first, and she opened her eyes to find the gentleman bending over her.

Now that she could see him more clearly, she realised that he was in fact exceedingly handsome, except that there was what she could only describe as a "darkness"

9

about his eyes and a cynicism in the deeply etched lines on his face.

He would, she thought, have persuaded her to drink even more of the wine, but she put up her hands in protest.

"Please," she pleaded, "I am . . . all right now . . . and I could not . . . drink any . . . more."

As if he realised she was speaking the truth, the gentleman moved to stand with his back to the fire. He was, the lady noted, so tall that his head almost touched the heavy ships' beams that supported the ceiling.

He did not speak and after a moment she said in a nervous little voice:

"Thank you for . . . being . . . so kind. The . . . accident . . . upset me."

"Whoever was driving you must have been a fool to take his horses out in this weather."

"It was . . . my fault."

As she spoke, the outer door opened and the Proprietor came back into the room.

He looked towards the lady but he did not speak. Instead, he held the door open, and a moment later two men appeared, carrying between them a man who was obviously unconscious.

There was blood on his face from an open wound on his forehead and his clothes were covered in mud as if he had fallen violently onto the dirty roadway.

"Upstairs and put him in th' Guest-Room, Joe," the Proprietor was saying, "then see if ye can get hold of th' Doctor. Ye'll find him at Th' Crown and Anchor. He be always there at this time o' night."

"Right ye are, Guv'," Joe replied.

His voice had become almost inaudible as he and the other man with their burden disappeared through the door at the side of the bar which led to the other part of the Inn.

The Landlord shut the outer door and followed them, and they could hear his voice admonishing the men to be careful as they negotiated the stairs which led to the first floor.

At the first sight of the injured man the lady had sprung from her chair to stand staring at his prostrate body until he was out of sight.

Now she said almost as if she spoke to herself:

"There . . . must be a ship . . . there must!"

The gentleman, standing in front of the fire, turned to look at her and realised that she appeared to have forgotten his presence.

"Is it your husband that you are so anxious to run away from?" he enquired. "Or your Guardian?"

He spoke mockingly and he thought the latter was the more likely.

The man who had been injured was obviously in his forties, but he judged the woman beside him to be little more than a girl of eighteen.

She turned her head at the sound of his voice, and now that he could see her more clearly in the light from the fire, he realised that her pointed face was extremely attractive and the lashes that fringed her eyes were long and dark.

It was an arresting face, but there was no admiration in his eyes as he said, almost as if he jeered at her:

"Surely it must be one or the other!"

Before she answered him she sat down again in the chair. Then she said:

"He is . . . neither! He is a man who is . . . abducting me and I have to . . . escape from him!"

"Abducting you? Then surely it is quite easy. You can hire a post-chaise to take you back to wherever you have come from."

The lady shook her head.

"That is . . . impossible!"

"Then suppose you explain! I am not asking out of idle curiosity, but I might—although I am not committing myself—be able to help you."

The expression on the lady's face altered immediately.

"Oh . . . could you help me . . . could you really? Do you mean you could find me a ship . . . or perhaps . . ."

She hesitated a moment; then, as if she was impressed by the manner in which the gentleman was dressed, she finished her sentence by saying:

". . . You have . . . one of your . . . own?"

"I am asking the questions," the gentleman replied. "Why are you running away, and from whom?"

The lady drew in her breath before she answered:

"From my . . . Stepmother!"

The gentleman raised his eye-brows. It was an answer he had not expected. Then he said:

"Perhaps before we go any further we should introduce ourselves. I am the Marquis of Elvington . . ."

Before he could say any more, the lady gave a little cry and said:

"I have heard of you! You are famous, and of course you have a yacht. That is why you are here. Oh, please . . . please, take me to France! I have to get away . . . and quickly!"

"From the man upstairs who is abducting you?"

"Yes . . . I never imagined . . . I never dreamt for one . . . moment that he would behave . . ."

Her words seemed to fail and she made a kind of helpless gesture with her hands that was somehow pathetic.

"I am waiting for you to tell me your name," the Marquis said.

"It is . . . Ola Milford. My father was Lord Milford and we live near Canterbury."

"I seem to have heard the name," the Marquis said cautiously.

"Papa did not often go to London. He preferred being in the country and he was not well for two years before he . . . died."

"You say it is your Stepmother from whom you are running away?"

"Yes . . . I cannot . . . stay with her any . . . longer! It is . . . impossible!"

12

"Why?"

"She hates me! She makes my life an absolute misery! She is my Guardian but she will not give me any of the money that Papa left me. It is mine, but I do not have the . . . handling of it until I am . . . twenty-one or am . . . married."

"That should not be too difficult," the Marquis remarked cynically.

"You do not understand!" Ola Milford replied. "My Stepmother, who married Papa three years ago when he was so unhappy after Mama's death, is . . . jealous of me."

She said the word a little hesitatingly, as if she felt uncomfortable at telling the truth. Then she continued:

"She keeps saying she wishes to be rid of me . . . but she prevents me from going anywhere . . . and if a gentleman comes to the house she will not let me talk to him . . . I think actually she wants to get married again herself."

"Surely there are other relations with whom you could live?" the Marquis suggested.

"I have thought of that, but when I suggested it," Ola replied, "my Stepmother refused to contemplate such an idea because she thought I would take my money with me."

She gave a deep sigh.

"It is my money that is at the bottom of all the trouble, both with my Stepmother and with my . . . cousin . . . upstairs."

She looked upwards as she spoke and the Marquis saw her give a little shiver.

"Your *cousin?*" he questioned. "How does he come into it?"

"I was desperate . . . absolutely desperate at the way my Stepmother was . . . treating me. You cannot know what it is like to live with hatred . . . and incessant fault-finding."

"I can imagine," the Marquis replied. "Go on!"

"I decided there was only one thing I could do and that was to go back to the Convent near Paris where I

13

was educated, and become a Nun, or else, as my Step-mother has suggested so often, a cocotte!"

The Marquis was visibly startled.

"A what?" he questioned. "Do you know what you are saying?"

"I do not know . . . exactly what it entails," Ola admitted, "but if she has said it once she has said it a thousand times: 'With hair like yours, you should be a cocotte and that is about all you are suited for!' "

As if to demonstrate what she was saying, she pushed back the hood of her cloak which she had worn ever since she came into the Inn.

Suddenly it seemed as if the flames from the fire had transferred themselves to the chair opposite the Marquis.

He had seen many women with red hair but never one whose colour was so vivid or indeed so beautiful as that of the girl opposite him.

Because her hair had been covered by the fur-lined hood for some time, it was for the moment flat on her small head.

Then, after she had unfastened her cape at the neck and let it fall down behind her in the chair, she ran her fingers through her hair and it seemed almost to come alive.

It glinted as it caught the light and its vivid hue made her skin seem almost dazzlingly white.

'It is not surprising,' he thought, 'that any woman, especially a Stepmother, would wish to be rid of a potential rival whose appearance is not only unusual but spectacular!'

The Marquis felt that Ola was waiting for him to comment and he said drily:

"I cannot commend either suggestion to you. You must think of an alternative."

"I have thought and thought," Ola replied, "but what can I do if Step-Mama will give me no money and will not permit me to live anywhere except with her?"

"I see there is some difficulty about that."

"Of course there are difficulties!" she retorted. "I assure you I do not intend to do anything stupid; I just wish to stay with the Nuns and discuss my future with the Mother-Superior who has always been very kind to me."

She paused before she added:

"Perhaps I should take the veil. It would certainly prevent me from being bullied and persecuted as I have been these last years."

"I am surprised at your being so faint-hearted."

As if the Marquis had stung her, not only with his words but with what she thought was contempt in his voice, Ola sat upright.

"It is all very well for you to talk," she replied. "You have no idea what it is like to be slapped and pinched and even occasionally beaten when Step-Mama has a whip in her hand."

She drew in her breath before she went on:

"The servants are not allowed to obey my orders or to bring me food if she says I am not to have it. When visitors come to the house I am sent to my bedroom, and if they are friends of Mama's I am locked in so that I cannot talk to them."

She gave a deep sigh.

"I have tried to defy her, I have tried to assert myself for two years, and now the only way I can remain sane is to run away."

"So you have decided to go to France," the Marquis said. "Where does your escort come in?"

He saw Ola's lips tighten and she replied in a very different voice:

"He has behaved despicably, utterly and completely despicably! I did not believe that any man could be so treacherous!"

"What did he do?"

"He is my cousin, but I always thought that although he is old, he was kind. When he came to stay, because I thought Step-Mama fancied him, I left a note in his bedroom begging him to see me alone, and he agreed."

She glanced at the Marquis to see if he was listening, then she continued:

"He gave me a perceptible nod when he came down to dinner, and after I had been sent to bed early so that Step-Mama could talk to him, I managed to jump from the balcony to his room next door. It was a dangerous thing to do, but I managed it."

"Was he surprised?"

"I think he thought I would come to him, but he did not know I was locked in my room at night."

The Marquis looked surprised and Ola said scathingly:

"That was to prevent me from finding out what my Stepmother was up to when she had her friends to stay. She need not have worried. I was not interested. I only . . . hate her!"

"I expect with hair that colour you are overemotional anyway!" the Marquis said.

"Any more references to my hair either from you or from anybody else," Ola snapped, "and I shall either cut it all off or dye it!"

She sounded like a small tiger-cat spitting at him, and almost despite himself the Marquis laughed.

"I apologise, Miss Milford. Go on with what you were telling me."

"I told Giles . . . that is my cousin's name . . . of my predicament . . . and to my delight he told me that he would take me to Paris and leave me at the Convent where I wanted to go."

"And you believed him?"

"I made him swear on everything he held sacred that he would not betray me to Step-Mama. After that he was really obliging about the arrangements."

"So what happened?" the Marquis asked.

"He left yesterday, but instead of going to London, as he told Step-Mama he intended to do, he stayed near our house at a Posting-Inn."

Ola gave a little sigh.

"I had to trust him. There was nobody else who I felt would make an effort to help me."

"What happened?"

"I crept out of the house soon after dawn, and I bribed one of the gardeners, who had always been attached to Papa, to come into the house before the rest of the staff had risen and to collect the trunk I had packed and put ready in my bedroom!"

There was a brief smile on her lips as she said:

"It was easier than I expected, because when I went downstairs to let him in, there was nobody about as I had been half-afraid there might be."

"No night-watchmen, no night-footmen in the Hall?" the Marquis enquired.

"They were all at the other end of the house."

"So you ran away with your luggage," the Marquis said. "What woman would not think of her appearance, even in the most desperate situation?"

"I have already told you," Ola replied, "that I had no money. It would be very silly to spend on clothes what I could obtain by selling my mother's jewellery."

"You have some jewels?"

"I suppose it was rather indiscreet of me to mention them, when I intend to travel alone," Ola answered, "but they are all I have between me and starvation!"

"I promise you I will not steal them!"

"I know that," Olga said scornfully. "But I was foolish enough to trust Giles, and now I will never trust a man again . . . never . . . never . . . not even you!"

The Marquis found himself smiling at the anger in her voice. Her eyes, which he now saw in the light from the fire, were green and seemed to have a glint of steel in them.

"I am interested," he said aloud, "to hear what your cousin Giles did that was so reprehensible."

"He helped me to run away. Then halfway to Dover he . . . informed me that he . . . intended to . . . marry me!"

The Marquis laughed.

"That was something you might have anticipated as you are wealthy."

"But Giles is old! He has turned forty, and as he has always been a bachelor, how could I have . . . imagined he would want to . . . marry me?"

She thought that the Marquis was once again going to refer to her money, and she went on:

"Giles said to me: 'I shall be delighted, when we are married, to administer your fortune, but as I find you unexpectedly attractive, Ola, I shall also enjoy being your husband.' "

"What was your reply to that?" the Marquis asked.

"I told him I would rather die than marry him, and I thought even to suggest such an idea showed that he was a treacherous swine, a Judas whom I should never have trusted in the first place."

"Strong words!" the Marquis said, laughing.

"You may think it funny," Ola cried, "but I knew at that moment I had not only to escape from my Step-mother but . . . also from . . . Giles!"

She drew in her breath before she said:

"There was something about him which . . . fright-ened me . . . it was not only because he was determined to have my fortune . . . it was the way he looked at me when we stopped for luncheon."

She glanced across the hearth-rug at the Marquis, then continued:

"I expect you think that if I had been clever I would have escaped then, but it was only a small Posting-Inn and there were no other visitors having luncheon except ourselves. If I had tried to run away, Giles could easily have caught me, and it would be difficult to run carrying my jewel-case."

As she spoke she glanced down to where it stood beside her chair.

"I am not criticising," the Marquis said mildly.

"I had originally intended that when I reached here I would take the ordinary cross-Channel ship to France,"

Ola went on. "But to escape him I must now hire a vessel of some sort."

"Why did he not marry you in England?"

"He had thought of that," Ola answered, "but he was afraid there might be difficulties as he had not my Guardian's permission. He told me he intended to say he was my Guardian, and he thought if he could pay them enough, the French would be more accommodating about performing the marriage-ceremony than an English Parson was likely to be."

"Your cousin had certainly thought things out carefully!" the Marquis remarked.

"Only to his own advantage, and I hate him! It is a pity the accident did not . . . kill him!"

As Ola spoke, the door of the Inn opened and Joe appeared.

"Oi'm sorry, Lady, but Oi finds th' Doctor at Th' Crown and Anchor an' he ain't in no state t' come 'ere tonight. Oi've left a message wi' his mates to tell 'im to be here first thing in th' morn' when he be sobered up."

"Thank you, Joe," Ola replied. "I am very grateful to you."

As she spoke she realised that Joe was waiting for the tip he had been told she had promised him.

She quickly drew a small purse from the inside pocket of her cape, which was still lying behind her on the chair.

Before she could open it, however, the Marquis flicked a gold coin from his side of the fireplace towards Joe, who caught it deftly.

"Thank ye, Sir!" he said with a grin. "O'll go upstairs now an' see 'ow th' patient be. The Guv'nor said as 'ow he'd stay with him 'til Oi comes back with th' Doctor."

He disappeared and Ola looked at the Marquis.

"Can we go now . . . at once?" she asked.

"I have not yet said that I will take you with me."

19

"But you will . . . please . . . say you will! You can leave me at Calais and I will find my own way from there to Paris."

"Alone?"

"There is nobody else to travel with me, unless . . . Giles recovers."

The mere idea made her look up at the ceiling as if she thought to hear the sound of his voice.

"He must not do that . . . he is determined . . . absolutely determined . . . to m-marry me!"

"You could of course tell your story to the Magistrates and ask them to return you to your Stepmother."

"How can you suggest such a thing when I have told you she hates me?" Ola asked. "No . . . I am going to Paris even if I have to buy a boat and row myself across the Channel!"

She gave an exasperated little sigh and added:

"Oh, why does England have to be an island?"

The Marquis smiled.

"It is something that stood us in good stead when Napoleon was trying to invade us!"

"That was a long time ago, and if there was not the sea between us and France, I could ride to Paris or drive there in a *diligence,* although I believe they are very uncomfortable. I saw them often enough when I was at the Convent."

"I cannot imagine either mode of travel would be particularly enjoyable," the Marquis remarked drily.

"I am not out to enjoy myself," Ola retorted. "You seem not to understand that I am trying to escape from a life of misery, and you must be very insensitive not to understand how much I have suffered."

"I am, as it happens, concerned with my own suffering at the moment," the Marquis commented.

"What can that be? Have you lost a fortune at the gaming-tables? Or been crossed in love? That is not compatible with your reputation, My Lord Marquis!"

She spoke sarcastically, and was surprised by the expression of anger which contorted the Marquis's face.

"You will keep a civil tongue in your head," he said sharply, "or I will leave you here to cope with your problems alone, which in fact I am certain would be the sensible thing for me to do!"

Ola clasped her hands together.

"I am sorry . . . please forgive me . . . it was, I know, very rude . . . and I should not have spoken as I did. Please . . . please . . . help me! If you refuse to do so . . . I think I shall throw myself into the Harbour. I doubt if anyone would notice, and I should just be discovered floating out to sea in the morning!"

She spoke dramatically, and although he was angry the Marquis was forced to laugh. Then he said:

"I accept your apology, but in the future, as you are at my mercy, I suggest you curb your tongue and your imagination, or I shall certainly abandon you to your fate!"

"Please . . . do not do that!"

"If I were wise that is exactly what I should do. It is no affair of mine whom you marry or do not marry, and I have an uneasy suspicion that if I were behaving with a vestige of common sense I should send you back to your Stepmother!"

"But you will not do so," Ola said softly.

"I hate to think what is the alternative."

"I can tell you that," Ola said in a small voice. "It is that you take me to Calais in your . . . yacht. Surely this fog will lift soon?"

As she spoke she rose as if to go towards the door and look out.

At that moment there were heavy footsteps coming down the stairs and a moment later the Proprietor came into the room.

"Oi don't know if ye wish to stay here the night, Ma'am," he said to Ola, "but Oi 'as a small bedroom empty an' could accommodate ye, 'though 'tis not so comfortable as the one th' poor gentleman be in."

21

Ola looked towards the Marquis.

"I am taking this lady with me," he said, and saw, as he spoke, the expression of delight that transformed Ola's face.

On the other hand, the Proprietor was obviously disappointed.

"What about th' gentleman upstairs?"

"He can look after himself when he gets better," the Marquis replied. "But I understand this lady had a trunk with her in the carriage in which she was travelling. What has happened to it?"

"The servant, who seemed unharmed," the Proprietor replied, "is a-taking th' horses to a stable at th' top of th' road."

"Then send your man Joe to collect the trunk," the Marquis ordered, "and he can follow this lady and me to where my yacht is tied up at the Quay. It is not more than fifty yards from here."

"I'll get him down, Sir," the Proprietor answered.

He went to the bottom of the stairs and started shouting for Joe.

Ola turned towards the Marquis.

"How can I thank you?" she asked. "Thank you . . . thank you! I think you must be an angel sent to save me."

"I think if the truth were told," the Marquis replied, "I am slightly touched in the head, or else the brandy I have imbibed was stronger than I anticipated."

"No, you are a Good Samaritan," Ola said, "for, as I told you, I really have fallen amongst . . . thieves!"

Again as she thought of her cousin upstairs her eyes went towards the ceiling, and the Marquis, seeing the lines of her long neck and the movement of light in her hair, told himself he really was behaving like a fool.

He had sworn when he left home that never again would he have anything to do with women except those who simply sold their favours to the highest bidder.

Never again—and this was a vow he intended to keep for all time—would he be fool enough to imagine himself in love.

Even to think of Sarah made him want to clench his hands and hit something—anything, anybody—to relieve the fury of his feelings.

And yet, despite a lesson which should have made any man hesitate before even looking at or speaking to a woman who called herself a lady, he had quite inadvertently become involved with this girl.

It was simply because it was impossible for him not to feel sorry for her in the predicament in which she found herself.

On the other hand, how did he know whether what she had told him was the truth? It might be a lie like the lies Sarah had told him.

He felt a sudden impulse to change his mind and tell her that after all she must find her own way out of her difficulties.

Or, easier still, he had only to say he was going outside to see what the weather was like, and then disappear in the fog and never come back.

That would be prudent and sensible, perhaps, but it would also, he thought, be a caddish trick such as he had never lowered himself to play in the past.

But nobleness, chivalry, or sheer decency, call it what you will, had only succeeded in making him the cynic he knew he now was and would be for the rest of his life.

"Never trust a woman—they always betray you!"

It sounded like a quotation he must have heard somewhere, unless it was a conviction that came from the depths of his heart.

The mere thought of Sarah made him feel as if his body were on fire, while his anger swept over him and there was a red film in front of his eyes.

He wanted to curse her aloud, and he wished now that he had given himself the satisfaction of telling her plainly what he thought of her before he had walked away, determined never to see her again.

'Dammit all—I am running away!' he had thought as he drove towards Dover.

But something sensitive and vulnerable within him shrank from the scene which would have followed had he told Sarah what he had discovered and seen with his own eyes.

She could have lied, she would have pleaded with him, and if she had finally suffered defeat and found that she could not again cajole him into wishing to marry her, she might have laughed at him!

That was something he knew he could not endure simply because he deserved it.

For the first time in his life, in his very successful career as both a sportsman and a lover, the Marquis, the most acclaimed and envied man in Society, had been "hoist by his own petard."

Even now, a whole day after it had happened, he found it hard to believe it was true.

He had become used to being a conqueror; he had grown used to knowing, although he told himself he was not conceited about it, that any woman he fancied was only too ready to fall into his arms.

Most of all, there was no woman in the length and breadth of the Kingdom who would not jump at the chance of becoming his wife.

As soon as he looked at them he would see the excitement in their eyes and it told him exactly what they longed for and undoubtedly prayed for.

"We will be married, my darling," he could hear himself say to Sarah, "as soon as you are out of mourning. I cannot wait a day longer than I have to."

"Oh, Boyden!" Sarah had cried. "I love you, and I swear I will make you happy, just as you have already made me the happiest woman in the world!"

Her voice was very soft and seductive as she said the last words, and as her blue eyes looked up into his, the Marquis had believed that he had found the pearl beyond price which he had always sought in the woman he would marry.

Then yesterday evening everything he had planned, his whole future, had fallen in pieces about his ears.

CHAPTER TWO

The Marquis awoke when he heard the anchor being raised and a few minutes later the yacht began to heel over as the sails were set and caught the wind.

He was aware that his head ached and his mouth felt dry, and he knew that last night, contrary to his usual habit, he had drunk too much.

First, the brandy had been surprisingly good at the Inn on the Quay, and secondly, when he had returned to the yacht he felt so depressed and incensed with life in general that he had sent the steward for a decanter of his best claret, which he had drunk until the early hours of the morning.

Then, when he thought of last night, he remembered that he had brought a woman aboard with him, and he asked himself if he had gone insane.

How, after all that happened, after an experience that should have been the lesson of a lifetime, could he have been mad enough to involve himself with yet another woman and one who, if he was not careful, would undoubtedly be an encumbrance?

Then, because it was impossible for his thoughts to linger for long on anything except the perfidy of Sarah, he recalled the reason why he was in Dover, why he had drunk too much, and why in the cold and unpleasantness of March he should be contemplating a voyage at sea.

Thinking back, he could remember all too clearly the moment when he had met Sarah.

He had been so occupied in London that he had not been down to Elvin last winter as much as usual.

He had been involved in many discussions and committees concerning the projected Reform Bill and in speaking frequently on other matters in the Chamber of the House of Lords.

He had also found that the new King, William IV, required his presence constantly at Buckingham Palace.

While it was flattering to be in such demand, it meant that he seldom had any free time for his own amusement.

It had therefore been almost with a feeling of playing truant that he had slipped away from London to Elvin, to enjoy a few days' hunting before the season ended.

He was well in the front of the field and enjoying one of the best runs he had experienced for a long time when, crossing some rough ground, his horse picked up a stone.

As he was riding one of his very best hunters, the Marquis dismounted, and, letting the hunt go on without him, he realised that he must either try to dislodge the stone himself or find someone to do it for him.

He had, as it happened, nothing he could use as a probe except for his fingers, and when he lifted his horse's hoof he saw that the stone was embedded half under the shoe and if it was not extracted carefully the shoe would come away with it.

He looked round and saw that he was on his own Estate, which was a very extensive one, and that only a short distance from where he was standing was the Manor.

He remembered his Agent telling him a year ago that it had been let to Sir Robert Chesney.

Ordinarily the Marquis would have called on a new tenant, but he had in fact forgotten Sir Robert's arrival, and when he had come to Elvin it had been with large parties and he had no time to pay courtesy calls on local people.

"I shall have to make my apologies now," he told himself as, leading his horse by the bridle, he walked towards the Manor.

He went immediately to the stables and found an elderly groom to whom he explained his predicament.

The groom recognised him and, touching his forelock, said:

"Now don' ee worry, M'Lord. Oi'll soon get th' stone away, then ye can rejoin th' hunt. Oi can 'ear 'em now, drawing through Chandle's Wood, but Oi doubts they'll find anything there!"

"I imagine that is where the fox has gone to earth," the Marquis replied.

"If 'e 'as, then they'll 'ave to dig deep!" the groom said with a smile.

He took the horse as he spoke and led it towards an empty stall.

"While you are busy," the Marquis said, "I will pay my respects to Sir Robert. He is at home?"

The groom's voice altered as he answered:

"Sir Robert died last week, M'Lord!"

"I had no idea!" the Marquis exclaimed.

He thought as he spoke that it was extremely remiss of his Agent not to have informed him of the fact.

It would have been polite to send Sir Robert's widow a letter of condolence or at least to send a wreath to the Funeral.

"Oi be sure 'er Ladyship'd wish to make yer acquaintance, M'Lord," the groom said.

The Marquis walked towards the front door, feeling uncomfortably that he owed Lady Chesney an apology.

An elderly man-servant led him across the small Hall and into what the Marquis remembered was a charming Drawing-Room which overlooked the rose-garden at the back of the house.

If he thought the room was charming, then so was its occupant.

She was certainly astonished to see him when he was announced, but he liked the manner in which her voice when she greeted him was calm and composed, and he certainly liked her appearance.

In a black gown which accentuated her clear skin, the gold of her hair, and the blue of her eyes, Lady Chesney was certainly very alluring.

She insisted on sending for some refreshment, and as the Marquis seated himself opposite her he said:

"I have only just learnt from your groom of your husband's death. I can only say how sorry I am not to have sent you my condolences and my sympathy, but now they are both yours."

"That is very kind of you, My Lord," Lady Chesney answered. "My husband had been ill for some years, and the reason why we came here was that the Physicians thought the fresh air and the quiet of the country might do him good."

She paused before she said with a little sob:

"Unfortunately they were . . . mistaken."

That was the beginning of an acquaintance that progressed rapidly into friendship, and from friendship into love.

The Marquis, riding away from the Manor, found it impossible to forget the blue eyes which had looked at him pathetically, curiously, and then undoubtedly admiringly.

He had returned the next day, feeling that since he had not sent a wreath to the Funeral, he could at least provide the widow with exotic fruit and flowers from his greenhouses.

She had been suitably grateful and of course had said how interested she would be to see Elvin, as she had always heard so much about it.

The Marquis was only too willing to be her guide, and her delight at the treasures that had been accumulated by his ancestors and at the innovations he himself had made in the house was very gratifying.

It was six months before the Marquis became what he had wished to be within a week or so after making her acquaintance—Sarah Chesney's lover.

But he had found that to accomplish this required all his powers of persuasion and ingenuity.

This was not because she did not love him.

She had told him that she had loved him at first sight and that he had captured her heart to the point where it was no longer hers but his.

However, she was anxious that there should be no breath of scandal, which, she had said, might so easily spoil the love they had for each other.

She had explained it in a way which the Marquis thought was good common sense.

"You are so fascinating and so handsome, My Lord," she had said, "that naturally every woman you meet falls in love with you. The world being a censorious place, no-one would believe that any one female could resist your magical charm."

"You flatter me!" the Marquis had said with a smile, but he had enjoyed it all the same.

"You will understand," Sarah had gone on in a soft, caressing voice, "that I could not be disloyal to my dear Robert's memory by getting myself talked about in a scandalous manner so soon after his death. While you can go back to London and forget me, I have to live in this small world in which people talk because they have nothing better to do."

"Do you really think I could forget you?" the Marquis asked.

"I hope you will not do so," Sarah replied. "But you are so important and of such consequence in the Social World, while I am just a little nobody who worships you because you have brought me such unbelievable happiness."

"You know that happiness is what I want to bring you," the Marquis said, "and I want to show you how much I love you. But as you say, it is impossible here at the Manor, where your servants might be suspicious of what we were doing."

"They are so kind to me," Sarah said. "They look after me and cosset me. But they would be deeply shocked if they thought you were anything more than a kind friend who wished to comfort me in my loneliness."

The situation had seemed hopeless until Sarah was asked to stay with some friends on the other side of the County with whom the Marquis had a slight acquaintance.

It had not been easy, but because he was determined he had somehow managed to get himself invited at the same time.

They pretended that they had never met before. Fortunately there were quite a number of other people staying in the house and their bedrooms were not far apart.

The Marquis, making love to a woman he had pursued for six months, found it a delight that made him feel as if he had won a victory after what had been a strenuous battle.

He believed too that he was in love with Sarah as he had never been in love before.

The only difficulty was how they could contrive to continue their love-making, which the Marquis was certain had been as unforgettable an experience for her as it had been for him.

There had been another month of frustration during which, despite his pleadings, Sarah had refused to agree to what he asked of her and had made him feel he was a brute to suggest anything that might damage her reputation.

"If I cannot come to your house and you will not come to mine," he asked, "what are we to do about each other?"

Her eyes filled with tears as they looked into his and she said in a broken little voice:

"Oh, Boyden, I love you so desperately! But . . ."

'There is always that "but"!' the Marquis later thought irritably.

Then it suddenly struck him that the answer to their problem was quite obvious. He would marry Sarah!

He had always known that sooner or later he must marry and produce an heir, but it had not seemed a pressing necessity until he was over thirty, which would not be for another year.

What was more, he enjoyed being a bachelor and had seen far too many of his friends unhappily married to women who had seemed desirable enough until they actually bore their husbands' names and sat at the top of their tables.

"Marriage is hell, Elvington!" Lord Wickham had said to him after being married for only three months.

"But Charlotte is so beautiful," the Marquis had replied.

"That is what I thought, until I saw her in the mornings when she is petulant, and in the evenings when she is tired. And I will tell you another thing," Lord Wickham had gone on, "it is not the looks of a wife that count, it is her intelligence."

His lips tightened for a moment before he had continued:

"Can you imagine what it is like to know exactly what a woman is going to say before she says it, for twenty-four hours of the day?"

The Marquis had not replied, and his friend had said bitterly:

"You are the only one of our crowd who has had the sense to remain a bachelor. George's wife takes laudanum, and Charles has married a harridan!"

"I have certainly no wish to be leg-shackled!" the Marquis said firmly not only to his friends but to himself.

And yet, he thought, Sarah was different, so different and so ideal in every way, so exactly what a man wanted in his wife, that he dared not risk losing her.

He knew even then that he hesitated before committing himself.

In fact, he was now considering Sarah from a somewhat different angle. She was not only a very desirable woman who set his pulses racing and his heart throbbing when she was near, she was someone he could trust.

She would also, he thought, be able to take his mother's place as hostess in the houses he owned and, more important still, be as acceptable at Buckingham Palace as he was himself.

He knew this involved something very different from what it would have meant under the last Monarch.

George IV up until his dying day had liked the men who surrounded him to be raffish and witty and, because it was what he himself had always been, promiscuous as regards women.

What was more, the ladies who were admitted to the Royal Circle were expected to be attractive to the opposite sex and not to be too particular or difficult as regards their morals.

But Buckingham Palace today had a very different atmosphere. The Marquis often thought it was not the same place now that the staid and prudish little Queen Adelaide was on the throne.

There was no doubt that she and her much older husband were extremely happy together, but while the King had enjoyed a riotous youth and had fathered ten illegitimate children by the actress Mrs. Jordan, he had now become so respectable that, as one Statesman had remarked to the Marquis:

"I always feel as I enter the Palace that I am attending a Prayer-Meeting!"

The Marquis had laughed, but he knew that if he wished to keep his place at Court, his life must be circumspect in every way.

If there was the slightest breath of scandal about his wife, Queen Adelaide would make sure that she was excluded from the Royal Circle.

Watching Sarah critically, the Marquis became more convinced every time he saw her that she would make exactly the wife he required.

Although he had to control his desires, which he found both irritating and frustrating, he still admired her for sticking to her principles and making him understand mentally, if not physically, that they were really necessary.

Only when finally he had proposed marriage, and she had said in a rapturous manner that her dreams and her ambitions had been fulfilled, did she relent a little and, as he put it to himself, "lower the drawbridge."

"I love you! How can I wait months before you can be mine?" the Marquis had asked.

"I want you too," Sarah had whispered, "and so, my darling, I have an idea!"

"What is it?"

"My lady's-maid, who I always feel watches me like a hawk, has left today to visit her mother, who is ill. That means there is only an old couple in the house, both of whom are deaf."

"You mean . . . ?" the Marquis had asked, his eyes brightening as he realised what she was saying.

"If you come to me tonight, dearest, nobody will know that you are here and I can be in your arms as I long to be."

The Marquis had kissed her until they were both breathless, then Sarah had said:

"Come to me across the garden. You can leave your horse tied to a tree in the shrubbery and I will open the French window after the servants have gone to bed."

"My sweet! My darling!" the Marquis had cried.

When later he had said a formal farewell in front of the old Butler, their eyes met and he knew that they were both counting the hours until they could be together again.

They had spent two nights of bliss. Then Sarah told him that her maid had returned, and because the Marquis could not bear to toss restlessly in his bed at Elvin, when he longed to be with Sarah in hers, he had gone back to London.

There was a great deal for him to do, and, because he was genuinely interested in politics, the difficulties of the Reform Bill fully occupied his mind during the days.

But at night he found it impossible to sleep, and like a boy at School he crossed the days off on his calendar until Sarah's official mourning would be over and they could be married.

She would be free on March third but they agreed that it would be politic to wait another month. To the Marquis the thought was like a light glowing in the darkness.

He had already bought Sarah an engagement-ring and several expensive jewels to go with it.

They were locked in a drawer of his desk, waiting for the moment when he could give them to her and the world could be told that she was to be his wife.

Then his longing to see her again made him know that he must go back to Elvin. Even if he could not make love to her as he wanted to do, he could at least hold her in his arms, kiss her, and hear her pay him compliments in her soft, musical voice.

He was wondering when he should go to her, when he received a letter and at the mere sight of her hand-writing he felt his heart turn over.

"I have never been so much in love as I am now!" he told himself.

He opened the letter and read:

Hannah, my maid, has been told today that her mother has died. She is therefore leaving immediately for the Funeral, and you know, dearest, wonderful Boyden, this means we can be together as we both long to be.

I know that you will be counting the hours, as I am, until we can touch the wings of ecstasy!

Come to me in the usual way across the garden tomorrow, at half-after-nine-o'clock. The servants go to bed early, and I shall be waiting for you . . . waiting . . . waiting until I feel your arms round me.

I love you!
Sarah

The Marquis read and reread the note and told himself that no woman could be so loving, so adorable, and so exactly right in every way to be the Marchioness of Elvington.

"I am the most fortunate man in the world," he said aloud, "and I shall see her tomorrow!"

Then he read the letter again.

She had said that her maid Hannah was leaving today. In which case, why wait until tomorrow and miss being together tonight?

He looked at the clock.

He had risen early and the letter had been waiting on his breakfast-table.

He calculated that if he left London within the next hour he could be at Elvington about eight o'clock.

After he had dined he would ride across the Park and through the fields as he had done before and be at the Manor by about ten o'clock.

The window would not be open for him but the servants would be in bed, and if Sarah was in her bedroom he could easily attract her attention from the garden without disturbing anybody else in the house.

"I will surprise her!" he told himself with a smile, thinking of her delight and what an excitement his arrival would be to both of them because it was unexpected.

He gave the order for his Phaeton and his fastest team of four horses to be brought round immediately, and soon he was on his way to Elvin.

His arrival was no surprise to his servants because his staff had instructions always to be ready to receive him and his Chef prepared to produce a superb menu without having any previous notice of his arrival.

The Marquis, having bathed and changed, ate an excellent dinner, waited on by his Butler and three footmen. At precisely nine-forty-five he went to the front door to find one of his fastest horses waiting outside.

Because he often rode at night after dinner, he thought his staff would not have the least suspicion as to where he was going. He would therefore have been extremely annoyed if he had known that everyone in the house, from the Butler to the youngest knife-boy, was aware of his infatuation for the widow who lived at the Manor.

"All I can say," one of the footmen said to another as he rode away, "is that she's been lucky to catch His Lordship.

There's not a gentleman to equal him in the sportin'
world."

"You're right there," his companion replied, "and I
suppose she'll suit him all right. But I'd never fancy a
widow meself."

"Why not?" his friend enquired.

"I likes to be first!" was the answer. "First past the
winning-post and first in bed!"

There was laughter at this, and it was fortunate that
the Marquis, crossing the Park in front of the house, was
unaware that his staff did not suppose he was just enjoying the evening air.

Once out of sight of the house, he galloped because
he was in a hurry to reach Sarah.

He thought romantically that the noise of the horse's
hoofs repeated over and over again the three words that
were uppermost in his mind:

"I love you! I love you! I love you!"

At the end of the Park he passed through a wood,
then over several fields, until at last he could see ahead
of him the shrubbery which bordered the garden of the
Manor.

He knew exactly where he could tether his horse, and
having done so he walked surely and without hesitating
along the twisting path which skirted the rhododendrons and ended at the edge of the rose-garden, in the
centre of which was a sun-dial.

It was then that he was aware that the lights were on
not only in Sarah's bedroom but also in the Drawing-
Room.

The Marquis stood still.

It suddenly occurred to him that perhaps Sarah was
entertaining, which would explain why she had asked
him to come tomorrow instead of tonight.

Then he told himself that she would never have
expected anyway that he would have received her letter
so early and have left London immediately.

She knew how meticulously he always planned his
various engagements, and in fact he had done some-

thing unprecedented for him when this morning he had sent messages to no fewer than four people to offer his regrets that he could not keep the appointments he had made with them.

"When I tell her, she will appreciate how much I love her," the Marquis told himself.

But now, looking across the darkness of the garden towards the light, he was uncertain.

The last thing he should do was to walk in unexpectedly if Sarah was entertaining their neighbours.

Then it struck him that despite the fact that there were lights in the Drawing-Room, everything seemed very quiet.

Although he was listening intently, he could hear no chatter of voices or laughter as might have been expected.

"Perhaps she has not yet gone to bed," he told himself. "She may be sitting reading or sewing in the Drawing-Room and if I knock on the window she will open it."

He took a step forward from the shelter of the rhododendrons and as he did so he saw the long French window open, and someone was standing against the light.

'She is waiting for me,' he thought.

They were so attuned to each other, he told himself, that she had known perceptively, almost clairvoyantly, that he was coming and had opened the window to welcome him in.

There was a rapturous smile on the Marquis's lips as he took another step forward. Then suddenly he saw that Sarah was not alone.

A man had appeared beside her and hastily the Marquis retreated into the shadows.

Now he saw Sarah turn her face up towards the man beside her, and the next moment she was in his arms and he was kissing her!

At first the Marquis could hardly believe that what he was seeing was not a figment of his imagination or a part of some terrible nightmare.

Then the moon came out from behind the clouds and he could see more clearly than he had before.

Sarah was wearing her blue negligé. He knew it well, and when he had last seen it she had been letting him out of the window, as she was doing now with the man she was kissing.

What was more, the Marquis recognised who he was.

He was the handsome younger son of a Peer whom the Marquis had found, since he had inherited Elvin, a considerable nuisance.

Because the boundaries of their two Estates marched together, Lord Harrop was always sending complaints of one sort or another to the Marquis.

He knew that the reason for most of them was that Lord Harrop was far from wealthy and was determined to extort from his rich neighbour every concession and help for his own Estate that was possible.

The Marquis was well aware that Lord Harrop's sons—and there were four of them—were jealous of the horses he rode at the local Point-to-Points and at the Steeple-Chases which he invariably won.

It was not his fault, but it flashed through his mind now that Anthony had his revenge in taking from him the only woman he had ever wished to marry.

Then as he watched Anthony kiss Sarah before he stepped out through the window and onto the terrace outside, the Marquis felt the blood rush to his head.

He wanted to fight Anthony, to knock him down and even to kill him.

Then, not only years of self-control kept him from moving, but a pride which told him that he had been made a fool of not only by Sarah but by a man younger than himself whom he had always thought too insignificant even to consider as a rival.

As the Marquis battled with himself, he realised that Anthony was walking towards him and in the space of a few seconds they would meet face to face.

He clenched his fists together.

Then as he was not quite certain what he would do, he heard Sarah's voice, soft and sweet as it had so often been to him, call out:

"Anthony, darling, I have something more to say to you."

His rival turned back and it was then that the Marquis knew he must escape.

He retreated, moving swiftly back the way he had come, and found his horse.

It was only as he mounted that he saw Anthony's horse about fifty yards farther along the side of the shrubbery.

In the darkness before the moon came out he had not noticed it, but now he could see it quite clearly.

The Marquis wasted no time, he just rode away, hoping that Anthony would not see him go.

It was only when he reached home and walked upstairs to his own room that he felt numb with shock, and there was at the same time a growing anger deep within him that seemed to increase as every minute passed.

He allowed his valet to help him undress but he did not speak, and only when he was alone did the Marquis ask himself what he should do.

He knew he could not stay in England to face Sarah and the explanations that would have to be made and the scene that would follow.

He knew too, because he was deeply humiliated by what he had seen, that it would take him some time to control himself to the point where he could appear indifferent.

At the moment he was angry and hurt, wounded and jealous, murderous and yet at the same time weak, with a kind of misery that he knew would increase because he had lost something which he had thought was more valuable than anything he had ever possessed before.

He asked himself a thousand times how he could have been so foolish as to be deceived like any greenhorn by what he knew now was a scheming woman.

He had no doubt that Sarah had intended to marry him from the first moment they had met.

He could see all too clearly that by playing "hard to get" she had excited and enticed him into offering her exactly what she wanted, which was marriage.

The Marquis admitted frankly that usually his love-affairs did not last very long.

Once a woman had surrendered herself, he found that the repetition of their love-making soon became tedious and he began to wonder what it would be like to pursue another beauty and whether she would be more original or more captivating than the one he was with now.

Sarah had been too clever to allow him to feel like that, and had driven him crazy by bestowing her favours after a long wooing and then withholding them again.

The Marquis gritted his teeth when he thought of how he had fallen into the trap that women have set for men ever since the days of Adam and Eve.

Each move had been traditional, almost like a game of chess, but he had not had the intelligence to see it until now.

Then he told himself in the darkness of the night that he could not face Sarah because all he could really accuse her of was being more astute than he was.

'I have to get away,' he thought, and remembered that his yacht was waiting ready for him at Dover.

It was three months since he had last used it, and then only for a short journey across the Channel with a friend who wished to fight a duel without anyone in England being aware of it.

He knew that on his orders the yacht was always ready to put to sea at a moment's notice.

He had risen before dawn and left Elvin when the stars' were still shining in the sky.

The Marquis could hear the slap of the sea against the bow of the yacht as they were under way, and as the timbers creaked and there was the rasp in the rigging, he felt the sails fill and knew there was a strong wind blowing.

"At least there will be nothing to hold us up," he told himself.

He had given his Captain instructions the night before, and it should take them less than five hours to reach Calais, where he would deposit his passenger. After that, he would be free to sail anywhere in the world that took his fancy.

He wondered now if Ola would manage on the way to Paris, then told himself that it was none of his business.

It must have been the brandy last night that had made him feel he ought to help her out of what must have been for her a frightening situation—that is, if he was to believe what she had told him.

There was no doubt that the man who had been involved in the accident through driving his horses in a pea-soup fog was elderly, and the girl with her flaming red hair was very young.

But perhaps she was deceitful and a liar, the Marquis thought scornfully, as all women were—damn them!

"When I return to England there will be no more 'Sarahs' in my life," he said aloud, "and no more games of pretence."

He could almost hear himself saying the loving words to Sarah which now made him blush with embarrassment.

Although he had thought she genuinely meant the sentimental promises which lovers make to each other, all the time she had been laughing at him.

Doubtless too she held him up to ridicule with the man she really loved, penniless Anthony, who had been her lover those nights when, alone at Elvin, he had felt frustrated and solitary because Sarah was worrying about her "reputation."

"Her reputation!"

The Marquis laughed bitterly.

These were the words he had repeated to himself when he drove his superb horses from Elvin to where the road joined the main highway to Dover.

At the first Coaching-Inn he changed his horses for those that were kept for him month after month, just in case he should need them.

There was another change later on, and these horses should have brought him easily to Dover before dusk.

But then they had run into the fog, and it was only by superb driving and because the Marquis knew the way so well that he had managed to board his yacht and inform the Captain that he wished to put to sea immediately.

"I regret, M'Lord, that's completely impossible!" the Captain had replied.

"You mean because of the fog?"

"No ship could move in this weather, M'Lord. There's not enough wind to fill a pocket-handkerchief!"

"Then we will leave as soon as it is possible."

"Where to, M'Lord?"

This was something the Marquis had not considered and he said after a moment:

"I will tell you later."

"Very good, M'Lord. I hope we have everything Your Lordship'll need aboard. We took on fresh water and supplies yesterday."

The Marquis nodded, but he was not interested in the details of his yacht-equipment. It was just a vehicle, almost a Magic Carpet, to carry him away not only from England but from Sarah.

When he dined he could not bear to be alone with his thoughts, and he walked through the fog to where he saw the lights of The Three Bells.

Now he wished he had made use of the fog to escape from yet another woman.

He had the uncomfortable feeling that he had made a fundamental mistake in agreeing to carry that red-head—what was her name?—Ola, to France.

If her Stepmother caught up with her and learnt that she had been assisted by the Marquis of Elvington, all sorts of constructions might be put on what had been a simple act of charity.

"I have been a fool once again!" the Marquis told himself. "What the hell is the matter with me? Of course I should have left her at the Inn."

Instead of being, as she had said, a Good Samaritan, he could easily find himself accused of being interested in the girl personally, and if her Guardian was anything near as ambitious as Sarah, he might be expected to make reparation by offering her marriage.

"I am damned if I will do that!" the Marquis said angrily.

Then he told himself that he was being needlessly apprehensive. He would do what the girl had asked, would drop her at Calais, and then would forget about her.

By the time she had got herself into trouble he could easily be on the other side of the world, but where he intended to go he had not yet decided.

'I suppose the Mediterranean would be best, at any rate as a start,' he thought.

He remembered that Smollet had eulogised over Nice and he knew that the climate would be springlike at the moment and there would be sunshine and a blue sea.

"It might as well be Nice as anywhere else," he told himself.

The sea would be blue! That made him think of Sarah's eyes.

"She is haunting me—that is what she is doing!" he exclaimed.

Then he thought of how she had put her arms round Anthony's neck and lifted her face in a way that was very familiar and which he confidently believed was the way she greeted only him.

Had she not said again and again that she loved him as she had never loved anybody else?

There was a red blaze of anger before his eyes and once again he found himself clenching his fists.

"Damn her! Damn her! Damn her!" he said aloud, and the sound of his voice mingled with the whistle of the wind and the sudden slap of the sails as the ship listed to starboard.

"We are in for a rough passage," the Marquis told himself.

CHAPTER THREE

Ola was so tired that, unlike the Marquis, she did not hear the anchor being raised or know that the ship was pitching and tossing as soon as they were out of Harbour.

Instead she slept deeply and dreamlessly until a knock on the door awakened her.

When she said: "Come in!" a steward appeared, moving unsteadily across the cabin to put a closed cup, such as she had heard was used at sea in rough weather, down beside her bed.

"We're in for a rough passage, Miss," he said. "I've brought you some coffee, and if you'd like something more substantial the Chef'll do his best, but it's a bit difficult to work in the galley at the moment."

"Coffee is all I want," Ola replied, "and thank you very much."

"I should stay where you are, Miss, if you'll take my advice," the steward said before he left. "It's easy for 'land-lubbers,' as we calls 'em, to break a leg when the weather's so bad."

Ola knew that he was being tactful in not suggesting she might be sea-sick, but as it happened she was aware that she was a good sailor.

Her father had been very fond of the sea and when she was a small child he had often taken her out in a boat and she had soon learnt that however rough it might be, she was unaffected.

When the steward had gone, she thought that she should have asked him at what time they would reach Calais.

She had the feeling that if she was not ready to go ashore as soon as they docked, it would irritate the Marquis.

When they had walked to the ship last night in the thick fog she had known, although he had said nothing, that he was annoyed by his own generosity in offering to take her across the Channel.

He had abruptly instructed a steward to show her to a cabin, and she had told herself that it had really been "touch and go" as to whether he fulfilled his role of being a Good Samaritan or abandoned her to her fate.

She shuddered now as she thought of how horrible it would have been to have to marry Giles. She had never really thought of him as a man until the moment when he had revealed his treachery because he desired her fortune.

'It is a great mistake to have so much money,' she thought to herself, 'and if Papa had had a son I would not now be in this predicament.'

At the same time, son or no son, she knew that her father had not been able to escape from her Step-mother once she had made up her mind to marry him.

Ola could understand only too well how easily it had happened.

She had been at the Convent in France when her mother died.

There had been no chance of her getting back in time for the Funeral, and her father had therefore not sent for her or even told her by letter what had occurred, but instead had come himself to break the news to her gently.

They had cried together for the woman they had both loved. Then her father had returned to England alone, and that, Ola had told herself over and over again, had been a fatal mistake.

Of course she should have gone with him to look after him, but it had never occurred to either of them that she should cease her education because of her father's bereavement.

It was only when she was seventeen and had completed the two years she was to spend in France, as had been arranged by her mother, that she returned to England, to find that she was too late.

Her father had been lonely, miserable, and without anyone near him to whom he could talk about his beloved wife.

Her Stepmother, who was a neighbour, had, with the charm and sweetness that she could switch on so easily when it suited her, wormed her way into his confidence until he felt she was indispensable to him.

They were married just two days before Ola arrived home, and she knew as soon as she met her Stepmother that the haste was deliberate so that she could not interfere.

She saw that her Stepmother, all too obviously, wanted more than anything else the social position of being Lady Milford and to be married to a man who could provide her with the money she had always craved.

The face she showed him was a very different one from what his daughter saw.

Ola supposed that she must have met her father's new wife in the past, but she could not remember when, and it was doubtful that Lady Milford would have paid much attention to the young daughter of a neighbour whom she did not often see.

But a child in the Nursery or in the School-Room was very different from a stepdaughter with a spectacular beauty, and when Lord Milford died, Ola inherited a large fortune that exceeded by a dozen times what had been left to his widow.

Lady Milford had from the first been jealous of Ola, but now she was also envious of her money, and her hatred exploded almost like an anarchist's bomb.

Ola had only very briefly described to the Marquis what she had suffered. It would have been impossible to tell him of the agony she had endured in what was a continuous mental persecution, besides being afraid of her Stepmother physically.

Because she knew that Lady Milford disliked her good looks to the point where even to see her aroused her anger, Ola had always been nervous that she would find some way of damaging her face, as sometimes in a temper she threatened to do.

Then, because she had both spirit and courage, Ola was determined to escape.

She was well aware that it was not going to be easy, but as she became more and more a prisoner in the home where she had once been so happy, she knew that somehow, however difficult it might be, she must get away.

Giles had proved to be an undoubted Judas when she had least expected it, and that had been a blow which might have made somebody with less character collapse completely.

Then like a miracle, Ola thought, she had found the Marquis, and now in his yacht she was safe for the moment, whatever difficulties lay ahead.

When she had drunk the coffee, being careful not to spill any of it on the fine linen sheets which were embroidered with the Marquis's monogram, she lay back against the pillows and tried to think.

She had spoken to the Marquis of the *diligences* but she remembered that they were slow and used by all sorts and conditions of people, some of whom might be very rough.

The most sensible thing, she thought, would be to take a post-chaise to Paris.

But it would be expensive and she would not have enough money to pay for one without selling some of her jewellery.

'I must talk to the Marquis about that,' she thought.

Then something fastidious made her feel that it was embarrassing to discuss money with the man who had befriended her against his will and would be wishing to be rid of her as soon as possible.

"There must be a good jeweller in Calais," she told herself. "I will ask what he will pay me for one of Mama's smaller diamond brooches. When I get to the Convent I will give the rest of the jewels to the Mother-Superior to keep safely until I require some more money."

Then a sudden thought struck her and she opened her eyes to stare unseeingly, but with a definite expression of desperate anxiety, across the small cabin.

It was after midday when the Marquis came down from the deck to where his valet was waiting for him at the bottom of the companionway to help him out of his oil-skin coat.

"Your Lordship's not wet, I hopes?" he asked solicitously.

"No, Gibson," the Marquis replied. "And it is an exhilarating experience to see how fast the *Sea Wolf* moves with the wind behind her."

"It is indeed, M'Lord," Gibson replied. "I always said Your Lordship was right in choosing this type of ship for what you requires."

"I am always right, Gibson!" the Marquis said half-jokingly, but with an inner conviction that told him it was in fact the truth.

There had been a battle to get the ship-builders to design a yacht on the exact lines that he required. But he had seen when he was a boy the performance of the Naval Frigates in the war, and he had sworn that if he was ever in the position of building a yacht of his own, he would build one on those lines.

When he was older he had made it his job to examine and sail in the fast Schooners to which the name "Clipper" was first attached.

Their hull design was to become a model for the famous square-rigged Clippers that were being built in the American ship-yards and were only slowly being adopted by the English.

What the Marquis finally evolved for himself was a Schooner with the swiftness of a Frigate but which fortunately did not require such a large crew.

When the *Sea Wolf* was finally launched it caused a sensation amongst sea-faring enthusiasts and the Marquis was congratulated not only by his friends but a great many Naval authorities.

This was the first time, however, that he had taken the *Sea Wolf* out in such a tempestuous sea.

Watching her this morning riding the waves in a manner which he could not fault, he had known that all his ideas which had been called revolutionary had been proved right.

Walking carefully but with the sureness of a man who is used to the sea, the Marquis went into the Saloon, saying as he did so:

"Tell the stewards I am ready for a good meal. I am hungry!"

Then as he finished speaking he saw that he was not alone.

In the comfortable Saloon, where he had designed all the furnishings himself, there was the woman whose very existence he had forgotten for the last two hours.

"Good-morning, My Lord," Ola said. "Forgive me for not rising to greet you, but I feel it would be rather difficult to curtsey when the ship is rolling at this angle."

"Good-morning—Ola!" the Marquis replied.

There was a pause before he said her name because it took him a moment to remember it.

He sat down in a chair not far from her before he asked:

"You are feeling all right? You are not sea-sick?"

"Not in the least," Ola replied, "and if you will allow me to do so, I would like to come up on deck after luncheon. I have never been in a ship that can travel as fast as this one."

"Are you telling me you enjoy the sea?"

"I love it!" Ola replied simply.

"I am glad to hear that," the Marquis said, "because I have some bad news for you."

Ola looked at him enquiringly and he said:

"Last night I ordered my Captain to make for Calais, but so strong a gale has blown up from the Northeast that we cannot make the coast of France. All we can do is run before it out into the English Channel."

As the Marquis spoke he had not really thought of what Ola's reaction would be.

Now as he saw her green eyes light up and a smile appear on her lips, he told himself he might have anticipated that she would prove an unwanted guest who had no wish to relieve herself of his hospitality.

As if she knew what he was thinking, Ola said:

"You are so kind, My Lord, in saying you would take me to France that you must not be . . . annoyed when I say I am . . . delighted to know that I do not have to . . . leave this lovely yacht as . . . quickly as I had . . . anticipated."

The Marquis was not quite certain how it happened, but as the steward brought them a meal he found himself telling Ola about his yacht and the difficulties he had had in having it built in accordance with his ideas.

"I had to fight every inch of the way, or rather every inch of the ship!" he said. "And only when it was finally finished did the ship-builders stop croaking that my design was impracticable, unworkable, and that she would sink or turn turtle at the first rough sea we encountered."

"I am glad she is doing neither at the moment," Ola said with a laugh.

"You are quite safe," the Marquis said. "She is the most sea-worthy ship afloat, and I am prepared to stake my fortune and my reputation on it!"

They talked of ships and of the *Sea Wolf* in particular the whole time they were at luncheon, and it was only when they had finished that the Marquis said:

"When the wind drops and we can make our way to the French coast, I have been thinking that if we overshoot Le Havre, which is likely, then I may have to take you as far as Bordeaux."

"Are you sailing through the Bay of Biscay?" Ola enquired.

"I am going to the Mediterranean," the Marquis replied, "and there I thought I would put into Nice."

He spoke almost as if he were talking to himself, then as he saw the expression on Ola's face he realised that he had made a mistake.

He had no intention in any circumstances of keeping her aboard one minute after it was possible to put her ashore.

"Bordeaux would suit me very well, My Lord," she said, "if it is not possible to make . . . Le Havre."

Her reply, the Marquis told himself, was one thing, but the hope he saw in her eyes was another.

'I should never have brought her in the first place,' he thought.

He remembered Sarah and the way she had cajoled him into doing what he did not wish to do, and his hatred of women, every one of them, swept over him.

"I can assure you that my Captain is doing his best to reach Le Havre," he said sharply, "and it would be a mistake for you to come on deck. It is extremely cold and you would get wet."

He rose from his seat as he spoke, and without looking at Ola he went from the Saloon.

She gave a little sigh.

She knew it would only make him angry if she argued.

"I wonder what has upset him," she pondered, and was quite certain in her own mind that it was a woman.

Because the Marquis was so good-looking and undoubtedly very rich, it seemed unlikely, if not impossible, that any woman he fancied would not throw herself into his arms if that was what he wanted.

Yet perhaps, like everybody else, he wanted the unattainable, although what that might be Ola could not imagine.

If she was not allowed to go on deck, she thought, at least there were a number of books in a bookcase on one side of the Saloon.

It had surprised her that there were books aboard the yacht, for she knew that when her father was at sea he was far too interested in what was happening on deck to have any time for reading.

It struck Ola that the Marquis was different from what she would have expected of a man of his age and position.

She had heard so much about the riotous behaviour of the Bucks and Beaux in London that she imagined his life would be spent in search of pleasure and amusement.

Then she remembered that she had read of him in the Parliamentary Reports besides seeing his name mentioned continually on the sporting-pages of the newspapers.

'He obviously has many interests,' she thought to herself, and decided she would discuss them with him at dinner if she was still aboard.

The mere idea that she would soon be leaving brought back all the apprehensions and worries that had beset her in her cabin until she could not bear to think about them any more.

"I will manage, of course I will manage," she told herself reassuringly. "After all, it is not as though I have never been abroad before, although never . . . alone."

She knew it would be very different travelling on her own. When her father and mother had first taken her to the Convent they had stayed on the way with friends at their grand *Chateaux* and had made the journey an adventure which Ola knew she would never forget.

When she had returned to England with two other girls who were English, they had two Nuns in attendance and a Courier to arrange their rooms and see to the luggage.

'Now I shall be alone,' she thought, and she could not help shivering and feeling a little afraid.

She was convinced that it would be wisest to hire a post-chaise. But she still would have to stay at Inns on the way, and she thought that they would think it strange that a lady should be travelling alone, especially when she was so young.

A memory came flooding back to her which was even more disturbing.

When she was returning to England with the Nuns, they had stopped at an Inn on the main Paris-to-Calais road. It was not large or as pleasant as the other Inns in which they had stayed, but, as the Nuns explained, it was the best available.

When they arrived it was to find that they were one room short, and while the Courier was arguing about it with the Proprietor, a woman had come up to the desk to speak to him and Ola had looked at her with interest.

She was French, with an extremely attractive face which also looked a little strange because, Ola realised, she used far more cosmetics than anyone she had ever seen before.

Her eye-lashes were mascaraed, her mouth was crimson, and there was definitely rouge on her cheeks.

Nevertheless, the clothes she wore were expensive and very elegant and she looked so pretty that Ola found it hard to understand why when she asked for a room the Proprietor's wife, who was attending to her while her husband was busy, said in a hard voice:

"Are you alone, *Madame*?"

"I have asked only for one room and that is the answer to your question," the lady replied.

"We do not let our rooms to women who travel alone," the Proprietor's wife had snapped. "You will find the type of Hotel you require farther down the street!"

She spoke in such a rude, uncompromising way that Ola expected the lady to reprimand her for her impertinence.

To her surprise, she merely shrugged her shoulders and walked out of the Hotel.

Now Ola wondered whether she, as a woman alone, would receive the same treatment.

She gave a little sigh at the thought, then told herself optimistically that at least there were some Hotels that would take women who travelled alone, and perhaps they would be quieter and less crowded.

The prospect of reaching Paris began to appear more difficult than she had thought at first, and there was so much to consider that, although she found several books which interested her amongst the Marquis's collection, while she was still thinking of her problems she fell asleep.

❦

The Marquis, after an enjoyable two hours of watching his yacht plunge through the sea, came below, having learnt from the Captain that it would be impossible for them to turn towards Le Havre.

"The only thing I can suggest, M'Lord," he said, "is that we tack back there when the wind drops, but it will take time, and at this time of the year one can never be certain what the weather conditions will be like."

"No, we will go to Bordeaux as you suggested previously," the Marquis said. "I am sure Miss Milford, who is my guest, can easily find her way from there to Paris."

"Surely the young lady is not travelling all that way alone, M'Lord?" the Captain asked in surprise.

The Marquis was instantly annoyed that he had mentioned it and moved away without replying to the Captain's question.

"I have brought her to France as she asked," he told himself, "and I will not in any circumstances make her my responsibility!"

He remembered how Sarah had first evoked his sympathy because she seemed so helpless and pathetic without a husband to protect and care for her.

He saw now with a bitterness that seemed to run through his veins like poison that a great deal of it had been an act to make him feel big, strong, and protective.

He could recall the things she had said to him to which he had made the obvious reply! He could see all too clearly the trusting look in her eyes when she told him she was bewildered, worried, anxious, or upset. To which the inevitable answer was that he would see to it for her!

"Fool! Fool!" he told himself, and he felt the sound of the wind in the rigging repeat the same words.

"It is something I will never be again," he vowed.

When he went below he was seeking the words in which to tell Ola that the moment they reached Bordeaux his responsibility would be at an end.

"Whether she reaches Paris or anywhere else is nothing to do with me, and doubtless she will find plenty of other men to help her."

He wondered how many men there had been in Sarah's life besides Anthony.

There was no reason to think that he was the only one, and there must have been other men before her husband died!

Men who she found had been only too willing to look after and help a woman who pleaded with them with eyes as blue as a clear summer sky, but which were actually as dark with deceit as those of Satan himself.

The Marquis's eyes were hard and his lips were in a tight line as he entered the Saloon.

For a moment he thought that it was empty and Ola had retired to her own cabin. Then he saw that she was curled up on the sofa, asleep.

The Marquis had decorated the Saloon in pale green because it seemed an appropriate colour to use at sea.

That in itself had been revolutionary as most yachts were upholstered in brown leather and it was fashionable to have oak panelling on the cabin walls.

He could not have chosen a colour that was a more effective background for Ola's fiery red hair.

As the Marquis moved towards her he saw that her eye-lashes were very dark against her cheeks, which were still pale from tiredness, and in fact as she slept she looked very young and vulnerable.

He sat down on the chair opposite her, and it struck him that it was not surprising that she was tired, seeing what a dramatic day it had been for her yesterday.

Running away at dawn must have been a nerve-racking experience in itself. Then to learn of her cousin's intentions towards her had been a shock which was bad enough, without the sudden fright of an accident in the fog.

The Marquis had seen far too many accidents with carriage-horses not to be aware that Ola was lucky to have escaped unhurt.

Her cousin, who had been driving, had obviously been flung onto the road and it was unlikely, the Marquis thought, that the wound caused by the stone on which he had fallen would be his only injury.

Usually in such an accident he would have fractured a limb, while in several cases the Marquis was aware that people had broken their necks.

He wondered whether the horses were hurt, then told himself sharply that it was none of his business.

It was the brandy which was responsible for his having burdened himself with Ola and the sooner he was rid of her the better.

Then, looking at her, he wondered how, after he had put her ashore, she would reach Paris.

A post-chaise from Calais would not have been difficult, for it was the usual route taken by travellers, and the French with their shrewdness for making money had everything organised to suit the pockets of every class of person visiting their country.

But Bordeaux was a long way from Paris, and the Marquis began to think it might in fact be impossible for Ola to find a post-chaise to take her, even with a frequent change of horses, directly to Paris.

"I will not concern myself with her—I will not!" he said firmly.

Then he told himself that she was so young, a lady, and as such she was used to having servants, relatives, teachers and Governesses looking after her.

"She will find herself a Courier," a critical part of his mind told him, but then he wondered if a Courier of any repute would take on a woman who was by herself.

Moreover, there were Couriers who were known to prey on travellers, charging them exorbitant sums and even being in league with robbers who would relieve them of their luggage and other valuables before abandoning them penniless in some isolated part of the country.

'Damn her! Why did I ever meet her in the first place?' the Marquis thought to himself.

As the words were spoken in his mind, Ola opened her eyes.

For a moment she looked at him as if she wondered who he was. Then some memory came back to her and there was a smile on her lips that was very attractive as she sat up and said:

"I fell . . . asleep. I am ashamed of my indolence when I might have been improving my mind with one of your books."

"What you were doing was very sensible," the Marquis said. "It is extremely rough outside now. The wind is cold and there are gusts of sleet which are very unpleasant."

"All the same, you look as if you have enjoyed it!" Ola said. "Perhaps you will let me go on deck tomorrow."

"It depends if it is safe."

Ola gave a little sigh.

"I believe you are afraid I shall break my leg, and then you will not be able to be rid of me unless you throw me overboard!"

What she was saying was so near to what the Marquis was thinking that he felt almost embarrassed.

He did not reply and Ola said:

"I promise you I will go ashore the moment you tell me to do so, but there is one thing I want to ask you."

"What is that?"

"As we are going to Bordeaux and it is a town I have never visited and therefore know very little about, do you think there is a good jeweller there?"

"A jeweller?" the Marquis asked in perplexity. "What do you want with a jeweller?"

It flashed through his mind that she might be expecting him to give her a present. He remembered so many women who had somehow lured him into a jeweller's so that he could demonstrate his affection for them in what to them was a very much more practical manner than by kisses.

Ola looked down, as if she was shy, then said in a small voice:

"I think . . . if I could have got off at . . . Calais . . . I would have had enough . . . money to reach Paris . . . but as Bordeaux is so much . . . farther away . . . I shall have to . . . sell some of my jewellery . . . and I do not wish to be . . . defrauded."

"Surely you did not set off from home without having enough money to carry you to Paris?" the Marquis asked. "How much did you bring?"

There was silence and he had a feeling that she was not going to tell him the truth.

"Do not lie to me!" he said sharply. "Quite frankly, I am not really interested in your finances one way or another. If you want my help you had better at least be honest."

"I . . . I was not going to . . . lie," Ola replied. "I just did not wish you to think I was . . . foolish to bring so little money with me."

"How much have you got?"

"F-four sovereigns . . . and some . . . silver."

Before the Marquis could speak she added quickly:

"Because Giles was coming with me . . . I thought it would be . . . enough."

"So you intended that he should pay for you, even before you learnt he wished to marry you?" the Marquis asked scornfully.

"Not at all!" Ola answered. "He knew that as Step-Mama has the handling of my fortune she could pay him back anything I owed him . . . or else I would have given him a piece of . . . Mama's jewellery. It is very valuable!"

"And you mean to say you are carrying it all in that case you had with you last night?"

Ola nodded.

"My dear child," the Marquis said, "do you really imagine you can reach Paris without having it stolen from you and perhaps being knocked about or killed in the process?"

"There is . . . nothing else I . . . can do," Ola said defensively.

She gave a little cry.

"Oh, it is easy for you to find fault and say: 'You should have known better!' now that everything has gone wrong, but I trusted Giles when he said he would take me to the Convent. Now last night I thought of . . . something . . . else."

"What is that?" the Marquis asked in an unsympathetic tone.

"Because Giles knows where I intended to go, he will, when he is better, look for me there . . . so I cannot now stay at the . . . Convent."

The Marquis looked at her.

"Then where do you intend to go?"

"I have not yet decided."

"But you have to go somewhere."

"Yes, I know, but there is no reason for me to worry you with my plans. You have made it quite clear that I am not your responsibility, which of course I am not."

"No, of course not," the Marquis agreed. "At the same time, shall I say I am curious! You did mention an alternative last night, I think."

"Yes. I told you that Step-Mama was always saying I would have to be a cocotte but that I was not certain exactly what that means."

She looked at the Marquis as if he could supply the answer. When he did not do so, she went on:

"I looked the word up in the French dictionary, and it said: '*Fille de joie*'—'woman of joy,' and I thought that must mean an actress of some sort. Is that not so?"

"Not exactly," the Marquis replied.

"I expect they will tell me what it is when I get to Paris. The trouble is, I can hardly walk down the street asking for an Instructor on how to be a *'Fille de joie'*! Perhaps they would be able to tell me at a Theatre?"

She gave him a mischievous little smile as she went on:

"The Nuns would be very shocked! They thought Theatres were the invention of the Devil and always warned us against visiting them, although we were allowed occasionally to attend the Opera House."

The Marquis was finding it almost impossible to know what he could say to this ridiculous, ignorant child. He made up his mind.

"The best thing I can do," he said firmly, "is to sail to Plymouth. There I will engage a responsible Courier who will take you back to your Stepmother."

Even before he had finished speaking Ola gave a cry of horror that seemed to echo round the cabin.

"How can you suggest anything so abominable, so cruel, so treacherous?" she cried. "You know I cannot go back to my Stepmother, and you have no authority to send me."

She paused to catch her breath.

"I called you a Good Samaritan, but you are a *wolf* in sheep's clothing and your yacht is aptly named . . . you are a *sea wolf* and I hate you!"

As she spoke he rose from his chair, and without looking at her, moved towards the door. It would have been a dignified exit except that a sudden movement of the ship made him stagger, and it was only with the greatest difficulty that he prevented himself from falling.

When he had gone, Ola stared despairingly at the door as if she could not believe that she had heard him aright.

He had seemed so kind, so helpful, and she had thought at luncheon-time, apart from anything else, how interesting it would be to talk to him.

Now suddenly for no reason he had turned against her and was behaving as badly in his way as Giles had behaved in his.

"How dare he! How dare he treat me as if I were a child to be taken here or there without even being consulted!" she cried aloud.

She wanted to scream in defiance at the Marquis, and yet at the same time her instinct told her that, sea wolf or not, it would be best for her to plead with him.

Then she knew by the tone of his voice and the squareness of his chin that he meant what he said and she would find it hard to dissuade him from doing what he intended.

'If he sends me home,' she thought, 'I shall have to run away all over again and it will be more difficult another time.'

She had the feeling too that the Marquis would make sure that she did not escape while she was with him, and she wished now that she had not entrusted her jewellery to him.

She thought she now hated the Marquis as much as she hated Giles.

'Men are all the same,' she thought. 'They do not play fairly unless it suits their own ends.'

She wondered why the girls at School were always talking of men as if they were something marvellous and more desirable than anything else on earth.

"I hate men!" Ola told herself. "I hate them as I hate my Stepmother! All I want to do is to live by myself and be allowed to have friends and do all the things I want to do without being ordered about by anybody!"

It had occurred to her a long time ago that when one was married one would always be at the beck and call of some man who thought he had authority over her.

Perhaps that would be endurable if one was in love, but otherwise it would be intolerable. She thought that because she was rich, she need be in no hurry to get married but could wait until she found somebody whom she would like to live with simply because he was kind and understanding and she would be able to talk to him.

She had often thought in the past that it was difficult to find people to whom she could talk when she was at the Convent.

The Nuns gave orders, and when she was with her father he talked to her but he did not converse. In fact, neither he nor anybody else was interested in her opinions or her ideas.

'When I talked to the Marquis at luncheon,' she thought, 'he listened to me when I was describing the different ships in which I have sailed in the past, and he explained the things I wanted to know about his own yacht.'

From the number of books in his bookcase it struck her that he was interested in a great number of subjects about which she wished to know more.

'We will talk about them tonight at dinner,' she had thought excitedly, but now he had made it very clear what he thought of her.

She was an unwanted piece of merchandise of which he would dispose as he saw fit, without even asking her opinion on the matter.

'I hate him!' she thought. 'I hate him because he has deceived me when I thought he was kind and honest.'

She did not want to cry when she thought of her future; it only made her angry.

Somehow, in some way, she would get even with the Marquis because he had disappointed her when she had least expected it.

"I am glad he is upset about something, and I hope a woman has really hurt him and made him unhappy!" she said to herself. "It will serve him right! If he ever told me about it I would laugh because I am pleased he has been made to suffer!"

This was all very well, but it did not solve her own problem and she told herself that now she had to escape somehow.

There seemed no possibility of her doing anything of the sort unless she was prepared to throw herself into the sea.

"If I do so," she mused, "I should be drowned and perhaps it would be on his conscience for the rest of his life."

Then she told herself sensibly that he would merely attribute it to an unbalanced mind and forget all about it long before he reached the Mediterranean.

But Ola was not going to be defeated.

She sat back against the cushions and began to plan how she could elude the Marquis and his ideas in one way or another.

'Perhaps if I stow away in the hold,' she thought, 'he will think I have gone ashore and I shall only be discovered when he is out at sea again.'

It seemed quite a possible idea, except that she had the feeling he would make very sure that the Courier he engaged acted as a jailor too and there would be no escape at least until he was too far away even to know about it.

"What am I to do? What *am* I to do?" Ola asked herself.

Then as there was a sudden rasp of the wind in the rigging which told her that there was still a gale outside, it occurred to her that perhaps the Marquis's intentions would be circumvented not by her but by nature and they would not be able to dock in Plymouth as he intended.

Chapter Four

Ola was sitting on her bed, an expression of despair on her face.

She had learnt from the steward that the *Sea Wolf* would dock in Plymouth either very late tonight or first thing in the morning, depending on the wind and the tides.

In the last twelve hours she had thought of nothing except how she could escape from the Marquis and prevent him from sending her ignominiously back to her Stepmother.

She had been sensible enough not to rage at him when they had luncheon together, but instead to talk about the races and horses which took part in them.

She knew he was surprised that she was not referring to what lay ahead, but after a little stiffness at the beginning of the meal he gradually relaxed and talked to her as if she were as knowledgeable as he was on the subject.

Every hour that passed brought her nearer to her fate, and she thought now that even her optimism was fading and there would be nothing she could do but leave the Marquis and set off on her homeward journey with the jailor he would provide for her.

There was a knock on the door and Ola started.

"Come in!" she said, and the steward who always looked after her stood there.

"'Scuse me, Miss," he said, "but do you happen to have any laudanum with you? The Captain's got such an aching tooth that he can't stay on deck."

"Oh! I am sorry," Ola exclaimed, "and I wish I could help, but laudanum is something I never take myself."

The steward smiled.

"You're too young, if I may say so, Miss, for such fads and fancies, but there was just a chance, and the Captain's groaning in his bunk like a lost soul."

Ola could not help smiling. Then she said:

"Tell him to soak a little wool or a rag in spirit . . . brandy is best, although I daresay rum would do . . . and pack it round it, if possible into the tooth that is hurting. I remember my father doing that once."

"I'll tell the Captain what you said, Miss," the steward replied. "I know he'll be very grateful."

He shut the cabin door and as he did so Ola gave a little exclamation.

She suddenly remembered that she might have some laudanum with her after all.

When she had left the Convent many of the girls of her age had given her presents and among them had been a beautiful chinoiserie enamel scent-holder made in the reign of Louis XIV.

It was very attractive and when she opened it she found it contained three little bottles shaped like triangles so that they fitted together to make a whole.

They each had enamelled stoppers and their glass was engraved with flowers.

Yvonne, the girl who had given them to her, had said:

"I have put the most exotic perfume I could find in one, an *eau-de-toilette* in the second, and you will have to fill the third yourself."

Ola had never actually used the bottles, but, because it was so attractive, the case had stood on her dressing-table, and when she was packing, thinking that she might see her friend when she was in France, she had put it at the bottom of her trunk.

She had not thought of it until now, but actually the third bottle contained laudanum.

Soon after she had returned from Paris she had suffered from the most acute tooth-ache which turned out to be an abscess.

The Doctor had been called to see her and he had promised to arrange for a Dentist to visit her the following day.

"Because I know what pain you're in, Miss Milford," he said, "I'm going to give you a little laudanum to take tonight so that you will sleep. Be careful not to take too much."

He had handed her a small bottle as he spoke and instructed her to take only a few drops.

It had certainly helped her to bear the pain, and when her tooth no longer hurt, Ola, thinking that the medicine-bottle looked untidy, had tipped what remained of the laudanum into the empty bottle in her chinoiserie case.

"How stupid of me!" she said aloud. "Of course I can help the Captain!"

She opened her trunk which she had already filled with her clothes, feeling that if she did not do so the Marquis would be informed and would think it was a deliberate act of defiance.

In the bottom corner she found, as she expected, the enamel case carefully wrapped in cotton-wool to protect it.

She drew it out and rose to her feet to call the steward so that he could take it to the Captain.

Even as her hand went out towards the door, she paused.

An idea had come to her, an idea that was so fantastic that she told herself it was impossible and would be quite unworkable.

And yet, fascinated by it, she sat down on the bed to consider it carefully, step by step.

❦

Wearing a very attractive gown and, because it was cold, a fur wrap round her shoulders, Ola was waiting in the Saloon when the Marquis came in to dinner.

Each night, despite the roughness of the weather, he changed into his evening-clothes, and he looked to Ola as elegant and impressive as if he were going to a dinner-party in London rather than dining alone with her.

"Good-evening, Ola!" he said. "I think the wind is dropping a little, and certainly the *Sea Wolf* is travelling more smoothly than she was yesterday."

"I have found that," Ola smiled. "But my elbows are black and blue from having to support me as I was thrown against the cabin walls."

"You should have stayed in bed!" the Marquis said automatically.

"That would be an admission of defeat, which I most dislike acknowledging at any time!"

He gave her a sharp glance, as if he thought she was referring to other things than the movement of the sea.

She quickly turned the conversation to the subject she wished to discuss with him but had not yet had the opportunity.

"I found in your bookcase a volume of Hansard," she said, "and I see that you made a speech in the House of Lords regarding the employment of young children in factories and coal-mines."

"You read it?" the Marquis asked in surprise.

"I only wish I could have heard it. It is something about which I feel very strongly, as every woman should."

It struck the Marquis that no woman he had known in the past had been in the slightest degree interested either in his speeches or in the children, as young as four and five, who were made to work sometimes as much as twelve hours a day and who were beaten if they fell asleep.

For a moment he thought that Ola was only toadying to him and would start pleading with him not to send her back to her Stepmother.

To his surprise, she not only talked with unmistakable sincerity on the subject, but she also had obviously read quite a lot of the reports which had been published in the newspapers besides being discussed in Parliament.

They argued over the rights and wrongs of employing child-labour and also as to what compensation could be given to the employers if it was forbidden.

The Marquis found himself waxing very eloquent about what he intended to bring before the House of Lords in the future, and he discovered that Ola was also interested in the Reform Bill.

"Is it true," she asked, "that the King scrawled on a piece of paper:

" 'I consider Dissolution
Tantamount to Revolution.' "

"Who told you that?" the Marquis enquired.

"I must have read it somewhere, but I cannot believe, old though he is, that the King does not realise that reforms are necessary."

"The trouble is," the Marquis replied, "he has a rooted dislike of elections and only with difficulty made up his mind to dissolve Parliament. I think too, as he is really a simple sailor, he finds the Bill in all its complexity very difficult to understand."

"I have always been sure," Ola said, "that he has not the brilliant brain of his brother, the late King George IV."

"That is true," the Marquis agreed, "but, though I am fond of His Majesty, I cannot help sometimes remembering that Greville wrote: 'He is but a plain, vulgar, hospitable gentleman, opening his doors to all the world with a frightful Queen and a posse of bastards.' "

As he spoke, he realised to whom he was speaking and said quickly:

"I apologise."

"No, please do not do that," Ola said. "I like to be talked to as if I were your equal rather than a foolish, unfledged girl without a brain in her head."

"I would certainly never say that about you," the Marquis replied.

A steward cleared the table but left a decanter of brandy and one of claret in front of the Marquis.

They were ship's decanters, made so that it was impossible to upset them or to turn them over as they had very broad bases and were of extremely heavy cut crystal.

Ola looked at them for a minute, then she said:

"As this is our last dinner together, My Lord, I would like to propose a toast."

The Marquis raised his eye-brows; then, feeling that as she was trying to be pleasant he must do the same, he replied:

"I shall join with pleasure in any toast you suggest, Ola. Will you drink claret or brandy?"

"I think claret," she replied, "but only a very little."

The Marquis half-filled the glass in front of her.

"I shall join you," he said, and filled his own:

Ola reached for her glass but as she moved she gave a little cry.

"Oh, my brooch!" she exclaimed. "I could not have fastened it properly and I heard it fall beneath the table."

As she spoke she dropped the diamond brooch she held in her hand down beside the hem of her skirt.

"How foolish of me," she said. "I should not have worn it, but it looked so pretty with this gown."

"I will pick it up," the Marquis said.

He pushed back his chair, looked down, and saw that the brooch was out of reach of his hands unless he went down on his knees.

As he did so, Ola bent forward to tip into the Marquis's glass of claret the contents of the little cut-glass bottle she had hidden beside her.

She had emptied it by the time he retrieved the brooch and emerged from under the table to sit in his chair again.

"There you are," he said.

As he held out the diamond brooch towards her, he said:

"It is certainly a very beautiful piece of jewellery."

Ola smiled.

"It was one of my mother's smaller brooches. My father loved her so much and gave her magnificent jewels on every possible occasion and anniversary!"

"Then you must keep it safe," the Marquis admonished, "and if you sell it, be careful that you are not defrauded."

"I will be," Ola said, taking the brooch from him.

She set it down on the table and lifted her glass.

"To the *Sea Wolf!*" she said. "May she find, wherever she sails, new horizons and eventually happiness!"

"A charming toast, Ola!" the Marquis exclaimed.

She knew he was surprised not only at the words but at the sincere way in which she had spoken them.

She smiled at him and the smile seemed to illuminate her face.

"No heel-taps," she said, and lifted her glass to her lips.

Because he was prepared to humour her, the Marquis tipped the entire contents of his glass down his throat.

But when he had swallowed and put his glass down on the table there was a frown on his forehead.

"I thought—that wine tasted—a little strange . . ." he began.

He reached out his hand as if he would take hold of the decanter, but before he could do so he leant back in his chair as if the effort was too great and after a second or so shut his eyes.

Ola watched him anxiously.

She knew she had given him a very large dose of laudanum, and she was not certain how soon it would act and whether he would have time to call a steward to his assistance.

It was soon obvious that he would not do so, though quite a long time passed while he sat with closed eyes before his head fell to one side and she knew he was asleep.

Fortunately, the chair in which he was sitting, which was battened to the deck, had a wing-back and his head rested against one of the wings, so that Ola knew it would be impossible for anybody coming through the door to know whether he was awake or asleep.

Just as she had planned, because she felt that the steward outside would be listening in case he was required, she went on talking.

Because she did not dare try to imitate the Marquis's voice, she made deep humming noises when he should have spoken, which made it sound, she hoped, as if he were speaking in a lower tone than she was.

After ten minutes had passed she rang the gold bell that stood on the table.

As she had guessed, the steward had been waiting outside, and as he opened the door she said in an excited tone, as if she were speaking to the Marquis:

"Oh, let me send the order! It is so wonderful of you! I am so happy!"

Then she turned her face towards the steward who stood just inside the door.

"Will you inform the Captain or the First Mate, if he is now in charge of the yacht," she said, "that His Lordship says that as the weather is better we will not now put into Plymouth as arranged, but will sail with all possible speed towards the South."

She was obviously so delighted with the command and her pleasure was so infectious that as she smiled at the end of what she had to say, the steward smiled back.

"I'll give the order to the First Mate right away, Miss," he said, and went from the Saloon, closing the door.

Ola went on talking as she had done before, lowering her voice to impersonate the Marquis's responses.

Then she lifted the decanter of claret and, moving from the table, poured the contents down behind the sofa.

As that piece of furniture was also battened down, she knew that the wine was most unlikely ever to be discovered since it would seep into the wood and be practically indiscernible.

Then she put the empty decanter back on the table and went on talking.

Nearly an hour later she rang the bell for the second time, and when the steward answered she said in a hesitating and rather nervous little voice:

"His Lordship has fallen . . . asleep . . . I think perhaps he is . . . very tired."

The steward came quickly to the table and Ola saw him glance at the empty decanter before he said:

"I'll fetch Gibson, Miss. I expects you'd like to go to your own cabin."

"I think that would be a good idea," Ola agreed, "and thank you very much."

A little later she heard the Marquis being carried towards the Master Suite, which was past her cabin door.

When she got into bed she knew with a little leap of her heart that she had got the better of the Marquis!

"At least by the time he wakes it will be too late to go back to Plymouth," she told herself.

She shut her eyes, determined that she would not worry as to what would happen when the Marquis awoke, but would try to sleep.

The Marquis stirred, feeling as if his head were filled with fog, and had a fleeting memory of walking through the darkness to the *Sea Wolf*.

He opened his eyes with an effort and somebody rose from the other side of the cabin and came towards him.

"If you're awake, M'Lord, I thinks Your Lordship should have something to drink," he heard Gibson say, and felt a glass pressed against his lips.

He took a few sips, then turned away petulantly to say in a thick voice:

"Leave—me alone—I am—tired!"

When he awoke again he was aware that there was sunshine coming through the port-holes and now his head felt clearer although his mouth was dry.

Once again Gibson came to his side, and this time he asked:

"What is the time? Where are we?"

"Sailing down the coast of Portugal, M'Lord."

It took the Marquis a moment to understand what had been said. Then with an effort, clutching at his memory, which seemed to be trying to escape him, he said:

"Portugal? You mean—Plymouth!"

"No, M'Lord. Portugal! We're already well past the Bay of Biscay."

The Marquis forced his mind to assimilate this information. Then in a voice that was a little stronger he asked:

"What the devil are we doing here? I gave orders to dock at Plymouth!"

"I understand you countermanded that order, M'Lord, and told the Captain to sail South as quickly as possible. We've had the wind behind us all the way and it's been the best passage I've ever known in the Bay. It's a pity Your Lordship weren't awake to appreciate it!"

There was silence for a moment, then the Marquis asked:

"Are you telling me that I have been asleep since before we were due to reach Plymouth?"

"Yes, M'Lord. I've never known Your Lordship sleep like it," Gibson replied. "And I've never known claret, not even a whole decanter, to have such an effect."

"I was drunk?" the Marquis enquired.

"I'm afraid so, M'Lord. And it's the first time I've seen Your Lordship so 'foxed'!"

"How long have I been in this state?"

"Three days, M'Lord!"

"I do not believe it!"

The Marquis forced himself to sit up in bed.

"Three days!" he said as if he was speaking to himself. "And you think that is possible on one bottle of claret?"

"Your Lordship had nothing else," Gibson replied defensively. "The stewards said that the brandy went untouched."

"I slept for three days on one bottle of claret?"

"There must have been two," Gibson conceded. "What Your Lordship drank at dinner, and a full decanter placed on the table after dinner."

Because the Marquis was sitting up it seemed that his head was swimming dizzily, so he lay back again.

"There is something wrong here, Gibson," he said. "Very wrong! I intend, when I am better, to get to the bottom of it."

"Yes, M'Lord, of course, M'Lord," Gibson agreed, "but Your Lordship should rest until you feel yourself again."

The Marquis was silent for a moment. Then as his valet was moving away from the bed he said:

"The young lady—what is her name?"

"Miss Milford, M'Lord."

"She is still aboard?"

"Yes, M'Lord. Enjoying every moment of the voyage. Up on deck from first thing in the morning to last thing at night. We've all been saying we've never seen a young lady so happy."

The Marquis lay still.

Now he was remembering what had happened.

He had been firm in his decision to put Ola ashore at Plymouth and send her back to her Stepmother so that he would no longer have any responsibility for her.

He remembered too how at first she had raged at him and accused him of treachery. Then she had been surprisingly pleasant, especially at dinner.

Slowly, because it was an effort, he tried to recall everything that had been said, everything that had happened.

Now he remembered the toast she had asked him to drink and how after he had poured a little claret into her glass and filled his own she had dropped her diamond brooch under the table.

He had retrieved it, then she had thanked him and had lifted her glass, saying:

"No heel-taps!"

He gave a little exclamation.

It was after he had drunk his glass of claret, and had thought it had a strange taste, that darkness had covered him and he remembered no more.

The Marquis was extremely intelligent, and although it seemed incredible that this sort of thing, like something out of a Walter Scott novel, could happen in real life, he felt sure that when he was picking up her brooch Ola by some means had drugged his wine!

74

But was she likely to carry a drug round with her? he wondered.

Then, knowing how he had felt when he first awoke, the heaviness of his head and the difficulty he had thinking, it struck him that he had felt like this once before.

It was after he had broken his collar-bone out hunting and the Doctor had been called to attend to him at Elvin. He had hurt him excruciatingly when he had put the bone back into place.

He had cursed and the Doctor had opened his leather bag and produced a small bottle, and from it he had poured some dark liquid into a teaspoon.

"Drink this, My Lord."

"What is it?" the Marquis had enquired.

"Only laudanum, but it will take the edge off the pain."

"Women's remedy!" the Marquis had said scornfully.

"Women are not expected to be courageous about pain like a man," the Doctor had replied, "but I have always believed there is no point in suffering unnecessarily."

"No, you are right," the Marquis had agreed.

He had taken the laudanum and found it helped him considerably, though the next morning he awoke with a heavy head and a dry mouth such as he had now.

Of course that was what Ola had given him—laudanum—and he told himself that he had been a fool not to be suspicious of what she was up to when she had made herself so pleasant and talked so agreeably to him.

He had known that she was determined not to return to her Stepmother, just as he was determined that she should.

'Damn the woman—she has won!' the Marquis thought irritably.

He slept intermittently for the rest of the day, and every time he was conscious he found himself growing more and more angry that Ola had managed to trick him.

But there was in fact nothing he could do at the moment but take her along with him to the Mediterranean.

He supposed that they were now long past Lisbon.

The next civilised port-of-call would be Gibraltar, and as that was a British possession there would be far too many explanations if the Marquis of Elvington left an attractive but very young woman stranded there while he sailed on alone.

'I suppose I can put her ashore at Marseilles or Nice,' he thought, and wondered whether, if he told her what he intended, she would find another means of circumventing his plans.

After a good night's sleep he felt remarkably well and in comparatively good spirits, except that he was still angry with Ola.

When he was dressed he went up on deck, and now he no longer needed an overcoat or oil-skins, for the sun was warm and the sea reflected the blue of the sky.

"Good-morning, M'Lord!" the Captain said as soon as he appeared. "I hope Your Lordship's in better health?"

The Marquis bit back the angry retort that there had been nothing wrong with his health except that he had been drugged without being aware of it.

But he knew it would be undignified to say anything of the sort, so he merely replied:

"I am sorry to have missed so much of the voyage, Captain. Gibson told me this morning that we have had the best passage he has ever known through the Bay."

"Fantastic, M'Lord!" the Captain replied. "The wind exactly right, the sea dropping after the storm, and I already feel as if the winter is over and we've found the spring."

"Yes, indeed," the Marquis agreed, feeling that the Captain was being quite poetic.

Because he looked surprised, the Captain said with an apologetic smile:

"Those are not my words, M'Lord, but Miss Milford's. We've all been thinking she looks like spring herself, and no mistake!"

The Marquis followed the direction of the Captain's eyes and saw Ola, whom he had not noticed before.

She was sitting on deck, protected by a piece of super-structure and looking, although he hated to admit it, very spring-like and undeniably beautiful.

She wore no hat and the lights in her red hair seemed to dance in the sunlight, her eyes were deep green like the waves as they broke against the bow of the ship, and her skin was dazzlingly white.

As she saw him looking at her she raised her hand in a wave and the smile on her lips seemed to welcome him.

He wondered how she dared to appear so unselfconscious about her misdeeds, but he told himself that this was not the moment to confront her with them.

He therefore made no effort to move towards her but stood talking to the Captain. As he watched the ship move with a speed that thrilled him, it was hard, despite himself, to continue to be in a bad humour.

"There's a little damage I would like to speak to you about, M'Lord," the Captain said, after the Marquis had been silent for some time.

"Damage?"

"Nothing very serious, M'Lord, but in the storm two of the water-butts broke loose and knocked against each other, spilling their contents."

"Two?" the Marquis asked sharply.

"They've been repaired, M'Lord, and as good as they ever were, but they are empty and I wondered if Your Lordship would consider putting into a bay I know of, a bit further down the coast, where there's a spring of sweet, clear water."

"You have been there before?" the Marquis asked.

"Twice, M'Lord. Once in the war when I was serving in a Brig and we were out of water completely, and we filled up there and very glad we were of it too. The second time was when I was on Lord Lutworth's yacht, M'Lord. Very mean, His Lordship was, and though I told him the water-butts were not sea-worthy he wouldn't listen to me.

Fell to bits, they did, when we encountered a storm off the southern coast of Portugal."

"That was unfortunate," the Marquis remarked.

"Soon, M'Lord, there wasn't a single drop of water left in the whole ship."

"That certainly must not happen to us," the Marquis said, "so we will drop anchor in your bay, Captain. How long before we get there?"

"About forty-eight hours, M'Lord; and you might like to stretch your legs on shore."

"It is certainly an idea," the Marquis agreed.

All the time he was talking he was acutely aware that Ola was watching him, and now, almost as if she was compelling him, he walked along the deck.

"I want to speak to you, Ola!" he said when he reached her.

He saw the light go out of her eyes as she asked:

"Here, or in the Saloon?"

"In the Saloon," he replied, and went below without waiting to assist her.

She joined him a few minutes later, and as she came into the Saloon he saw that the expression in her eyes was apprehensive even though her hair seemed like a flag of defiance.

She did not wait for him to speak but moved across the cabin to sit down on the sofa she usually occupied, saying as she did so:

"I am sorry . . . very sorry . . . I know you are . . . angry with me."

"What did you expect me to be?" the Marquis asked.

"I had to save myself from my Stepmother . . . and it was the only way I could . . . do so."

"What did you give me?"

"Laudanum."

"How much?"

"I am afraid . . . nearly a whole bottle . . . it was only a small bottle . . . but I knew it was . . . a very strong dose."

"You might have killed me!" the Marquis said sharply.

"There was really no chance of that," Ola replied, "but you did sleep for a long time. I was glad when we reached the coast of Portugal."

"I suppose you realise that your behaviour is so outrageous, so incredible, that I find it difficult to express what I feel about it?"

"I have said I am sorry," Ola answered, "but it was the only way I could prevent you from sending me home unless I threw myself overboard. I did seriously think of . . . that."

"You do not frighten me with your dramatics."

"I know that, and as I have abused your hospitality I am prepared to leave when we reach the South of France."

"That is certainly very kind of you," the Marquis said sarcastically, "and I suppose you will be up against the same difficulties as before—no money and nowhere to go."

"I have told you . . . I will go to Paris."

"Oh, for God's sake!" he said in an irritable tone. "We cannot go over all that again. For the moment we had best talk of something else, otherwise I shall feel inclined to give you the beating you thoroughly deserve."

She gave a little exclamation but she did not speak, and the Marquis went on:

"It is obviously a punishment that was neglected when you were young, and your over-fertile imagination was given too much licence."

He spoke not angrily but in the bitter, sarcastic tone that Ola thought was almost as wounding as if he actually used the whip with which he had threatened her.

Then suddenly as she thought of how she should reply to him she gave a little chuckle.

"It was clever of me, was it not?" she asked. "I despaired . . . I really despaired of how I could prevent you from putting me ashore at Plymouth. Then the steward asked me if I had any laudanum with me as the Captain had a tooth-ache."

"And you refused to help the Captain?"

"I refused because I had actually forgotten I had it in my trunk," Ola answered. "Then I remembered it and suddenly thought of a way to prevent you from sending me home from Plymouth and to contrive that you should take me South with you."

She saw the steel in his eyes and put out her hand impulsively on his arm.

"Please . . . please forgive me . . . and let us go on talking together as we did before. It was so exciting for me . . . so different from . . . anything I have enjoyed before, and although I know you will not admit it . . . you seemed to . . . enjoy it too."

The Marquis looked at the pleading in her green eyes, and despite his resolution to refrain firm and very annoyed, he found himself weakening.

"I am extremely angry with you," he said, "but I suppose there is nothing I can do but accept this ridiculous situation, which incidentally is extremely reprehensible from the point of view of your reputation."

"I stopped worrying about my reputation long ago," Ola replied, "and who is to know or to care where I am, except my Stepmother, who will only be afraid that I shall be found, which will prevent her from keeping my fortune all to herself."

"It is your fortune, as you call it, that is at the bottom of all this trouble," the Marquis said.

"Of course it is, and I was thinking that if Papa had had a son I should not be so rich and then no-one would have worried about me," Ola said. "Let that be a lesson to you! When you have a family, have lots of children, not just one tiresome daughter."

"I can simplify things far more easily than that," the Marquis said, "by not getting married and not having any children."

He spoke bitterly and without thinking, simply because the word "marriage" made him remember Sarah once again.

As he did so, it struck him that in the days when he had been unconscious, and today when he was himself, he had not once thought of her.

"I have decided never to marry too," Ola said confidingly. "I have been ordered about too much in my life, and a husband might easily be worse than my Stepmother, worse than Giles, and worse than you!"

"You cannot spend the rest of your life alone!" the Marquis remarked.

"I shall make friends," Ola replied, "and friends are easier to dispense with than relatives and husbands."

"You are talking nonsense!" the Marquis snapped. "Of course you will have to marry, and the quicker the better, so that you will have a man to look after you."

"And order me about?"

"Undoubtedly, and, what is more, you will have to obey him."

"I refuse, I absolutely refuse!"

Then she was smiling at him mischievously as she said:

"Although I daresay I shall manage to do what I want to do, one way or another."

"I can quite believe that, and your future husband will have all my sympathy."

He saw her eyes twinkle and had the feeling that she was not taking him seriously and was in fact so relieved that he was not really angry with her that she was laughing at his helplessness.

"You are an extremely irritating brat!" he said. "God knows what will happen to you in your life, but I refuse to let it worry me."

He reached out for the bell and rang it.

"I am going to have a glass of champagne," he said. "Would you like to join me?"

"It sounds very luxurious and exciting," Ola said, "especially for me."

"You must have had champagne before?"

"Yes, but not at sea in a magnificent yacht with a handsome nobleman all to myself!" Ola replied. "What could be a better opening to a dramatic story of adventure and romance?"

For a moment the Marquis glared at her, then found himself laughing.

He was right, she was incorrigible, and there was nothing he could do about it.

He had never in his life expected to encounter a woman who could behave in so outrageous a manner and yet make him laugh at her behaviour.

"A bottle of champagne!" he said to the steward.

When the champagne came, the steward opened it in front of him and poured a glass for the Marquis and one for Ola.

When the man had left the cabin the Marquis said:

"I have no intention of taking my eyes off this glass before I drink it, so if you drop anything on the floor you can pick it up yourself."

"I was so afraid," Ola admitted, "that you would be too grand to lower yourself and would ring for a steward to find my brooch, in which case everything would have been much more difficult."

"It is something I shall remember to do in the future," the Marquis said, "especially if there is someone like you about."

"You are quite safe now where I am concerned. I would never do such an unimaginative thing as to perform the same trick twice."

"You are not going to play any more tricks on me," the Marquis said. "Let us make that quite certain, otherwise I swear I will throw you overboard!"

"I warn you, I can swim!" Ola retorted. "And I shall either reach the shore or wait for another yacht to come by, which, with my good luck, will contain a handsome, wealthy, unmarried Duke. I intend to go one higher each time!"

The Marquis laughed again.

"Perhaps we should confine ourselves to a quieter, less eventful life, at least until we reach the South of France."

There was silence, until Ola asked in a rather small voice:

"Then what are you . . . going to . . . do with . . . me?"

"I have not yet decided," the Marquis replied, "but of course a lot will rest on your behaviour in the meantime."

"Then I will be good," Ola said, "very, very good, and perhaps if I am . . ."

She paused before she said quickly:

"No, I will not say it. It might be unlucky."

"You are right, it might be terribly unlucky," the Marquis agreed, "but you are to promise me that there will be no more tricks, and you have to swear that you have no drugs, poisons, or lethal weapons of any sort hidden in your possessions."

"Very well then, I promise," Ola said. "And do you know what I have been doing while you were asleep?"

"What?" the Marquis asked in an uncompromising voice.

"I have been reading about the Reform Bill. I found quite a lot of papers about it in a drawer in your desk."

She looked up at him quickly as she asked:

"You do not mind my looking for them and reading them?"

"I presume, as I am allowed to have no privacy where you are concerned, that I have to accept your somewhat high-handed methods. I realise that nothing is sacred from your curiosity."

"If I had found any love-letters or anything like that," Ola said, "I would of course not have thought of opening them or reading them, but printed leaflets are different. I could see quite clearly what they were."

The Marquis gave up the hopeless task of explaining that he did not expect his guests, whoever they might be, to rifle the drawers in his desk.

Instead he said:

"I should be interested to hear your opinion on what has been proposed so far in the amendments which I expect you have read and which were included in the Second Bill."

"Quite frankly, I did not think they went far enough," Ola said.

Then, almost despite himself, the Marquis found himself defending the Government and refuting Ola's contention of "too little and too late" as if he were speaking to a man of his own age.

CHAPTER FIVE

*T*he *Sea Wolf* sailed into a small bay surrounded by high cliffs.

They peaked so high that they looked like mountains rising from a small sandy beach, and Ola, watching every movement, exclaimed with delight when the anchor went down.

"What an ideal place!" she said to the Marquis. "I do wish we could swim in this clear water."

"I am afraid you would find it very cold," he said, "and the sea can be very treacherous at this time of the year."

"There is always some excuse for my not doing what I want to do," Ola pouted, and he laughed.

"I do not intend to feel sorry for you," he said. "You get your own way far too much already."

She gave him a mischievous glance from under her eye-lashes, and he knew that she was being provocative in a manner which he had grown used to yet still found alternately irritating and intriguing.

The sailors had already lowered the boat into the water, and as Ola and the Marquis climbed down a rope-ladder into it, other men were bringing the empty water-butts up from below-decks.

"I want to see the spring," Ola said as they were rowed away towards the shore.

They went to the spring first, and it was in fact rather disappointing to look at.

There was only a small amount of water flowing from the dark rock, but when they tasted it the Marquis knew that the Captain had been right in saying it was both pure and clear.

"If we were enterprising," Ola said, "we would start a Spa here and sell the water to people with ailments, most of which I am convinced are imaginary."

"I think the Spanish might object to that," the Marquis replied with a smile.

They moved away from the spring, and as they walked over the soft golden sand, Ola looked up at the cliffs rising above and said:

"Think what a wonderful view there must be from the top, not only over to the sea but over the land behind it. I have always wanted to see Spain."

"Are you suggesting we should climb it?" the Marquis asked.

"Why not?" Ola enquired. "It would be very good for us to take some exercise after being cooped up in the yacht for so long."

"I admit to missing my riding," the Marquis agreed, "but I think you would find it a hard climb."

Ola did not answer for a moment. She was looking at small tracks up the side of the cliff which she thought must have been made by wild goats.

Then with a smile she exclaimed:

"That is a challenge! And because I always accept one, I am quite prepared to race you to the top and beyond!"

"Nonsense!" the Marquis replied. "It would be far too much for you. If you would like to sit on the sand you can watch me climb some of the way up, then I can inform you what the view is like."

"I am not going to tell you what I think of that suggestion," Ola replied, "because it would be rude, and I have every intention of climbing the cliff. I am wearing sensible slippers, and I think you will find it far more difficult in your Hessian boots."

"They may certainly prove a handicap," the Marquis replied, "but let me assure you that I am extremely sure-footed, and if you faint by the way-side, or rather on the cliff-side, I shall be quite prepared to carry you down."

"You insult me!" Ola cried.

She put down her sunshade as she spoke and looked at the cliff to find where the best place was to start climbing.

She had worn no bonnet all the time she was on the yacht, for the simple reason that she had only the one she had travelled in, and when she sat on deck she either wore a chiffon scarf over her hair or, if it was very sunny, held up a small sunshade.

She did not, however, have to take much trouble over her skin because, as the Marquis had already noted, it had a magnolia-like quality that was the prerogative of some women with red hair and yet even so it was very rare.

It did not brown in the sun, and although she had been out on deck in wind, rain, and sunshine, it still had its dazzling whiteness which was in such direct contrast to the fiery hue of her hair.

The Marquis could understand only too well why women would not only envy her but also dislike her because it would be impossible for her not to draw the eye of every man present, wherever she might be.

It would be simple to dismiss her as looking theatrical, but that was a very superficial view of her looks, which were far more subtle than that.

She had, the Marquis thought, the same colouring and the same almost spiritual beauty he had seen in a painting but he could not remember where.

Suddenly he knew where he had seen the colour of her hair before—in a picture he himself owned.

By Rubens, it was a portrait of Marchesa Brigida Spinola-Doria. He had always thought not only that it was lovely but also that the gleaming red curls of her hair would be soft and silky to touch and at the same time would have a springing vitality.

He was sure that that was what Ola's hair would feel like.

Then he told himself severely that he had never admired women who were not fair and blue-eyed like Sarah.

Strangely enough, when he thought of her now there was no longer that stabbing pain in his heart, nor was there a red mist before his eyes, and his hands no longer clenched as if he wished to hit somebody.

He felt instead that Sarah, like England, was far away, and when Ola was talking to him so interestingly, drawing him out on his favourite subjects and listening with a rapt expression in her eyes which told him that she was genuinely entranced by what he was saying, Sarah no longer mattered.

Her power to hurt him had gone, and so too had her power to make him feel that he was a fool to have been betrayed.

He told himself firmly that he still distrusted and disliked all women and would never put himself in the same position again.

At the same time, when the sun was shining and the yacht he had designed himself was showing how remarkably easy she was to handle, there was no point in worrying over what was done and finished with.

Now he was amused by Ola's insistence that they must climb the cliff, as he was quite certain that she would find it too much for her.

They both started, with only a few feet between them, to scramble up the rough rocks and onto the tiny twisting paths which led them higher and higher.

The Marquis was remarkably fit, owing not only to the fact that whenever he was in London or in the country he rode one of his spirited horses every morning.

Although he had not bothered to mention it to Ola, he was an experienced pugilist and sparred in the

Gymnasium which was patronised by a great number of his friends.

He was also a swordsman, and although duelling with pistols was far more fashionable, fencing was still a skill in which the Marquis excelled.

Altogether he was extremely proud of being so strong and had no intention of becoming flabby through drink and debauchery like many of the Bucks under the last Monarch.

The King had certainly changed the fashion for large meals which had been set by George IV.

He had just saved fourteen thousand pounds a year by dismissing his brother's German Band and replacing it with a British one—a patriotic but less skilful substitute.

He had then sacked the squadron of French Chefs who had followed the previous King from residence to residence.

This was an economy which was deplored by a number of those who were habitually at the Royal table.

"I find it detestable and depressing," one Statesman had said to the Marquis; while Lord Dudley, who was celebrated for grumbling *sotto-voce* and caused a lot of embarrassment in doing so, had remarked:

"What a change, to be sure! Cold pâtés and hot champagne!"

But while the late King's habitual companions suffered, the public were delighted that William IV had dispensed with the luxurious extravagances of his brother's way of life.

They cheered when they learnt that the number of Royal yachts had been cut from five to two, the stud reduced to half its original size, and that one hundred exotic birds and beasts which had been the delight of George IV were presented to the Zoological Society.

The King was applauded wherever he went, and actually there were few people, if they were honest, who did not admit that a change was overdue.

As the Marquis climbed steadily up the cliff he told himself that for the moment it was a relief to be away from London, free from all the complaints and criticisms which inevitably were voiced amongst those who found the King different in every way from the late Monarch.

For one thing, the Marquis, who was extremely diplomatic when he was acting in an official capacity, found King William's indiscretions dangerous.

He had winced with the Ministers when William had referred to the King of the French as "an infamous scoundrel!"

The Duke of Wellington had given the King a stiff rebuke which had kept him quiet for some weeks, but actually he was irrepressible; and another time, angry at the conduct of affairs by the French, he had startled a Military Banquet at Windsor Castle by expressing the hope that if his guests had to draw their swords, it would be against the French, the natural enemies of England!

"I deserve a holiday," the Marquis said to himself, remembering how he had had to smooth down the incensed feelings of the French Ambassador.

Then he realised that, deep in his thoughts, he had not noticed that Ola was ahead of him.

He told himself she would soon grow tired, but at the same time he moved a little quicker to get level with her.

"Be careful," he admonished. "If you slip you will fall a long way and doubtless end up with a cracked head and a broken leg."

She managed a little smile.

"Stop croaking at me," she said. "I am as sure-footed as any chamois, which, by the way, is an animal I would like to see."

"They are more likely to be found farther inland," the Marquis replied.

"You have visited Spain?"

"I have been to Madrid and Seville."

"How lucky you are! I was just thinking as I was climbing that if I were a man I would be an explorer. What is the point of sitting in one place when one might be travelling all over the world, finding fascinating places where no white man has ever been before?"

"That would certainly be no life for a woman!" the Marquis said.

"I thought that would be your answer," Ola remarked in disgust.

She looked at him, then moved towards the cliff-top so quickly that he had to make a very strenuous effort to catch up with her.

Then suddenly there was a flat rock and as they reached it at almost the same time, Ola gave a little exclamation.

"Look!" she cried. "Caves! How exciting!"

The Marquis stepped onto the flat rock, aware that he was breathing quickly from the exertion and the climb, which had certainly exercised every one of his muscles.

It astounded him to see that Ola was completely composed and the only outward sign of her exertion was that her gown was stained by the moss and lichen that grew on the rocks.

She was looking wide-eyed at the caves behind them, large, dark openings. Then, almost as if with an effort, she turned round to look out to sea.

Below them, and it was a long way down, they could see the yacht riding at anchor and the men carrying a water-butt, which they had filled at the spring, back towards the boat.

Then beyond was a vista of sparkling blue sea which, in the sunshine, seemed to shimmer with light to where in the indefinable distance the horizon met the sky.

"It is lovely! Absolutely lovely!" Ola exclaimed.

"I agree with you . . ." the Marquis began.

"I wonder . . ." Ola said.

Then she gave a little cry that was stifled as suddenly a rough hand was placed over her mouth and she was lifted off her feet.

She found herself being carried away into the darkness of a cave.

For a moment she could not think what was happening. Then as she struggled and realised that the hands that held her were strong, and that there were four of them, she knew any resistance was useless and could only wonder desperately to where she was being taken.

She had not long to wait, since the dark passage down which she was carried opened suddenly into what was a large cavern lit by flaring torches, with a wood-fire at the far end of it.

Now she was set down on the ground, but she was still unable to speak because the hand was kept across her mouth.

But she could see, and she saw that standing in the centre of the cave was a man who looked so exactly like the popular conception of a Brigand that it was difficult to believe that he was in fact real.

He had long, dark, greasy hair, a moustache which turned down at the sides of his mouth, and he wore a brightly coloured handkerchief round his head.

In a wide red belt which encircled his waist were knives with ornamented handles, and in his hand he held an old-fashioned pistol.

Standing round the cave were a number of other men dressed like him, the only difference being that the majority of them held knives in their hands instead of a pistol.

The Marquis had obviously put up a fight, for Ola had been in the cave for a few seconds before he was dragged in by three men.

A fourth man was concerned only with keeping his hand over the Marquis's mouth so that he could not speak, and Ola realised that the Brigands were afraid that if he shouted, even though they were so high up, he might alert the attention of the sailors.

The Marquis, seeing the Chief Brigand with his loaded pistol, realised that it was useless to fight any further and he stood still, although his captors kept a firm grip on his arms, and now the man standing behind him covered his mouth with both his hands.

The Brigand Chief merely looked the Marquis up and down, then glanced at Ola.

"What are you waiting for?" one of the men asked. "Kill him and let me have his boots!"

"I could do with his coat," another jeered, "and I bet there's some gold in his pockets!"

The Chief cocked his pistol and Ola saw an expression of delight in his followers' eyes as they bent forward, obviously excited at the thought of seeing a man die.

She could not believe this was happening, but the Brigand Chief had raised his pistol and she knew that he was in fact going to shoot the Marquis, just as he stood there, in cold blood.

Frantically, she bit hard into the hand which covered her mouth, taking her captor by surprise.

He had been far too intent on watching what his Chief was doing to be concerned with her, and when he took his hand away she started to speak.

"No, no, *Señor*, listen a minute!" she shouted in Spanish.

As her voice rang out in the cave the Brigand Chief looked at her in surprise.

"You must hear what I have to say," Ola went on, "because, *Señor*, if you shoot this nobleman without listening to me first, you will make a very great mistake because you will lose a great deal of money."

She spoke slowly although it was difficult for her because she wanted to scream at the Brigands.

But she realised when they spoke that their Spanish was not the pure Castilian language she had learnt and that they might in fact find her hard to understand.

Then she thought, and she was not mistaken, that the Brigand Chief was better educated and doubtless better bred than his followers.

"So you speak our language, *Señora?*" he said. "What is this man to you—your husband?"

"That is not important," Ola replied. "What you should know is that he is very rich. You do not want his boots, nor his coat. You want the gold he has aboard his ship, which can make you rich for the rest of your lives."

The Brigand Chief and the rest of the party were listening to her almost as if they were spellbound. Then the Chief laughed.

"You paint a very pretty picture, *Señora*," he said. "And how do you suggest we collect the gold? Ask the seamen to hand it over?"

"They would be prepared to do so in exchange for their Master's life!"

"We are more likely to receive a bullet in the gullet, *Señora*," the Brigand answered. "No, no, your idea is impracticable. I have seen ships here before, but it is the first time anyone travelling in them was fool enough to trespass on what is my property."

"In which case we can only apologise, *Señor*," Ola said, "and I assure you that if this nobleman gives you his word of honour he will reward you for taking us back in safety to his yacht."

As she spoke the Brigand was looking at her sceptically, and she added:

"Surely I do not have to explain to a Spaniard that no *nobleza* would break his word of honour, as you would not break yours?"

"You are very eloquent, *Señora*," the Brigand Chief said, "but my men do not want money. They are not hungry, as there is plenty of wild game in this part of the country, and if we fancy a fat sheep or a succulent pig for dinner the farmers are too frightened to prevent us from taking them!"

He gave a supercilious smile as he went on:

"No, *Señora*, what my men hanker after are fashionable boots, a coat that will keep out the rain, and perhaps some pretty jewels that a man can wear in his ears or on his fingers."

"Those I can definitely promise you," Ola said quickly. "I have jewels—diamonds, sapphires, pearls. They are there in the yacht and if you take me back I will give them to you."

There was silence, and she hoped she had made some impression on the Brigand, and yet she was not sure.

He had certainly listened to her and was looking at her now as if he was considering her proposition but could not make up his mind whether to accept or refuse it.

One of his followers rose from where he had been sitting and went up to him to whisper in his ear.

Ola wished she could hear what he was saying, but it was impossible.

The Chief nodded his head, then shook it as if he said "No," and then nodded again.

Ola looked at the Marquis and thought that if perhaps he was looking at her and their eyes met, she would know if he approved or disapproved of what she was trying to do.

But he was watching the two men whispering together in the centre of the cave, and now Ola felt her heart beating apprehensively and was aware that the position they were in was a critical one.

There were several men in the cave and she thought they were more ferocious and in a way more terrifying than any creature she could have imagined in her wildest dreams.

She was sure that they terrorised the countryside and that murder to them was as commonplace as killing the food they wanted to eat.

She found herself remembering the stories she had been told of the bands of ruffians who preyed on travellers all over Europe, to which she had paid little attention.

The girls at the Convent had told her how their relatives or friends had been held up by robbers even on the main highways and to save their lives they had been forced to hand over everything of value they possessed.

But these Brigands seemed to be different.

She could understand, if they lived in a cave like this, that money would not mean a great deal to them.

It was perhaps the excitement of living wild, beholden to no-one, outside the law, that was more attractive than possessions.

Frantically she began to think that her offer of what they could have in exchange for the Marquis's life was not forceful enough, and she said urgently:

"*Señor*, I have another idea!"

The Chief had been in the process of shaking his head at something his follower had suggested and now he looked at her and said:

"What is it?"

"Suppose one of us, either this nobleman or myself, goes back to the yacht to collect anything you want, clothes, food, boots, gold, jewels. We will put everything on the beach where you can see it quite clearly, and then when your second prisoner is released we can . . . sail . . . away. . . ."

Her voice faltered as if she felt she had not convinced him, and she added:

"What have you to lose by such a suggestion? You could not be identified, nobody could shoot at you, and you would have everything you want."

She thought, although she was not certain, that there was a murmur of approval from some of the other men listening.

The Chief said sharply:

"It is too complicated, and anyway why should we trust you? We have you here and the man shall die, but you will stay with us."

For a moment Ola did not understand what he meant. Then with an unpleasant smile on his lips he said:

"We have no women with us at the moment and some of my men find you attractive, *Señora*."

Ola gave a little cry of sheer horror.

"No! No! Do you really think I would . . . stay with you?"

"You have no choice," the Brigand said.

As he spoke he lifted his pistol again, and Ola, with a sudden strength which took them by surprise, fought herself free of her captors and rushed towards the Marquis.

She flung herself in front of him, facing the Brigand and crying as she did so:

"If you shoot him, you will have to shoot me first! You are murderers and the curse of God will strike you sooner or later!"

The words sounded more impressive in Spanish than in English and there was a cry of protest from the Brigand's followers.

At that moment the Marquis struggled wildly with his captors and managed in doing so to release his mouth from the restriction of the hands that had held him.

"Curse you! Yes, curse you!" he shouted, speaking, to Ola's surprise, in Spanish.

Then he was engaged in resisting the men who were struggling to regain their hold on him, while Ola stood between him and the Chief with his loaded pistol.

She knew that if she moved he would fire it. Then, glancing back at the struggle going on behind her, she saw that one of the Brigands had drawn a knife from his belt and had raised it high to strike the Marquis in the chest.

Without thinking, without even considering what she was doing, Ola threw herself at his arm, forcing the long, sharp, evil-looking blade upwards.

Then as she knew she had not the strength to prevent the Marquis from dying, there was a sudden explosion which seemed so loud as almost to break her ear-drums.

At the same moment she felt the knife pierce her own shoulder, searing its way into her flesh.

As she fell to the ground there were more explosions and the noise of them seemed to bring a darkness that covered her completely. . . .

The Marquis quietly opened the door of the cabin and walked towards the bed, and Gibson, who had been sitting in a chair beside it, rose to his feet.

"How is she?" the Marquis asked in a low voice.

"Running a high fever, M'Lord, and hasn't regained consciousness, which is what's to be expected."

"I thought I heard her voice during the night," the Marquis said.

"She was delirious, M'Lord, and I didn't know what she were saying."

"I will stay with her now," the Marquis said. "You go and rest, Gibson, and that is an order!"

"Thank you, M'Lord, but I'm all right. I'm used to doing with very little sleep."

"You will be watching over Miss Milford tonight, unless you allow me to do so," the Marquis replied.

"I'll stay with her, M'Lord, as we arranged. But if you'll stay with the young lady now, I'll do as you tells me and have a bit of 'shut-eye.' "

"Do that," the Marquis said. "If she is thirsty, is there anything for her to drink?"

"Yes, M'Lord. There's lime-juice in one jug and fresh water in another."

"The water which nearly cost us dear!" the Marquis remarked as if he were speaking to himself.

Gibson did not reply.

He only gave a last look at Ola to see if there was anything more he could do, then went from the cabin.

The Marquis, left in charge, looked at Ola and thought that they both were extremely fortunate to be alive. He had been sure that there was no hope for either of them.

He was aware now that it was her brave effort in trying to save his life that had allowed time for the sailors to climb the cliff and appear at precisely the right moment to shoot down the Brigand Chief and six of his men before the rest fled.

"I blame myself, M'Lord," the Captain had said when the Marquis had reached the yacht in safety.

They had had great difficulty in getting Ola, who was unconscious, down from the flat rock outside the caves. They had in fact to lower her with ropes, and the

Marquis was afraid that any rough movements would make her shoulder bleed more than it was doing already and she might die from loss of blood.

"Why should you blame yourself?" the Marquis asked.

"It never struck me that Your Lordship and the young lady would climb the cliff," the Captain replied, "and when you started I was actually below, making sure that the water-butts when they came on board would not get loose again, however bad a storm we might encounter."

The Marquis looked as if he approved, and the Captain went on:

"Then when I saw you and Miss Milford climbing upwards, I remembered that the last time I was in this bay I was told to watch out for Spanish Brigands. 'Nasty customers, they are!' one seaman on Lord Lutworth's yacht informed me. 'Cut your throat before they ask your name, and some of 'em are armed with pistols and muskets!' "

"When you remembered this, what did you do?" the Marquis enquired.

"I sent a man up aloft, M'Lord, with a glass, and told him to watch you and the young lady. When he shouted that he could see you being dragged inside the caves, I knew only too well what was happening."

"It was certainly an Act of Providence that your quickness of action saved our lives," the Marquis remarked.

"I'd never have forgiven myself," the Captain said fervently, "if anything had happened to Your Lordship."

"I have been near to death many times in my life," the Marquis replied, "but this was too near for me to wish to encounter such a situation again!"

"I can only thank God that you and Miss Milford returned without worse injuries," the Captain said sincerely.

The Marquis knew that he himself echoed those sentiments.

Now, looking at Ola, he thought it almost impossible to believe that any woman could have been so brave and so resourceful.

He had been surprised to find when he reached the cave that she was not crying or collapsing in the hands of her captors.

Then when she had managed to free her mouth he was aware that she was deliberately speaking slowly in Spanish so that the Brigands could understand what she was saying, and he thought it amazing that she was neither cringing with fear nor pleading.

Then as she stood in front of him to save his life and actually grappled with the Brigand who was trying to knife him, he thought it was an act of heroism he would not have expected from any woman, especially one as young and frail as Ola.

He supposed her fiery red hair reflected the indomitable spirit within her. Certainly only a woman of exceptional bravery could have been involved in so many strange and desperate situations since she had entered his life.

The last was almost incredible, and it was tragic that she, rather than himself, must be the one to suffer what had happened.

The Brigand's knife had gone deep into her shoulder, and by the time they had got her back to the yacht the blood had seeped over her gown in a crimson tide, and her face was so pale that the Marquis was half-afraid that she was in fact dead.

Gibson, who was as skilled as any Surgeon and better than a large number of those the Marquis had known in the Army, took charge in his usual efficient manner.

He and the Marquis had cut Ola's gown off her, to save her from being moved more than was necessary. Then they had cleansed the wound with brandy for fear that the knife had been dirty.

Fortunately, Ola was unconscious when Gibson had stitched the flesh together with such skilled neatness that the Marquis was sure no professional Surgeon could have done better.

The valet had bandaged her deftly and they both knew that the next twenty-four hours would be critical in case the inflammation would be so severe that gangrene would set in.

Gibson had insisted on staying with Ola that night.

"Leave her to me, M'Lord, and you get some rest. Your Lordship can take your turn tomorrow; it's going to be some time before th' lady's on her feet again."

The Marquis had seen the common sense of what his valet said, but although he had gone to bed he found it difficult to sleep while his brain went over and over what had occurred, and his thoughts kept returning to the injured girl in the next cabin.

As he looked at her now, he thought it would be difficult to find anywhere else in the world a face so lovely and at the same time so unusual.

He realised for the first time that her eye-lashes were dark at the tips and shaded away to gold where they touched her skin; similarly, the winged eye-brows above them were dark, while her hair against the white linen pillow was like a flame.

It made him think of the torches flaring in the Brigands' cave, and he wondered if any of the men who had fled in terror when the sailors had killed their comrades would ever go back.

He had the feeling that as their Leader was dead this particular gang of ruffians would be disbanded, and at least a few wretched travellers would escape persecution at their hands in the future.

At the same time, the Marquis told himself it was a salutary lesson that he should have learnt long ago, not to take chances in foreign countries.

There were so many parts of Europe that were wild and uncivilised, and he was aware that even if Ola had travelled on the main highway to Paris she would have been in danger.

She might have been molested, perhaps not by Brigands but certainly by thieves who would relieve her of the jewellery she carried, and by men who would find her looks irresistible and would be equally prepared to use violence to get what they wanted.

"How can any woman take such risks with herself?" the Marquis asked himself angrily.

Then he realised that he had forgotten how young, innocent, and inexperienced Ola was.

Since they had been talking to each other on equal terms he had found it hard to remember her age and that she was in some ways, little more than a child.

He found himself remembering how she had puzzled over the word "cocotte" and supposed it referred to some kind of actress.

'Some man will take it upon himself to enlighten her about such things, one of these days,' the Marquis thought cynically. 'Then she will be like every other woman—pursuing men and, having caught one, prepared to manipulate him to suit her own ends.'

Once again he was thinking of Sarah. Then he recalled how Ola had told him that she had no wish to marry and submit to being ordered about by a husband.

'He will be an exceptional man to get his own way,' the Marquis thought with a smile.

A sudden movement caught his attention.

She was moving her head from side to side and now she said in an indistinct murmur:

"I . . . must . . . escape . . . I must! . . . Help . . . me . . . oh . . . help me!"

The Marquis rose and put his hand on her forehead. It was very hot and he knew that her temperature was rising.

She moved again restlessly, and although Gibson had bound her arm tightly to her side, the Marquis was afraid that she might break open the wound.

He went to the basin where Gibson had left a clean linen handkerchief and beside it a bottle of *eau-de-Cologne*.

The Marquis soaked the handkerchief in the Cologne and some water, then squeezed it out, and when it was moist and cool he put it on Ola's forehead as she murmured:

"It is . . . foggy . . . do . . . be careful! . . . Look out!"

He knew she was back in the post-chaise, reliving the difficulties and the drama of her escape from her Stepmother.

"It is all right, Ola," he said gently, "you are safe and you must go to sleep."

She was still for some minutes, as if the handkerchief on her forehead was soothing.

Then with a little cry she said agitatedly:

"I . . . cannot go back . . . I have to . . . escape again . . . I hate him! I . . . hate him! How . . . can I . . . save . . . myself . . . ?"

There was something pathetic in the last words and the Marquis said softly:

"You have saved yourself. Listen to me, Ola, you are safe, and you do not have to go back to your Stepmother—do you understand?"

He was not certain whether his words reached her or not, but he thought, although he was not sure, that some of the tension seemed to go from her body.

Then once again she appeared to fall asleep.

"I suppose I have committed myself now," the Marquis told himself ruefully. "Whether she heard me or not, I have told her she will not return to her Stepmother, and that is a promise I have to keep!"

CHAPTER SIX

I congratulate you, young lady, on having been lucky enough to have your wound treated so expertly," the Doctor said.

He was a hearty man who had been summoned on board at Gibraltar to examine Ola's wound, and he could in fact find nothing wrong with it.

"I expect you're feeling exhausted after your fever," he went on, "but with rest and good food you'll soon be on your feet again."

"What about a tonic?" the Marquis suggested, who had come into the cabin after the Doctor had finished examining Ola.

The Doctor glanced round the luxurious surroundings and said with a twinkle in his eye:

"The best tonic I can prescribe comes from France."

The Marquis smiled.

"I presume you mean champagne?"

"It's what I always prescribe for my richer patients," the Doctor said, "but the poorer ones expect a bottle from me, which is usually little more than coloured water!"

The Marquis laughed.

"At least you are frank."

"I believe it's a patient's will-power that counts," the Doctor said. "If they want to get well, they get well; if they want to die, they die!"

The Marquis noted that Ola, weak though she was, was smiling at this exchange of words and now she gave a little chuckle.

"I come into the first category," she said, "and I want to live."

"Then as I've already said, we shall soon have you up and dancing," the Doctor answered.

He glanced at Ola's hair before he left the cabin, and she heard him say outside the door:

"It's seldom I have the privilege of attending so beautiful a young lady!"

Ola listened for the Marquis's reply but they had moved too far away, and she wondered if he had qualified the Doctor's compliment by complaining that she was also a nuisance, a positive encumbrance.

When she had regained consciousness she had learnt how much trouble she had given.

It was Gibson who had told her that the Marquis had sat with her every day when she was delirious and running too high a fever to be left alone.

'He must have been terribly bored,' she thought.

Then she told herself that she had upset him in so many different ways that one more would make little difference.

But when she was on the way to recovery, she realised that the Marquis was sitting with her when there was really no need for him to do so.

He read to her and was not offended when she fell asleep, and as soon as she could sit up in bed they played chess and piquet and, what she enjoyed more than anything else, they talked.

It was after they had left Gibraltar and were moving over the blue sea of the Mediterranean that Ola began to feel more like her former self.

Gibson was sure that it was due not to the champagne but to the fresh oranges and lemons he had been able to buy in Gibraltar.

"I've seen too many sailors, Miss, suffer from lack of fruit when they were a long time at sea," he said, "not to realise how important it is, especially when there's a wound that needs healing."

Because Ola was prepared to believe that he was right, she drank glass after glass of the juices he prepared for her, and she had to admit that they seemed to speed the healing of her wound.

"Will I have a scar?" she asked Gibson when he was dressing it.

"I'll tell you no lie, Miss," he replied. "You'll carry a mark there to your dying day, but fortunately it's not in a place where it'll show unless your evening-gowns are cut over-low."

Ola laughed.

"I must remember to make them discreetly modest."

When she told the Marquis what Gibson had said, he laughed too.

"You will certainly not be expected when you go to Court to have a very low décolletage," he said, "not with Queen Adelaide's eye upon you."

He spoke without thinking, and only as he saw Ola blush did he remember that if her behaviour at this moment were known in Society, she would receive no invitation to Buckingham Palace and would be ostracised by all the important hostesses of the Social World.

He thought with a frown that that must not happen, and he decided that before they reached Nice he must find some solution to Ola's problems. Above all, she must have a Chaperone.

As if she knew what he was thinking but felt too tired to argue about it at the moment, Ola shut her eyes.

He thought she was asleep and after some minutes he very quietly left her cabin. Then she lay staring at the ceiling and wondering once again despairingly what would happen to her in the future.

After four days' sailing in the Mediterranean, Ola was well enough to be carried up on deck.

"What you wants Miss, is some good fresh air, to put the colour back in your cheeks," Gibson said.

Ola thought he sounded exactly like her old Nurse, who had always believed that fresh air was a cure for everything, including a bad temper.

When she was on deck she realised why the Marquis looked so well and did not seem to mind that they were sailing more slowly towards Nice than they would have done if she had not been on board.

Although the sunshine was warm the sea was cold, but he swam in it twice a day, once in the morning and again in the afternoon.

She liked to watch him swimming until his head was only a little spot in the distance, but she would feel anxious in case anything should happen which would prevent him from returning to the yacht in safety.

She found herself remembering the stories of men who had cramps in the sea and sank before anyone could rescue them.

When she enquired about sharks she was told that there were none in this area and the only thing the Marquis had to be afraid of was catching a chill.

"He's unlikely to do that," Gibson said, and added with pride in his voice: "There's few men as strong as His Lordship, and whether he's riding or hunting it's always the horse as tires before His Lordship."

Ola found that when he was not swimming the Marquis liked to take the helm of the yacht and sail the *Sea Wolf* himself.

She realised how expert he was and that he could sail closer to the wind than anyone else aboard without letting the sails flap.

She thought it must give him the same thrill as driving his Phaeton to break a record or riding his own horse past the winning-post in a steeple-chase.

Lying comfortably on the soft couch which Gibson had constructed for her on deck, and propped against silk cushions, Ola found the activities going on all round her far more fascinating than being alone in her cabin.

She was taken down below when the sun began to sink, and, as often happened, a chill wind blew up and the Marquis usually came with her.

Then they would talk and to Ola's delight they would discuss subjects as diverse as Oriental religions and the Abolition of the Slave Trade.

The Marquis was astounded not only at the subjects which interested her but because she knew so much about them.

"How can you have read so much at your age?" he asked one evening after they had had a long and animated discussion on the conditions in the coal-mines.

"I have not only read a lot," Ola replied, "but Papa was an extremely clever man. The only trouble was that he wished to expound his own theories and not listen to anybody else's."

The Marquis smiled.

"So that is why you are so verbose on these subjects."

"That is a rather unkind way of putting it," Ola objected, "but the answer is 'yes.' I have been bottling up my own ideas for so long that now, because you are obliging enough to listen to me, they burst out like a volcano."

The Marquis laughed and thought that while he was the first man Ola had ever been able to talk to, she was the first woman who had ever been interested in every subject in the world except himself.

He had never before in his life, the Marquis thought, talked for hours with a woman, and an attractive one at that, when there had been nothing personal in what they said to each other.

With Ola there were no flirtatious glances, no fishing for compliments, and, most of all, none of the sharp, witty *double entendres* which the sophisticated women in London used as a weapon of attraction.

Thinking back, he could not remember ever having a conversation with Sarah which had not involved her feelings or his, and which had not ended in his making passionate expressions of his love for her.

He realised now how cleverly she had led him on, how she had aroused, then tantalised him by refusing to "risk her reputation" by surrendering herself as he wished her to do.

Yet all the time she was amusing herself with another man.

To his surprise, he found that his hurt pride as well as his anger had now subsided to the point where he could wonder quite calmly what Sarah must have thought when he did not arrive the following night as she had expected.

He imagined that she would have waited for him, then must have decided that he could not have received her letter.

She would therefore have expected him the next day and perhaps the day after that, until finally she would either have made enquiries or somebody would have told her that he had stayed one night at Elvin and then had left at dawn the following morning.

It was then, he thought, unless she was more stupid than he gave her credit for being, that she would have realised what had happened and been aware that she had lost him irretrievably.

"I hope she is upset," he told himself, and found that he was not even feeling very vindictive about it.

She had gambled and lost, as many men and women had done in the past and would do in the future.

For the first time the Marquis said to himself:

"Thank God I was lucky enough to find out the truth before it was too late!"

He had had a lucky escape and he knew he should be grateful for that, just as he was grateful that Ola had saved his life when, if she had not been there, he would undoubtedly have died at the hands of the Brigands.

Several days before they reached Nice, Ola was able to go up on deck without being carried, and she was well enough not only to have luncheon with the Marquis in the Saloon but also to stay up for dinner.

"I have been given strict instructions by Gibson that I am to go to bed before you drink your first glass of port," she said, "so please do not be in a hurry to do so."

"You know Gibson has to be obeyed when it is a question of your health," the Marquis said with mock seriousness.

"I am well aware of that," Ola replied. "He gets more like my Nurse every day until I find myself almost saying: 'Yes, Nanny!' and 'No, Nanny!' to everything he tells me to do."

The Marquis laughed and she added quickly:

"But I am not complaining! I realise that if Gibson had not been on board I might not be here with you now."

"He is really rather a wonderful little man."

"He thinks the sun and the moon rise and set for you," Ola said. "He sings your praises until I too bow to your importance."

"You are trying to make me feel embarrassed," the Marquis complained, "and I suspect there is a sting somewhere in what you are saying."

"Now you are being nasty," Ola teased. "You are omnipotent and I feel that by the end of this voyage I shall be saying my prayers to you."

She spoke without considering her words.

Then as the Marquis saw a sudden wary look in her eyes and the colour rise in her cheeks, he knew she was thinking that if she was praying to him, it would be to beg him not to send her back to her Stepmother, which he could quite easily do from Nice.

He hesitated, as if he intended to say something, but before he could do so the steward came into the Saloon and the opportunity did not seem to arise later.

The *Sea Wolf* sailed into the Harbour at Nice early in the morning, and Ola could see the white Villas and Hotels built along the sea-front and above them the surrounding hills, and silhouetted against the sky in the far distance the snow-capped, rugged head of Mont Chauve.

Everything seemed to glow with a warmth and radiance which made her feel as if Nice gave her a special welcome, and before they dropped anchor she could see the palms, the graceful feathery tamarisks, the oleanders, and, what she longed for more than anything else, the yellow mimosas.

"I want to go ashore immediately!" she cried excitedly to the Marquis.

Then as he did not reply she looked up at him and saw a frown between his eyes.

"You think that would be . . . unwise?" she asked quickly.

"What I would like to do," he replied, "is to have a quick look round to see whom I know here. This, as you are well aware, is a fashionable time of the year for people to come to Nice, and I would not wish you to be embarrassed until we have made our plans."

"Yes . . . of course," Ola said quickly.

She realised now that they should have discussed what she was to do before they had actually arrived.

But she had been content to let the days drift by without forcing the issue, and she had the idea that the Marquis was being kind to her because she was still weak from her wound.

"I am sure you are right," she said. "You must go ashore, and I will wait until you return."

He smiled as if he thought she was being not only sensible but conciliatory in a way he had not expected.

"I shall not be long," he said. "I know where to make enquiries and I shall come back as quickly as possible."

"I will sit and look at the view," she said. "It is so lovely—like a picture by a master-painter of which one would never grow tired."

The Marquis left the yacht and Ola thought he looked extremely elegant with his top-hat at an angle on his dark head.

She wondered if there were many of his old loves staying in Nice who would welcome him with open arms.

She hoped that if they did so it would not make him linger for long, because without him the yacht seemed empty and she felt lonely.

After a while she went down to the Saloon and, choosing a book, settled herself down to read.

It was full of interesting things she thought she would like to discuss with the Marquis, and yet she kept wondering if, now that they had reached Nice, this would be the end of the voyage as far as she was concerned.

She could hardly believe that he would be so cruel or so heartless after what had happened to send her back to her Stepmother as he had threatened to do before she had drugged him.

But what was the alternative? Unless she went, as she had first intended, to the Convent and risked her cousin Giles finding her there.

It struck her that she had not thought about Giles since the moment she had left Dover with the Marquis, and she supposed that he would have been well looked after wherever he was staying.

If he was not, it could hardly be her fault. He had no right to behave as he had or to threaten that he would force her into marriage just so that he could possess her fortune.

"He is horrible and I have no wish to think about him!" Ola told herself.

She was quite certain that the Marquis would never behave in such an ungentlemanly manner however much in need he might be of money.

Besides, she was sure that, unlike Giles, in straitened circumstances the Marquis would be clever enough to find some way of making money and would not just sponge on his friends or relations.

'He would be too honourable,' Ola thought.

She had picked up her book to go on reading, when she heard footsteps outside the Saloon and thought with a leap of her heart that the Marquis had returned.

She looked eagerly towards the door as it opened and a steward appeared to say:

"A gentleman to see His Lordship!"

Then a man walked into the Saloon and as Ola stared at him incredulously she realised with astonishment that it was Giles.

After his first start at seeing her, he said harshly:

"So this is where you are! I might have suspected it when I was told that the Marquis of Elvington had taken you across the Channel to Calais."

"Why . . . are you . . . here?"

"I was looking for you," Giles replied, "although I did not expect to find you in Nice!"

She did not speak, and as if he thought he must explain himself he said:

"When I was well enough to travel, I went to the Convent, expecting to find you there."

That was what Ola had guessed he would do, and she drew in her breath as he continued:

"I was not certain where I should go next, and I came to Nice to convalesce after my accident. You have not asked after my health and it may interest you to know that I fractured two ribs and my head still aches."

"You got what you deserve," Ola replied sharply, "and I was lucky to escape from you!"

"To the Marquis of Elvington!"

There was no doubt from the way Giles spoke that he was sneering, and Ola said:

"His Lordship was kind enough to help me when you were trying to force me into marriage just so that you could get your hands on my fortune."

"I was at least prepared to marry you," Giles sneered, "but I always thought that with your hair you would become a strumpet sooner or later!"

He spoke so aggressively that he was not aware, as Ola was, that the Marquis had come into the Saloon behind him.

Now as he finished speaking he turned his head and saw who was there.

"You will kindly apologise for speaking to your cousin in such a manner!" the Marquis said quietly.

"I shall do no such thing!" Giles retorted. "I called her a strumpet, which she obviously is, but because we are related I am still prepared to make an honest woman of her, which is more than you are prepared to do."

He spat the words at the Marquis, then as Ola gasped the Marquis knocked him down.

It was a blow to the chin, and as Giles sprawled on the deck of the Saloon the Marquis said:

"Get off my yacht! If I ever find you here again, or speaking in such an insulting way to a woman, I will give you the thrashing you deserve!"

For a moment Giles did not move, and Ola thought the expression on his face was so unpleasant that it was positively evil.

Then as he picked himself up he said:

"If you think you can get away with this, Elvington, you are very much mistaken! When I get back to London I shall make it my business to see that everybody in the Social World is aware of your behaviour in abducting a young and defenceless girl. I cannot believe His Majesty or the Queen will countenance such immorality on the part of one of their privileged entourage."

As he finished speaking Ola gave a little cry of horror, then as Giles walked from the cabin, stroking his chin where he had been hit, and the Marquis following him, she ran to her own cabin.

She knew that Giles had not spoken idly in saying that the Marquis would be in disgrace if the King and Queen heard his distorted version of her being alone and unchaperoned on the Marquis's yacht.

The Queen had been generous enough to accept the burden of His Majesty's illegitimate children and to become devoted to them, but in every other way she had shown herself to be prudish and extremely censorious about anything that offended her particular ideals of morality and respectability.

Having been brought up in a narrow and provincial Court, she had a very clear vision of what conventional life should be and had no idea of modifying her beliefs to suit an alien land.

Ola was intelligent enough to realise that the Marquis was not only proud of the confidence placed in him by the King but also made it his duty to try to prevent the Monarch from making the many mistakes in which his impetuosity involved him.

She had also learnt quite casually in their conversations that when people at Court and even the Prime Minister wanted something done, they asked the Marquis to help put their point of view to the King simply because His Majesty was so fond of him.

"How can I take that from him? How can I spoil that part of his life?" Ola asked herself.

Because she could think of nothing else she could do, she frantically began to pack her trunk, taking her gowns from the cupboard in which they hung and her other things from the drawers which were in a cleverly contrived piece of furniture which fitted against the side of one of the walls of the cabin.

Because she was agitated it took her longer than it would have done normally, apart from the fact that because she was using her injured arm it began to hurt her.

But at last everything was packed, and she took her bonnet from the top of the cupboard, put it on her head, and tied the ribbons under her chin.

Then she went to the cabin door and called for a steward.

There was always one in attendance when she and the Marquis were in their cabins, but it was not the steward who came in answer to her call; it was Gibson.

"I wanted the steward," she said.

"I'll do whatever it is you want, Miss."

Ola hesitated a moment, then she said:

"Please have my trunk strapped down and taken onto the Quay, and I want a hackney-carriage."

Gibson did not reply and after a moment she said firmly:

"At once!"

"I'm afraid that's impossible, Miss."

"What do you mean . . . it is impossible?" Ola enquired.

"Before the Master went ashore, Miss, he says to me: 'Look after Miss Milford, Gibson, until I gets back.' "

"What His Lordship said or did not say does not concern me," Ola said with dignity. "I have to leave, Gibson, and I would be obliged if you would carry out my orders."

"I'm sorry, Miss, but that's something I can't do!"

"You mean you are refusing to have my trunk taken ashore?"

"If it comes to that, Miss, I'm refusing to let you go," Gibson answered. "Besides, you're not strong enough to go gallivanting about, and you knows that as well as I do."

"I . . . have to . . . go, Gibson."

He shook his head; and then instead of raging at him as she was sure she would have done in the past, she sat down helplessly on the bed.

"Now, what I'm going to do, Miss," Gibson said in a different tone, "is to fetch you a nice cup of tea. There's nothing like a cup of tea when you feels upset."

He went from the cabin as he spoke, shutting the door behind him, and Ola put her hands up to her eyes as if in an effort to think.

"If I stay here I shall hurt the Marquis," she said, "and that is something I must not do."

She decided that if Gibson was going to be so obstructive she must leave without her luggage.

She knew he would have gone to the galley to make her tea, and she thought that if she hurried she could slip up on deck and get away before he was aware of it.

The *Sea Wolf* was tied up alongside the Quay and there was a gangplank by which she could step ashore.

She therefore picked up her jewel-case, and, moving very quietly in case there was anyone listening, she went to the door and turned the handle.

It seemed surprisingly stiff, and then as she turned it again she realised indignantly that Gibson had locked her in!

It was intolerable behaviour on his part, and she walked to the port-hole, wishing that she were small enough to squeeze through it and swim to the shore, just to show her independence.

Then she knew that that was impossible and once again she sat down on her bed, and taking off her bonnet she threw it down in a display of temper, which, however, only made her feel more tired than she was already.

Then she heard Gibson returning and thought she would tell him in no uncertain terms what she thought of his impertinence in daring to treat her as if she were a child.

He had been so kind and skilful when she was ill, but now he was exceeding his authority.

She heard the key turn in the lock and then the door opened, but it was not Gibson who stood there but the Marquis.

He came into the cabin and she saw him glance at her packed trunk and thought he already knew what she was trying to do.

Then as his eyes met hers, she found that her words of protest died on her lips. She could only look at him and think how handsome he was and how strong he had appeared when he had knocked Giles down.

"I am sorry to have been so long," the Marquis said. "You must have been wondering where I had gone."

"I . . . I wanted to . . . leave . . . but Gibson would not let me."

"Where were you going?"

"Away . . . so that Giles cannot . . . hurt you by the things he would tell the . . . King and Queen."

"I think your leaving in such a precipitate manner would hardly alter his story if he was permitted to tell it."

Ola's eyes widened.

"You stopped him from doing so?"

The Marquis nodded.

"But . . . how? What have you . . . done?"

It flashed through Ola's mind that the Marquis had injured Giles or even killed him. Then she knew that that would mean he would be in worse trouble than he was already. Besides, it seemed somehow out-of-character.

She was still sitting on the bed, and now the Marquis walked to the end of it to lean his arms on the ornate brass end, where he stood looking at her.

Unexpectedly Ola found herself apologising.

"I am so sorry," she said, "I did not think when I . . . forced you to bring me away from England . . . that I could hurt you . . . and now . . . after what Giles has said

. . . I realise what I have . . . done, and I can only say how . . . very . . . very sorry I am."

"Because you have said that," the Marquis answered, "it makes it easier for me to tell you how I have contrived that Giles will not be able to damage either of us with the tale he wished to relate in London, and he would undoubtedly have done so had I not prevented it."

"What have you done? You must tell me!" Ola said.

"I told your cousin," the Marquis said, "that we are married!"

For the moment Ola felt as if she could not have heard him aright. Then as she looked at him, her eyes so wide in her pale face that they seemed to fill it, she saw the confirmation in his and said:

"How could you have said such a thing? When he finds out it is not true it will only make things worse."

"But it is true," the Marquis said quietly. "We are, in fact, already married legally, although I am sure you would like a Church Service. So I have arranged one for this evening."

He saw that Ola was so astonished that she was speechless, and he explained:

"In France one has to be married first in front of the Mayor at the Town Hall, and it is permitted that one of the persons concerned be represented by proxy."

He smiled before he continued:

"The proxy has to be a responsible person and so, as I thought the Captain would qualify in that capacity, I took him with me!"

"Are you really saying . . . that I . . . I am your . . . wife?" Ola asked.

"I have the document to prove it," the Marquis answered, "but as I think every woman is entitled to be present at her own wedding, we will be married very quietly tonight after sunset at the Protestant Church. The Vicar is not only very willing to perform the ceremony but has promised to keep it a secret."

For a moment there was complete silence in the cabin, until Ola said in a frightened little voice:

"B-but . . . you said you . . . hated women and did not want to . . . marry anybody!"

"And you," the Marquis replied, "said you hated men and had no wish to be married."

There was again a long silence. Then he said:

"I feel sure, Ola, you will be sensible and intelligent enough to know that we both have to make the best of a difficult situation that has been brought about through your cousin. It is actually something I should have anticipated, but while you were convalescing I did not wish to trouble you with plans for the future."

"That was . . . kind of you," Ola said, "but this is . . . all my fault . . . and I am . . . ashamed."

"I think any blame you might attach to your action in forcing yourself upon me is certainly fully compensated and erased by the way in which you saved my life."

"I saved you," Ola said, "but you would not have climbed the cliff and gone into . . . danger had I not . . . challenged you to do so."

"You can think that now," the Marquis answered, "but if I had been alone I might easily have climbed for the exercise and the same thing would have happened, only with a far different ending to the story."

He saw that she was not convinced and he added:

"What has happened has happened and there is never any point in looking back in life and saying: 'If I had done that, or something else, it would all have been different.' "

He gave a little laugh before he said:

"Neither of us can rewrite history, but what we can do is to be wise enough not to fight against the inevitable or, as you are very fond of doing, to run away, as that will solve nothing."

"I thought if I . . . left you . . . you would be able to persuade Giles not to . . . tell anybody that I had been on the *Sea Wolf*. I am sure, because he is always short of money, that you could have . . . bribed him to keep silent."

"And have him blackmail me for the rest of my life?" the Marquis enquired. "No, thank you, Ola! I prefer my own solution, and perhaps you will not find it so unpleasant being married to me as it would have been if you had married your cousin or were on your own."

"I . . . thought," Ola said in a low voice, "that when he was lying on the . . . floor he looked really . . . evil . . . and I am sure he will try to . . . hurt you if he can."

"I think we can be sure that he will be unable to do that," the Marquis said. "As I intend to send a notice of our marriage to the *Gazette* immediately, he will find when he reaches England that nobody will listen to anything he has to say."

Ola thought this over for a minute, then she said in a very low voice:

"He called me a . . . strumpet. Is that the same as being a . . . *fille de joie?*"

The Marquis hesitated for only a moment before he answered:

"Yes."

"And 'cocotte' . . . means the . . . same?"

He nodded.

"Now . . . I . . . understand how horrible and insulting my Stepmother was being to me . . . and perhaps . . ."

She paused for a moment before she added:

"P-perhaps your friends will think it . . . very wrong of you to . . . m-marry somebody who looks like . . . me."

The Marquis smiled.

"My friends when they see you, will think I am very lucky to have married somebody who is, beyond all question, extremely beautiful!"

He saw by the expression on her face that Ola did not believe him, and he exclaimed:

"Good Heavens, child, you cannot be unaware that because you are so lovely your Stepmother and, I imagine, many other women you meet are wildly jealous of your looks?"

"Do you . . . mean that?" Ola asked. "I have always felt there is . . . something wrong . . . because people are so surprised at the colour of my hair."

"They are surprised because it is very rare for a woman to have that particular colour and be so beautiful."

He was paying her a compliment, and yet she thought his voice sounded almost indifferent, as if he were discussing an inanimate object rather than a human being.

"I am glad . . . very glad that you need not . . . be ashamed of me," she said after a moment.

"I can promise you I will never be that," the Marquis said. "And now, as there need be no more restrictions on your appearance with me in Nice or anywhere else, I suggest after luncheon I take you for a drive. The views from Villefranche, which is just along the coast road, are very fine."

"I would love that! May I really come with you?"

"I will order luncheon to be served immediately," the Marquis replied.

He went from the cabin and Ola sat down in front of the dressing-table to tidy her hair.

As she stared at her reflection in the mirror she thought of how the Marquis had said that she was beautiful, at the same time with a note in his voice which made her sure that it meant nothing to him personally.

"I want him to think me beautiful," she told herself.

Then she remembered that she was now his wife, and she felt herself shiver because she was afraid that after all he hated her because he had been tricked into marriage, against every inclination to remain a bachelor.

"How could I have known that this would happen?" she asked herself.

She was suddenly ashamed of the fact that she had behaved in such an outrageous way that would make any man dislike her and decide to keep out of her way.

She had drugged him so that for three days he had been unconscious. Then when he could have rid himself of her at Gibraltar or Marseilles, he had been too kind to do so because she had a knife-wound in her shoulder.

And now, to save his reputation and hers, he had been forced to marry her. She could see that it was a conclusive answer to keep Giles's mouth shut, but it was a heavy price to pay.

"He will never forgive me . . . never!" she told herself, and felt something like a physical pain in her heart at the thought.

Then strangely she found herself praying that somehow she could persuade him not to hate her.

She prayed that he would find her, although it was unlikely, the type of wife he wanted, who could talk to him about his ambitions, the work he was doing in the House of Lords, and try to run his houses in the way he wanted them run.

"I will make no demands on him," she told herself.

Then she wondered if that was all a man wanted in marriage. Surely he would want more?

She knew the answer almost as if somebody had said it aloud.

A man would want love; but was that something she could give the Marquis?

She asked the question and saw her own eyes staring back at her, wide and a little frightened.

Then she knew the answer but was afraid to put it into words.

CHAPTER SEVEN

"Forasmuch as Boyden and Ola have consented together in Holy Wedlock and have witnessed the same before God, and thereto have given and pledged their troth each to the other, and

*have declared the same by the giving and receiving of a ring and
by joining of hands, I pronounce that they be man and wife
together, in the name of the Father, and of the Son, and of the
Holy Ghost. Amen."*

*I*t was true, Ola thought. She was married to the Marquis!

She had felt ever since leaving the yacht that she was
moving in a dream and that everything had such a sense
of unreality that she might still be in the fog in which
they had first met.

In fact nothing had seemed real since he had told her
that they were already married legally and that he had
arranged a Church Service in the evening.

Immediately after luncheon, when conversation had
been a little difficult, the Marquis had taken her, as he
had promised, driving round Nice.

It had been a short drive because after they had seen
the view from Villefranche he had ordered the carriage
to return to the yacht.

"I want you to rest," he said. "You have been through
another dramatic experience today, and nothing is
more tiring."

Although she was thrilled by the sunshine, the sea, and
the flowers, Ola knew that the way Giles had behaved and
the packing she had done herself had left her somewhat
exhausted.

When they arrived back on the yacht she had obeyed
the Marquis and had gone to her cabin and got into
bed.

She had thought she would lie awake thinking about
their marriage, but as soon as her head touched the pillows she had fallen asleep.

It had been a deep and dreamless sleep, and she had
awakened only when Gibson came to her cabin to insist
on looking at her shoulder.

"It is all right," she said quickly.

"I've warned you, Miss, against doing too much," Gibson said sternly, adopting his Nanny role again as he always did when he was tending to her wound.

Because she knew it was hopeless to argue with him, she let him take the light dressing from her shoulder and put on another one.

She suspected that as the wound had healed so well even a dressing was unnecessary, but she had the feeling that Gibson enjoyed nursing her and was determined not to relinquish his authority until the very last moment.

"Now, I think you should get dressed, Miss," Gibson said, "and there's a special gown here for you to wear."

"A gown!" Ola exclaimed in surprise.

"Yes, Miss. His Lordship bought it this afternoon, and as I gives him the exact right measurements, I'd be surprised if it doesn't fit."

Ola was astonished not only at receiving a present of a new gown but because the Marquis had taken so much trouble over her.

She knew, now that she was awake again, that it was impossible for her thoughts not to keep returning to him, remembering that while he had no wish to be married he had been pressured into it through circumstances.

She had been glad that Giles's evil intentions towards them both had been circumvented by their marriage and that the Marquis would not lose his special relationship with the King.

At the same time, it was not his public life with which she was concerned, and when she thought of how she had forced herself on him when he had wished to be rid of her she felt more and more ashamed.

She was now an encumbrance not only on a voyage but for life!

When Gibson returned to her cabin carrying a gown in his hands she could only think that the Marquis was not only making, as he had said, the best of a situation in which they were both involved, but was actually embellishing it in a way she had not expected.

The gown was lovely and when she put it on she knew that it made her look exactly as a bride should—ethereal, spiritual, and like a fairy-Princess.

The full skirt swept the ground in front and had a train at the back, the bodice tapered to a tiny waist, and the white gauze of which the gown was made was ornamented with silver ribbons caught with orange-blossoms.

It seemed part of the golden mimosa trees she had seen with the Marquis, the shrubs heavy with brilliant flowers, and the shimmering sunlight which gave everything a glittering glow which seemed to come from Heaven itself.

"It fits like a glove, Miss!" Gibson exclaimed.

Ola knew he was delighted not only with her but with himself for having got her measurements right.

He went from the cabin and came back with a wreath of orange-blossoms which matched those on her gown, and with it a lace veil so fine that it might have been made by a spider.

Ola allowed him to arrange it over her red hair and she knew that nothing could be more becoming and that it gave her a look of purity and innocence which every bride should have.

"It's a pity, Miss, that you can't wear one of them tiaras that His Lordship has in the safe at Elvin," Gibson said. "Very fine they are, and there's emeralds which will suit you when you goes to a Ball."

"I am very happy with the orange-blossoms," Ola said in a low voice.

She thought it would be pretentious of her to think that she would ever wear the family jewels that belonged to the Marquis, and she knew that today she had no wish to open her own jewel-case.

Somehow at the back of her mind she had the feeling that because her wedding was so strange and unusual, everything about it should be very simple.

That she looked like a bride was the choice of the Marquis and she would leave in his hands everything which concerned herself.

In a way it would be an apology to him, she thought, and she wondered if he would understand.

When she was ready she suddenly felt afraid of leaving the cabin and she thought that perhaps when she went into the Saloon she would see a frown between the Marquis's eyes and would know how much he was disliking the ceremony which was awaiting them.

"Perhaps he would like to run away, as I have always run away when things became too difficult," she told herself.

Then she remembered that they were in fact married already, although she was sure that no-one on the yacht knew anything about it except the Captain.

Only because Gibson insisted and because she could think of no reason not to do so, she walked into the Saloon proudly, with her chin up.

As she had expected, the Marquis was there, and when she saw him she was astonished at his appearance because he was wearing evening-dress.

Then she remembered that the girls at the Convent had told her that in France the bridegroom always wore evening-dress whatever time of day the ceremony took place.

But as her wedding was in the evening it actually was entirely appropriate.

He certainly looked magnificent, and looking at him she forgot her own appearance.

She saw that he was not frowning or looking disagreeable but was regarding her with a smile on his lips.

"Thank you," she said hurriedly, "thank you . . . so much for my . . . gown. I did not expect you to think of . . . such things . . . but I am . . . very grateful."

"If you are ready, I suggest we leave for the Church immediately," the Marquis said. "There is a carriage waiting on the Quay. In fact there are two, as the

Captain is coming with us as a witness and will be travelling in the second one."

Ola did not reply, she merely followed the Marquis onto the deck and was glad both for the darkness and for the veil over her face, which was a protection from any curious eyes that might be watching her.

However, there appeared to be nobody about, and when she stepped into the closed carriage which was waiting by the gangplank the Marquis joined her and they set off immediately.

She thought she ought to speak to him, but as he did not say anything to her they drove in silence and there were only the lights of the Villas and Hotels lining the road to make her feel as if she were going on a strange voyage to an unknown destination.

The Church, however, was not far away and when they arrived the Marquis got out first to help her alight, then offered her his arm.

It was only a few steps to the porch, then they were inside the Church and by the light of the candles on the altar Ola could see that it was small and had stained-glass windows and stone pillars.

What made it different were the mass of lilies in the chancel and the profusion of white carnations which decorated the base of the pillars and the empty choir-stalls.

It gave the Church a beauty she had not expected and the fragrance of the flowers filled the air almost like incense.

The Marquis took her up the aisle to where the Parson was waiting for them and when they stood in front of him he immediately began the Service.

The Marquis made his responses in a firm voice, but to Ola her own voice sounded so strange that she barely recognised it.

She knew that she was frightened and she felt as if she were making an irretrievable step into the unknown, and yet there was nothing she could do and she felt as if she were being swept along on a tide which carried her into an unknown sea.

When the Parson blessed the ring Ola felt the Marquis's fingers holding her hand and the strength of them seemed to give her courage.

They knelt and she found herself praying that somehow their marriage would be a happy one and that the Marquis would not hate her because it was all her fault that he was married.

The Parson blessed them, and as they rose to their feet he said in a kindly voice:

"I shall pray for your happiness."

Then to the Marquis he added:

"You may now kiss the bride."

Ola felt herself stiffen, feeling that perhaps the Marquis would refuse to do such a thing, but he lifted her veil from her face and threw it back over her wreath.

Then as her eyes met his and widened a little in fright, he looked down at her before his lips sought hers.

It was a very brief kiss, more a symbolic gesture than a real kiss, and yet it gave Ola a sensation she had never known before when she felt her mouth possessed by the Marquis and her lips made captive by his. . . .

The Marquis offered her his arm and they walked slowly down the aisle.

Ola, looking up above her where the light of the candles did not reach the shadow of the roof, felt that they were not alone but were being watched by celestial beings who wished them happiness.

When they reached the porch she gave a little gasp of surprise, for outside, lining the way to their carriage, was a Guard of Honour consisting of the sailors from the yacht.

She knew that the Marquis was surprised too, but he smiled as he led Ola through the ranks of his own men, dressed in their smartest rig.

The carriage was no longer closed, and as they reached it Ola saw that the hood was decorated with

127

white carnations like those inside the Church, and the horses had gone.

Instead there were two lines of sailors to draw them, and as soon as Ola and the Marquis were seated they moved off with the Guard of Honour following them.

"Did you know this was going to happen?" she asked.

"I had not the slightest idea," the Marquis replied. "In fact, I thought the only people who knew our secret were the Captain and Gibson."

Ola gave a little laugh.

"I am sure it was Gibson who thought of anything so exciting and so dramatic. It was just what he would enjoy."

"Are you enjoying it too?"

The Marquis's voice was deep and it made her a little shy so that she could not look at him as she replied:

"Of course . . . it is very . . . exciting for me, and how could we have a more . . . wonderful setting for our . . . wedding?"

As she spoke, she looked up at the stars which were now brilliant overhead, and as they drew nearer to the Harbour they could see the moonlight shimmering silver on the sea and the masts of the yacht silhouetted against the whole glory of the Heavens.

The Marquis's eyes were on the rounded softness of her neck as she looked up, but he did not speak and Ola gave him a shy little smile.

"Thank you, thank you!" she said to the sailors as they brought the carriage to a standstill at the gang-plank.

Then as she smiled at them they cheered her and the Marquis, waving their caps above their heads until they had reached the deck and disappeared inside the yacht.

"How can they have thought of such a lovely surprise?" Ola was asking as she went into the Saloon and found that the surprises were not at an end.

There were white lilies standing in huge vases on each side of the sofa and there were lilies on the Marquis's desk, and a profusion of white flowers decorated the table at which they were to dine.

Ola clapped her hands together.

"Who can have thought of anything so lovely?" she asked.

"I will see that everyone is thanked in the most practical manner," the Marquis said with a smile.

She heard him ordering the stewards to serve rum to all the ship's company and for champagne to be sent to the Captain and the other Officers.

It was time for dinner and the Chef had excelled himself in producing a meal that was better than anything Ola had eaten since she had been aboard the *Sea Wolf*.

Finally, when dessert was put on the table, the stewards carried in a large wedding-cake.

"I am prepared to claim credit for this," the Marquis said. "I bought it today when I was choosing your gown."

It was certainly a very impressive cake, of three tiers decorated in the traditional manner with horse-shoes and artificial orange-blossoms, surmounted by a tiny but very French-looking bride and bridegroom under a silver canopy of love-buds.

"We must cut it together," Ola said.

Then she wondered if the Marquis would think that such a demonstration of unity was unfitting.

But he agreed, saying as they rose:

"I should really have brought my sword with me, but I did not think it would be necessary on this voyage."

Ola glanced at him quickly to see if he was talking bitterly, but he was smiling as he handed her a long, sharp knife, saying:

"I am sure, however, that this will be far more effective."

Ola put her hand on the knife and the Marquis covered it with his and once again she felt the strength of his fingers.

They gave her the same strange feeling which she had known when he had kissed her, but she told herself that it was only because she was feeling shy.

The cake was cut, and the stewards, having left two slices on the table, carried it away to offer the rest to everyone aboard the *Sea Wolf*.

A decanter of brandy was set before the Marquis and it made Ola think of the night she had drugged him. As if he was thinking the same thing, he said after a moment:

"We have been through some strange experiences together, Ola, and perhaps the strangest of them has happened today."

She thought he was reproaching her, and after a moment she said in a small voice:

"I . . . am . . . sorry."

He raised his eye-brows.

"For what?"

"Having brought all . . . this about, I know . . . what you must be . . . feeling."

"I rather doubt that."

"But of course I know," she insisted. "You had sworn never to marry, and you told me that you hated women as I hated men, and yet because I . . . forced myself upon you I am now your . . . w-wife."

It was somewhat difficult to say the last word and she stumbled over it because it sounded so intimate.

She felt the colour rise in her cheeks.

"I think we have a great deal to learn about each other," the Marquis said, "and as we are both intelligent people we are both well aware that what we said yesterday does not necessarily apply to today."

Ola gave him a little smile.

"You are being kind to me," she said, "but I want to say something to you."

"What is it?" the Marquis asked.

He had made no effort to help himself to brandy. He was sitting back in his chair, his eyes on her face, and he seemed relaxed, yet almost as if he were seeing her for the first time.

"We are . . . married," Ola said in a small voice, barely above a whisper. "I know it was . . . necessary and there was, as you said, nothing else we could do in the circumstances. But I want you to be happy, and I will do . . . anything you decide when we return to England."

"What do you mean by that?" the Marquis enquired.

For a moment Ola could not reply. She was trying to find words to express the thoughts that were in her mind and yet would not formulate themselves as clearly as she wished.

She said after a long pause:

"If you want me to live . . . apart from you, or if we are together at times because people would think it strange if we were not, I will try to . . . please you and behave in a way that the wife you would have chosen for yourself would behave."

The Marquis did not speak, and Ola, in the light of what she had said, thought perhaps he was considering her suggestion that they might live apart to be a good one.

She glanced at him and thought how handsome he looked and that there was something about him which would make him stand out in whatever company he was in and however many men there were round him.

'He is so distinguished,' she thought to herself, 'and, in a way, magnificent.'

It suddenly swept over her that he was her husband—she bore his name and she was his wife!

Then almost as if a voice from Heaven spoke to her, she knew that she did not want to leave him. She wanted to be with him; she wanted to talk with him . . . to listen to him. . . .

She wanted . . . she could barely express it herself . . . she wanted him to . . . kiss her . . . again!

As the whole idea was so revolutionary, so different from anything she had ever thought about the Marquis before, she felt her heart beating tempestuously in her breast!

In a panic, she wanted to run away from the room in case he should be aware of what she was thinking.

As if he had made a decision, the Marquis said:

"Give me your hand, Ola."

He put out his own as he spoke and obediently she put hers on it and felt his fingers close.

"I think there should be no misapprehensions or misunderstandings between us," he said. "I should tell you now exactly what I want of the future and what I feel about you at this moment."

He felt her fingers quiver as he went on:

"It may be hard to make you believe it, but when we were being married just now I knew it was what I wanted and that you were in fact the wife I would have chosen for myself had we met under different circumstances."

Ola was so surprised that she could only stare at him, her eyes very wide in the light of the candles.

"Do . . . you . . . mean that?" she whispered.

"I mean it," the Marquis replied, "and it is true. Perhaps I should explain to you, although it seems unimportant now, why I said I hated women and why in fact I came on this voyage in the first place."

"No!" Ola said quickly. "No, please do not tell me! I have felt, in fact I am sure, that you have been hurt and wounded and it was a woman who did it, but I would rather not know!"

The Marquis looked at her in surprise and she went on:

"What has happened in the past has nothing to do with me, except that you were there when I needed you most! So if it is possible . . . I would like us to start our life together anew . . . with none of the . . . miseries, the problems, and the . . . difficulties which have happened before we . . . met each . . . other."

She made a little sound which was almost a sob as she said:

"I have called you my Good Samaritan, and that is what you were. If you had not taken me in your yacht when I was . . . desperate, my life would have been very . . . different. It would have been a . . . horror I cannot bear to . . . contemplate!"

"I understand what you are saying," the Marquis replied, "and I think there is no other woman who would be so sensible."

He smiled and it seemed to illuminate his face as he added:

"But then you have always been very original, Ola, and extremely unpredictable ever since we met."

"I know," she agreed, "but I will try, I will try . . . desperately hard, not to do anything . . . outrageous again, but to be quiet and . . . well-behaved so that you will be . . . proud of me."

"I have a feeling that if you tried too hard to alter yourself it might be rather dull," the Marquis said. "After all, I have by this time grown used to dramatics and I have a feeling I might miss them if they were no longer there."

He was teasing her, but his hand still held hers closely as Ola said:

"You . . . know I want to . . . please you."

"Why?" the Marquis asked.

She was surprised at the question and she felt he was waiting for an answer as she said:

"You have been so . . . kind and it is only . . . right that I should want to . . . please the man who is my . . . husband."

"Is that all?"

She looked at him enquiringly, and then because of the look in his eyes she felt her heart beating even more violently than it had done previously.

What was more, it was impossible to look away, and although the Marquis did not move, she almost felt as if his hand was pulling her nearer and nearer to him.

She did not speak and after a moment he said:

"I think, Ola, with your hair it would be impossible for you not to feel very strongly about anything one way or another, and I am therefore asking you what you feel about me. Not as a Good Samaritan or as a wolf, which you told me I was, but as a man and your husband."

Now there was a depth in his voice that made Ola feel as if she listened to music. She felt too that there were vital vibrations passing from his hand to hers.

"What can I . . . say?" she asked a little helplessly.

"The truth!" the Marquis replied. "That is what I want from you, Ola. The truth, now and always. I cannot bear to be lied to."

The way he spoke told her that a woman had lied to him in the past and left a wound that was not yet healed.

Because she had no wish, as she had said, to think of what had happened to him before their meeting, she merely said simply:

"I will never lie to you. But what I feel is difficult to put into . . . words."

How could she describe to him, she asked herself, the feeling she had now in her breast which seemed to be rising into her throat and moving toward her lips?

How could she tell him that she wanted him to kiss her again?

Perhaps he would be shocked that she had such thoughts! Perhaps he would think her fast and immodest, or, in Giles's words, behaving like a strumpet!

Because she was suddenly agitated in a manner which she could not understand, she released her hand from the Marquis's and rose from the table.

"I think . . . perhaps it is . . . getting . . . late," she said a little incoherently. "It has been a . . . long day and I . . . should go to . . . bed."

The Marquis did not move but merely looked at her standing in the centre of the Saloon, her red hair gleaming beneath her veil, the exquisite lines of her figure revealed by the clinging white gauze against which her hands, wearing only the gold ring that he had put on her finger, moved restlessly.

"I am waiting for an answer to my question, Ola," he said.

"I do not know . . . how to . . . reply. I cannot find the . . . right . . . words."

The Marquis rose from the table.

"Words are often quite unnecessary."

He moved towards her as he spoke, and as she looked up at him, very conscious of his closeness, his arms went round her. He pulled her against him, saying:

"Let us express our feelings in a far easier way!"

Then his lips were on hers.

As he kissed her Ola knew that this was what she had wanted, this was what she had longed for, for a long time.

But as his lips held her captive it was impossible to think of anything but the wonder of his kiss.

She felt as if the silver of the moonlight on the sea rippled through her body as the strange sensations that had been in her heart seemed to move from her breasts into her throat and onto her lips.

She was not certain whether she gave the wonder and the beauty of them to the Marquis or he gave them to her. She only knew that they were joined with a rapture that was too perfect to find an expression in any other way.

What she was feeling was love. The love she had thought she would never find.

The Marquis's arms tightened, his lips became more demanding, more possessive, and she wanted to be closer to him, so close that she lost herself in him. She was his completely and was no longer alone and afraid.

He raised his head.

"I love . . . you! I love . . . you!"

The words seemed to burst from Ola's lips.

"That is what I wanted you to say, my darling," he answered.

Then he was kissing her again; kissing her fiercely, passionately, and with an insistence that made Ola know that he dominated her, and yet she was not afraid.

She felt as if her whole body had come alive and she was no longer human but was flying through the sky towards the stars. She was part of the universe and of life itself and very much a part of the Marquis!

'Why did no-one tell me,' she wondered, 'that love is so majestic . . . and so . . . irresistible!'

The sound of the anchor awakened Ola.

As she realised where she was, she gave a little cry of joy.

She was in the Marquis's arms, her head was on his shoulder, and she could feel his heart beating against hers.

"I love . . . you," she murmured.

Then as she looked up to see him in the pale sunlight coming between the sides of the curtains which hung over the port-holes, he was smiling.

"It is . . . true? Really . . . true?" she asked. "I am . . . here in your . . . arms and you . . . love me?"

"Do you still doubt it, my darling?" he asked.

"I thought I must be dreaming."

"You are awake," he said, "and if you have been dreaming about me, then it is true!"

She gave a little laugh which was one of sheer happiness and moved closer to him.

"Were we . . . really married . . . last night?"

"I hope so!" he replied. "Otherwise I can only think, my precious, that your behaviour at this moment is somewhat reprehensible!"

She kissed his shoulder with a passionate little gesture which brought fire to his eyes.

"No-one could be more adorable," he said, "but why did I not recognise the moment I saw you that you were what I had been seeking all my life but thought did not exist?"

"I am . . . ashamed too, of being so . . . unperceptive," Ola said. "But even though you hated women you were kind to me, and as really kind men are few and far between, I was very . . . very lucky to find . . . one."

The Marquis kissed her forehead, his lips lingering against the softness of her skin, before he asked:

"Am I still a wolf in sheep's clothing?"

"A very magnificent, exciting, and . . . demanding wolf, whom I . . . love very much."

The Marquis laughed.

"I might have known you would give me an answer different from what I expected! So let me tell you that I shall be a very ferocious wolf and a very jealous one! If I see any other man admiring your hair or wanting to touch the softness of your skin, I will kill him!"

"There will be no need for you to be jealous," Ola said in a soft voice. "I still hate all men except you, and

I love you so much that there is no room for anyone else in my mind, my heart, or my soul."

"And I possess all three?"

"You know you do."

"I also possess your body," the Marquis said, "and it is the most alluring and perfect possession I have ever had."

"Perhaps when you get used to it you will put it on a . . . shelf and . . . forget it."

The Marquis's hands were touching her as he replied:

"I think it is very unlikely, and if I tried to put you on a shelf, my naughty one, I cannot believe you would stay there."

He paused before he went on:

"I think really I am rather apprehensive about what surprises you will have for me in the future. You have already told me that you never repeat your tricks, so I need not be afraid of being drugged with laudanum or murdered by bandits. But there are quite a number of other atrocities in various parts of the world!"

Ola gave an exclamation of sheer indignation.

"How can you be so unfair?" she asked. "The bandits had nothing to do with me, and I did save you. Oh, darling! . . . I am so glad I did! Suppose . . . you had . . . died!"

The Marquis pulled her a little closer.

"I am very much alive," he said, "and at the moment determined to make the very best of it!"

His lips found Ola's as he spoke.

He kissed her until she felt the fire that was burning in him light a response within herself which felt like a flame flickering through her body.

She put her arm round his neck, pulling him even closer.

"You are so . . . magnificent . . . so wonderful," she whispered. "Please . . . teach me to love you as you . . . want to be . . . loved."

"I do not think you need many lessons, my precious," the Marquis replied, "so all I want is to teach you to love me as much as I love you."

"How can you love me after the way I . . . behaved?" she asked. "And when did you first . . . think you . . . did?"

"I knew I loved you when you threw yourself in front of me to save my life," he replied. "But before that I found myself fascinated by your looks, by your clever little brain, and most of all by the magic that makes you different from any other woman I have ever known."

Ola gave a sigh of happiness.

"How could you say anything so marvellous!" she murmured.

"As I sat by your bed when you were unconscious," the Marquis continued, "I knew that I wanted to look after you and protect you in a way I had never felt about anyone else. And what was more, I wanted you to stimulate my mind and inspire me, which I never thought any woman could do!"

He smiled as he said:

"Before, I had felt myself completely self-sufficient as a man, but now I know you have so much to give me that is mental as well as physical, and that is something I had never even thought of until now."

"Suppose I . . . fail you?" Ola asked in a frightened little voice.

"You will not do that," the Marquis said positively, "because I believe we were intended by fate for each other, long before we met."

As he spoke, he thought that it was fate which had prevented him almost at the eleventh hour from marrying Sarah, fate which had made him find out about her treachery, fate which had sent him running away as a solution to his problems, and fate which had taken him to The Three Bells in the thick fog to meet Ola.

From that moment, everything that had happened seemed, in retrospect, incredible, and yet fate had meant it to culminate in this moment, when the Marquis knew he was happier than he had ever been or had ever expected to be in the whole of his life.

This was love, yet he had the feeling that he and Ola had only touched the fringe, that there was so much more to discover and to savour.

He had known, when he made love to her last night and made her his, that Ola was different from any other woman he had ever known, and the feelings she aroused in him were not only the rapture of desire but something far more ecstatic and sublime.

Because he loved her he had remembered her youth and her innocence and had been very gentle and controlled so that they had both touched the Divine and become for the moment like the gods themselves.

He felt a surge of gratitude sweep over him because, when he had least expected it, life had brought him the greatest reward that is possible for mankind to have.

A love which is true and perfect!

Then, because the softness and the beauty of Ola aroused him, because his body was throbbing and burning for her, his lips sought hers again.

As he kissed her he knew that she too desired him, and, innocent and inexperienced though she was, she had an instinct that made her respond to everything he asked of her and give him not only what he sought but so much more besides.

"I love you, my darling," he said, "and we will spend our lives finding a happiness that is greater than anything we even thought of or imagined."

"That is the . . . happiness I want to . . . give you," she whispered.

And then as the Marquis took the words from her lips, she felt them merge together into one person.

She knew that the voyage ahead of them towards an indefinable horizon would carry them over an unknown sea that was sometimes smooth and sometimes rough and tempestuous.

But fate had saved them for each other, fate had brought them together. It was also fate which would bring them safely into harbour because their ship was guided by love.

LOOKING FOR LOVE

Author's Note

During the Armistice between the French and English in 1803, Napoleon Bonaparte's espionage in England was extensive. The smugglers who operated in the Channel carried spies to and from France, and a number of émigrés in London found it an easy way to augment the pittance on which they had been forced to live after the Revolution of ten years earlier.

The fears that Bonaparte had aroused over the whole of Europe and ominous reports that the Armistice was just a breathing-space before he invaded England resulted in a witch-hunt through the corridors of Whitehall, with repercussions all over the country.

Chapter One

1803

"Ye're quite certain ye'll be all right, Miss Gilda?"

"Of course I will, Mrs. Hewlett. Do not worry about me, and I hope you enjoy your wedding."

"Oi'm sure Oi shall, Miss. It's reel lucky for our Emily, when her thinks she be on th' shelf, for that farmer t' come along, an' a very nice man he be, too."

Gilda smiled, knowing that Mrs. Hewlett had been worried in case she would have to provide for her niece and was grateful as much for her own sake as Emily's that the "nice farmer" was ready to marry her.

Mrs. Hewlett was the worrying sort and Gilda often thought she was the only person who really cared what became of her now that she was alone after her father's death.

"Now leave everythin' that needs washing up for me when Oi gets back on Monday," Mrs. Hewlett was saying. "Ye don't want t' trouble yerself t' do anythin' but have a bit o' rest."

That, Gilda thought, was something she had been doing for a long time, and the amount of washing up that would be left after her frugal meals would hardly make a pile even if she did leave it for Mrs. Hewlett.

But she knew it was no use arguing, or Mrs. Hewlett would be worrying about her while she was away in the next village attending Emily's wedding.

Having struggled into a heavy coat even though it was a warm day, Mrs. Hewlett picked up the wicker-basket which she always carried whether there was anything in it or not, and taking a last look round the kitchen lifted the latch of the door.

"Now take care o' yerself, Miss," she admonished, "an Oi'll be back on Monday afternoon if th' stage-coach be punctual, which it's unlikely t' be!"

When the door had closed behind her, Gilda gave a little sigh and, leaving the kitchen, went down the passage to the front of the house.

It was only a short way, for the small Manor in which she had lived ever since she was born had at one time seemed only just large enough for her father, her mother, her sister, and herself.

Now it seemed much too large for one person, and she wondered, as she had been wondering ever since her father had died, whether she should try to sell the house and move into a small cottage.

It would, she thought, be the sensible thing to do. At the same time, she could not bear to part with the furniture, shabby though it was, which she had known all her life and which seemed a part of herself and the only thing she had left.

Her father's desk, her mother's inlaid work-table, and the Chippendale bookcase were all like old friends, and she felt that without them she would be even lonelier than she was already.

At the same time, she had to face facts. She had so little money that she could barely afford to buy enough food to eat unless she could supplement her tiny income in some way.

Her father's pension had died with him. He had served in the Grenadier Guards, and when he was alive his pension as a Major-General had kept them in comparative comfort, or would have done if her father had not amused himself in his old age by investing in stocks and shares.

Gilda could understand the excitement of it, but while the General might have been a very experienced soldier, he knew nothing about finance.

Invariably the companies to which he entrusted his money either went bankrupt or paid such tiny dividends that they were hardly worth the paper on which they were written.

Now all that Gilda had was the very small amount of money her mother had brought into the marriage-settlement, the income from which had been left to the children of the marriage.

Gilda had often wondered what would have happened if her sister had claimed her share.

After Heloise had gone to London to live with her rich Godmother she had shown little or no interest in her impecunious relatives, and Gilda sometimes thought she was ashamed of them.

Sitting now at her father's desk, Gilda pulled open a notebook in which she was trying to jot down all her expenditures.

It seemed to her to come to an uncomfortably large total, despite the fact that she was trying to economise on food, clothing, and in fact everything that was personal.

One economy she had thought of was to dispense with the services of Mrs. Hewlett, but when she had actually suggested this, Mrs. Hewlett had been horrified to the point of being insulted and had even offered to work for nothing.

"Oi've come here for nigh on ten years," she said, "and if ye think ye can do without me now, Miss Gilda, ye're very much mistaken. What's more, yer dear mother'd turn in her grave, she would, at the very idea!"

Mrs. Hewlett had been so voluble on the subject that Gilda felt it was impossible for her to say any more, and she also admitted to herself that without Mrs. Hewlett's incessant good humour she would be very lonely indeed.

147

In fact, there would be no-one to talk to at all except the Vicar, who was growing very deaf, on an occasional visit, and old Gibbs the gardener.

He was long past work but came because he liked to potter round the place where he had worked for so long and could not bear to see his labours being stifled by weeds or obliterated by overgrown brambles.

Gilda added up the total of what she had spent, checked it again, and knew there was no mistake. It was too much.

"What can I do?" she asked herself.

She wondered whether she had any talent which could bring her some money.

She was well educated compared with many other young women of her age. Her mother, who came from a Cornish family which had held very distinguished posts in the County for many generations, had seen to that.

The fact that her grandfather and great-grandfather and the generations before them had been High Sheriffs, Judges, and even Lords Lieutenant, did not, Gilda thought, make her own brains any the more marketable.

Her father too had been an intelligent man.

His contemporaries who had visited him when he was alive always told Gilda that no General had more skill in deploying his troops or a better grasp of tactics in battle.

"Your father could always be relied on to inflict the maximum losses on the enemy with the minimum to his own men," one of his brother Officers had told Gilda.

She had realised that this was high praise, but it did not solve her own problem.

"I shall have to do something . . . I must!" she said to herself, and rose from the desk to walk to the window.

The Manor stood back from the small country road down which it was nearly a mile to the village. It had a short drive to a gate that was badly in need of repair, while the gravel sweep in front of the house was overgrown with weeds.

Gilda, however, saw only the daffodils under the ancient trees, the lilacs white and purple just coming into bloom, and the first buds on the almond tree which by next week would be a poem of pink and white petals.

'If only I could paint,' she thought, 'I could paint a picture that everybody would want to buy!'

But she knew she could not afford either the canvas or the paints, so the only person who could enjoy the miracle of spring would be herself.

Because the sunshine seemed to call her, she thought the accounts could wait and the best thing she could do would be to go into the garden.

There was plenty of work for her to do there, not only amongst the flowers and shrubs but in the kitchen-garden, where unless she weeded the vegetables and planted those that she would want later in the year, she would be very hungry indeed.

At the same time, she wanted to look more closely at the white lilacs which her mother had always loved and which, if she picked some and placed them in a chest in the Hall, would scent the whole house.

There was a smile on her lips as she turned to leave the window. Then as she did so she looked down the drive and was suddenly still.

To her astonishment she saw coming through the gate a pair of well-bred horses.

Then she saw that the coachman driving them was wearing a cockaded high hat, and incredibly there was a footman beside him.

No-one in the County who was grand enough to have a footman on the box was likely to call, and as the horses drew nearer Gilda thought there must be some mistake and whoever was arriving must be coming to the wrong house.

As they came nearer still, she could see that the horses were drawing a very elegant travelling-carriage with a coat-of-arms painted on the door.

"There is a mistake," Gilda said to herself. "I must tell them so."

As the carriage drew up outside the front door, she hurried from the Sitting-Room, patting her hair into place as she did so, and conscious that she was wearing one of her oldest cotton gowns which had been washed until the colour had faded and it was too tight and too short.

However, it was of no consequence, for the visitor would not be for her, and when there was a loud rat-tat on the knocker she opened the door, feeling not embarrassed but curious.

A footman, resplendent in a liveried coat embellished with crested silver buttons, was outside.

However, he was not waiting to ask whose house it was, but turned back to open the carriage-door.

Then Gilda gave a little cry of surprise, for stepping out was a vision in blue silk taffeta with a lovely face framed by a bonnet surmounted by ostrich feathers of the same colour.

"Louise!" Gilda exclaimed, then quickly corrected herself. "Heloise!"

After she went to London her sister had changed her name to one that she thought was more unusual and more aristocratic. She had written to her father saying that in the future she was to be addressed as "Heloise."

"I am thrilled to see you!" Gilda said. "But you did not let me know you would be coming."

Heloise bent forward so that Gilda could kiss her cheek.

"I did not know myself until the last moment," she replied.

She turned to the footman.

"Take my trunk upstairs, James," she said in an authoritative voice, "and make sure you return here early on Monday morning. You are not to be late. Do you understand?"

"I understands, Miss."

He started to loosen the cords that bound the trunk to the back of the carriage.

Before Gilda could tell him to which room to take them, Heloise said:

"As Mama's room is the best, that is where I wish to sleep. Tell someone to show him the way."

"Yes, of course," Gilda replied, "but Mrs. Hewlett is not here today."

"Then you will have to show him yourself," Heloise answered, "and make sure that he undoes the straps and opens the lid before he leaves."

"I will do that," Gilda agreed.

Heloise walked into the Sitting-Room and Gilda waited in the Hall until James came in through the front door carrying her sister's trunk.

Then she went ahead of him up the stairs to open the door of the room which her mother had always used and which had been shut up after her father's death.

Hastily Gilda pulled back the curtains and opened the windows.

The room was clean, since Mrs. Hewlett "turned out" every room in the house regularly whether they were used or not.

There was a Holland cover over the bed, which Gilda removed as the footman set down the trunk near the door.

"'Twill be all right 'ere, Miss?" he asked.

"Yes, thank you," Gilda replied, and thought that if it was not to Heloise's liking she would move it for her.

She noticed that the footman looked round the room with a somewhat contemptuous air, as if he saw how shabby and worn everything was and compared it very unfavourably with the house in which he was employed.

Then unexpectedly he grinned at Gilda and said:

"Nice to be in th' country, Miss. I were brought up on a farm meself an' often misses it."

"I am sure you do," Gilda answered. "London must be very hot and dusty in the summer."

"'Tis all o' that, an' thick wi' mud in th' winter. Good-day, Miss."

He grinned at her again before she heard his foot-steps running down the stairs, and, thinking that Heloise would want her, she hurriedly followed him.

By the time she reached the Hall the carriage was driving away, and she went into the Sitting-Room with a look of apprehension in her blue eyes.

"I am so very . . . very glad to see you, dearest," she said, "but why are you here?"

Her sister had taken off her bonnet and Gilda saw that there was a blue band round her head, while her golden hair curled riotously round her oval forehead.

It was as lovely as the face beneath it and very elegant, as was the gown of white muslin with a high waist and blue ribbons which crossed over her breasts and hung down the back.

"You look lovely . . . simply lovely!" Gilda said impulsively, and Heloise smiled at the compliment.

"I am glad you think so, and the reason I am here is to make somebody say to me exactly what you have just said."

Gilda looked puzzled and Heloise said:

"I have run away—I have disappeared—but the question is, will he or will he not worry as to what has happened to me?"

Heloise was sitting on the sofa and Gilda sat down on the edge of an armchair opposite her.

"You are talking in riddles," she said. "Explain to me . . . tell me exactly what is happening."

Heloise gave a little laugh.

"It is quite simple," she said. "Somehow I have got to bring a certain gentleman 'up to scratch,' and this is the only way I could think of that had anything original about it!"

"Oh, Heloise, how exciting! And what do you think this gentleman will do when he finds you are gone?"

"That is the question," Heloise replied. "He was to have driven me to Ranelagh this afternoon. I was to have dined at his house this evening at a dinner-party where a great number of people will ask why I am not present."

"Have you told him you will be here?" Gilda asked.

"No, of course not! How can you be so stupid? I have just vanished into thin air."

"Oh, Heloise, I think it is very brave of you!" Gilda cried. "But will your Godmother not tell him where you have gone?"

"I took no chances of his coaxing my address out of her," Heloise replied. "I left her a note which my maid will have read to her when she was called this morning."

Gilda looked puzzled and Heloise said:

"Oh, I forgot to tell you. Her Ladyship has an affliction of the eyes which has made her blind."

"Blind!" Gilda exclaimed. "How terrible! What is wrong?"

"The Doctors, who are fools anyway, think it is only a temporary blindness," Heloise said impatiently, "but her eyes are bandaged so that everything has to be read to her. It is my duty as a rule and a very boring one."

"I am so sorry for her."

"Keep your sympathy for me, because I need it," Heloise answered. "Oh, Gilda, if my desperate gamble does not come off I shall be in despair."

"Are you so much . . . in love with . . . this gentleman?" Gilda asked.

"In love?" Heloise repeated. "That really has little to do with it! I want more than I have ever wanted anything in my whole life to be the Marchioness of Staverton."

"That is the name of the gentleman from whom you are hiding?" Gilda asked.

"Yes, of course," Heloise answered. "Do not be nit-witted, Gilda! Try to understand what is happening. He has been paying court to me in his own way for over a month. I have been waiting, feeling certain two weeks ago that he intended to propose, but . . ."

"What happened?" Gilda interrupted.

"He paid me compliments—he sent me flowers—he has taken me driving—he has given dinner-parties for me."

She paused before she said impressively:

"He has even on two occasions asked me to dance with him, and you have no idea what an honour that was! He hates dancing, and I thought then that I had finally caught him—but no, the words I want to hear have never passed his lips."

Gilda clasped her hands together.

"Oh, Heloise, I can understand how frustrating it must be for you."

"Very, very frustrating!" Heloise agreed. "I have dozens of admirers, really dozens, but none of them measure up to the Marquis."

"Tell me about him."

Heloise gave a sigh.

"He is one of the wealthiest men in the *Beau Monde*. He is a close friend of the Prince of Wales. He is a Corinthian and a Beau, although he does not like one to say he is. And his possessions—oh, Gilda, I cannot begin to describe them!"

"Why has he not been married before?"

"You may well ask," Heloise replied. "He has every girl in London at his feet, or, if they are married, women in his arms!"

Gilda looked shocked and Heloise laughed, but the sound had no humour in it.

"He is not such a fool to make love to an unmarried girl, otherwise her father would pretty soon march him up the aisle!"

The way Heloise spoke was sharp and, Gilda thought, unpleasant.

"I expect," she said a little hesitatingly, "the Marquis has been waiting to . . . fall in love . . . and that is what he must have done . . . with you."

"That is what I thought the moment we first met," Heloise replied, "but it is taking him a long time to say so, far too long for my liking."

"And now that you have disappeared you think that he will realise how much you matter to him?"

"That is what I have come here for," Heloise said. "In fact, that is what he must do, damn him!"

Gilda gave a little start.

It was strange and very shocking to hear her sister swear.

However, she was too wise to say so, and after a moment she said:

"I am sure, Heloise, it is very remiss of me, but I never asked you if you would like refreshments after your journey."

"Now that you mention it," Heloise answered, "I am thirsty. Is there any wine in this benighted place?"

Gilda looked startled.

"There may be a bottle of claret in the cellar. I have really never looked since Papa died."

"I suppose not," Heloise said. "I cannot imagine you drinking anything but milk or water."

The way she spoke did not sound like a compliment, and Gilda said:

"There is tea if you would like some."

"I suppose I shall have to if there is nothing else!" Heloise said. "But it must be nearly luncheon-time. Have you something decent to eat?"

Gilda thought quickly.

"There are eggs, so I could make you an omelette, or there is some cold ham which Mrs. Hewlett brought me which her son who has the farm next door had cured."

Heloise wrinkled her nose.

"It does not sound very appetising. You had better make me the omelette. If nothing else, I suppose a star-vation diet is good for my figure."

Gilda made no answer to this. Instead she picked up the blue silk travelling-cape which Heloise had thrown down on a chair and carried it into the Hall.

She hung it up in the carved oak cupboard which contained two of her father's overcoats and a rather disreputable cloak she wore in the garden when it was cold.

As she hung Heloise's cape beside them she was conscious that it exuded a fragrance which she was sure came from Paris.

Then she hurried into the kitchen and started preparing the omelette.

It took her a little time to build up the fire in the stove, which had begun to die down after Mrs. Hewlett had left, to boil a kettle for the tea, then to heat the frying-pan for the omelette.

There were three eggs in the larder, which she broke into a bowl, thinking as she did so that she would have to go to the farm to get some more for Heloise's dinner and certainly for her breakfast tomorrow morning.

She was mixing the eggs when Heloise came into the kitchen.

She looked so lovely that for a moment Gilda could only stare at her, thinking that with her fashionably dressed golden hair and her blue eyes she was like the Goddess of Spring.

"It looks just the same," Heloise said disparagingly. "I had forgotten how small and shabby the house was. How you can stand it, Gilda, I do not know!"

"I have had no choice," Gilda answered. "In fact, I have been wondering what I should do, because quite frankly, Heloise, I cannot afford to live even here."

As she spoke she saw her sister stiffen, and she knew instinctively that Heloise was afraid she was going to ask her for money.

"What did Papa leave you?" Heloise asked after a moment.

"His pension died with him," Gilda replied. "If Mama had lived she would of course have been entitled to a widow's pension, but children are not provided for."

"I expect if they are boys they are expected to earn their own living, and if they are girls to get married," Heloise said. "That is what you will have to do."

Gilda laughed.

"An opportunity would be a fine thing! The only unmarried man in the village is the Vicar and he is over seventy."

"If you married him at least you would have some money!" Heloise remarked.

Gilda laughed again, but she had the uncomfortable idea that Heloise was not intending to be funny.

Her sister sat down on a kitchen chair and looked at her.

"You know, Gilda," she said after a moment, "we are not unalike. If you took a little more trouble with yourself, you might easily attract some country squire, but that gown you are wearing is a disgrace!"

"I know," Gilda said humbly, "but the last thing I can afford is clothes, and it would be no use being smartly dressed if I have to starve to death."

"Are things really as bad as that?"

"They are worse."

Heloise sighed.

"I suppose I could have brought you some of my gowns which I have no further use for. One thing about Her Ladyship is that, although she is a bore to live with, she is very generous in wanting me to look my best."

"Surely she has been very, very kind to you," Gilda said. "After all, it was her idea that you should go to live with her when Mama died."

There was a moment's silence. Then Heloise said:

"Actually, it was mine!"

Gilda put down the fork she held in her hand with a clatter.

"Your idea?" she exclaimed. "Do you mean . . . are you really telling me . . . ?"

"I wrote to her," Heloise interrupted. "She is my God-mother, and I saw, as no-one else did, that if I lived here in this hole I might as well be buried alive."

"But . . . how could you be so . . . daring?" Gilda asked.

"Nothing ventured, nothing gained!" Heloise replied. "I wrote her a pathetic letter, one that would have brought tears to the eyes of a stone-image, saying how much I missed Mama, how poor and deprived I was, and how Papa did not want me."

"Oh, Heloise, how could you tell such lies? You know Papa adored you. After all, you were the first baby, and Mama always said it was the most wonderful moment of their married life when you were born, and they thought you were a gift from God."

"Well, as God was not very generous when it came to the things I wanted," Heloise replied, "I had to take things into my own hands."

"You have certainly been very successful about it."

"It was clever of me, was it not?" Heloise said. "Actually it is very nice for Godmama to have me with her. She has had to admit herself that because I am such a success in London, far more interesting and distinguished people come to the house than if I were not there."

"But it is still very kind of her to give you lovely clothes and make it possible for you to go to the Balls and parties. You used to write and tell me about them when you first left."

"I have had no time to write now," Heloise said quickly. "There is never a moment when I am not being entertained, fêted, and of course made love to by attractive men."

"I am not a bit surprised," Gilda said. "You were always beautiful, but never as beautiful as you are now."

The note of sincerity in her voice was very touching, and Heloise preened herself before she said:

"You are right, Gilda. I do look my best, but sometimes I get tired when there is a Ball every night and so many delightful things to do in the daytime."

"But how do you manage since Her Ladyship is blind and cannot chaperone you?"

"I write letters to her friends asking them to chaperone me," Heloise replied, "but what more often happens is that invitations to the big dinner-parties and Balls come from people who are well aware of her affliction and therefore they take it for granted that they will look after me."

"It must be very exciting for you to be such a success."

There was a pause before Heloise said in a hard voice:

"This is my third Season, and I have to be married! No beauty, however much acclaimed, lasts forever, and I intend that the Marquis shall *marry* me."

She accentuated the word so that it sounded positively aggressive, and Gilda said in a small voice:

"Suppose he does not?"

"I have an alternative," Heloise replied, "but not nearly such an attractive one."

"Who is he?"

"Nobody of great importance, except that he is extremely wealthy. But I refuse to consider him. I can see myself only as the Marchioness of Staverton, and that is what I intend to be!"

Again she spoke in a way that made Gilda look at her apprehensively.

She thought that as Heloise was so lovely it spoilt her when she spoke in a hard voice that seemed somehow to vibrate through the kitchen and jar on the sunshine coming through the window.

She had beaten the eggs and now she said:

"I suppose you will want to eat in the Dining-Room?"

As she spoke she took a tray from one of the shelves.

"Of course," Heloise replied. "Although I am sure you eat in the kitchen when you are alone, I am not sinking to that level!"

"No . . . of course not," Gilda said humbly. "Go into the Dining-Room, Heloise, and everything will be ready for you in a moment."

She put some knives and forks on the tray and a plate at the front of the stove to warm, then started to make the omelette.

She knew there would not be enough for two, and thought she would take in a piece of the ham for herself in case Heloise did not wish to eat alone.

Then she thought it was unlikely that her sister would notice what she was eating.

She remembered that although it seemed unkind, she had often thought when Heloise was living at home that as far as she was concerned no-one else existed in the whole world except her.

"It is understandable because she is so beautiful," Gilda had excused her sister's selfishness then, and she was thinking the same now.

As she skilfully tipped the beautifully browned omelette onto the warm plate, she found herself wondering if Heloise would be happy when she had attained her desire and married her Marquis.

She supposed that wealth and position and a leading role in Society would bring happiness to some people, although it was not anything she wanted herself.

'When I marry,' Gilda thought, 'I want a man who will love me and whom I will love, and we will be content to be together, whether our home is a very grand one or a very poor one like this.'

She remembered how happy her mother had been with her father when he was not away with his Regiment and after he had retired.

The General had been a lot older than his wife and they had not had children until they had been married for some years. Gilda could only vaguely remember days when they had followed their father to Salisbury Plain and other Army depots.

Once he had gone abroad for two years, and when he returned her mother had been so happy it had seemed to Gilda as a little girl that every day was like a Fête Day.

Then when there were no more journeyings and they had settled down at the Manor, she could remember how content her father and mother had been in the garden or reading together in the Study.

There had been laughter at meal-times, and before she became old enough to go down to dinner, Gilda could remember listening at the top of the stairs to the chatter of voices in the Dining-Room.

Afterwards there had been the sound of music coming from the Drawing-Room as her mother played and sang old songs to which her father liked to listen.

"They were happy," Gilda told herself, "and that is what Heloise should want, not just material things."

But she knew her sister would never listen to her if she tried to explain the difference. Anyway, she doubted if she would understand.

Heloise had always craved for luxuries and for all the things that money could buy.

She remembered her sister on her fifteenth birthday, when she herself had been thirteen, stamping her foot because her presents were not what she wanted.

"I asked Mama for a new gown," she said angrily, "and a coat trimmed with fur! All she has given me is this rubbish!"

As she spoke she had thrown across the room a pretty bonnet trimmed with blue ribbons with a small reticule to match and a pair of satin slippers.

"But they are so pretty!" Gilda had expostulated. "And you know you needed some new slippers."

"I also wanted a new gown and a new coat!" Heloise had raged.

"I do not think Mama can afford those things at the moment," Gilda said.

"Well, she could have sold something to get me what I want," Heloise retorted. "I think Mama is selfish and beastly, and I hate my nasty dull presents!"

Gilda had been shocked at the time, but she had not been surprised when a month later Heloise had coaxed and wheedled what she wanted out of her mother, although later she had said to Gilda:

"We shall have to economise, Gilda, to make up for the things I have bought Louise. But they have made her happy, so I can easily go without a new coat myself this winter."

Yes, Heloise had always been the same, Gilda thought as she carried the omelette to the Dining-Room.

Although she had nothing to do but sit and wait, Heloise had made no attempt to lay the table-cloth, and now as Gilda quickly arranged it for her she sat back in her father's armchair and looked almost disdainfully at the omelette.

"Is this what you call a square meal?" she asked. "It is lucky that I am prepared to admit that it will do me good to fast for the next forty-eight hours, for it is very difficult not to over-eat in London."

"Is the food superb?" Gilda asked, aware that Heloise was ready to gossip.

"It is when one dines with the Prince of Wales."

"Do you mean to say that you have dined with him?"

"Yes, I have, and I am quite certain it was the Marquis who made him invite me. He is always curious about anybody new who is beautiful, although he is not really interested in young girls."

She paused to note that Gilda was listening intently and went on:

"And when I received my invitation I was naturally overjoyed."

"I am sure you were," Gilda agreed.

"It was a terrible rush to get a new gown, and as I said to Godmama, I could hardly go in the old rags I was wearing at the time."

"Was that not rather rude, when she had given them to you?"

"Not at all! She agreed," Heloise said carelessly, "and sent me to the very best dressmaker in Bond Street. It cost a great amount of money, but it was worth it to have the Prince paying me compliments, as did every other man of consequence who was at the dinner."

"But did that not make the Marquis jealous?"

There was a frown on Heloise's small white forehead before she replied:

"I am not certain—and this is the truth, Gilda—what he really feels about me."

She stopped eating for a moment before she said:

"He is the most infuriating, exasperating man I have ever met in my whole life. One never knows what he is thinking or feeling."

"Then why do you want to marry him?"

"Do not be so silly! I have answered that question once!" Heloise answered sharply.

"Yes, of course . . . I am sorry," Gilda said quickly. "But he sounds frightening."

"He does not frighten me," Heloise said. "He just makes me very angry and very frustrated, but I will get his ring on my finger or die in the attempt."

"Do you really think you will be happy when you are married to such a man? Suppose he continues to upset you?"

Heloise shrugged her shoulders.

"It will be too late then for him to do anything about it, and though you do not know it living here in the back of beyond, most couples in the *Beau Monde* each go their own way."

Gilda looked surprised and Heloise went on:

"I am sure that after the first year, when I suppose I shall have to produce an heir to the title, I shall have my friends and the Marquis will have his, and neither of us will ask too many questions."

There was silence for a moment. Then Gilda said:

"Do you mean that he will have . . . lady-friends?"

"Of course I mean that," Heloise replied. "He would be a monk or a Saint if he remained faithful to one woman, and I have every intention of keeping my admirers happy until I am a ripe old age."

Gilda wondered exactly what this entailed, but she was too nervous to ask. Instead, as Heloise finished her omelette she took away her empty plate, saying:

"I am afraid there is nothing else except cheese."

"I hate cheese!" Heloise said petulantly.

"I will try to get something better for you this evening, and I will cook you a pudding. Do you still like treacle tart?"

"Good Heavens! I had forgotten such things existed!" Heloise exclaimed. "But now that you speak of it, I remember when we used to have treacle tart one day, plum duff the next, and roly-poly pudding the third. How we ever endured such horrors I cannot imagine!"

"Tell me what you eat in London," Gilda said, to change the subject.

Soon Heloise was expatiating on the delicious dishes that she had enjoyed in distinguished houses.

At the same time, she made it very clear that once she had the Marquis's Chef under her orders, the food that would be served in any house of which she was chatelaine would exceed anything she had enjoyed at anyone else's.

They talked, or rather Heloise did, all through the afternoon, and only when she said she would lie down for a little while before supper did Gilda have the chance to hurry to the nearest farm, which was owned by Mrs. Hewlett's son.

As she went, she calculated what it would cost to buy a small leg of lamb for Heloise's dinner.

She would also want eggs, and if she was fortunate Farmer Hewlett might have made some sausage-meat, which Heloise used to enjoy when she lived at home.

Gilda knew that all these things would come to a considerable amount of money, and although she knew it was wrong of her, she could not help feeling a little relieved that Heloise did not intend to stay long.

She was quite certain that she would not offer to pay for anything while she was at home.

Although it was exciting to see her again and hear all the things she had to tell her, Gilda was a little hurt that this was the first time she had heard from Heloise for over a year.

It was quite obvious that while she was in London she had forgotten her sister and her shabby home and was completely absorbed in her new life.

'She is very lucky, and Lady Neyland has been so kind to her,' Gilda thought.

She wished that Heloise did not sound so bored by her Godmother's blindness and so ungrateful for all she had received from somebody who was not even a relative.

Lady Neyland had in fact been a close friend of her mother's before she married, and although they had seen each other only spasmodically in the years that followed Mrs. Wyngate's marriage, they had continued to correspond.

Because Lady Neyland had no children, she had always been interested in her friend's family. Presents had come at Christmas for both girls and Heloise had always received something on her birthday.

"It is a pity my Godparents died when I was young and omitted to remember me in their wills," Gilda said to herself with a faint smile.

Then she told herself it would be very wrong to be jealous of Heloise.

It was her sister's right to have the best that was available, and she had been very happy for the last two years after her mother's death when she had been alone with her father.

She loved listening to him talk about his life in the Army and they read interesting books together.

Thinking back, she knew that not even the Balls that Heloise described so vividly could make up for their companionship, which she found difficult to put into words but which had enriched her life.

"I loved Papa and he loved me," Gilda told herself.

That meant a great deal more than pursuing a Marquis who, if she was honest, she thought sounded extremely unpleasant.

CHAPTER TWO

*H*eloise had decided to spend most of Sunday in bed, and Gilda had carried first her breakfast upstairs at a very late hour, then her luncheon.

She had cooked the lamb very carefully, and Heloise, having eaten two helpings, had actually said that she found it tender.

Now she sat up in bed looking exceedingly beautiful and was ready to talk.

"I am so glad you had such a good night," Gilda said. "You must have been very tired to sleep so late."

Heloise laughed.

"It was not so much being tired as taking an extra-large dose of laudanum."

Gilda was horrified.

"Laudanum!" she exclaimed. "You know Mama always disapproved when the Doctor used to suggest that Papa should take a spoonful at night when his rheumatism was bad."

"I could not sleep without it."

Gilda was looking disapproving and Heloise continued:

"It is all very well for you to criticise, but if you were dancing until three or four o'clock in the morning and drinking champagne, when you did get to bed you would find it impossible to get to sleep."

Gilda could not help feeling that she would like to try the experience of dancing until the early hours, but she

felt it was important that Heloise should realise that laudanum was bad for her.

"I am sure you would find it easy to sleep if you drank
some warm milk. Mama always said honey and milk . . ."

"Oh, do not fuss!" Heloise interrupted sharply. "I
want to tell you what a success I was at the Ball given by
the Duchess of Bedford. Everybody said I looked sensational, and it was after that that the Marquis began to
pay me attention."

She was back again talking about the Marquis, although Gilda had no wish to complain.

She found it fascinating to listen to Heloise's descriptions of the Balls she had attended, the compliments she
had received, and her descriptions of her best gowns,
which cost more money than she herself had to live on
for a whole year.

She was not jealous of her sister and never had been.
Heloise had always taken first place in her father's affec-
tions and in everything they had done as children.

It was true that she was eighteen months older than
Gilda. At the same time, she was so beautiful that it
seemed to be her right to be given the best of everything
that was available, and for Gilda to be content with what
was left over.

"When the Marquis said to me," Heloise was saying
now, " 'I will give a dinner-party for you at my house in
Berkeley Square,' I knew I was being specially favoured."

"Is that the party to which you did not go last night?"
Gilda asked.

Heloise nodded.

"Surely that will make him very angry?"

"It will make him jealous," Heloise replied. "He will
be quite certain I am doing something which I find
more amusing and attractive than dining with him, and
the mere idea will give him a shock."

Gilda could not help thinking that it was very bad
manners for her sister to run away at the last moment
and without notice from an entertainment which had

been specially provided in her honour, but she was too wise to say so.

"The trouble with the Marquis," Heloise went on, "is that he is spoilt. He has everything he wants in the world, and from all I hear, no woman has ever refused him her favours or anything else he asked of her."

She said this in a voice which surprised Gilda and made her wonder what exactly her sister meant.

But before she could ask questions Heloise continued:

"I worked it out in my own mind that the one thing which would really make the Marquis consider me more seriously than he has done up to now is for me to appear reluctant to be with him and not pressure him in the same way that every other woman does."

She laughed before she added:

"Of course I am in fact doing so! I am determined to catch him and make sure he does not get away."

"And when you have caught him?" Gilda asked.

"Then I will be the Marchioness of Staverton and my worries will be over."

Gilda smiled.

"Have you really any worries? You certainly do not look troubled."

"Of course I am worried," Heloise said. "I have told you I have to be married. I shall be twenty, as you well know, in July, and most girls who were débutantes at the same time as I was have already found husbands."

There was a little frown between her blue eyes as she went on:

"But they were so lucky. They had fathers and mothers who arranged marriages for them, as is usual in aristocratic circles."

"But could not your Godmother . . . arrange a . . . marriage for . . . you?" Gilda asked hesitatingly.

She thought as she spoke that an arranged marriage sounded a very cold, almost unpleasant way of being married.

But if it was the customary thing to do, then of course it was something Heloise would want.

"Godmama is so stupid!" Heloise replied contemptuously. "She really does not understand what is expected of her. When I suggested last year that she might approach Lord Cornwall, whose eldest son was interested in me for a short while, she said it was too embarrassing as she did not know the Cornwalls!"

"I can understand her feelings."

"You would, because you are as stupid as she is," Heloise retorted, "and I daresay that Mama if she were alive would have been no better. One does not have to be sentimental when it comes to social advancement."

Gilda was silent for a moment. Then she said:

"Is the Marquis expecting to have an arranged marriage?"

"I am sure he has been approached by every Duke and Duchess and every Earl and Countess who want to push their plain daughters off onto him," Heloise said. "But I am quite certain he wishes to choose his own wife."

"Then we must just pray that he chooses you," Gilda said.

"It is not prayers which are needed at the moment, but intelligence," Heloise answered, "and that is what I have. I am sure by this time the Marquis is wondering frantically what has happened to me and whom I am with."

"Will you tell him you have been here?"

"You must be crazy!" Heloise replied. "I shall look down my nose and say I have had a delightful time. If I speak in a soft, rather passionate little voice, he will think somebody has been making love to me and kissing me. That will make him jealous, and then anything might happen!"

She lay back against the pillows and turned her blue eyes up to the ceiling as if she was thinking ecstatically of what it would mean when the Marquis proposed to her.

Gilda did not speak for a moment. Then she said:

"Of course I am very . . . ignorant about such things . . . but would the Marquis not think you were rather . . . fast if you allowed men to . . . kiss you?"

"He would think it very strange if no-one wished to!" Heloise replied.

"I can understand their wanting to," Gilda said. "You are so lovely, dearest, that I am sure every man finds you irresistible, but . . . should you kiss them?"

"You do not know what you are talking about," Heloise said. "Just leave me to get the Marquis in my own way. I know what I am doing."

"Yes . . . of course," Gilda said humbly.

When it was tea-time, Heloise decided she was far too comfortable in bed to move, so Gilda brought her tea upstairs.

She arranged her mother's best china on the tray with a pretty lace cloth and hoped Heloise would enjoy the shortbread biscuits that she had hastily baked while the oven was still hot.

When tea was finished she said in a small, rather shy voice:

"I have . . . something to . . . ask you, Heloise."

"What is it?" her sister enquired.

"If I came to London . . . would it be . . . possible for you to find me . . . employment of some . . . sort?"

Heloise sat up abruptly.

"Come to London? What would you want to come to London for?" she demanded.

"I have been . . . thinking things over," Gilda said. "I really cannot afford to stay here . . . unless I earn money somehow . . . but I cannot . . . think what I can . . . do."

"What do you expect to do in London?" Heloise asked.

She spoke aggressively and Gilda thought uncomfortably that her eyes looked hostile.

"I . . . wondered if it would be . . . possible for me to . . . give lessons to . . . children or to . . . look after them."

"Do you mean become a Governess?" Heloise asked in tones of horror.

"Well . . . something like . . . that."

"How do you think I would feel," Heloise enquired, "with my sister nothing more or less than a superior servant? How can you suggest anything so abominable?"

"I am . . . sorry," Gilda replied. "I did not . . . think it would . . . upset you."

"Of course it upsets me!" Heloise snapped. "I am a Lady of Fashion, and naturally I have never admitted to anybody that my home is a crumbling, tumble-down Manor and my father had no money except what he earned as a soldier."

Gilda thought uncomfortably that she had often suspected that Heloise was ashamed of her family. But now that she put it into words, it came as a shock that made her clasp her fingers together because they were trembling.

"I am . . . sorry, Heloise," she said quickly. "I did not mean to . . . upset you. I will manage . . . somehow."

As she spoke she thought of how last night she had looked at her cash-book again and knew it was really impossible to live at the Manor on the small amount she could draw from her mother's money.

"If you have to teach children, you can teach them here!" Heloise said in a hard voice.

"There is already a teacher in the village," Gilda replied. "It is only a Penny School, and I am afraid poor Miss Crew would starve to death if she had not a little money of her own."

There was silence. Then Heloise said:

"I have told you, you will have to get married. There must be a farmer or perhaps even a well-to-do tradesman who would think it an honour to have you as his wife."

Gilda rose from the bed and walked to the window.

She stood there not looking out at the afternoon sunshine and the overgrown garden, but fighting back the tears that came into her eyes.

Now she knew exactly what Heloise thought of her and that she had no affection either for her or for her mother's memory.

To suggest that she should marry a farmer or tradesman rather than become a nuisance showed all too clearly the contempt that Gilda had always felt in her heart Heloise really had for her.

Her mother had always been proud of her distinguished Cornish ancestry, and her father's family had all served their country either as soldiers or sailors for generations.

Her grandfather who had been a General had been Knighted, and her great-grandfather had his place in the history-books.

As Gilda fought back her tears, a voice from the bed said:

"I suppose what it comes down to is that I shall have to give you some money, although I do think it is extremely tiresome that you should want it."

Gilda turned from the window.

"It is . . . all right, Heloise," she said. "I will . . . manage somehow."

Heloise, however, was not listening.

She looked so cross and disagreeable that it spoilt her pink and white and gold beauty, and for a moment she looked exactly as she had when as a small girl she flew into a tantrum whenever she could not get her own way.

"I tell you what I will do," she said. "I will give you twenty pounds a year until you are married, and it will be no use whining for any more."

"I am not . . . whining," Gilda said.

She tried to speak proudly, but her voice broke on the words and two tears ran down her cheeks.

"I will give it to you," Heloise went on as if Gilda had not spoken, "but on the condition that you do not come to London, nor do you ever at any time make any other claims upon me."

"I would . . . certainly not do . . . that."

"What I mean," Heloise went on, "is that when I marry the Marquis I shall not tell him I have a sister, nor are you at any time to appear in my life or ever to tell people outside the village that we are related."

"I promise I will do that," Gilda said, "but, Heloise, I will not take your money. In fact, after what you have just said, I would rather scrub other people's door-steps than accept a penny from you!"

She walked out of the bedroom as she spoke, shutting the door behind her. Then she ran to her own room to fling herself down on her bed and burst into tears.

Because Heloise was the last member of her family left, she had always thought of her with warmth and love, but now as she lay there she knew that that feeling was more imaginary than real.

She had imagined herself into thinking that she loved Heloise and Heloise loved her, simply because without that love she was completely and utterly alone.

Now that she knew exactly what Heloise felt about her, it was as if she had lost something precious and it had left a void in her life which nothing could heal.

She cried for a long time.

Then she realised that Heloise would soon be wanting dinner and she must cook the ox-tongue which Farmer Hewlett had persuaded her to buy.

"Oi won't charge ye much fer it, Miss Gilda," he said. "An' it'll be a nice mouthful for the two o' ye."

Gilda had thanked him, and now she remembered that she had told Farmer Hewlett that she had a visitor but fortunately she had not said it was her sister.

She had felt he would not be interested as his mother would have been, and anyway she had been in a hurry and had just bought the lamb and the eggs and had only added the tongue when he insisted.

She washed her face in cold water and went downstairs.

All the time that she was cooking she was wondering despairingly how she would be able to manage when Heloise had gone and the tithes on the Manor soon became due.

"Perhaps I was silly to refuse the offer of twenty pounds she made me," she told herself.

Then she thought of her Cornish ancestors and lifted her chin.

She had been born with the same pride with which they had carried their arms into battle first against the Normans, then against the Barons who had threatened their freedom.

173

"I will manage . . . of course I will manage," Gilda told herself.

She felt a little embarrassed when she carried Heloise's tray upstairs, but her sister merely said when she appeared:

"I cannot think why you have been away for so long. I had to light the candles myself."

"I am sorry," Gilda said, "but I have been cooking the supper, and I hope you will enjoy it."

"I expect so," Heloise replied indifferently, "and I hope you had the sense to bring up the bottle of claret you were talking about."

"Oh, I am sorry," Gilda said. "I never thought of it, but do you think claret is good for you? Mama always said that too much wine could ruin a woman's complexion."

"Mama talked a lot of nonsense!" Heloise replied. "I have to drink in London, although some young girls are forbidden to do so by their mothers."

"Then why do you drink?" Gilda asked.

"Because I want to, for one thing," Heloise replied, "and because it makes me enjoy myself more."

"I have always heard that the Prince of Wales drinks a great deal and so do the Bucks and Beaux," Gilda remarked.

"They sometimes get unpleasantly drunk before the end of an evening," Heloise admitted, "but not those who are Corinthians, because they want to be fit for when they are racing."

"I always imagined that the right sort of gentleman would also be athletic," Gilda said.

"Well, that is certainly what the Marquis is," Heloise replied, getting back to her favourite subject. "Because he is so big and tall he has to keep his weight down for the Steeple-Chases he always wins, and they say he is the finest swordsman in the whole of the *Beau Monde*."

"Have you ever seen him fence?"

"No," Heloise replied, "because ladies are very seldom invited to the Gymnasiums where the duellists exercise. Not that I am interested."

"But you must be!" Gilda cried.

"Oh, I pretend to be," Heloise answered, "but I do not want to watch the Marquis doing things. I want to listen to him talking to me and telling me how beautiful I am."

She picked up a hand-mirror which she had beside her on the bed and contemplated her face in it.

As she did so, Gilda said:

"Do you know, Heloise, at the moment . . . you look exactly like Mama. She always said we were both like her and her grandmother, who was a great beauty."

"I do not suppose anybody ever heard of her outside Cornwall," Heloise said scornfully. "I am a rival of Georgina, Duchess of Devonshire! In fact most people think I am more beautiful than she is!"

"I am sure you are," Gilda said loyally.

When the supper was over Heloise said she was going to sleep.

"I want to have a long night tonight because tomorrow I shall be dancing and I want to look my best."

She told Gilda to fetch her another nightgown so that she could change from the one she had worn all day.

She also made her pin her hair into curls round her forehead and became quite angry when at first Gilda did not do it as skilfully as the lady's-maid she had left behind.

"I am sorry," Gilda said, "I am trying to do exactly as you tell me, but it is something I have never done before."

"That is obvious from the mess your own hair is in."

However, Heloise conceded that her lady's-maid had been taught by an experienced hairdresser what to do before she finally got it right.

"Of course, whenever I am going to a Ball, a *Coiffeur* comes to the house to attend to me," Heloise boasted. "He always says I am a great advertisement for him and everybody wants him because I look so lovely."

Gilda put the last pin into her sister's golden hair.

"Now, is that all right?" she asked.

"Not too bad," Heloise conceded.

On her sister's instructions Gilda put a fine lace cap on her head to hold the pins in place.

Then Heloise anointed her face with a lotion which came from Bond Street.

"It is made from the roots of irises," she said, "and keeps the skin clear and white. It is very, very expensive."

"You have always had a beautiful skin," Gilda replied, "and I do not believe that irises or anything else have much to do with it."

Heloise laughed.

"I am glad Godmama cannot hear you say that," she said. "She complained about the last bill and said that I was too young to need such aids to beauty."

"I am sure she is right," Gilda said. "You do not need any lotions except fresh air and water."

She spoke positively. At the same time, she did not want Heloise to go away hating her because she was critical.

"After all, whatever she may say, and however much she may be ashamed of me, she is still my sister," Gilda argued with herself, "and perhaps one day—who knows?—she may need me again."

Heloise, who had been sitting on the stool in front of the dressing-table, got into bed.

"Now shut the window," she said to Gilda, "and make quite certain the curtains are properly closed. I do not want the light to wake me."

Gilda obeyed, thinking that the room would be rather stuffy, but she did not wish to argue.

"One last thing," Heloise went on, "bring me my bottle of laudanum. It is on the washing-stand, and I shall want a spoon."

"Oh, Heloise, do not take it!" Gilda begged.

"I have every intention of sleeping from now until eight o'clock tomorrow morning, when you must call me so that I can be ready when the carriage comes," Heloise said.

There was nothing more Gilda could say, and she fetched the bottle from the washing-stand, feeling as she carried it across the room that the dark liquid in it looked sinister.

Heloise took three teaspoonfuls, then when Gilda would have taken it away she said:

"Leave it by the bed. I sometimes find difficulty in getting off to sleep and take another spoonful."

Gilda did as she was told, then blew out one of the candles by the bed.

"If there is nothing more you want," she said, "I will bring your breakfast up at eight o'clock and pack your trunk."

"If I am drowsy, wake me," Heloise said. "I must be in London before luncheon, as I expect the Marquis will be waiting to see me."

"I hope he is, for your sake."

Gilda blew out the candles on the dressing-table and walked towards the door.

"Good-night, Heloise," she said. "It has been nice for me to have you here, and whatever you may feel about me, I shall always pray for you and hope that you get everything you want in life."

"I will!" Heloise replied firmly.

Gilda went from the bedroom down the stairs to the kitchen.

She had the dinner-plates to wash up and she also laid everything ready on a tray for Heloise's breakfast, thinking as she did so:

'I must try to keep the Manor so that there will be somewhere for Heloise to come if things go wrong.'

She did not know why, but she had the feeling that her sister would not marry the Marquis, however determined she might be to do so.

There were times when Gilda had presentiments about people which were illogical and not based on fact, but invariably they came true.

She knew it was due to her Cornish blood, and her mother had often told her how, like the Scots and the Welsh, the Cornish people were Celts and therefore had instincts which were at times clairvoyant.

"I have always known when your father was in danger," Mrs. Wyngate used to say in her soft voice. "At first I thought it was my imagination, but later when these feelings came I used to jot down the dates and time of day."

Her voice deepened as she continued:

"When your father came home, I found they coincided exactly with the moment when a native spear missed him by a hair's breadth, or he was fighting a battle in which many other soldiers lost their lives."

Gilda had found that she too had this power of clairvoyance.

She always knew when she met people if they were honest and true or twisted and crafty.

She also was invariably aware whether what she was being told was the truth or not.

Afterwards, she thought to herself that because her presentiments were invariably accurate they were extremely embarrassing.

Now when Heloise had been talking of the Marquis and of her conviction that he would propose marriage, Gilda had known it was something he would not do and her sister was doomed to disappointment.

"I am wrong . . . I am sure I am . . . wrong," she tried to tell herself when finally she went to bed.

But as she undressed, her feelings were too strong to be denied.

Because she did not wish to think about them, she pinned her hair into curls as she had pinned Heloise's.

As it happened, Gilda's hair curled naturally, while Heloise's had always been straight.

'If it is too curly in the morning, I shall look like the top of a mop!' Gilda thought.

At the same time, she thought that when she combed her hair out, the fashion would be as becoming to her as it was to Heloise.

She thought of the beautiful gowns her sister had to wear and the bonnet in which she had travelled with its small blue ostrich feathers.

'I wish I could try it on,' she thought, but knew if she asked her sister would refuse.

Heloise had made no further reference to her offer of twenty pounds a year, which Gilda had refused, and in the light of what she had said it was obvious that unless a real crisis occurred, once she had left she would never return.

She also wished to forget that she had a sister.

It hurt, but Gilda told herself she had to be sensible. There was no point in trying to alter people from what they were.

☙❧

Gilda awoke and realised that she had plenty of time to prepare Heloise's breakfast.

Then she got up and went downstairs to tidy the house and dust the Sitting-Room.

It was something she usually did anyway, leaving the other rooms for Mrs. Hewlett but preferring to handle herself the small chic ornaments her mother had loved instead of trusting them to Mrs. Hewlett's heavy hands.

The fire was burning brightly in the stove by the time she had finished, and she thought that before she cooked the eggs it would be a good idea to call Heloise and make quite certain she was properly awake to enjoy her breakfast.

She therefore went upstairs a few minutes before eight and crept quietly into the room to pull back the curtains.

The sunshine poured in, and glancing out the window Gilda thought there were more blossoms out on the lilac bushes than there had been the day before.

Then she turned towards the bed.

As she had expected, Heloise was fast asleep.

She stood looking at her sister and thought how lovely she was and that she looked very much younger when she was unconscious than when she was awake.

Now there was a faint smile on her lips and her skin seemed almost translucent.

"Heloise!" But there was no response.

Gilda called her name again. Then she bent forward to touch her shoulder.

Her sister did not move.

"Heloise, you must wake up!" Gilda said. "It is eight o'clock, and you know you have to hurry to London to see the Marquis."

She thought that, if nothing else, would arouse her, but still Heloise did not stir.

Then Gilda touched her hand which lay outside the sheets, and when she did so she started.

Heloise's skin was cold, so cold that it was almost like touching a marble statue rather than a human being.

It was then that Gilda glanced at the laudanum bottle which stood beside the bed.

It was not in the same position as where she had put it last night, but was nearer to Heloise, and the spoon which she had wiped after her sister had used it had obviously been used again.

Gilda felt frightened.

Holding Heloise's hand in both of hers, she rubbed it, saying as she did so:

"Wake up, Heloise! Wake up!"

There was no response and Heloise's hand was still cold.

'As cold,' Gilda thought, 'as death!'

It was then that frantically she put both her hands on her sister's shoulders and shook her. As she did so, Heloise's head fell forward limply like that of a rag doll.

It took Gilda some moments to face the truth. Then she knew unmistakably that Heloise was dead.

Because her mother had always called on the villagers when they were ill and Gilda often went with her, she had seen a number of dead people.

Only after she had felt Heloise's heart and pulse and got no response did she wonder desperately what she should do.

There was no Doctor in the village.

She would have to send to the nearest town, which was five miles away, where a young man had taken over the practice of the old Doctor whom Gilda had known since she was a child.

This meant he would have to be paid, and Gilda could not help feeling it would be a waste of money when there was nothing he could do or say except what she knew already, that Heloise had taken an overdose of laudanum.

The laying-out locally was always done by Mrs. Hewlett and she would not be back until the afternoon.

'I will wait until she returns,' Gilda thought. 'Then I will tell the Vicar.'

She then remembered that the Vicar was away and would not be home for nearly three weeks.

That meant that a Clergyman from another village would have to be contacted to perform the burial service.

"How could this have happened?" Gilda asked herself unhappily, and wondered if she could have done anything to prevent it.

She thought again how lovely Heloise looked and how very, very young.

'She is young,' Gilda thought, 'and yet, how much more Heloise has already done in her life than I shall ever do!'

She wondered if many people in London would mourn her sister or whether she would soon be forgotten. Perhaps there would be somebody new, an even more beautiful young girl whom the Beaux would admire and never have another thought for Heloise, who had died when she was not yet twenty.

"It is all the Marquis's fault," Gilda told herself. "If he had proposed to her she would never have come home. She would have stayed in London and been with him and been so happy that she would not have needed laudanum."

The thought of the Marquis made Gilda realise that she would have to tell him and Heloise's Godmother, Lady Neyland, that her sister was dead.

"I will write a letter," she decided, "which can go back with the carriage when it arrives."

She wondered if it would be more polite to go in person to Lady Neyland, as she was blind, to tell her what had happened.

"I am sure that is what Mama would think I should do," Gilda told herself. "And if Lady Neyland would be kind enough to send me back in her carriage, I would be able to return late in the afternoon."

Then she told herself that if she did go to London she had no clothes fit to wear. Although Lady Neyland would be unable to see her, the Marquis might be waiting at the house as Heloise had expected he would.

'If Heloise was ashamed of me, he would certainly be shocked at my appearance,' Gilda thought.

She decided that, rude or not, she would write to Lady Neyland and a maid could read it to her.

It would certainly come as a terrible shock.

She walked across the room to pull the curtains so as to leave Heloise in the dark.

As she did so, she took one last look at her sister, thinking it was cruel that she should die and leave behind everything that had been so important to her.

She was beautiful, she was a success, and if she had not married the Marquis she would have had the chance of marrying another rich man.

"How could she die at this particular moment and in such a stupid way?" Gilda asked herself.

She was quite sure that Heloise had not meant to die.

She had just taken more laudanum, not anticipating for a moment the tragic effect it would have upon her.

'Mama would have been dreadfully upset,' Gilda thought, but now Heloise was with her mother and father and they were all together.

"I am the only one of the family left," she said aloud, "and perhaps, as I am likely to die of starvation, it will not be long before I join them!"

It was a bitter-sweet thought, and once again she turned to draw the curtains.

Then suddenly an idea came to her!

It was so sensational, so explosive, that she could only stand still, staring out the window with unseeing eyes.

She asked herself how she could even consider such a thing.

And yet, the idea was there and it persisted.

Then insidiously, as in one of her clairvoyant moments, the conviction came that it was something she could do, although it was hard to believe she would be successful.

"No, it is mad! Crazy! Impossible!" Gilda exclaimed.

And yet still she could feel her brain working, turning the idea over and over, looking at it from every angle, and at the same time being convinced with a perception that could not be denied that it was something which was possible.

"However outrageous it seems, it would be better than staying here and starving," she told herself.

After what seemed a long time, she turned from the window and walked to the mirror.

She sat down as Heloise had done on the stool to look at her reflection.

As she had taken the pins out of her hair this morning it had fallen into little curls round her forehead, resembling the way her sister had looked yesterday.

Now it seemed as if the face beneath the curls were not her own but that of Heloise, and she knew there was and always had been a remarkable likeness between them, just as they both resembled their mother.

Gilda looked at herself and went on looking.

The shape of her face was the same as her sister's and so was her small, straight nose.

If anything her eyes were a little larger, or perhaps Heloise had been tired when she arrived and her eyes were not shining as brightly as they might have done.

On the dressing-table in front of her was the lip-salve which Heloise used, the hare's foot with which she added a little colour to her cheeks, and the powder which made her skin even whiter than it was naturally.

As if she moved in a dream, Gilda applied the cosmetics she had watched her sister use on her face.

After luncheon on the Saturday of her arrival, Heloise had gone upstairs to her bedroom to change from her travelling-gown into something cooler and lighter. She had sat down at the dressing-table and exclaimed:

"Heavens! I look dreadful!"

It was then that she had added the faint pink blush to her pale cheeks, made her lips glow with lip-salve, and added a dusting of white powder which Gilda had thought made her look different and in a way older than she did without it.

"Does everybody in London use cosmetics?" she had asked.

"Of course they do!" Heloise replied. "I would feel naked without them."

"It makes you look strange, but at the same time very beautiful," Gilda had said.

As she spoke she had seen the reflection of her own face above Heloise's in the mirror and thought she looked dull in contrast and rather washed out.

Now the cosmetics seemed to transform her not into a more vivid image of herself but into Heloise.

"I am the duplicate of Heloise!" Gilda told herself as she rose from the stool.

"How can I think of doing anything like this?" she asked herself, half-expecting her sister to sit up in bed and denounce her for such presumption.

But Heloise lay very still, while the sunshine touched the gold of her hair and somehow made it seem like a halo.

"I am sure she would have been kind to me if she had lived," Gilda said defensively. But she knew that was not true.

Then as if she forced herself to obey an impulse that was stronger than her own will, she went to the wardrobe.

❦

Half-an-hour later Gilda pulled Heloise's packed trunk from the room to the top of the stairs.

Then she went back to pick up her bonnet, gloves, and reticule.

She then pulled back the curtains and went to stand beside the bed.

For a moment she looked down at her sister in the dim light before she went down on her knees.

Then she prayed fervently that Heloise might find peace and happiness and that she herself would be forgiven if what she was doing was a sin.

"If only you could tell me, Mama," she said to her mother, "that what I am about to do is wrong or right, it would be much easier for me. But I swear on everything I hold holy that if I do this, I will try to be kind and helpful and understanding to everybody I meet!"

She sighed and went on:

"There are not many people I can help here, but perhaps in London there will be those who will need my comfort as so many people needed yours. Help me, Mama, to be like you. And forgive me if you disapprove of what I am doing now."

When she had finished her prayer, Gilda wiped the tears from her eyes, then bent forward to kiss Heloise's cold cheek.

"Good-bye dearest," she whispered, "and may God keep you safe."

Then picking up the things she had laid down as she prayed, Gilda went from the bedroom, closing the door quietly behind her.

CHAPTER THREE

———— ❦ ————

*A*s the carriage neared Curzon Street, moving slowly through the traffic, Gilda began to panic.

'Perhaps,' she thought, 'the best thing I can do is to tell Lady Neyland that I came to London to tell her of Heloise's death and, having nothing to wear, was obliged to borrow her clothes.'

Then the same pride which had made her refuse her sister's money told her she was being ridiculous.

To go back and struggle to live on potatoes and vegetables from the garden would be to admit defeat before she had even entered the battle.

She tried to convince herself that this was an opportunity which had appeared unexpectedly to save her, and she would be not only foolish but extremely cowardly if she let it pass her by.

Before she had left the Manor she had tried to think of everything which could allay suspicions regarding "her" death.

When she had reached the Hall she had gone upstairs again to remove the bottle of laudanum from her sister's side.

She had then thrown it away into the bushes where it was never likely to be discovered, before she went into the small Study to sit down at her father's desk to wonder how she could make things easier for Mrs. Hewlett.

Returning from her niece's wedding, she would find, as she thought, that her young mistress had died in a room she did not habitually use.

But there was no-one to whom she could turn for advice, except to send five miles for the Doctor.

"She must have some money," Gilda told herself.

It was then that she looked into Heloise's reticule which she had brought downstairs with her bonnet and gloves.

To her surprise, she found quite a considerable sum of money inside it, far more than she would have expected a lady would require if she went to the country for two nights.

She then supposed that she was being naïve and ignorant and the golden guineas were what people in London considered an ordinary amount to carry with them.

Anyway, it solved her problem, and she put the book in which she had written down her expenses on the desk as if she had been working out her accounts before she went to bed.

Then she put a sum of money beside it and marked on a piece of paper in her elegant writing:

"Mrs. Hewlett's wages for two months."

Another pile was labelled:

"Tithes due on the 1st May."

The third pile was for bills owed locally, including three sovereigns which were loose in the drawer, which Gilda thought would pay for her Funeral.

It all appeared very neat, and as there was nobody who came to the house except Mrs. Hewlett, who was absolutely trustworthy, it would not be considered strange that she had left lying about what money she had.

When the carriage arrived James fetched her trunk from the top of the stairs, then he and the coachman

187

bade her "good-morning," and Gilda drove away, unable to look back at the house where she had lived for so many years because she felt it might make her cry.

For a long time she sat thinking of Heloise and her own desperate adventure and fighting against an urge to tell the carriage to turn back.

Then as they journeyed on she became interested in the countryside, while at the same time her brain was busy trying to remember everything Heloise had said in their conversations.

She had to prevent herself from making mistakes when she reached Lady Neyland's house in Curzon Street and it was not going to be easy.

She knew the first difficulty would be to find her way about the house, but she recalled that when she had asked Heloise if it was noisy at night in London, she had replied:

"Not in Curzon Street, which is filled with houses belonging to aristocrats, and anyway Godmama and I both sleep in rooms which overlook the garden at the back."

"That is one thing I must remember," Gilda told herself.

Then there were the servants' names.

She tried to remember if her sister had mentioned them. If she had, she could not recall them.

Fortunately, her mother had explained to her the different appearance of senior servants in a grand house, and during her father's last year in the Army when he was a full General they had employed a Butler and a footman because they had done so much entertaining.

"Housekeepers wear black with a chatelaine at their waists," Gilda told herself; "lady's-maids wear black dresses without an apron, and housemaids wear mob-caps."

Nevertheless, when the carriage finally stopped outside the porticoed house in Curzon Street, her heart started to beat frantically and her lips felt dry.

A footman in the same smart livery as James wore came running down the steps to open the door of the carriage.

At the front door, a man with grey hair who Gilda knew was the Butler was waiting to receive her.

"Good-morning, Miss Heloise," he said respectfully. "It's nice to see you back. Her Ladyship's waiting for you."

"Thank you," Gilda said.

She walked towards the staircase, wondering frantically how she would find Lady Neyland's bedroom.

Then when she reached the top of the stairs she saw waiting a middle-aged woman in black without an apron and knew it must be her lady's-maid.

"Good-morning," she said, wishing she knew the woman's name.

"Good-morning, Miss Heloise," the maid replied. "Her Ladyship's been waiting for your arrival. She was upset on Saturday when she found you'd gone without saying good-bye. It's not right that Her Ladyship should be upset, seeing the state of health she's in!"

The maid was scolding her exactly like a Nanny, Gilda realised, and she thought that Heloise had been quite unnecessarily inconsiderate in going away as she had.

"I am sorry," she said humbly, and thought the maid gave her a sharp glance as if she was surprised at her reply.

They walked a little way along the passage and the maid opened a high mahogany door.

"Miss Heloise's back, M'Lady!" she announced, and Gilda walked into a very attractive bedroom, the sunshine coming through the window on the far side of it.

She saw Lady Neyland sitting in an armchair with a bandage over her eyes.

This, Gilda knew, was a test which she might fail.

She was well aware that when people were blind they were more sensitive to voices than if they could see, and she only hoped that hers would sound like Heloise's and she would not immediately be denounced as an imposter.

Lady Neyland held out her hand.

"Heloise, my dear," she said. "I have been so worried about you travelling without a Chaperone or even a maid with you."

Because her voice was so kind and not in the least reproachful as the maid's had been, Gilda moved quickly across the room.

"I am sorry . . . Godmama, very, very sorry," she said, "for upsetting you. It is something I should not have done."

"Well, you are back safely," Lady Neyland said, "and I am sure Carter and James looked after you."

"They did indeed," Gilda said.

She took Lady Neyland's hand in hers and bent forward to kiss her cheek.

"I am sorry if you missed me," she went on, "but now I will make amends by reading you all the morning newspapers."

Lady Neyland laughed.

"I will certainly appreciate that. But just take off your bonnet and cloak, then tell me how you found everything at home. I heard from the servants that was where you had gone."

Gilda thought it was stupid of Heloise not to realise that although she had tried to deceive her Godmother, she had only to ask her own servants where they had driven her.

"Everything was all right," she said, "but I am glad to be back, very, very glad."

"That is what I want you to say," Lady Neyland replied, "and your ardent admirers will be delighted that you have returned, especially the Marquis."

There was a little pause before Gilda asked, as she knew Heloise would have done:

"Was he . . . upset when I did not . . . attend his . . . dinner-party?"

"I do not know if he was upset," her Godmother replied. "He called to take you driving in the afternoon

and certainly seemed surprised that you had left without informing him of your change of plan."

Lady Neyland smiled before she went on:

"I got the impression that it was the first time any
woman had refused one of his invitations in such an off-
hand manner."

Gilda thought that Heloise had been right. Her
action had surprised the Marquis, and perhaps it would,
as she had hoped, make him "come up to scratch," as
she had put it.

"Anyway, I expect you will see him this evening and
you can make your own explanations to him."

"This evening?" Gilda questioned without thinking.

"Surely you have not forgotten that my friend the
Countess of Dorset has invited you to a dinner-party she
is giving before her Ball? She told us when she was here
the other day that she had seated you on the Marquis's
left."

"Yes . . . of course . . . I remember," Gilda said hastily.

"Run and take off your things, dear child," Lady Neyland said. "Then we must discuss what you are going to
wear. I shall want you to look your very best."

"I will try," Gilda said, "but I wish you could come too."

She thought Lady Neyland was pleased as she replied:

"I too wish I could. Nevertheless, you will tell me later
all about it, so that I can feel I am not missing everything by sitting here blind as an old bat!"

She tried to laugh, but there was a little throb in her
voice which told Gilda how much she minded.

"Godmama," she said. "I was thinking about you, and I
remembered how Mama always said that carrots helped
our eyesight and of course green vegetables also."

She saw that Lady Neyland was listening intently, and
she went on:

"I was reading a book about somewhere in the East
where it was very dry and dusty and the rains came only
once a year."

She paused before she continued:

"I cannot remember which country it was, but in the book it said the native inhabitants had poor physiques and suffered badly with their eyesight until after the rain, when everything sprouted. Then they ate the green shoots of the plants and trees and immediately they regained their strength and especially their eyesight."

"That is very interesting!" Lady Neyland exclaimed. "I think, dearest child, you must speak to Chef and see if he can buy fresh carrots and lettuces and other green vegetables."

"You can at least try to see what they will do," Gilda said.

"I certainly will," Lady Neyland replied, "and thank you for thinking of me."

"I will go and take off my bonnet," Gilda said. "Then I will read to you."

As she walked towards the door she was wondering where her room would be.

Fortunately, Lady Neyland's maid was waiting outside the door.

She thought the woman looked a little less disagreeable, and Gilda said quickly:

"I wonder if you would come with me to undo the back of my gown? It will not take me a minute to change, and I feel rather hot after my journey."

She took off her travelling-cape as she spoke, and almost mechanically the lady's-maid took it from her and walked down the passage in what Gilda knew must be the direction of her bedroom.

The house was not large and her bedroom in fact was only two doors away from Lady Neyland's, and when they reached it she found that her trunk had already been brought upstairs and a young housemaid was kneeling beside it, taking out her clothes.

"So you are here, Emily!" the lady's-maid said. "Miss Heloise wishes to change her gown, so you can undo the buttons for her."

She moved away and Emily got to her feet and started to unbutton Gilda's gown.

"Miss Anderson's got a monkey on her shoulder this morning," she said confidingly.

"I am afraid that I upset her," Gilda replied, glad to know the name of the lady's-maid.

"She's angry wi' me too," Emily said, "because I scorched one of the table-cloths I were a-pressin'."

Then she looked at Gilda apprehensively as if she thought she had said too much, and asked quickly:

"Which gown do you want to wear, Miss?"

"Oh, anything cool and simple," Gilda replied.

The maid went to the wardrobe and when she opened it Gilda drew in her breath.

She had never before seen such an array of wonderful gowns. They looked as if somebody had captured a rainbow.

Because she did not wish to keep Lady Neyland waiting, she changed quickly into a crisp muslin not unlike the one Heloise had worn at home, but this one had pale green ribbons instead of blue ones, and the muslin was sprigged with tiny white flowers and pale green leaves.

It was so pretty that Gilda felt it was a gown she would have worn at a smart garden-party.

But she knew that she would have to leave it to Emily to choose what she would wear normally, and after thanking the maid she hurried back to Lady Neyland's room.

The newspapers lay on a stool not far from the chair in which Her Ladyship was sitting, but when Gilda came towards her she asked:

"Tell me what you are wearing. I want to visualise you, and one of the problems of being blind is that people forget that descriptions are very important when one cannot see with one's own eyes."

"I will try to describe everything to you," Gilda replied, "and let me say that it is a lovely day, the sun is shining, and in the country the lilacs are coming into bloom and the daffodils are gold among the trees."

She went on trying to paint a picture, and when she stopped Lady Neyland said:

"You have described it beautifully, dearest. I had no idea you were so poetical."

"Now let me tell you about my gown," Gilda said quickly.

She remembered that Heloise had never shown an interest in nature.

"Talking of flowers," Lady Neyland said, "I have just remembered that Anderson tells me there are a great number of bouquets for you downstairs. I expect you will want to go see them."

"I will see them later," Gilda replied. "For the moment I would much rather talk with you."

It was obvious to Gilda that Lady Neyland was both surprised and pleased.

She described the gown in which she had travelled to London and also her impressions of the countryside she had seen on her drive.

She was still talking when Anderson came in to say:

"Your luncheon's just coming upstairs, M'Lady, and Miss Heloise's is ready for her in the Dining-Room."

"Oh, how disappointing that I cannot eat with you!" Gilda exclaimed.

There was a slight pause. Then Lady Neyland said:

"But you must remember, dearest child, you said only a short while ago that you hated eating off trays in bed-rooms."

Gilda drew in her breath. Then she gave a little laugh.

"If I said that, it must have been when I got out of bed on the wrong side," she said. "I would much rather have luncheon with you. In fact, to be truthful, I find it depressing to eat alone."

She thought of how many meals she had eaten alone since her father had died, and how when Mrs. Hewlett had gone home the house seemed so quiet and oppressive that sometimes she talked to herself.

"I would like you to eat with me," Lady Neyland said, "but I must learn to be adventurous and come downstairs to dinner."

"Why not?" Gilda replied. "It must be boring sitting here all the time, and I am sure your friends would like to join you sometimes if you did not find it too tiring."

"I am perfectly well except for my eyes," Lady Neyland replied, "but I thought it might be embarrassing if because I cannot see I am messy with my food."

As she spoke, Gilda was quite certain that Heloise had put such ideas into her head.

"I will tell you what we will do," she said. "You will ask some of your very special friends to dinner, and I will choose dishes which you do not have to cut up but can eat with a spoon. Besides, they will understand if you do not seem very hungry and talk and listen rather than eat."

Lady Neyland gave a little laugh.

"You are making it a game! At the same time, I feel better already. Oh, Heloise, do you think my eyes will ever get better so that I shall be able to see again?"

"I know they will," Gilda said positively.

As she spoke, she knew that what she was saying was true. The conviction was there in her intuition.

She told herself that she would see the Chef immediately after luncheon and speak to him about the carrots and green vegetables, and, what was more important than anything else, she must make Lady Neyland believe that she would soon be able to see again.

Anderson, with a rather sour face, went downstairs to say:

"Miss Heloise would have luncheon upstairs with Her Ladyship."

When the two trays arrived, a table was arranged for Gilda opposite Lady Neyland's, and they talked animatedly all the time that the luncheon was being served by the Butler and two footmen.

"This is fun," Gilda exclaimed, "and much, much better than having luncheon on my own."

"That is something which does not often happen to you," Lady Neyland answered. "I think you will find there is a pile of invitations waiting for you, and now we must talk about tonight."

"I have an idea!" Gilda said. "Because the Countess is such a close friend of yours, Godmama, I am going to drop her a note and suggest that you would like to come in for an hour or so after dinner. You could listen to the music and your friends could talk to you. That would be far better for your health than sitting here all alone."

Lady Neyland was very still.

"Do you really—think I could do—that?" she asked after a moment. "I would not be a bore and an—encumbrance?"

"If the Countess is a true friend, you will be nothing of the sort," Gilda said. "In fact, I am sure she would welcome you with open arms. Please, Godmama, let me send her a note and suggest it."

"I do not know—what to say," Lady Neyland said helplessly.

"Leave it to me," Gilda said.

She wondered where she should write the note, then felt sure that there would be a Writing-Room.

She ran down the stairs and when she reached the Hall she said to one of the footmen on duty:

"Will you look and see if there is plenty of ink in the ink-well? I have to write a letter and I want somebody to take it to the Countess of Dorset's house where I am dining this evening."

"Henry'll take it, Miss," the footman replied.

As Gilda expected, he went ahead of her into a room which opened off the Hall, and when she followed him she saw that it was obviously a Study which would have been used by Lady Neyland's husband when he was alive.

There was a huge mahogany bookcase filled with books, which Gilda glanced at with delight, and a large flat-topped desk with elegant gilt handles and feet and on which were a blotter and a number of white quill-pens ready to be used.

The footman looked at the ink-well and said:

"There's plenty of ink there, Miss."

"That is all right then," Gilda replied, and sat down at the desk.

She wrote quickly, hoping she was addressing the Countess respectfully enough as she suggested that it would give her Godmother so much pleasure if she could come for a short while after dinner and listen to the music and meet some of her friends.

She wrote:

Her Ladyship is in good Health, except for the Affliction in her Eyes, but I feel sure with Care and Faith her Sight will soon be Returned to Her.

She signed the letter when she had finished, addressed it, then gave it to the footman who was waiting in the Hall.

Then as she was about to go back upstairs, another footman opened the front door.

As he did so, a man came into the house and as Gilda looked at him she knew who he was without being told.

She had imagined, from the description Heloise had given of the Marquis, that he would be tall and good-looking, but she had not expected him to be so handsome and so overwhelmingly magnificent that he took her breath away.

She knew that because she had seen very few gentlemen since she grew up, any man she met in London would look different from those she had encountered in the country.

At the same time, she was quite certain that the Marquis would be outstanding wherever he was.

As he walked towards her she felt as if he overwhelmed her and for the moment she could not speak and it was also impossible to think.

"So you are back!" he said, and his voice was sharp. "I want an explanation, Heloise, of where you have been and why you should have behaved in such an unaccountable manner."

Gilda thought frantically of what she could reply, but somehow she could only stare at the Marquis, fearing that as his dark eyes searched her face, he had already penetrated her disguise.

Then she told herself that there was no reason to think he might be suspicious, and, lifting her chin in a way that she felt Heloise might have done, she said:

"If I have inconvenienced Your Lordship I must of course apologise."

"You certainly must," the Marquis said grimly, "and perhaps we should discuss this where we can be alone."

He did not wait for her to agree but walked towards another door in the Hall, which Gilda felt must lead into the Drawing-Room.

She followed him and found that she was not mistaken.

She saw a very attractive room with a large crystal chandelier hanging from the ceiling and elegant gold-framed French furniture upholstered in blue brocade.

She thought it might have been chosen as a background for Heloise, then remembered that it would also frame herself.

The Marquis closed the door behind him. Then he walked in a purposeful manner to stand with his back to the mantelpiece.

Feeling a little shy, Gilda went to a sofa not far from where he was standing and sat down on the edge of it.

She knew it was foolish, but she felt like a School-girl who had been caught out playing truant, and she told herself that as he had not proposed to her sister, he had no right to behave as if he owned her.

At the same time, because he was so overpowering she felt her heart fluttering unpleasantly and found it hard to look at him.

There was silence until the Marquis said:

"I am waiting!"

"For what?"

"You know that you have behaved unpredictably, if nothing else," he replied. "I am not in the habit of giving dinner-parties for young women who do not turn up and have not even the good manners to send their excuses."

"I am . . . sorry," Gilda said, feeling there was nothing else she could say.

"That is not at all an explanation."

"I am sorry to have upset you," Gilda said, "and most of all to have upset Godmama. I can only say I am very . . . contrite and it will not . . . happen again."

She was not looking at the Marquis as she spoke, but she had the feeling that he was staring at her in a way which she felt was intimidating.

Then he said:

"You surprise me, Heloise, and I suppose it is best if we say nothing more about this escapade. At the same time, I was extremely angry at having my plans disrupted at the last moment."

"I can understand that," Gilda said, "and it was, I admit, extremely rude of me. So I can only repeat that I am very sorry if I inconvenienced you."

The Marquis did not speak, and she managed to steal a glance at him.

She thought he was the most handsome man she had ever seen.

At the same time, there was something about the squareness of his chin and perhaps the strong line of his lips which told her that he could be not only difficult but perhaps also at times cruel.

Gilda did not believe that Heloise would have been happy with him, however much he could have given her in the way of worldly advantages.

"We will forget it," he said magnanimously.

Gilda rose to her feet.

"I know you will excuse me, My Lord," she said, "if I go back upstairs to be with my Godmother. She, too, was upset that I ran away in that foolish manner, but now that I am back I am trying to forget my misdeeds, and I am arranging for her to come to the party this evening."

"To the Dorsets'?" the Marquis enquired. "But surely as she is blind that will be impossible?"

"Why should it be?" Gilda asked. "She is not ill in any other way. It is just that her eyes are affected, and I can imagine nothing more depressing than sitting at home night after night and thinking of her friends having a lovely time while she cannot join them."

"And what do you intend to do about it?" the Marquis asked.

"I have just sent a note to the Countess asking if Godmother can join the party after dinner. She naturally feels embarrassed at having to eat in front of people, but she can sit and listen to the music, and I will be able to tell her what is happening, and what I forget you can describe to her."

"Me?" the Marquis questioned. "Are you expecting me to take part in this charade?"

"Why not, My Lord? It would certainly be a kindness, and I am sure she would appreciate your attention."

Unexpectedly the Marquis threw back his head and laughed.

"You are certainly full of surprises at the moment, Heloise," he said. "Never before have I been asked to be the eyes of somebody who is blind."

"There is always a first time for everything," Gilda replied, "and as there is quite a lot of preparation to be done, I hope you will excuse me."

"I came here to ask you to drive with me," the Marquis said. "My Phaeton is outside."

"It is very kind of you to think of me, My Lord," Gilda replied formally, "but perhaps another time."

He looked at her in a manner which told her without words that he was astonished that she could turn down his invitation. Then he said:

"If that is what you wish, of course I understand that your Godmother has a right to your company rather than myself! I shall see you tonight at dinner, Heloise, and naturally it is something to which I shall look forward."

He spoke with a touch of sarcasm in his voice, which made Gilda think that he was not being quite sincere.

Then it suddenly struck her that he thought her concern for her Godmother was just an act put on to impress or rather to intrigue him.

She guessed that he was intelligent and was quite sure that in consequence the wiles that had been practised on him by dozens of other women besides her sister had not gone undetected.

'He thinks I am trying to trap him,' Gilda thought to herself.

She thought it would be amusing if the Marquis knew she was not in the least interested in him as a man, but rather was a little afraid that he might be perceptive enough to realise that she was not her sister.

She wondered why on such short acquaintance she had received such a strong impression of him.

She in fact was vividly aware that he was clever, intuitive, and had a way of looking deep into the person he was with, almost as if he searched for something he did not expect to find.

There was no reason for her to know this, and yet she did, and her clairvoyant powers told her that if she was not careful, the Marquis might be a very dangerous enemy.

'The best thing I can do,' she thought, 'is to keep away from him as much as possible.'

Without waiting for him to say any more, she walked towards the door.

When she reached it she looked back and saw that he had not moved from the fireplace, perhaps thinking she was merely putting on an act and actually had no intention of leaving.

She dropped him a little curtsey.

"Good-day, My Lord, and thank you for your invitation to go driving. I shall of course look forward to meeting Your Lordship again this evening."

She could not help just a touch of mockery in her voice, which echoed the note she had heard in his.

Then, because actually she was shy and a little afraid, she pulled open the door.

She ran through the Hall and up the stairs before there was any sign of his leaving the Drawing-Room.

❦

"Now tell me exactly what you are wearing," Lady Neyland said as Gilda came into her room before leaving for the dinner-party.

"I feel very beautiful," Gilda replied with a little laugh, "and that is not conceited, for it is all due to my gown, to the hairdresser, and of course to Anderson's help in making my face prettier than it really is."

As she spoke, Gilda was amused to see Anderson look quite proud.

The maid had in fact been surprised when Gilda had asked her help in using the cosmetics that she knew her sister had always applied to her face.

It was after the hairdresser had left, having arranged her hair in a fashionable style that was both becoming and elegant, that she had gone to Lady Neyland's room to ask her help.

She had chosen her words with care.

"I think, Godmama," she said, "from something somebody said the other night, that I am using too much powder and perhaps also too much rouge. I wonder if you would allow me to borrow Anderson to help me? I notice how lovely your skin looks, and that is how I would wish mine to be."

Anderson was gratified, and she certainly had a skilful and experienced touch that Gilda herself did not possess.

"The trouble with young people," Anderson said, "is that they always think they know better than anybody else. I've always wanted to tell you, Miss Heloise, that you were using too much rouge and the wrong colour. Your powder should be applied so sparingly that it is virtually invisible unless somebody looks closely."

"I am sure you are right," Gilda answered. "I will watch very carefully to see what you do."

She knew when Anderson was finished that the maid had only very gently accentuated the natural colour in her cheeks and on her lips, and the colour of her skin seemed almost natural, except that there was no shine on her small nose or her pointed little chin.

Anderson had thoroughly approved Gilda's suggestion that Her Ladyship should attend the party.

"What she wants is taking out of herself," she said.
"Moping about here all the time with no-one to talk to
is not the way for her to get well again."

"I agree with you," Gilda replied.

"Her Ladyship has always liked parties and being with
her friends, and I can't think now why we never thought
of her going to one before. She can listen and talk, even
if she can't see."

"Yes, of course, and she shall not be left behind in the
future," Gilda said. "I will write to every hostess who has
asked me to a party and say that my Godmother must
come too."

"It's kind of you to think of it, Miss Heloise," Anderson said.

She spoke in a way that made Gilda feel uncomfortably that she was thinking how self-centred she had been
in the past.

But she did not wish to compare what she was doing
with what Heloise had done.

She had no wish to face the fact that her sister was so
selfish that it would never have crossed her mind to
think of anybody else's pleasure but her own.

'I must make up for my deception by trying to give
happiness to everyone with whom I come in contact,'
Gilda thought, and she knew that was the only way she
could make retribution for the lie she was acting.

When she thanked Anderson for attending to her face
and told her how clever she was, the maid had quite a
flush on her pale cheeks, and Gilda thought that the
almost open antagonism she had encountered when she
arrived was now forgotten.

She spent a long time choosing first which gown she
should wear, and secondly which gown would be most
becoming to Lady Neyland.

She too had a wardrobe filled with beautiful dresses,
most of them in soft shades of mauve or grey, which

Gilda heard she had worn ever since her husband had died.

"As soon as you can see again," she said, "I am going to make you buy a gown to celebrate, which will be as brilliant as the sunshine and as gay as the flowers in the window-boxes."

Lady Neyland laughed.

"If you want me to look like a bird-of-Paradise," she said, "when I am able to see for myself, we will go to the most expensive and best dressmaker in Bond Street and you too shall have some new gowns."

"I shall never be able to wear all those I have already!" Gilda expostulated.

"Of course you will!" Lady Neyland replied. "And then you will tell me you have nothing to wear! No woman ever has enough clothes."

They both laughed, but Gilda wished she could tell Lady Neyland how much the gown she was wearing meant to her personally.

After the dresses she had grown out of and which had faded and shrunk in the wash, it was like being transformed from a chrysalis into a butterfly.

Her gown was made of a gauze which was so delicate that she felt it revealed rather than concealed her figure, and it was trimmed with silver ribbons which made her think of the moonlight.

She had silver slippers to match, and a little wreath of leaves studded with diamanté which encircled the knot of curls which the *Coiffeur* had arranged at the back of her head.

"I look like a Greek goddess," she said to Lady Neyland when she described her appearance, "or perhaps Diana the Huntress, and I should be carrying a spear in my hand."

"You have already speared enough hearts as it is," Lady Neyland replied with a smile, "but we have talked so much about my gown that you have not yet told me what the Marquis said to you."

"He was both surprised and angry at my behaviour."

"I hope you apologised properly," Lady Neyland admonished. "I find him charming, but he is very conscious of his own consequence."

"That describes him exactly!" Gilda exclaimed. "I also think he is a little intimidating."

There was a pause before Lady Neyland said:

"As I have told you before, dearest, I think you are flying too high in wishing to catch the Marquis. After all, Sir Humphrey Grange is just as wealthy, if not of such great importance."

Gilda noted the name and knew that he was the other suitor for Heloise's hand, who she had said was not important enough.

"There are plenty of men in the world," she said lightly, "and quite frankly, Godmama, I am in no hurry to be married."

She spoke impulsively and knew that Lady Neyland was astonished.

"But, dearest child, you have been so insistent that you must be married! I told you over and over again that there is no hurry, as I love having you with me! You have time to think, and you must be very careful to choose the right husband to ensure your future happiness."

"Yes, I know you said that, Godmama, and you are quite right," Gilda replied, "and so I shall refuse everybody who asks me for at least another year."

Lady Neyland clapped her hands together.

"That is what I want to hear and it gives me great pleasure. Oh, Heloise, I have been so afraid that you would rush into marriage and then be as desperately unhappy as I was."

"Were you?" Gilda asked curiously. "How very sad!"

"I do not talk about it," Lady Neyland said. "My husband had many other—interests besides me, and after our marriage he really had no use for me, except as a hostess for his more—respectable friends."

Gilda understood what her Godmother implied, and she reached out to take Lady Neyland's hand in hers.

"I am sorry, so very sorry for you," she said. "It must have been very hurtful."

"What I minded more than anything else," Lady Neyland said in a low voice, "was that in consequence we had no children. I would love to have had a dozen sons and daughters to look after and to plan for as they grew older."

Gilda bent forward to kiss her cheek.

"Now you can plan for me and make sure that I do not marry the Marquis of Staverton or Sir Humphrey, but wait until somebody as charming as Papa comes along. Then I know I shall be happy, even if I have to live in a small house in the country with very little money."

Gilda spoke dreamily, thinking of her mother and how happy she had been. Then she realised that Lady Neyland, still holding her hand, had not spoken.

After what seemed quite a long pause she said:

"You have changed, Heloise, changed in a way that is difficult to describe. I have never heard you say such things before, and certainly you have never thought of me until now."

Gilda realised she had made a mistake, but there was no turning back.

"If I have changed," she said, "it is because when I went away from you I realised how terribly kind you have been to me and how selfish I was in thinking only about myself and not about you."

Her voice rose a little as she went on:

"Now everything is changed, and we are going to do things together. If a hostess will not have you at her party, then I shall stay at home and we will gossip like two old spinsters!"

She had intended to make Lady Neyland laugh, and she succeeded.

"You are being ridiculous, child," she said, "but I love you for it. Now hurry or you will be late for the dinner-party, and do not forget, I shall be arriving at nine o'clock, and I will be feeling like a débutante going to her first Ball."

"I will be your Chaperone," Gilda said, "and see that the most eligible men sit beside you whispering sweet nothings into your ears."

Lady Neyland laughed again.

Then as Anderson put a velvet wrap trimmed with marabou round her shoulders, Gilda went downstairs feeling that it was a good thing that no-one guessed she was in fact making her début tonight in the first evening-gown she had ever worn.

She was going to the first dinner-party she had ever attended and would be dancing at her first Ball.

It was all like a dream!

As she reached the Hall she saw the carriage waiting outside to take her to the Countess of Dorset's house, and she only hoped that she would not wake up too soon and it would last at least until midnight.

CHAPTER FOUR

Gilda lay in that delicious state between sleeping and waking, thinking how happy she was.

Last night had been a revelation and had in fact exceeded all her wildest anticipations.

She had always dreamt of seeing a Ball-Room filled with beautiful women and handsome men dancing under the glittering light of crystal chandeliers, with a Band playing softly and the atmosphere fragrant with the scent of flowers.

The dinner-party too at the Countess of Dorset's had been an enchantment.

They had sat down fifty to dinner, and the large table stretching down the middle of the room was a magnificent sight with its gold ornaments, huge golden candelabra, and decorated with orchids.

Gilda had sat staring about her wide-eyed until she realised that the Marquis was watching her and remembered that she was supposed to have been familiar with such scenes of beauty for the last two years.

Nevertheless, as the candles glittered on their hostess's enormous tiara, which was almost like a crown, she could not help murmuring more to herself than to her dinner-companion:

"This is just like a fairy-tale!"

"Why especially tonight?" the Marquis asked with what she thought was a bored note in his voice.

"Perhaps it seems more glamorous than usual," Gilda said quickly, "because I am feeling happy."

"Why?" he persisted.

"Does one have to have a reason for happiness?"

"If a woman says she is happy, it usually means that she is in love!"

Gilda laughed.

"Then I am the exception. I am happy because everything is so beautiful and everybody is so kind to me."

"In what particular way?"

She thought his questions were rather tiresome and she evaded them by turning to talk to the gentleman on her other side, who plied her with compliments.

She felt that they came too easily to his lips to be sincere, but at the same time they gave her confidence.

She was determined not to get involved in private conversation with the Marquis, and when Lady Neyland arrived it was easy to avoid it.

She caused quite a stir when she came into the Drawing-Room on her host's arm, looking, Gilda thought, very elegant in a beautiful mauve gown with a tiara on her head and a huge necklace of amethysts and diamonds round her neck.

Gilda had been clever enough to suggest before she left that Lady Neyland not wear the eye-bandage she usually wore on the Doctor's orders, but instead should substitute for it a piece of the same material as her gown.

Anderson had made up Her Ladyship's face skilfully, and with amethyst and diamond earrings hanging from her ears it was easy to forget that she looked any different from any other attractive Dowager in the Ball-Room.

The Earl of Dorset led her to a comfortable chair that had been specially arranged for her on a small dais. When Gilda joined her Godmother, she said:

"This is all due to you, dearest child, and I am so excited at hearing the music and the voices of my friends."

Her last remark gave Gilda an idea of how she could overcome a difficulty that had been worrying her all day.

She was well aware that many of the people who would wish to speak to her Godmother must have been known to Heloise for some time, and it was therefore perfectly obvious that she would be expected to say:

"Here is Lady 'X' or Lord 'Y,' " as they approached.

Instead, she said:

"Now, Godmama, let us see if you recognise the voices of your friends."

Lady Neyland was only too eager to enter into the game, and nine times out of ten she guessed right the first time.

When the Marquis approached, Gilda was sure that he intended to talk to her, and she said quickly:

"Here is the Marquis of Staverton, and he has promised, Godmama, to describe to you how some of your favourite people are looking, although I am afraid he may be critical of them!"

Lady Neyland laughed.

So the Marquis, after he had kissed her hand, could do nothing but sit down beside her, which gave Gilda a chance to slip away and dance with some of the many young men who were begging her to do so.

As each dance ended she returned to her God-mother's side, but she soon found that she was not needed, for as Lady Neyland's friends circled round her she was holding Court and, as Gilda well knew, enjoying every moment of it.

Gilda had just finished dancing with the young man who had been on her left at dinner when a large, rather florid-looking man came up to her and said:

"How could you be so cruel and so unkind, Heloise, as to disappear without telling me where you were going?"

Gilda was tense, wondering who he could be, but fortunately her partner interrupted:

"You are bumping and boring, Sir Humphrey, which is something you dare not do on the race-course. Miss Wyngate is my partner until the next dance starts."

"I am not going to apologise," Sir Humphrey replied, "because I have something very important to say to Miss Wyngate and you must therefore forgive me if I take her away from you."

He did not wait for an answer but drew Gilda by the arm onto a balcony outside the Ball-Room.

Although she had no wish to go with him, she had little choice in the matter.

Fortunately, once they were on the balcony she saw that there were a number of other couples who had come out to enjoy the coolness of the evening air, and the only way Sir Humphrey could be intimate was to lower his voice.

"You are driving me crazy!" he said. "When do you intend to give me an answer? I am tired of waiting."

Gilda thought he must be referring to the fact that he had offered to marry her, and after a moment she answered hesitatingly:

"It is . . . not a . . . thing one can . . . decide in a hurry."

"Hurry!" Sir Humphrey exclaimed. "I have been down on my knees to you for over six months!"

Gilda did not speak, and after a moment he said:

"I hoped that you would encourage me by wearing my sapphires tonight. After all, although your Godmother is here, she is unable to see them."

Gilda had no answer to this, as she did not know what he was talking about. Instead she said:

"I think I must go back to Godmama. I am sure she would like to talk to you. It is very exciting for her to come here this evening after being shut up in the house for so long."

"I am not concerned with your Godmother but with you," Sir Humphrey said, and Gilda thought that he came a little nearer to her.

There was something about him that she did not like, although she thought that perhaps her feelings were unreasonable.

She did not know why, but she did not trust him and she could understand her sister's reluctance to marry him.

'If he were as rich as Midas I would not marry him,' Gilda thought.

As two more people came from the Ball-Room onto the balcony she said quickly:

"I must go and see that Godmama is all right," and escaped before Sir Humphrey could do anything to prevent her.

However, he was hovering in the background all evening, and Gilda found that she was trying to avoid not only the Marquis but also him.

At the same time, her first Ball was everything she had expected it to be.

There was no doubt that Heloise's beauty had made her a success, and even the most blase Beaux and those who, Gilda suspected, usually stood about looking bored and contemptuous paid her compliments and obviously thought it smart to be in her company.

Going home with Lady Neyland, she thought again how terribly sad it was that Heloise should have died at the very zenith of her success.

Unimportant as far as the *Beau Monde* was concerned, she had managed to make an impression on the most critical Society in the whole of Europe.

Almost as if she was following her thoughts, Lady Neyland said:

"You were greatly admired tonight, dearest child, and I was very proud. Also, I want to thank you too for being so kind to me."

"I should be thanking you," Gilda said quickly. "If I had not such a beautiful gown and were not your God-daughter, I feel nobody would pay any attention to me."

"Nonsense!" Lady Neyland said. "Your face is your fortune, as the saying goes, and all the gentlemen who talked to me tonight were quite lyrical in their praise of you, including the Marquis!"

"I think he is still astonished that I should have run away from him," Gilda remarked.

"I am sure he is," Lady Neyland said. "At the same time, dearest, I do not think he would make you a very good husband. The Countess was telling me that she is sure he has never been in love with anybody in his whole life."

Gilda thought that probably was true, as Lady Neyland went on:

"I cannot help feeling that he is pursuing you primarily to annoy all your other admirers and show them that he can beat them not only on the race-course but in the Ball-Room."

"You are right!" Gilda exclaimed. "And let me assure you, Godmama, I do not take him seriously."

"I am so glad, dearest, for I was so afraid that he might break your heart as he has broken so many other women's."

"He will not do that," Gilda said confidently.

When they arrived home and Lady Neyland was telling Anderson what a wonderful evening it had been, Gilda kissed her Godmother good-night, thanked her again, and went to bed.

Because she was so unused to dancing and staying up late, she had fallen asleep almost immediately.

Now she could look back in retrospect and the only thing that puzzled her was Sir Humphrey's reference to his sapphires.

What sapphires? And if he had given them to Heloise, though she could hardly believe that was true, then where were they?

Emily came in a little later with her breakfast, and Gilda found that by the time she had finished it, half the morning had gone.

"I must get up," she said to Emily.

"There's no hurry, Miss," Emily replied. "Her Ladyship's still asleep. But there's bouquets of flowers downstairs and I've some notes which came with them."

She put them down in front of Gilda on the bed, and when she opened the first she saw that it was from Sir Humphrey, and he had written:

I must see You, Enchanting Seductress. Will You drive with Me this afternoon, or may I call on You at about four o'clock?

Gilda realised that she had no wish to accept either suggestion, then almost laughed at herself to think how exciting such an invitation would have been if she were still at the Manor House.

There was no note from the Marquis, and in the majority of the *billets-doux* she had difficulty in identifying the writers.

When finally she was dressed, she said to Emily tentatively, feeling her way:

"This gown really needs a small brooch in the front."

"You are quite right, Miss," the maid said. "Why not wear that pretty pearl one which you told me belonged to your mother?"

Gilda was still.

She knew quite well that all her mother's jewellery had been sold by her father when he wanted money to invest in his dubious stocks and shares.

When she did manage to reply, she said:

"Yes, of course. That is a good idea. Where is it?"

"In your jewel-case, Miss," Emily replied.

Gilda thought it would be a mistake to ask where that was, but Emily went to the wardrobe and opened it.

Gilda saw to her astonishment that on the floor beneath her gowns was a box made of leather, which looked like a jewel-case and appeared large enough to contain the Crown Jewels.

Suppressing her astonishment, she said vaguely:

"Now, where did I put the key?"

"I wasn't prying, Miss," Emily said quickly, "as you told me never to interfere, but I happened to notice 'twas in your reticule last night, the way you always take it with you."

"Yes, of course," Gilda answered. "I am tired this morning and feeling rather stupid."

Emily fetched the pretty satin reticule trimmed with lace that she had carried by its ribbons over her arm and which she had thought contained only her handkerchief.

But when she pulled it open she found that at the bottom beneath the handkerchief there was a small key.

As she drew it out, to her surprise Emily said:

"I'll wait outside, Miss, 'til you calls me," and went from the room.

Gilda thought this was obviously the way Heloise had instructed Emily to behave, so she said nothing, but as soon as the door shut behind the maid she went to the wardrobe and knelt down to open the jewel-case.

It was certainly very large, and she could only suppose that Lady Neyland had given it to Heloise as a present, or perhaps it had been one of her own for which she had no further use.

She turned the small key in the lock and raised the lid.

Then she stared in sheer astonishment, for on the tray which lay inside on the top of the case there was a remarkably large amount of jewellery.

"How can Heloise have owned all this?" Gilda asked herself.

There was the pearl brooch which Emily thought had belonged to her mother but which Gilda had never seen before, and there were pearl earrings to match it and a very pretty gold bracelet set with diamonds and pearls.

In another velvet pocket there were two earrings of sapphires and diamonds and a pendant to match them.

She knew these were what Sir Humphrey must have been referring to last night, and she was horrified that her sister had accepted such an expensive gift from a man whom she had not promised to marry and apparently had no wish to do so.

"I must send them back," she told herself.

There was also on the tray a small string of pearls which she had the uncomfortable feeling might be real.

Then she lifted up the tray and drew in her breath.

She could hardly believe that what she was seeing was not a mirage.

In the bottom of the jewel-case there were dozens and dozens of gold sovereigns!

She stared at them, feeling that what she was seeing could not be true, but if it was—where on earth could Heloise have obtained so much money?

There must, she calculated, be at least fifty sovereigns lying there.

Then it flashed through her mind that perhaps Lady Neyland was generous in giving Heloise money for tips or small purchases, and therefore there was nothing very peculiar in the fact that she had saved the money rather than spent it.

Then she saw that there was a small pile of papers amongst the gold, and she picked up the first one and opened it.

The top of the paper was headed "*Coutts Bank*" and Gilda read:

Dear Madam:
We have the honour to inform you that your Deposit Account now stands at £1,959.10s.

We wish to express our deep appreciation of your continuing custom, and remain, Madam, your humble and obedient servants.

Coutts.

Gilda thought there must be some mistake. Then she saw that her sister's name, *Miss Heloise Wyngate,* was written there at the top of the letter.

"I cannot believe it!" she said beneath her breath. "How can Heloise have accumulated so much money?"

She could not help thinking of her sister's reluctance to offer her twenty pounds a year and the conditions attached to it.

Then, as if she was afraid of what she had learnt, she put the paper back into the jewel-case, replaced the tray, and locked the box.

Then she walked over to the dressing-table to sit down on the stool and stare at her reflection in the mirror. But she did not see her own face, only that of Heloise, and heard the questions that she kept asking herself over and over again in her mind.

What did it mean? Where had this money come from?

After what seemed a long time she suddenly remembered that Emily was waiting outside. She crossed the room and opened the door to say:

"I am going to Her Ladyship's room."

"Did you find your brooch, Miss?" Emily enquired.

"I have changed my mind," Gilda replied, and her voice was somehow hard. "I have no wish to wear any jewellery."

The Marquis of Staverton, having ridden in the Park before his contemporaries were awake, came back in a good humour for breakfast at this house in Berkeley Square.

The new stallion which he had purchased the previous week at Tattersall's had given him an even better ride than he had anticipated when he bought it.

He decided that when he went to the country he would take the horse with him and try him over some fences he had erected as a miniature steeple-chase course.

He found this an excellent way to train his horses not only for racing but also for hunting.

As he settled down to enjoy one of the well-cooked dishes which his Chef had provided, his Butler said respectfully:

"Excuse me, M'Lord, but there's a messenger from the Foreign Office asking if you'll call on Lord Hawkesbury at your earliest convenience."

The Marquis looked at the clock on the mantelpiece.

"Ask the messenger to inform His Lordship that I will be with him at eleven o'clock."

"Very good, M'Lord."

The Marquis finished his breakfast, then went into his Library, where his secretary was waiting with a large pile of invitations besides a number of letters from the Agents on his Estates, asking for his instructions regarding various improvements, renovations, or alterations which had to be done.

The Marquis worked for an hour-and-a-half before the pile of correspondence on his desk had diminished considerably, then he went upstairs to change his clothes.

Looking as usual resplendent without being in the least dandified, he set off for the Foreign Office, driving a high-perch Phaeton with an expertise that was the envy of every passerby who watched him as he drove into Piccadilly, then down St. James's Street.

At the Foreign Office there was a Senior Clerk waiting to conduct him to the Foreign Secretary's Office, and as soon as he entered the room Lord Hawkesbury rose to his feet, holding out his hand in welcome.

"It was good of you to come at such short notice, Staverton," he said.

"I was naturally curious as to why you needed me so urgently, My Lord," the Marquis said.

He sat down in a comfortable armchair on the opposite side of the desk, and as the Foreign Secretary seated himself there was a worried expression on his face.

There was silence for a moment. Then Lord Hawkesbury said:

"Quite frankly, Staverton, you are my last hope."

The Marquis raised his eye-brows but did not speak, and Lord Hawkesbury said almost as if the words burst from him:

"You will hardly believe it, but I am convinced, although I have little proof of it, that there is a leak of information going out from this Office!"

This was certainly surprising, and the Marquis sat upright.

"From this Office?" he repeated. "How can you be sure?"

"I am not sure, and that is the trouble," Lord Hawkesbury replied, "and I admit that to a certain extent I am guessing. At the same time, I am desperately afraid that secret information is being carried from Whitehall to Bonaparte in some devious manner."

There was silence, and the Marquis was thinking that while the Treaty of Amiens, which had been signed a month ago, had delighted the world, Ministers like Lord Hawkesbury had been suspicious that Napoleon Bonaparte was just playing for time and was consolidating his forces.

If this was true, then in a very short while hostilities between England and France would recommence.

However, it would be useless to say such things to the Prime Minister.

Henry Addington, who had succeeded William Pitt after his resignation the preceding year, had proved himself to be weak, vacillating, and complacent to a degree which the Leaders of the Armed Forces thought extremely dangerous.

The Marquis had on various occasions in the past been of service to the Ministry of Foreign Affairs and Lord Hawkesbury in particular, and now he was sure that if the latter was suspicious, he had grounds for it.

"What can I do about a leak if there is one?" the Marquis enquired.

"That is what I am asking you!" Lord Hawkesbury said with a faint smile.

"Explain the position," the Marquis said.

The Foreign Secretary lowered his voice as if he thought the room might have ears.

"I have investigated and had under observation, secretly of course, every member of my staff."

"And you have a suspect?"

"It is slanderous to say so, because I cannot find anything specific against him," Lord Hawkesbury answered, "and yet my instinct tells me that Rearsby is not all he appears to be."

The Marquis frowned for a moment.

Then he remembered Lord Rearsby, a rather overdressed young man whom he had seen at parties and on race-courses but had never wished to make his acquaintance.

He was not the type, the Marquis thought, that one would suspect of being dangerous in any way. He merely hung round the rich and the famous and was the sort of man who would belong to a good Club because it would advance him socially.

"Do you know him?" asked Lord Hawkesbury, who had been watching the Marquis's face.

"By sight," the Marquis replied. "He is not a man who interests me either as a friend or as an acquaintance."

"That is what I thought," Lord Hawkesbury said. "His father was the first Peer, and Rearsby went to a good School. He has a small Estate in Sussex, where he spends little time, and he is, I am told, ambitious to be recognised by the Prince of Wales."

The Marquis gave a little laugh.

"That might apply to quite a number of men."

"Exactly!" Lord Hawkesbury replied. "That is what makes me think I must be 'barking up the wrong tree.' At the same time, there seems to be nobody else."

"Why is he working here at all?"

"He came here during his father's lifetime because Lord Rearsby, who received his title as a reward for distinguished work for us, was eager for his son to follow in his footsteps."

There was a pause before he went on:

"When his father died, everybody expected young Rearsby to resign immediately and spend the money he had been left on riotous living. But strangely enough he remained, and as he is really quite conscientious in his work, there is no reason at all why we should not continue to employ him."

"And what makes you suspicious?"

"Quite frankly, I do not know," Lord Hawkesbury said. "It is just that there seems to be nobody else whom I would not trust implicitly, and also there is no-one else who has been here very much longer than Rearsby, although that has little to do with it."

"It certainly sounds very difficult," the Marquis said. "What do you expect of me?"

Lord Hawkesbury laughed.

"Again, I do not know. I am having Rearsby watched, but he has not been seen in contact with any of those whom we suspect of being sympathisers or supporters of our enemies. If he does in fact pass on any information, I cannot think to whom he gives it."

"And what can I do?" the Marquis asked again.

"Just keep your eyes open, Staverton. You have been so lucky in the past, or shall I say so astute, and as I have already said, you are my last hope."

"Is there any information within Rearsby's knowledge which could be of great advantage to the French?"

"Anything they learnt about our Army or Navy would be helpful to Bonaparte, who I am quite certain is intending to invade this island sooner or later."

"You really believe that?" the Marquis asked. "I thought it was just a weapon with which to scare old ladies and the 'fuddy-duddies' in the Cabinet."

The Foreign Secretary shook his head.

"No, I am completely serious. My information is that the French are building barges in which to convey enough troops across the Channel to attack us when we are quite unprepared for it."

"Quite unprepared?" the Marquis ejaculated. "Then why the devil are we disbanding the Navy and the Army with such unprecedented haste?"

"You must ask the Prime Minister that question," Lord Hawkesbury replied. "All I can say is that I have protested vigorously at two Cabinet Meetings, only to be overruled as usual by those who think that if they believe in peace strongly enough, their wishes will come true."

"It is crazy!" the Marquis said sharply.

"I agree with you," Lord Hawkesbury replied, "but nobody is going to listen to me unless we can prove, and I am very anxious to do so, that Napoleon has spies who keep him well informed about everything in England, so that he will strike at a moment when, because we are so defenceless, he is bound through sheer numbers to be victorious."

"That is something we must prevent!" the Marquis said fervently.

"Amen!" the Foreign Secretary replied.

The two men sat talking together for over an hour, and when the Marquis left the Foreign Office he was looking serious.

As he drove home he was doubting whether even with his proverbial good luck he would be able to find what he knew was a "needle in a haystack."

He went to luncheon at White's because he thought he would see Lord Rearsby there, and he was not mistaken.

The first Lord Rearsby had been a member of the Club, and his son had been put down for membership when he was still quite young.

There was no doubt, the Marquis thought cynically, that Rearsby found it a "happy hunting ground" in which he could further his ambitions.

There was no other Club where he could meet socially the *crème de la crème* of Society, and where as members men put aside their prejudices against one another, and a member was accepted at his face value.

The Marquis noticed that Lord Rearsby was sitting with some friends who were not important and was neither eating nor drinking to excess.

It seemed almost absurd to suspect that he was a spy for Napoleon.

At the same time, if he really had ambitions to be a great social success, he would need more money than the amount that the Foreign Secretary suspected he had been left by his father.

It was well known in the Foreign Office that Napoleon was extremely generous to those who furnished him with the information he required, and the smugglers who carried spies back and forth across the Channel found such a cargo far more lucrative than the usual ones of brandy and tea.

Immediately hostilities had ceased, there had been the usual witch-hunt for those who had been disposed to sympathise with the French, and there were endless tales of spies listening in at Cabinet Meetings or even hiding in corners at Buckingham Palace.

The Marquis had not believed any of it. He knew only too well that patriotism could blow up something very trivial into a menace from which people shrank in terror.

What was more, without the excitement of battle, women particularly enjoyed tales of intrigue and conspiracy.

Without appearing to do so, he watched Rearsby for some time, and decided that Lord Hawkesbury was mistaken.

How would it be possible for an unimportant young man to get in touch with Napoleon's spiders'-web of espionage in the first place?

If Hawkesbury had had him followed, he would surely have been detected at some moment or other in contact with those émigrés now living in London who were always suspected of trying by any means, fair or foul, to return to their native land.

"I am sure the whole thing is just imagination," the Marquis told himself.

At the same time, having worked with Lord Hawkesbury for some years, he knew that he was conscientious, level-headed, and noted for being meticulous in separating the grain from the chaff.

Because the Marquis could find nothing of interest at White's, he decided that he would call on Heloise.

He was finding her behaviour so strange that it made him curious.

He was used to women trying to be different from one another and attempting to arouse his interest by being original, and he thought he knew all the tricks they used and all the bait they threw so carefully under his nose in an effort to catch him.

But Heloise Wyngate for the moment had him completely puzzled.

He had at first been extremely angry when she had upset the numbers at his dinner-party and had not even paid him the courtesy of letting him know that she was leaving London.

If there was one thing he really disliked, it was bad manners, either in a man or a woman, and he told himself that as far as she was concerned he was finished with her.

Then he laughed and decided it was just another carefully conceived plan to trap him into finding her irresistible.

He told himself he was far too old and too clever to be caught in such a way.

All the same, she was in fact the most beautiful girl he had ever seen, and he knew that if one of her other admirers swept her away when it was thought that he was still interested, it would definitely be a feather in his cap.

He had therefore decided that he would call and try to find out what she was doing, although he was quite certain he knew.

He was well aware how skilfully she had managed not to have any intimate conversation with him last night and had appeared to be enjoying herself with a child-like excitement which was different from anything he had noticed in her before.

When she left London, he had known perfectly well that Heloise had been concentrating fervently on him to the exclusion of everybody else in any Ball-Room or anywhere else they might be.

But last night she had been as elusive as a piece of quicksilver, and he had the strange idea, although he could not account for it in any way, that when their eyes had met there was a touch of fear in hers.

"I am imagining it," he told himself.

But the idea persisted, and he was convinced that he was not mistaken.

It had been Lord Hawkesbury who had first become aware that beneath the Marquis's Corinthian surface there was an astute, ultra-critical, highly perceptive brain.

He had therefore cultivated the young Marquis's friendship until he was in a position to ask his help in various problems which originated in the Foreign Office but overflowed into the Social World and came within the Marquis's orbit.

Because he had been so remarkably successful, Lord Hawkesbury had not only congratulated himself on discerning the Marquis's ability, but he had also begun to admire him more and more and also to rely on him.

He was quite certain that if anybody could solve the problem of what he suspected was a major leak in his department, it would be Staverton.

When the Marquis agreed to try, Lord Hawkesbury had sighed with relief, as if he had transferred a burden from his shoulders to those of a younger man.

The same intelligence and the same probing mind which the Marquis was prepared to exercise in finding Napoleon's spy, he was now concentrating on Heloise Wyngate.

He wanted to know why she had appeared to be so frightened.

❦

Gilda worried over the contents of her sister's jewel-case until it was difficult to think about anything else.

When Anderson had insisted that after such a late night Lady Neyland should lie down after luncheon, Gilda had gone to the Study to read.

She had found a dozen books which she thought would be extremely interesting, but when she curled up in the window-seat with one of them, she found the pages dancing in front of her eyes.

Instead, she could see only the letter from Coutts Bank addressed to her sister and the pile of glittering sovereigns at the bottom of the jewel-box.

She was wondering for the hundredth time what could be the explanation, when the door opened and the Butler announced:

"The Marquis of Staverton, Miss!"

Gilda started and her book fell from her lap onto the floor.

She would have risen to pick it up, but the Marquis crossed the room swiftly and gave it back into her hands.

As he did so, he looked down at the title and saw that the author of it was Rousseau.

"You read French?" he asked.

"Quite well, and this is a book I have always wanted to read," Gilda replied.

"Why?"

"I thought it would be interesting. Both Papa and Mama enjoyed his works, although Papa really preferred books about soldiering."

"I did not know you were a reader," the Marquis remarked.

Too late, Gilda remembered that Heloise had never read a book if she could possibly avoid it and was in fact extremely bad at French.

She only hoped that the Marquis did not know such facts about her sister, and she said quickly:

"Godmama was not expecting you to call this afternoon."

"As you are well aware, I am calling on you," the Marquis said.

"For any particular reason?"

"Do I have to have a reason?" he asked. "I thought, although perhaps I was mistaken, that we were such good friends that we liked being in each other's company."

There was that mocking note in his voice which Gilda had learnt to expect, and after a moment she said:

"I have a feeling, My Lord, that you are laughing at me!"

"Why should I do that?"

"I do not know, but perhaps it is because I have always heard you find young girls boring."

She had not heard this, but she felt certain that that would be the Marquis's attitude about most unmarried women.

"You are quite right," he answered, "but you can hardly put yourself in the category of 'young girls,' who are invariably gauche, unfledged, and extremely ignorant."

Gilda gave a little laugh.

"You are very unkind about them. They do their best, and remember, girls grow up and become beautiful and witty women."

"Sometimes!" the Marquis agreed enigmatically. "But you are very beautiful, Heloise, and you cannot imagine to what state you have reduced the male population of St. James's."

Gilda laughed again.

"You are too skilful with your compliments. I have a feeling that either you have uttered them so often that you have become word-perfect, or else you think them out in your bath."

"Now I think you are insulting me!" the Marquis said, but he was smiling.

Gilda looked at the clock over the mantelpiece.

"I think Godmama will soon have finished her rest, and I have to change my gown."

The Marquis's eyes twinkled.

"If that is an excuse to be rid of me, it is hardly up to standard. I cannot believe, unless you had luncheon particularly early, that Her Ladyship has had time to rest, and you look so charming in the gown you are already wearing that I doubt if you will trouble to change it again."

Gilda was silent, not knowing what to say, and he went on:

"What has happened? Why are you trying to avoid me?"

"I am . . . not doing . . . that," Gilda murmured rather ineffectually.

"I am not a fool," the Marquis said. "First you run away, then when you come back you make it quite obvious that you have no wish to be alone with me. I want an explanation, Heloise, and I think I am entitled to one."

"I do not know why you should think you are . . . entitled to . . . anything," Gilda said. "You have no . . . jurisdiction over me . . . as you well . . . know."

"No?" the Marquis queried.

"No!" Gilda said firmly.

He looked at her for a long moment, and she had the feeling that his eyes were probing beneath the surface, looking deep down into her heart, and she was afraid.

Then as she struggled vainly to find a new subject of conversation, the Marquis said:

"I have an idea that we should celebrate your Godmother's return to Society by giving a dinner-party for her."

There was a sudden sparkle in Gilda's eyes.

"Do you mean that?" she asked. "It would indeed please her enormously. She enjoyed herself so much last night, but she is rather dubious this morning about my intention to write to everybody who has invited me and inform them that she must attend the parties too."

She looked at the Marquis and added:

"As you noticed last night, Her Ladyship has no wish to push herself onto anybody."

"I am aware of that," the Marquis said, "and so I will give a party for her, and you shall tell me who are her special friends whom she would like me to invite."

"May I tell Godmama of your plans?" Gilda asked.

The Marquis shook his head.

"No, I think it should be a surprise!"

"That would be even more exciting."

Gilda paused for a moment before she said:

"I had always thought that Godmama had had such an enjoyable life, until she told me how unhappy she was with her husband and how much he neglected her. I think that is why now she is very grateful for any love or kindness she receives."

Gilda spoke in a low voice, and for the moment she was thinking not of the Marquis but of Lady Neyland.

When her Godmother had talked at luncheon-time she had understood how much the attention she had received last night had meant to her.

She thought too that because Lady Neyland was still comparatively young and attractive, it must have been very depressing for her to know that Heloise was going to parties every night while she had to stay at home, just as she had done when her husband had "other interests."

The Marquis was watching the expressions that crossed Gilda's face. Then he said:

"Leave everything to me. I will arrange the party for tomorrow night."

"Are you able to do that so quickly?"

"Why not?" he asked. "We will be about twenty at dinner. I will ask about the same number of people to come in afterwards, and I expect you will want to dance."

"Not if you do not want to," Gilda said quickly. "I shall be quite happy just to sit talking or to watch your guests playing cards."

The Marquis looked at her as if he thought she could not be speaking the truth, but again she was concentrating on Lady Neyland, and after a moment she said:

"Of course cards are no use to Godmama, but she would like to hear music, even if no-one dances."

"Then we will have music," the Marquis agreed.

"And please," Gilda said quickly, "could we choose a special dinner that Godmama can eat easily?"

"I see that like me you think of every detail," the Marquis said. "I have already decided that whatever the rest of us eat, your Godmother shall have food which she can eat with a spoon."

"That is very kind of you," Gilda said, "and thank you very, very much. I am sure that nobody has given a party exclusively for her in a very long time."

"Then I shall take care to invite her special friends," the Marquis said. "And what about you? If you are still determined to avoid me, you will need your special admirers there."

Gilda thought of Sir Humphrey and gave an involuntary little shiver.

"Tomorrow evening is nothing to do with me," she said. "Please ask only those people who will amuse Godmama and of course yourself."

"You are very self-effacing all of a sudden."

To his surprise, Gilda blushed and the colour rose up her throat towards her eyes.

Then as if she felt shy she rose to her feet.

"Are you trying to be rid of me before I am ready to leave?" the Marquis enquired.

"I thought . . . perhaps you . . . would have . . . a lot to do."

"You still have not told me why you have an aversion to my company."

"It is not that . . . I promise it is not . . . that!" Gilda said without thinking.

"Then what is it?"

She searched for words but could not find them, and after a moment she said unhappily:

"I do not . . . like having to . . . answer questions."

"I am curious," the Marquis said. "I find it annoying when people are unpredictable and I cannot discover a reason for it."

Then as if Gilda was amused that he was puzzled she gave a little laugh.

"I had the feeling before you said that," she said, "that you could solve any problem that presented itself to you."

The Marquis was startled by her reply because it seemed almost as if it might have some connection with what Lord Hawkesbury had said to him, and as if she were somehow reading a message.

Suddenly he had the feeling, although it was a vague one, that when there had been French words or phrases introduced into the conversation in the past, Heloise had not understood them.

It was considered smart—a fashion set by the Regent— to intersperse one's own language with smatterings of the languages of other nations.

The Regent often spoke in French or in Italian, and the Marquis was proficient in both languages, but there were few women of his acquaintance who could do the same.

To test Heloise he quoted the French adage which, roughly translated into English, meant:

"A little learning can be dangerous for little minds."

There was a quick laugh before she replied in extremely good French:

"Now you are really being insulting, and I think, *Monsieur le Marquis,* you are insinuating that I was boasting when I said I enjoyed Rousseau."

There was no doubt that she could speak French very well indeed, and the Marquis said:

"Ten out of ten! And may I apologise for doubting you?"

"That is something you should certainly do," Gilda replied. "And perhaps I should ask why you are so good at French, unless of course you are an admirer of Napoleon?"

"I am told that all the ladies who visit Paris," the Marquis said, "find him a most impressive figure. In fact, those who have recently returned from there go into eulogies over the manner in which the First Consul received them and the pomp and grandeur they found at the Tuileries Palace."

Gilda did not speak, and after a moment the Marquis said:

"Perhaps you would like to visit Paris with your God-mother when she is in better health?"

"Certainly not!" Gilda said so sharply that her voice seemed to ring out. "I think Bonaparte is a monster! And the sufferings he has inflicted in all the countries of Europe should ensure that no decent person would ever speak to him again."

The Marquis was astonished.

He had found few women interested in the war except for the fact that it deprived them of the silks and ribbons they required for their gowns.

If they thought of the conflict at all, it was the short-age of eligible males for social occasions which annoyed them, rather than the suffering of those who became involved in the war.

"I have seen some of the men recently discharged from the Army and Navy," Gilda went on in a low voice, "coming home without legs or arms, crippled for the rest of their lives. It is cruel . . . it is horrible for human beings to inflict such . . . injuries on one another . . . and so many of those who die are very young and have not really begun to live before they are buried."

The Marquis was stunned into silence, and the tears were in Gilda's eyes as she said:

"It is not only the soldiers who suffer in battle. Papa told me how horses scream when they are wounded and often are left to bleed slowly to death. They do not know what is happening . . . and how can they . . . understand why they should be . . . slaughtered for no . . . apparent reason?"

Now the tears ran down her cheeks, and as if she could not bear him to see her weakness she brushed them quickly away with the back of her hand.

Then she said hastily before the Marquis could speak:

"I must go to Godmama. Thank you . . . My Lord, for your . . . kindness in giving . . . a party for her . . . and please tell me if there is . . . anything I can do to . . . help."

Her words seemed to fall over one another, and without looking at the Marquis she went quickly from the room, leaving him staring after her in sheer astonishment.

CHAPTER FIVE

The Marquis returned home after a luncheon-party which had been of particular interest to him because all the guests except himself were politicians, and they had talked of the situation between France and England in a frank manner which he had found extremely informative.

As he went to the Library he was followed by his secretary with a list in his hand.

"What is it, Carrington?" the Marquis enquired.

"I thought you would like to see the names of the guests who have accepted for your party this evening. My Lord," Mr. Carrington said. "I am afraid there will be rather more than you first intended."

"I anticipated that," the Marquis said as if to himself.

He was well aware that when he sent out invitations there were very few people in the *Beau Monde* who would refuse, and although he had planned his party for Lady Neyland at the last moment, everybody to whom he had spoken about it had accepted with delight.

He took the list from his secretary and glanced down it, thinking that he had been clever in choosing both men and women who he knew would interest Lady Neyland, while there were also a number of younger men who would want to meet Heloise.

The Marquis thought he was being rather magnanimous in arranging that she would be admired and flattered as usual.

At the same time, he had a reason for it.

Because Heloise's behaviour towards him had surprised him so considerably during the last few days, he wanted to see her behaviour with the other men who he knew were paying her court.

In the past he had thought that while she was making it obvious that she wished to be with him, she was deliberately flirtatious and provocative with the rest in order to make him realise how much she was admired.

He was, however, aware that at the Ball the other night she had not appeared to be in the least flirtatious but had talked quietly and sensibly with her partners, and as far as he could ascertain, she had appeared to hurry away from those who were too ardent.

"Why has she changed?" he asked himself. "Or is this a new way of making me interested that has not been tried before?"

He thought he knew every move of the game and that every approach, however subtle, had been made to him before until he could almost sense exactly what would happen next.

But Heloise was now surprising him, and why she continued to run away from him when they might be together left him baffled for an explanation.

Mr. Carrington broke in on his reverie as he said:

"At the moment, with those who are coming in after dinner, your guests total sixty, My Lord."

"I think we can accommodate them," the Marquis said with a smile.

He looked down at the list once more. Then he said:

"Add Lord Rearsby to the list and send a groom with the invitation right away."

Mr. Carrington thought for a moment. Then he said:

"As Lord Rearsby has never been invited before, My Lord, I am afraid I do not know his address."

"White's Club," the Marquis said, and turned to the letters on his desk which were waiting to be signed.

He knew that Rearsby and quite a number of his friends would be very surprised at his invitation, but he thought he owed it to Lord Hawkesbury to have a closer look at the man who he suspected might be a spy.

'Not that I am likely to learn anything on so short an acquaintance,' the Marquis thought. 'At the same time, what else can I do?'

He knew he was not likely to meet Lord Rearsby at any of the parties given by his intimate friends, and because of his own reputation of being extremely fastidious in choosing those with whom he associated, he had deliberately avoided making his acquaintance in White's.

What was more, to do so would undoubtedly make those who knew him well question his reasons for approaching Rearsby, and if the young man was in fact involved in espionage, it would put him on his guard.

"No," the Marquis said to himself. "If he is here tonight it will merely be assumed that he has come with a party of some of my other friends, and nobody will think it strange."

There were other letters waiting for him, but he picked up the list which Mr. Carrington had left beside him on the desk and read it again.

It struck him that Heloise had not contributed any of the names to the party he was giving for her Godmother, and he thought it might be a good idea to consult her again as to whether there was any particular friend of Lady Neyland's who should be included.

He also, although he would not admit it to himself, was anxious to see Heloise again, and last night after he had gone to bed he had found himself quite unexpectedly puzzling over her behaviour towards him.

It was only a short distance from the Marquis's house to Curzon Street, but as his Phaeton was outside he stepped into it without thinking, drove himself round the Square, and a few minutes later had drawn up outside Lady Neyland's house.

He noticed that there was another Phaeton being walked up the street to keep the horses from becoming restless and wondered if it was somebody calling on Heloise.

The front door of Lady Neyland's house was open, and as he walked in there was only one footman on duty, who hurried to take his hat and riding-gloves.

"Is Miss Wyngate at home?" the Marquis enquired.

"She's in the Drawing-Room, My Lord," the footman replied.

"Do not bother to announce me," the Marquis said, and walked across the Hall to the Drawing-Room.

As he put his hand on the handle he heard Heloise scream.

Gilda had awakened that morning with a feeling that tonight would be very exciting because it would please her Godmother.

235

At the same time, she knew it would also be exciting for her because she wanted to see the Marquis's house and, if she was honest, to see him again.

Despite the fact that he frightened her, especially when he asked probing questions which made her afraid that he might guess at her deception, she found him very different from the other men whom she had met since she came to London.

It was difficult to explain even to herself exactly what that entailed.

She supposed it was because the Marquis was so much more intelligent than the young men who paid her fulsome compliments or talked in bored, blasé voices because it was the fashion.

'It would be very interesting to be friends with him,' she thought to herself, but she knew that such a thing was impossible.

She was perceptive enough to realise that he must have been aware that her sister was pursuing him, and she had the suspicion that he had known that Heloise's precipitate departure for the country was a ruse to bring him to the point of proposing marriage.

Gilda was quite certain in her mind that this was something the Marquis had no intention of doing, and certainly not to an obscure young woman called "Heloise Wyngate," who had no other attributes to recommend her except her beauty.

Her mother had always said that the great aristocrats of England invariably had arranged marriages because it benefitted their families either with money or with land.

"Anyway," Mrs. Wyngate had gone on, "those of blue blood, like Royalty, are allied with their equals, and although I hope, dearest, that you and Heloise will both make advantageous marriages from a social point of view, what is more important than anything else is for you to be in love with the man you marry."

Her voice had softened as she had said:

"Your father had no reason to marry me except that he loved me, and I not only loved but admired him so tremendously that I never thought I would be fortunate enough to become his wife."

Gilda had thought then that the one thing she wanted was to marry for love.

But as she had looked round the Ball-Room at the Countess of Dorset's, she had thought that however glamorous the guests looked, quite a number of them did not appear to be particularly happy.

At the same time, this was the Marquis's life, though it was not hers, and if she was honest it was not Heloise's either.

"Perhaps in the end," she told herself, "Heloise would have had to marry Sir Humphrey."

Then she shuddered at the mere idea of it, knowing that for some reason she could not explain, he made, in Mrs. Hewlett's words, "her flesh creep."

When Lady Neyland had gone to lie down after luncheon, having protested that there was no reason for it and that she was not tired, Gilda had gone to the Drawing-Room to arrange some flowers that had arrived for her that morning.

They consisted of bunches of tulips and daffodils, and as she put them into a big crystal rose-bowl she thought it strange that Society spent most of the summer in London when the country was so attractive.

"If I were the Queen," she said to herself, "I would arrange to be in London during the winter, where it would be much warmer, and spend the summer months in the country, where the flowers are blooming, the sun is shining, and it is lovely to be out-of-doors."

Then she remembered that if she were at home at the moment, she would not be enjoying the flowers but working hard in the vegetable-garden.

Digging often made her hands hard with occasional blisters on her palms, and she had been afraid at first that somebody might notice that her hands were not as soft or as white as Heloise's.

But as a result of having nothing strenuous to do they were becoming softer, and she thought now that few people would guess how vigorously she had had to dig and hoe to have enough vegetables to eat.

"I am so very, very lucky to be here," she told herself, and she was humming a little tune when the door opened and a footman announced:

"Sir Humphrey Grange has called, Miss."

Gilda gave a little start and was just about to say that she was not at home, when suddenly she had an idea.

"Show Sir Humphrey in, Henry," she said, "but give me a minute to go upstairs and tidy myself."

As she spoke she slipped across the room and left the Drawing-Room by another door which took her through an Ante-Room and out into a passage where she climbed the back stairs to the First Floor.

She ran to her bedroom, opened the jewel-case, and took out the sapphire earrings and pendant.

She wrapped them in a piece of tissue-paper, and without bothering even to look in the mirror and tidy her hair she ran downstairs again.

She had decided during the night that she had no intention of keeping the present that Sir Humphrey had given to Heloise.

She knew that until she had returned the sapphires she would always feel more uncomfortable in his presence than she did anyway and would also find it difficult to rid herself of his attentions while ostensibly she was under an obligation to him.

When she returned to the Drawing-Room, entering by the same door as she had left it, Sir Humphrey was standing by the mantelpiece, looking even more florid and flamboyant than he had at the Dorsets' Ball.

"Good-afternoon, my fair enchantress!" he said as Gilda advanced towards him.

She held out her hand and to her consternation he raised it to his lips, not in the perfunctory manner that

was customary but kissing it passionately in a manner
which made her shudder.

His lips were warm and possessive, and when he tried
to turn her hand over so that he could kiss the palm, she
snatched it away from him.

"I adore you!" he said. "Your beauty blinds me, and I
hope today you will be a little kinder than you were the
other night."

"I have something for you, Sir Humphrey," Gilda
said in what she hoped was a quiet, calm, but firm
voice.

"What is that?" he enquired.

"It was . . . kind of you to give me those . . . fine sapphires," Gilda began, "but I should have . . . explained
when I . . . received them that I cannot accept such a . . .
valuable gift. It would not be right."

"Now what do you mean by that?" Sir Humphrey
enquired.

He spoke aggressively, and although Gilda felt nervous she stood her ground.

"Please . . . understand," she said, "that I appreciate
your . . . thoughts of me . . . but you know as well as I do
that it is . . . wrong for a . . . lady to accept . . . any gift . . .
except perhaps flowers . . . from a man who is not . . .
connected with her in . . . any way."

She stammered over the words because she could not
quite think of how she should put it, and Sir Humphrey
said:

"That is easily remedied. I have asked you to marry
me. I am waiting for you to say 'yes.' "

Gilda drew in her breath.

"The answer . . . Sir Humphrey, is 'no'!"

He stared at her and now she felt as if his eyes had a
most ferocious expression in them.

"What do you mean 'no'?" he snapped. "You have
played me along very skilfully until now, with: 'perhaps,'
'someday,' 'sometime.' What has occurred that you
should suddenly shut me out?"

"It . . . is not . . . that," Gilda said hesitatingly.

"Of course it is!" he answered. "Are you telling me that Staverton has popped the question? The betting at White's was fifty-to-one against him doing so."

"No . . . no . . ." Gilda said quickly. "It is just that I have no . . . wish to be . . . married at the moment . . . and please . . . Sir Humphrey . . . take back your present."

She held out the sapphires as she spoke, but Sir Humphrey made no effort to take them from her.

"Something has happened," he said. "Something has changed you. You made it quite obvious until now that I was at least the second string to your bow."

Gilda thought that he was more intelligent than she had given him credit for. At the same time, she knew it would be dangerous if he became too inquisitive.

"It is only . . . to tell you," she said, "as I have told my Godmother, that I am . . . happy to stay with her for at least . . . another year before being . . . married to . . . anybody, and she is very pleased with my . . . decision."

"Stuff and nonsense!" Sir Humphrey ejaculated. "I do not believe a word of it! You have some reason for getting rid of me, and I want to know what it is."

"It is . . . not like . . . that," Gilda said unhappily.

"Then what is it?" he demanded.

He stood looking at her. Then the aggressive expression in his eyes changed to something very different.

Gilda had no idea how lovely she looked with the sunshine coming through the windows picking out the gold in her hair, her eyes worried and a little anxious, and, because she was nervous, her lips trembling.

"I love you!" Sir Humphrey said suddenly. "I love you and I will teach you to love me! Let us have no more of this nonsense, Heloise. I will deck you in diamonds and give you everything you want in life."

As he spoke he put his arms round Gilda and pulled her roughly against him.

She was not expecting such a move and it took her by surprise.

"Please . . . please . . . !"

Sir Humphrey seemed very large and overpowering. He was also very strong, and although she struggled against him, pressing her hands against his chest to free herself, she realised that she was helpless in his arms.

"I will make you love me!" he said, and as his mouth came towards hers she knew he intended to kiss her.

She twisted her head, but she felt his lips passionate and demanding on her cheek, and as his arms tightened she knew it was only a question of time before he kissed her lips.

"No! No!" she cried.

Then, because she was frightened of the passion she felt rising within him and the insistence of his lips against her skin, she screamed.

It was not a loud scream but one of fear such as might be given by a small animal which was caught in a trap.

Then as she thought she was lost and the next second Sir Humphrey's mouth would hold hers captive, the door of the Drawing-Room opened and she heard a voice ask angrily:

"What the hell do you think you are doing?"

She knew then that she was safe, and with a cry quite different from the one she had given before, she struggled free of Sir Humphrey as he loosened his grip and ran across the room.

Without thinking what she was doing, she threw herself against the Marquis, holding on to him because for the moment he stood for everything that was secure and safe in a nightmare of terror.

He stood still just inside the door, and as Gilda hid her face against his shoulder he put one arm round her.

He was looking at Sir Humphrey, who was glowering at him ferociously like a turkey-cock that has been challenged by another.

"I asked you a question, Grange," the Marquis said, and his voice was sharp, like the crack of a whip, and icy.

"What has it got to do with you?" Sir Humphrey asked in a furious tone. "Heloise tells me you are not engaged,

241

and I had asked her to marry me, which I understand is more than you have done!"

"Whatever I may or may not do," the Marquis returned coldly, "I do not force my attentions on a woman who is unwilling and who screams for help."

"Doubtless knowing that her Saviour was within hearing!" Sir Humphrey sneered.

He bent down and picked up the sapphires, which had fallen to the floor while they struggled. Then he said angrily:

"Very well, Miss Wyngate, I will take back my jewels and my offer of marriage. You have made it quite clear where your ambitions lie. I only hope that you will not be *disappointed*."

He accentuated the last word and walked past the Marquis and out of the room, slamming the door behind him.

For a moment it was impossible for Gilda to speak. Then she raised her head and said incoherently:

"I . . . I am . . . sorry."

The Marquis looked at her face, which he saw was very pale, and he was aware that she was still trembling although not so convulsively as when she had first reached him.

She walked away from him towards the window to stand with her back to the room, fighting for composure.

She had been terrified by Sir Humphrey in a manner which now seemed to her rather foolish.

Yet, because such an encounter had never happened to her before, she had been unable to think but could only struggle for freedom as if her very life depended on it.

As she stood trying to get her breath back, it flashed through her mind that after what Sir Humphrey had said, the Marquis would be aware that he had given her jewels, and she could imagine nothing more humiliating.

'I cannot explain,' she thought, 'and it is best to say nothing. I am sure he despises me anyway.'

The beat of her heart had almost returned to normal, and after what seemed a long time she said again in a small, hesitating little voice:

"I am . . . very sorry."

"So you should be," the Marquis said in an unfeeling tone. "If you encourage a man like that, you must expect him sooner or later to behave like a beast."

"He . . . he frightened me."

"I should have thought that by now you were used to handling men who lose their heads and their self-control under what I imagine is severe provocation."

The Marquis spoke in a cynical, sarcastic manner which Gilda thought was worse than if he had shouted at her.

Then once again she was trembling, but in a different way from before.

"Come and sit down, Heloise," the Marquis said suddenly. "I want to talk to you."

"No . . . please . . . !" Gilda protested. "There is nothing to . . . talk about. I cannot explain . . . but I only hope that Sir Humphrey . . . meant what he said . . . and will not speak to me again."

"You mean that?" the Marquis enquired.

"Of course I mean it! I thought from the first moment I saw him that he was . . . horrid, and there is . . . something about him which is very . . . unpleasant."

Only as she finished did she realise that she was speaking as herself instead of as Heloise.

It must have been obvious to the Marquis or to anybody else who knew her sister well that she had in fact encouraged Sir Humphrey as an admirer and, as Gilda now knew, the donor of expensive presents.

"I . . . cannot talk . . . about it," she said quickly. "Please . . . leave me alone!"

"I will in a moment, if that is what you really want," the Marquis answered. "In the meantime, I came here to talk to you about tonight."

Because it was a relief that he did not insist on talking any further of what had just occurred, Gilda moved slowly from the window towards him and sat down in one of the chairs near the fireplace.

As she did so, she knew that the Marquis was looking at her in that penetrating manner which she had noticed the first time she saw him.

Quite unexpectedly he said sharply:

"Look at me!"

Obediently Gilda turned her face up to his, feeling suddenly shy but at the same time unable to take her eyes from his.

"I believe you really are frightened," the Marquis said almost as if he spoke to himself.

"It is . . . very stupid of me but I . . . cannot help it."

"I will see that Grange does not worry you again," the Marquis said. "If he calls, refuse to see him. If he persists, let me know, and I will deal with him."

"I . . . I do not want to . . . put you to any . . . trouble."

"It will be no trouble," the Marquis said. "I dislike the man and always have."

He looked at her for a moment. Then he said:

"But we will not talk about him. I have brought you the list of guests I have invited to my party tonight for your Godmother, and I thought you might tell me if there is anybody you wanted me to add to it."

"Thank you. That is very . . . kind of . . . you."

She took the list which the Marquis held out to her and wondered what he would say if he knew that she had very little idea who any of the people were whose names had been neatly inscribed by Mr. Carrington.

She thought that she ought to contribute something. At the same time, for the moment she felt as if her mind was a blank and she could not even remember the name of the gentleman who had been so pleased to see her Godmother at the Countess of Dorset's Ball.

She forced herself to read the list slowly, knowing that the Marquis would expect it of her. Then she said:

"It looks perfect to me. I am sure Godmother will be thrilled to meet so many old friends."

"They really are her friends?" the Marquis asked.

"I think so."

The Marquis looked at her with a faint smile on his lips.

"You have lived here for two years," he said. "You must have some idea by now who Lady Neyland likes and who she does not."

"Of course!" Gilda said quickly. "All the people she . . . likes best are . . . included on your list."

She thought as she spoke that he must think her very insensitive and very selfish.

In fact, she was sure that he was condemning her for being so inattentive to Lady Neyland that she did not even know the names of her personal friends.

But there was nothing Gilda could do about it except to say again:

"I am sure you have thought of everybody who is . . . important."

"I gather you do not wish me to ask Sir Humphrey?" the Marquis asked.

Gilda gave a little cry of protest, then realised that he was teasing her.

"That is not . . . funny!"

"Why have you this aversion to him suddenly?" the Marquis asked. "And what did he mean by saying he had given you jewels?"

Quickly, because she was frightened, Gilda gave the only possible reply to that question.

"He . . . he offered me . . . some," she said, "but I . . . refused them."

"Curse his impertinence!" the Marquis exclaimed. "Surely he realises that you are a lady? Jewels are what one offers to . . ."

He stopped as if he felt he was being too outspoken, but Gilda guessed what he had been about to say.

She knew, because she had read about it and her father had mentioned it once inadvertently, that mistresses received jewels as well as money from the men who became their protectors.

She realised that the Marquis thought Sir Humphrey was treating her as a "fast woman" whose favours could be bought, and the idea brought the colour flooding into her face.

It was not only the embarrassment to herself, but it suddenly struck her that perhaps in some way she could not understand, Heloise had obtained the pearls, the brooch, and the other objects of jewellery in her case in such a manner.

Because she was so agitated, she rose to her feet and without really thinking what she was doing took a few steps towards the door as if she would leave the room.

"Running away from me?" the Marquis asked. "There is no reason for you to do so, Heloise, because I am about to leave."

Gilda turned towards him.

"I should . . . thank you," she said in a low voice, "for saving me and for arriving at . . . exactly the . . . right moment."

She could not help a little shiver passing through her as she thought that if he had not come when he had, Sir Humphrey would have kissed her, and she could imagine nothing more unpleasant or degrading.

"Forget it," the Marquis said sharply, "and I have told you that if he is troublesome I will deal with him. But in future try not to incite men to indiscretion, although that appears to be a pastime in which most women indulge."

"It is certainly . . . something I have no wish to do," Gilda replied, "and I promise you it is something I would . . . never do . . . deliberately."

She thought that the Marquis looked at her again to see if she was really being truthful in what she was saying.

Then he smiled and held out his hand.

"*Au revoir,* until this evening, Heloise. We will see, if nothing else, that your Godmother enjoys herself."

"I shall enjoy it too," Gilda said, "and thank you very, very much for being so kind."

"You can thank me if it is the success I intend it to be," the Marquis replied. "You had better go and lie down now and get over the shock of what has just happened."

He spoke kindly in a way he had never spoken to her before, and Gilda replied impulsively:

"You told me to forget it, and I intend to obey you."

"That is certainly a step in the right direction," the Marquis said, "and something you have often omitted to do in the past."

She put her hand in his and he found it was very cold.

"Good-bye," he said, "and think only that this evening is going to be, I hope, extremely amusing."

"I know it will be," Gilda said.

As he took his hand from hers, she had the feeling that she wanted to hold on to him.

She knew it gave her a feeling of safety and security and that he protected her not only from Sir Humphrey but from the fear of being discovered.

Then she told herself she was being absurd. The first person who might become aware of her deception was the Marquis, and she should in fact be more afraid of him than of anybody else.

As he reached the door he turned to smile at her once again, and she knew, however inconsequential it might be, that she was not now afraid of him.

❦

The Marquis's house always looked very attractive by candlelight. In fact, the Prince of Wales had said to him quite angrily on one occasion:

"I have spent a fortune on Carlton House, and dammit, Staverton, I cannot achieve the same artistic effect at night that you contrive to do."

The Marquis, who had no wish for the Prince to be jealous of him, had quickly eulogised over the house that was the talk of London and the pride and joy of the Prince himself.

It was not yet finished but had already cost an astronomical amount of money, most of it in the form of debts which were unlikely to be met for a long time.

247

To Gilda the Marquis's marble Hall with its pink granite pillars and exquisite statuary set in lighted alcoves was so beautiful that she found it hard to move up the carved and gilded staircase which led to the First Floor.

When she had left her own wrap upstairs and that of Lady Neyland, who had said she would wait for her rather than struggle up the stairs, she had returned to the Hall and her Godmother had taken her arm.

"Where are we, dearest child?" Lady Neyland had asked.

"It is to be a surprise," Gilda answered, "and when you meet your host you must guess who he is."

A few minutes later the Marquis received them in a huge Salon lit by three enormous crystal chandeliers, and Lady Neyland exclaimed at his first word of greeting:

"I know who you are, My Lord! Are you my host for this evening?"

"I am indeed," the Marquis replied, "and may I welcome you as my Guest of Honour, for the party is given for you!"

"How wonderful!" Lady Neyland exclaimed excitedly. "I cannot believe it. How could you be so generous and so kind?"

There was no doubting the excitement in her voice, and Gilda smiled at the Marquis and he smiled back.

With Lady Neyland on his arm, he presented to her all the other guests for dinner, and Gilda noticed that the majority of them were in fact old and dear friends.

"The Marquis has been very clever," she told herself, and thought how inadequate she had been in contributing to the guest-list.

At the same time, she thought it would be difficult for him, however critical he might be, to find fault with either her Godmother's appearance or her own.

She had ordered the *Coiffeur* early so that he could spend a great deal of time arranging Lady Neyland's tiara to its best advantage, then adding to the newest style in which he had done her own hair several white camellias which echoed the decoration of her gown.

It was such an expensive gown that she felt guilty at wearing it, almost as if she felt she must apologise to her sister for doing so.

But she knew she had made the right choice when as she described her appearance to Lady Neyland she had exclaimed:

"Oh, I am so glad you are wearing that gown tonight! When I chose it I thought it was one of the prettiest I had ever seen, but I also thought, although I may have been mistaken, that you did not care for it."

"You were very mistaken!" Gilda said quickly. "I think it is absolutely beautiful! I cannot thank you enough for giving me something in which I feel like a Fairy-Princess."

Lady Neyland laughed.

"Let us hope there is a Fairy-Prince at the party to tell you how beautiful you look."

Gilda did not reply.

She thought, although she was not sure, that the Marquis, as the party was being given for her Godmother, would invite much older men and there would be no-one to pay her the compliments which she had received the other night from her various dancing-partners.

But she was pleasantly surprised when she noted that there were several young men in the Salon who moved eagerly to her side and vied with one another in trying to keep her attention.

Strangely enough, Gilda found it difficult to listen to them, because she found her eyes straying towards the Marquis.

He was at Lady Neyland's side, putting a glass of champagne very carefully into her hand so that there was no chance of her spilling it, and making sure that the new arrivals who came after dinner were informed for whom the party was being given.

'No-one could be more kind,' Gilda thought.

She wondered, because it was something she had not suspected, whether kindness was characteristic of the Marquis or if in fact this was something which had never happened before.

At dinner Lady Neyland was on the Marquis's right, and although Gilda was much farther down the table she could not help noticing how he was explaining to her what she had to eat, and frequently he moved her plate a little nearer to her or handed her a spoon or whatever piece of cutlery she required.

'He *is* kind,' Gilda thought again, and was sure that very few men of the Marquis's standing would take so much trouble over a blind woman.

When the dinner, which had been more delicious than any other meal she had eaten, was over the ladies retired to the Drawing-Room and almost immediately afterwards people began to arrive.

It was then that Gilda saw that the room opening out of the Salon was as big, if not bigger. It had been cleared of furniture and there was a small String Band at the far end of it.

The room was beautifully decorated with flowers and there were French windows opening out onto the garden where fairy-lights edged the paths and Chinese lanterns hung from the trees.

It was only a small garden, and she was not aware that the Marquis's father had converted it from a piece of wasteland into what in the daytime was an exquisitely landscaped garden with a miniature waterfall and rock plants which had been brought from all over the world.

The garden was surrounded by a high wall so that anybody using it could do so in private, and tonight it seemed mysterious and undoubtedly very romantic.

When the Band started to play, the Marquis took Lady Neyland into the Ball-Room where some chairs had been arranged in one corner, where she could sit with her friends who could watch those who danced and describe to her the attractive gowns the ladies were wearing.

"Tell me who looks lovely," Lady Neyland asked, "apart from my Goddaughter, of course."

"She is the Belle of any Ball-Room she graces," the Marquis replied, "but I think perhaps you would admire the Princess de Lieven more than anybody else."

"Is she here?" Lady Neyland enquired. "I have always admired her, but feel I am not really grand enough for her to know."

"Then you must certainly meet her tonight," the Marquis said. "The Russian Ambassador is unfortunately not able to be present, but his wife is an old friend of mine, and I am honoured to learn that at such short notice she cancelled an important engagement in order to come here."

A little later when the music stopped he introduced Lady Neyland to the Princess and the handsome young Russian Diplomat with whom she had been dancing.

"You are full of surprises, My Lord!" the Princess de Lieven said to the Marquis, touching his arm with her fan. "What could be a more delightful surprise than this intimate party which I find is full of my most charming friends and none of my detested enemies!"

The Marquis laughed, knowing that the Princess because she had a sharp tongue had many enemies.

When he had left her to talk to Lady Neyland, he went to greet some other newcomers, noticing as he did so that for Gilda there was no shortage of partners.

The younger men in the party vied with one another in dancing with her, then taking her into the garden.

She would not let them take her too far from the lighted windows, knowing it would be indiscreet to venture into the shadows or to sit in any of the secluded arbours she could see in the faint light from the Chinese lanterns.

"You are being very prim and proper all of a sudden, Miss Wyngate," one of her partners said to her.

Gilda's chin went up and she looked at him sharply, and after a second or two's silence he said:

251

"Are you shocked that I should speak in such a way?"

"Yes, I am," Gilda replied.

"Then I must apologise," he said. "But the last time we met you were very much kinder to me than you have been this evening."

This made Gilda feel uncomfortable, wondering what he meant by being "kind," and having the embarrassed feeling that perhaps this was one of the young men whom Heloise had allowed to kiss her.

Because she knew she had nothing to say, she was forced to resort to her old trick of running away.

"I must go to my Godmother," she said hastily. "I have a feeling she needs me."

She sped back through the long windows and crossed the now empty floor to Lady Neyland's side.

She was talking to a gentleman sitting next to her, and Gilda waited for a pause in the conversation before she said:

"I just came, Godmama, to see if there was anything I could bring you."

"How sweet of you, dearest," Lady Neyland said. "No, I have everything, and I cannot begin to tell you how much I am enjoying this lovely party."

"You have been keeping yourself away from us for far too long," the gentleman beside her said, "and now that you have come out of seclusion, I assure you no party will be complete without you."

Lady Neyland laughed with sheer delight and Gilda turned away, knowing that there was no need for her to worry about her Godmother.

'The person to worry about is me,' she thought. 'I wonder how many other pitfalls dug by Heloise are waiting for me to fall into?'

At the same time, she could not feel anything but elated and excited because she could dance and look attractive enough for the gentlemen to compliment her.

And also because she was in the Marquis's house, which was more impressive than any house she had ever seen before in her whole life.

She thought also as she looked across the room to where he was talking with some friends that no man could be more handsome or more majestic.

"No wonder Heloise wanted to marry him," she said to herself, and found it difficult to attend to what the young man who had just come to her side was saying.

CHAPTER SIX

I find the dancing very warming," Gilda's partner said as they finished a spirited quadrille.

"So do I," she replied.

They walked towards the open window and out into the garden.

It was slightly cooler but there was no breeze, and Gilda moved towards a seat that was beneath one of the trees on which there were several Chinese lanterns.

"Can I get you a drink?" her partner enquired.

"Thank you," Gilda replied, "a glass of lemonade would be very refreshing."

He walked back towards the house, looking for a servant, and Gilda opened her reticule to take out her handkerchief.

She had found that Heloise had a small reticule to match every one of her gowns. They were only little bags made of the same material as the gown, but usually trimmed with lace and ribbons which made them very pretty.

She had just drawn out a tiny lace-trimmed handkerchief which was embroidered with her sister's initial when she heard a low whisper behind her say:

"Drop your reticule!"

For a moment she felt she could not have heard aright.

Then the whisper came again.

"Drop it, I say!"

She was so surprised that she did as she was told, pushing it off her knee.

A second later a gentleman came forward, saying in a clear voice:

"Allow me, Miss Wyngate!" and picked the reticule up from the grass on which it had fallen.

Gilda looked at him, thinking that she had never seen him before.

He was young, dark, and quite good-looking, but there was nothing particularly distinguished about him.

He handed her the reticule with what was almost a flourish, and she said automatically as she took it:

"Thank you very much!"

"It is a pleasure!" he replied.

He bowed to her with a graceful courtesy and walked away, vanishing into the crowd who were now coming from the Ball-Room in search of fresh air.

Gilda stared after him in bewilderment.

She found it difficult to believe that she had actually heard the whisper which had told her to drop her reticule to the ground.

There seemed to be no point in it.

Then as she replaced her handkerchief in the small bag she realised that there was something at the bottom of it which had not been there before.

She could feel that it was narrow and hard, but before she could investigate further her partner returned, a servant behind him carrying a silver salver on which were two glasses.

Instantly Gilda closed her reticule by pulling the ribbons tight, and placed it over her arm where it had been before while she was dancing, and accepted a glass of lemonade from the salver.

Her partner took the other glass, which was filled with champagne, and sat down beside her.

"Do I need to tell you that you are undoubtedly the most beautiful person here?" he asked. "But of course you must get bored with hearing that."

"Not really," Gilda replied, "only surprised when there are so many beautiful women present."

She thought as she spoke that she had grown quite clever at treating compliments lightly, as if she were used to them, and did not behave as might be expected of a country girl who had never received one before.

They continued their conversation for a few minutes, but Gilda could not help thinking how much more interesting it would have been if she had been talking with the Marquis.

She wondered what he was saying to the Princess de Lieven, with whom she had seen him talking before she left the Ball-Room.

The Princess was noted for her wit, and Gilda thought dismally that she would never be able to interest the Marquis in the same way.

Then she asked herself why she should be so anxious to interest him, and was afraid of the answer.

The music had started again and she rose to her feet.

"I suppose," her partner said, "it is useless to ask you if you will dance with me again?"

"Perhaps later in the evening," Gilda replied, knowing she was booked for at least the next six dances.

They went towards the house, but instead of going in through the Drawing-Room window she changed her mind and deliberately went in through a door.

A number of the guests were returning to the house that way, and Gilda was sure they were heading for the Supper-Room.

The crowd pressed in round her and she realised that her partner was no longer beside her. Suddenly she was aware of a sharp pull on the ribbons of her reticule, which was over her left arm.

She put out her free hand to draw it close to her, and as she did so the pull came again, this time sharper than it had been at first.

She looked round and saw that behind her there was a tall, rather distinguished-looking man, and felt that it could not be he who was pulling at her bag.

It was difficult to turn in such a crowd and she had only a fleeting glance of him before her right hand touched her bag, but at the same time she found to her astonishment that his hand was on it too.

She gave an exclamation of surprise, and immediately he withdrew his hand, saying as he did so: *"Pardon."*

Then he seemed to be swallowed up in the crowd.

Gilda moved forward and a moment later was back in the magnificent Hall with the staircase in front of her.

She hurried up it and went to the room where she had left her and her Godmother's wraps when they had arrived before dinner.

The bed was now piled with elegant cloaks, shawls, furs, and stoles.

There was a maid in attendance who curtseyed when she entered, and there was a lady sitting at the dressing-table.

Gilda passed through the bedroom into another, smaller room where there were also cloaks on the bed, but here there was no maid in attendance.

She went to the wash-hand-stand and, with her back to the open door behind her, opened her reticule.

She knew it was impossible to go on dancing without satisfying her curiosity as to what the strange gentleman who had whispered to her had placed inside.

She drew out first her handkerchief, then beneath it she saw a very small roll which appeared to be made of writing-paper.

She looked at it, wondering what it could possibly be, and it struck her that it might be a love-letter written to Heloise by the gentleman who had placed it there, but he was of course unknown to Gilda.

The small roll, little thicker than one of Gilda's fingers, was sealed with a wafer such as was used on letters.

Carefully she removed it and undid what was, as she suspected, just a piece of writing-paper.

It was inscribed in such minute lettering that she found it difficult to read what was written. Then as she held it in the candlelight she managed to decipher the words:

H.M.S. Dreadnought *has been laid up.*
H.M.S. Endeavour *in dock.*
H.M.S. Invincible *leaves for the West
Indies on May 15th.*

Gilda stared in astonishment at what she had read. Then there was a space and she read on:

. *Two Battalions of King's Dragoon Guards
move to Dover on May 11th.
One Battalion of Dragoon Guards at
present on manoeuvres at Folkestone.*

Gilda looked curiously at what was written.

Suddenly an idea came to her which was so horrifying that she felt the small piece of paper tremble in her hand.

There was another message a little farther down but she did not stop to read it.

Instead she rolled the paper back as it had been before and pressed the wafer into place.

Then she wondered frantically what she should do.

She heard voices in the next room and quickly replaced the tiny roll in her reticule.

As she did so, she realised that there was another piece of paper flat on the bottom of the bag, which she had not touched before.

She pulled it out and opened it, and then she saw, incredibly and unbelievably, that it was a note for one hundred pounds!

For a moment it was impossible to breathe!

Then as she crinkled the note and pushed it back into her reticule she knew why her sister had so much money in her jewel-box and what the paper she had just read meant.

She remembered how her father used to tell her of spies who carried information to the enemy and who were always a menace to any Commander who wanted to move his troops into position without being detected.

It was apparently an operation at which her father had excelled, and he also had had what seemed to be almost a "sixth sense" in his ability to detect amongst his own men those who were traitors and who were prepared to accept bribes.

"I flatter myself," the General had said, "that I have never made a mistake and have never punished an innocent man unfairly."

At the same time, Gilda realised what harm could be done and how many lives lost if the enemy was aware of the strength of the forces against them and where they were being deployed.

When the Armistice had come, even among those living in the country there had been some who said they did not trust Napoleon's overtures of friendship and were quite certain he was "up to no good."

Gilda did not have to be very perceptive to guess that what had been put in her reticule was in fact information for the French.

That her sister had been a messenger between the man who had whispered to her to drop her reticule and the other who had tried to take it from her in the crowd was horrifying.

Yet it was a clever idea, with the two men closely concerned never in contact with each other, and the only communication between them the pretty reticule of a young girl.

"How could Heloise do . . . anything so . . . abominable, so . . . wicked?" Gilda asked herself.

Then she wondered frantically what she should do
now that she knew her sister's secret, and worse still, she
was left in possession of the vital information.

For a moment she wished frantically that she had let
the reticule drop to the ground as the man who pulled
it expected, instead of holding on to it tightly.

He doubtless would have picked it up in the same cour-
teous manner and handed it back to her and nobody
would have thought there was anything strange about it.

Had he now gone away discomfitted? Or would he
approach her again?

Suddenly Gilda was very frightened.

She had not listened to her father without realising
how ruthless an enemy could be when it concerned
important information, and downstairs he would be
waiting for her.

Then she knew that whatever the dangers she ran
personally, whatever terrors she might experience, they
were completely unimportant beside the necessity that
the secrets of the country should not pass into the
hands of the enemy.

"What . . . shall I . . . do? What shall I do?" she asked
herself.

Suddenly she knew the answer.

She would take the roll she had received to the Marquis.

For a moment she felt overwhelmed with relief that
she had found a solution. Then she remembered it was
not as easy as that.

He would undoubtedly question her closely as to how
and why it should happen to her. How could she possibly tell him that the message recording the movements
of British ships and Regiments was accompanied by a
note for one hundred pounds?

It meant that Heloise was accepting money for taking
part in espionage against England, and this, unless she
was mistaken, was a criminal offence for which she
could be shot as a traitor.

Gilda felt herself tremble at the thought of facing the interrogation that was inevitable if she got in touch with the Marquis.

What was more, she could give no answer to his questions without not only incriminating her sister but being forced to admit that she had deceived him and Lady Neyland by taking Heloise's place.

'I cannot do that,' she thought.

She realised frantically that time was passing. If she did not quickly take action of some sort, the Marquis might think it strange that she was not in the Ball-Room and send somebody in search of her.

"What . . . shall I do? What shall I . . . do?" she asked herself again.

She felt there must be an answer to her problem, but she could not imagine what it could be.

The maid came into the room to look for a wrap which lay on the bed, and Gilda picking up her reticule from the wash-hand-stand walked through the other bedroom and out into the passage.

As she did so a servant came out of a door which was almost opposite, and Gilda knew by the way he was dressed that he was a Valet.

On his arm he was carrying a coat which she thought she recognised as one worn by the Marquis.

In his hand he had a pair of highly polished Hessian boots.

The man saw Gilda looking at him, and shutting the door behind him he made a respectful bow of his head and passed on down the passage.

Gilda stood still until he was out of sight.

Then looking round and seeing that there was no-one in sight, she swiftly opened the door of the room from which the Valet had just emerged and went inside.

As she had suspected, it was undoubtedly the Marquis's bedroom.

There was a large four-poster bed hung with red silk, the Staverton coat-of-arms embroidered over the head of it.

She had time for only a very quick look in the light of the candles burning on a dressing-table.

Opening her reticule, she drew out both the roll of paper and the hundred-pound note, and hurrying swiftly to the bedside she thrust them as far as she could reach under the turned-back sheet down the middle of the bed.

Then she opened the door again and slipped back into the passage.

It had taken her only a few seconds, but as she hurried down the staircase and back into the Ball-Room she felt as if she had passed through a traumatic experience which had taken hours.

A gentleman was waiting for her and he reproached her because he thought she had forgotten their dance.

When he took her onto the dance-floor Gilda looked round for the Marquis, wondering what he would think if he knew what had happened.

He was talking to an elderly man and she longed to run to his side and tell him how frightened she was.

Supposing the man who had tried to pull the reticule off her arm was watching her?

When the dance was over she went to Lady Neyland's side.

"You are enjoying yourself, dearest?" her Godmother asked.

"It is a lovely party," Gilda said, "but I think it is time, Godmama, that you returned home. I am sure the Doctors would not approve of your being up so late, or rather I should say 'so early,' as it must be long after midnight."

Lady Neyland laughed.

"I feel as if I were a débutante and you my worried Mama!"

"That is exactly what you are!" Gilda replied with a smile. "And you must not get over-tired."

Lady Neyland protested a little half-heartedly that it was too early to leave, and Gilda's partners with whom she had promised to dance protested vehemently.

They had no idea that she was afraid to leave the safety of the Ball-Room, and although she could not see the man who had pulled at her bag in the crowd, she sensed that he was somewhere near, waiting so that he could get her in a quiet place and demand what was no longer in her keeping.

She did not in fact feel safe until the Marquis had seen them into Lady Neyland's carriage and they were driven away back towards Curzon Street.

As Lady Neyland went into the carriage first, the Marquis asked Gilda:

"You have enjoyed yourself?"

"It has been a wonderful evening!" she replied.

He looked at her in the light of the flares which the linkmen were holding outside the house and asked unexpectedly:

"What is worrying you?"

He was too perceptive, Gilda thought. At the same time, she had the feeling that he stood for safety and security in a world that was suddenly, frighteningly menacing.

She did not answer his question, and he said quickly:

"I will see you tomorrow," and helped her into the carriage.

As Gilda led her Godmother up the stairs of her house in Curzon Street, Lady Neyland said:

"I have never known the Marquis to be so kind or so considerate. I always thought he was a hard man, but now I have a very different impression."

Gilda did not speak and Lady Neyland went on:

"Lord Hawkesbury was telling me tonight how clever he is and how he admires him more than any other young man in the *Beau Ton*. That is a great compliment from the Secretary for Foreign Affairs."

Gilda drew in her breath.

"He was there tonight?" she questioned.

"Yes, of course. His Lordship was sitting beside me for a long time. You must remember him. He came to luncheon about three months ago before my eyes became bad."

"Y-yes . . . of course," Gilda said quickly.

"He gave me an impression of the Marquis quite different from what I had thought of him before," Lady Neyland went on.

They reached the landing at the top of the stairs, and as Gilda led Lady Neyland towards her bedroom she said:

"I think I have changed my mind, dearest. Perhaps he would make you a good husband, especially if he loves you."

Gilda did not answer, and as Anderson started to take off Lady Neyland's tiara she kissed her Godmother good-night and went to her own room.

Only then did she feel as if those last words were echoing in her mind.

"If he loves you!"

She gave a little laugh that was more of a sigh.

He was never likely to do that!

She could not help feeling that it would be very, very wonderful to be loved by the Marquis, but it would be something which would never happen to her.

She knew that Heloise had wanted him because he was rich, because he had a great position in Society, and because of his vast possessions.

Thinking of him as she stood still in the centre of her bedroom, Gilda knew that none of those things mattered.

That the Marquis was a man was all that concerned her, and like a blinding light shining from the Heavens she knew that as a man she loved him.

It seemed ridiculous, absurd, something she had been quite certain would never happen, yet when as she stepped into the carriage he had said: "I will see you tomorrow," she had felt her heart turning a somersault.

The worry in her mind vanished, to be replaced with a strange excitement that came from within her breast.

He wanted to see her, and whatever other horrors might be lurking in the shadows, waiting for her, she would be able to see him.

She walked across her bedroom to sit down on the stool in front of the dressing-table as if her legs would no longer carry her.

"How can this have happened?" she asked herself. "How can I have fallen in love with somebody who is as far away from me as the moon?"

She thought she had known ever since she came to London that Heloise's aspirations where the Marquis was concerned were absurd.

He had no intention of tying himself to a young, unimportant girl, however beautiful she might be, and what was more, he was aware that Heloise, like so many other women, was trying to trap him into marriage and their transparent manoeuvres had merely amused him.

He had saved her from Sir Humphrey, he had given a party for Lady Neyland, but he had not asked her to dance.

He had in fact made no effort to talk to her except casually when they had first arrived and again when they left.

"Why could I not have fallen in love with one of the young men who were so eager to dance with me?" Gilda asked herself, and knew the answer was that the Marquis was so different from any other man.

"I am a fool!" she told herself.

Yet when she got into bed and blew out the candles, all she could see in the darkness was the Marquis's face and all she could hear was his voice when he said:

"I will see you tomorrow."

Then she thought of what was waiting for him in his bed, and told herself that he must never, never know who had placed it there.

Somehow, whatever terrors the future might hold from the men who had used Heloise as their messenger, she must not turn to the Marquis for help.

Then because even that was unimportant beside her own feelings, she hid her face in her pillow and whispered despairingly:

"I love him!"

Dawn was just coming up over the horizon and the last evening stars were fading in the sky when the Marquis said good-bye to the last of his guests.

Everybody told him it was one of the best parties they had ever attended.

"The trouble with you, Staverton," one of his friends said, "is that you do everything better than we do, even being a host."

"Thank you!" the Marquis said with a smile.

"I am complaining, not complimenting you," his friend retorted, and they both laughed.

Lord Hawkesbury had left soon after Lady Neyland and Gilda had departed.

He had not said anything intimate to the Marquis, but when he put his hand on the younger man's shoulder as they walked towards the front door, the Marquis knew that the Foreign Secretary was tired and worried and was thinking, as he had said earlier in the day, that he was his last hope.

"It has been an enchanting evening, my dear Raleigh," the Princess de Lieven said as she left.

She and the Marquis had had a brief *affaire de coeur* the previous year.

It had been a fiery encounter between two people who enjoyed each other's brains and who knew that for both of them such a liaison was just a way of passing the time with nobody being hurt in the process.

Now they were friends, and as a friend the Princess said:

"That Wyngate child is very lovely and very well behaved. I was watching her tonight, and I thought how much she has improved since I last saw her. It is strange, but she gives the impression of being much younger than she was last year."

The Marquis looked at the Princess in surprise and she laughed.

"I am perhaps being ridiculous, but my Russian instinct tells me she has changed from what she was and she might in fact be the secret jewel you are always seeking and so far have failed to find."

The Marquis merely smiled and kissed her hand, but when she had gone he thought that it was typical of the Princess with her Russian intuition to put into words what he had been thinking himself.

When at last he could go to bed he walked up the staircase thinking that his guests had been sincere, and it had, for some reason he could not quite ascertain, been one of the best parties he had ever given.

Also, there was no doubt who had been the most outstandingly beautiful person present.

He had thought when Gilda arrived before dinner that she seemed to be enveloped with a light which came from within herself, and she had no need of jewels because the candlelight shone on the gold of her hair, and her eyes, because she was excited, were like the blue of the sea.

"She is certainly very lovely," he said to himself.

As he went to his bedroom he remembered that the evening was entirely due to her because in the first place it had been her idea that Lady Neyland should attend the Ball given by the Countess of Dorset, and it was also due to Gilda that he had suggested giving a party for Lady Neyland at his own house.

But why, he wondered, should Heloise suddenly have thought of taking her Godmother with her when there had been dozens of parties she had attended without her? And never in her conversation had she indicated that she was even aware of her Godmother's existence.

He was so puzzled that it occupied his mind the whole time his Valet was helping him undress.

Then when the man had left him the Marquis stood for a little while at the open window, watching the dawn creep up the sky and breathing in the early-morning breeze which swept away the heat of the night.

The Marquis was so strong that he did not feel particularly tired, and although he had risen early and it had been a long day, he was looking forward to his ride before breakfast.

He had taught himself when he was in the Army to sleep very little when occasion demanded, and he knew that if he had three hours now it would be enough.

Harris had blown out the light on the dressing-table and there was now only the one left beside his bed.

He closed the curtains and walked to the bed. He got in and was just about to blow out the candle when his foot struck something that felt hard.

The Marquis thought it strange and threw back the sheet he had already pulled over him to investigate.

There, lying in the centre of the bed, he saw the little roll of paper that Gilda had put there, and beside it a crumpled note.

Sitting up and pushing aside the curtain which hung between him and the lighted candle, the Marquis investigated.

❦

Lord Hawkesbury listened incredulously as the Marquis, who had been his first caller as soon as he arrived at the Foreign Office, related what he had found.

Then as he undid the roll of paper which the Marquis had handed him he exclaimed:

"I was right, Staverton! This information must have come directly from this Office, and it was in fact communicated to me by the First Lord of the Admiralty only yesterday."

"And the reference to the Regiments?" the Marquis asked.

267

"I learnt that the previous day from Lord Hobart."

"The Secretary of State for the Department of War!" the Marquis said as if he was recalling Lord Hobart's office for himself.

"Exactly!" Lord Hawkesbury said.

"It is incredible!" the Marquis said. "But, having obtained such information, why should they hand it over to me?"

"It certainly narrows the field," Lord Hawkesbury said.

"You mean it must have been somebody who was at my party?" the Marquis said.

"It makes it easier for us to eliminate them one by one," Lord Hawkesbury said.

"I have been doing that already," the Marquis replied, "and I cannot believe that there is a traitor amongst my personal friends."

"If there is a traitor," Lord Hawkesbury said, "then there is also a patriot. The person who placed this information in your bed was obviously saving it from falling into the hands of the enemy, or perhaps having a somewhat belated change of heart."

"Yes, of course," the Marquis agreed, "and I have thought that too. But it still seems clear that the information was obtained from this Office, carried by somebody unknown to my house, and placed for no possible reason I can think of in my bed, so that I should find it when I retired."

"It sounds rather like something out of a Play," Lord Hawkesbury agreed. "At the same time, you know as well as I do that it is damned serious. It brings us back to my first suspect, Rearsby, who was at your party. In fact I was very surprised to see him there."

"I invited him so that I could take a better look at him," the Marquis said. "If in fact it was Rearsby who was passing on the information, why should he then relinquish it, and to me of all people?"

"I agree there is no easy answer to that question," Lord Hawkesbury said, "but at least I am now completely convinced in my mind that Lord Rearsby is at the bottom of all this."

The Marquis was silent. Then he said:

"I am going home now to find out from my servants if they noticed anyone entering my bedroom at any time during the evening. I felt I should not question them until I had seen you."

"Quite right," Lord Hawkesbury replied. "It is important that as little as possible is said about this. At the same time, I must leave enquiries to your good sense, which has never failed us in the past."

"I must say that whatever has happened before has never been quite so strange or so unexpected," the Marquis said with a smile.

"The most important thing that you have already established, as far as I am concerned," Lord Hawkesbury said, "is that Rearsby is a thief and a traitor. But we must hold our hands and not let him be suspicious that we are on his trail until we find out who his connections are regarding this very important piece of paper."

He looked at the roll again and said angrily:

"This is just the sort of information Napoleon needs if he is to invade these shores, as he intends to do."

"At least this will not reach him," the Marquis said soothingly, and rose to his feet.

He held out his hand, saying:

"There is no need for me to emphasise, My Lord, how important it is that Lord Rearsby should not suspect that we are on his track. If he learns from the intended recipient that this information has not been received, then he may try again, in which case we will be able to apprehend him at once and stop another spy from accomplishing the destruction of our country."

"That is Napoleon's whole aim and object," Lord Hawkesbury said sharply, "and if you and I can prove conclusively what is happening, perhaps it will wake even the Prime Minister out of his lethargy."

"We can only hope so," the Marquis agreed.

As he drove away from the Foreign Office he was wondering which of his servants he should question first, and decided that Harris, his Valet, should be the one.

Accordingly when he arrived home in Berkeley Square, he went to the Library and sent a servant for Harris.

The Valet had been with him for over ten years and he came into the room with a slightly cocky air about him which the Marquis knew meant that he was worried in case something had gone wrong.

"Your Lordship sent for me?" he asked.

"Yes, Harris. I need your help."

He realised that the man relaxed a little, but he did not speak, and the Marquis went on:

"Last night somebody went into my bedroom during the party and left a note for me. Unfortunately it was not signed, and I am anxious to know who wrote it."

"Left a note for you, M'Lord?" Harris questioned. "I never saw it."

"It was in my bed," the Marquis said.

Harris gave an exclamation of surprise.

"I'll lock the door in the future, M'Lord, when there's anyone strange in the house. It's not right that these young ladies who are always chasing you should walk in and out of the rooms as if they owned the place!"

The Marquis was amused to think how fiercely protective his Valet was of anything that concerned him personally.

"Well, it has happened," the Marquis said, "and it is embarrassing for me to receive *billets-doux* and not know who wrote them."

"That might be any number of ladies, M'Lord," Harris said.

This was an obvious impertinence and the Marquis frowned. Then there was silence before Harris said:

"I think I've got an idea as to who it was as wrote to Your Lordship."

"You have, Harris?" the Marquis enquired.

Harris nodded his head.

"I was just taking Your Lordship's things downstairs last night when I sees a lady standing in the doorway of the room opposite."

The Marquis was listening intently and the Valet was aware of it.

"Very pretty she looked, too, M'Lord. She stops when she sees me, an' I thinks as how she looked interested in what I was holdin' on my arm."

The Marquis was well aware that Harris liked to tell a story in his own way, and to encourage him he asked the obvious question.

"What were they, Harris?"

"Your riding-coat, M'Lord, and your new pair of Hessians which I had a job to get polished right."

"And who was this lady you thought was watching you?" the Marquis asked.

"The prettiest of any of the ladies as have come to the house in the past, M'Lord," Harris said, "and they was saying downstairs last night as how there was no-one to touch her in the Ball-Room."

The Marquis waited and Harris finished:

"I'm speaking, M'Lord, of Miss Wyngate!"

"I thought you might be," the Marquis replied, "and you really think it was she who left the *billet-doux* for me to find?"

"It must have been," Harris replied, "but nobody's had the impudence 'til now to place them in Your Lordship's bed."

The Marquis frowned again.

Then after what seemed a long pause he asked:

"You noticed nobody else who might have been responsible?"

"No, M'Lord. There was nobody else about at the time, and when I leaves her she was still standing in the open door where the cloaks was left."

"Thank you, Harris, for your help. That will be all," the Marquis said sharply.

When he was alone he sat thinking of the information his Valet had given him and found it incredible.

How could Heloise Wyngate possibly be mixed up in something like this?

His frown deepened as he remembered that when she had been frightened by Sir Humphrey Grange and he had entered the Drawing-Room of Lady Neyland's house, she had run to him for protection.

When she clung to him he had felt her tremble against him convulsively and had realised how frightened she was.

And last night, when he had said good-bye to her, he had thought that she looked worried, and there may have been an expression of fear in her eyes.

The Marquis turned the idea over in his mind. Then he told himself that she had been afraid and once again had turned to him for protection.

He sat for a long time thinking it over, determined to do nothing in a hurry.

Then he knew it would be best for him to talk to Heloise when she would be expecting him, which would be immediately after luncheon when her Godmother went to lie down.

It seemed a long time to wait, but the Marquis told himself it was the sensible thing to do, though he knew it would seem to him even longer than the two or three hours involved.

But it mattered—it mattered to him tremendously— that Heloise should not be involved in what was undoubtedly a very unsavoury mess.

Thinking back, he remembered, because unconsciously he had been watching her, that she had not come back into the Ball-Room until the dance before she and Lady Neyland left was already half-finished.

He had noticed her absence because she had danced every previous dance from the beginning until the end.

He had thought how graceful she was and how very lovely in her youthful simplicity, compared to the other women in the room, who were all much older.

He had in fact invited no other young girl. Yet he knew it was not only Heloise's youth which made her

stand out, but the excitement in her very expressive
eyes, the smile on her lips, and the way every movement
she made seemed to express a joy that came from her
heart.

Then she had come back into the Ball-Room where
her partner had been waiting for her for some minutes.

That must have been when, according to Harris, she
was upstairs.

She had then suggested to her Godmother that they
should leave, and when he said good-night to her she
had seemed worried.

It all fitted neatly into the puzzle which the Marquis
was turning over in his mind, but he knew he had not
unravelled the whole truth as to how or why Heloise was
involved.

Where had she found the incriminating piece of
paper? Or if she had been handed it unexpectedly, then
why had she not brought it to him directly?

Why had she gone to the trouble, and indeed taken
the somewhat reprehensible step, of going into his bedroom and slipping it under the bed-clothes?

She had known he would find it there, and she must
have realised he would know the significance of its contents.

It seemed to be the act of somebody very stupid, but
Heloise was not stupid.

The Marquis suddenly struck his clenched fist down
hard on his desk.

"Dammit!" he said aloud. "I will get to the bottom of
this!"

Then as he heard his own voice vibrate round the
room, he knew he would do everything in his power to
prevent Heloise from being involved.

CHAPTER SEVEN

s they finished luncheon, Lady Neyland said: "I admit to being tired today and am looking forward to a rest."

"We were very late," Gilda answered with a smile.

"I know, but it has done me good," Lady Neyland replied. "I feel quite different, and I am sure when the Doctor comes tomorrow he will say I can take off my bandage."

"You must not do anything too quickly," Gilda warned.

"I promise you I shall be careful," Lady Neyland replied, "and if I am able to see again, I shall be very, very grateful for my eyes."

"Mama always said we were never grateful enough for the things God gave us."

"I was thinking about your mother this morning," Lady Neyland said, "and how fond I was of her. I was also wondering if you ever hear from your sister."

Gilda was very still.

"My . . . sister?" she asked after a moment.

"You told me," Lady Neyland went on, "that she had gone to live with relatives in the far North. Surely she writes to you?"

Gilda drew in her breath.

"I have not heard from her for . . . some time," she answered.

When she had taken Lady Neyland upstairs to rest, she knew she had been hurt once again by Heloise's indifference and dislike of her.

The truth was that her sister had been afraid that Lady Neyland might want to include her in some of the parties and Balls to which she was invited and had therefore disposed of her unwanted relation by putting her out of reach.

"How could she have been so unkind after all we were to each other as children?" Gilda asked herself.

Then she knew it was no use being hurt over something which could not be remedied.

She did not want to think of Heloise's unkindness and selfishness but rather to remember how pretty she had been as a little girl when they had played together in the garden and shared their dolls.

When Gilda had left Lady Neyland in her room, she went down to the Salon knowing that once again there would be a number of flowers to arrange.

It was a task she had taken over from the housemaids, who disliked flower-arranging and said they had no time for it.

"It's most kind of you, Miss, to do it," they had said gratefully.

One of her admirers of the evening before had sent her a huge bouquet of lilies and another one of roses that were just coming into bloom.

Gilda carried the flowers into the Drawing-Room where a footman had already left two vases ready for her and filled them with water.

The sunshine was coming through the open windows, and having arranged the roses she was standing with an armful of lilies when the door opened and somebody came into the room.

She turned her head, then felt her heart leap as something came alive to vibrate through her whole body.

It was the Marquis, and because he had not been announced it was almost a shock to see him.

For a moment she could not move, and the Marquis looking at her with her hair haloed in the gold of the sun and the lilies in her arms thought she might have just stepped out of a stained-glass window.

"I thought I would find you alone at this time," he said in a deep voice.

He walked towards her and only when he reached her did Gilda manage to take her eyes from his and drop him a small curtsey.

"I must . . . thank Your Lordship for a . . . wonderful party last night . . ." she began in a hesitating little voice, wondering why it was so difficult to speak and thinking that he must hear the frantic beating of her heart.

"I want to talk to you."

She put the lilies down on the table and smoothed down her gown a little nervously as she walked towards the sofa.

She seated herself on the edge of it and looked up at the Marquis enquiringly.

It was then that she realised he was looking serious, with a slight frown between his eyes, and she wondered if he was annoyed about anything.

There was silence as if he was feeling for words. Then abruptly, so that his words rang out almost like a report from a pistol, he asked:

"Why did you leave that incriminating piece of paper in my bed last night?"

His question was so unexpected that it took Gilda completely by surprise.

For a moment she stopped breathing. Then the colour swept up her face in a crimson tide which proclaimed her guilt without words.

Because she could think of nothing to refute his accusation, she bowed her head and was silent until the Marquis said:

"I am waiting for an answer to my question!"

"H-how did you . . . know it was I . . . who put it . . . there?" Gilda asked, and her voice was so low that it was almost impossible to hear what she said.

"My Valet saw you upstairs at a time when you were not in the Ball-Room," he replied, "and I cannot think of anybody else amongst my friends who would be involved in anything so reprehensible."

Gilda lowered her head even farther.

She felt that he was condemning her and after this would never speak to her again. She would have to go away, perhaps back home, but anyway into obscurity.

Then in a very different tone of voice the Marquis asked quietly:

"Will you tell me what happened?"

Gilda thought there was nothing else she could do but tell him the truth.

"Someone . . . a man . . ." she said a little incoherently, "when I was sitting in the . . . garden told me to . . . drop my . . . reticule."

"You obeyed him?"

"He told me twice in a whisper . . . and I do not know why . . . but I did as he said."

"Then what happened?"

"He picked it up and . . . gave it . . . back to me, and when I . . . thanked him he said it was . . . a pleasure and . . . walked away."

"Do you know who he was?"

"No . . . I had never . . . seen him . . . before."

There was a pause. Then the Marquis asked:

"Did you realise he had put something into your reticule?"

"Only a few minutes later . . . when I replaced my . . . handkerchief in it."

"You were not expecting anything of this kind to happen?"

The question was sharp, as if, Gilda thought, he suspected that she was not telling the truth.

"No . . . of course . . . not!" she answered. "How could I . . . imagine anything like that would . . . occur at a . . . party given by . . . you?"

"Or at any other party, I should imagine," the Marquis added ironically.

"No . . . of course . . . not!"

"You swear to me," he said, "that you had no idea when this happened what this strange man had put inside your reticule?"

"None . . . whatever."

"What happened after that?

Because she was frightened it took Gilda some time to relate that her dancing-partner had returned with a servant carrying lemonade for her and champagne for him.

As the music had started again they had walked back to the house.

"I felt there was something hard in my reticule," she said, "and I decided to go . . . upstairs and see what it was. Then in the . . . crowd I suddenly felt the ribbons on my arm tighten . . ."

It was difficult to go on, but after a moment she continued:

"I . . . I thought my bag was just being . . . caught by someone moving . . . beside me, until it . . . happened again. Then when I tried to hold . . . on to it with my right hand, I . . . touched a man's fingers!"

"What man?" the Marquis enquired.

"I do not . . . know."

"You saw him?"

"Yes . . . yes . . . I turned my head . . . he was tall with a high forehead . . . but I only had a quick . . . glimpse of him."

"Did he speak to you?"

For a moment Gilda could not remember. Then she answered:

"He said '*Pardon*' and . . . disappeared."

"Then what did you do?"

"I went upstairs to the . . . bedroom where I had left my . . . wrap when I arrived . . ."

"And opened your reticule!"

"Y-yes."

"What did you think when you looked inside?" the Marquis asked.

"For a moment . . . I did not . . . understand," Gilda said in a very low voice. "Then when I read about the . . . ships and the . . . movement of the troops, I was sure that what I was . . . carrying was . . . information that could be useful to the . . . enemy . . ."

Her voice died away as she said the last words, and she thought nothing could be more humiliating than to have to confess to the Marquis that she had been involved even inadvertently in enemy espionage.

"So you were perceptive enough to understand the importance of what had been placed in your reticule?" the Marquis asked.

She thought by the way he spoke that he was accusing her not only of being aware of the seriousness of what was written on the piece of paper but also of having been somehow instrumental in its being there.

"I swear to . . . you," she said, "I swear by . . . everything I hold . . . holy, that I have no . . . idea why this should . . . happen or what I was . . . supposed to do . . . about it."

Even as she spoke she knew that was untrue.

She was aware why she had been chosen and that it was because the spies or traitors, whatever they were, had thought her to be her sister.

With a sense of horror she remembered the jewel-case upstairs at the bottom of her wardrobe with its sovereigns at the bottom of it and the letter from the Bank saying how much money was deposited in Heloise's name.

It was Heloise's money—money she had obtained by betraying her own country—which might cost the lives of English soldiers and sailors, and even perhaps eventually English civilians like themselves.

Because the idea was so horrifying Gilda rose to her feet.

The Marquis looked at her face and saw it was deathly pale, and as she stood beside him she asked:

"What . . . could I do? How could I . . . explain to . . . anybody what had . . . occurred?"

"So you hid the incriminating papers in my bed," he said slowly. "Why did you not give them to me?"

She looked away from him, knowing that she could not tell him the truthful answer to that question.

"I was afraid."

"Afraid of me, or afraid that you would be discovered with such papers in your possession and be brought to trial?"

His voice sounded hard and Gilda gave a little cry of sheer terror.

"Are you . . . saying that I shall be arrested?"

He did not answer and she gave a little sob and covered her face with her hands.

"I am . . . frightened . . . please . . . please . . . help me," she begged.

Then suddenly, as the Marquis did not reply, she looked up at him with the tears running down her face and asked:

"You are . . . not saying that I could be . . . hanged . . . or shot as a . . . s-spy?"

Because the idea was so terrifying and she thought the Marquis's expression was as grim as that of a Judge, she threw herself against him as she had done before and hid her face against his shoulder.

"S-save me . . . please . . . save me!" she sobbed. "It is not only that I am . . . afraid of . . . d-dying . . . but as Papa's daughter . . . how could I . . . disgrace him?"

Her words tumbled over one another, and as the Marquis felt her tremble against him convulsively as she had done before, he put his arm round her as if to support her.

In her misery Gilda just sobbed with her face against his shoulder, until after a little time he said very quietly:

"Stop crying! You came to me for protection, and I will protect you."

Gilda controlled her tears but she did not move away from him. She only held on to him as if comforted by the strength of his arm and the fact that she was close against his chest.

"C-can you . . . save . . . me?" she asked after a moment, her voice breaking on the words.

"I will save you," the Marquis said, "but I agree with you that it would be intolerable for your father's good name, which is venerated by those who served with him,

280

to be dragged in the filth and shame which an enquiry would involve."

The relief of what he said made Gilda feel so weak that she thought she might fall to the ground.

Without being conscious of what she was doing, she moved even closer, as if only by doing so could she lose the terror which still left her trembling.

"But the only way I can help you," the Marquis said, "is if you tell me the whole and absolute truth."

He felt Gilda stiffen and went on:

"There is no other way by which I can sift the facts and extricate you from the position in which, perhaps through no fault of your own, you have become involved."

He thought that Gilda was very tense and after a moment he asked beguilingly:

"Will you not trust me?"

There was a pause before Gilda said:

"I . . . want to do so . . . but I . . . I am . . . afraid."

"Of me?"

"Of what you . . . might think."

There was a faint smile on the Marquis's lips which Gilda did not see as he asked:

"Does it matter to you what I think?"

"Of . . . course it . . . matters."

"Why?"

The question was sharp, and Gilda felt it was almost like an arrow piercing into the very depths of her being.

Now she was trembling again, but it was different from the way she had trembled before.

Unexpectedly the Marquis put his hand under her chin and turned her face up to his.

He looked down at her cheeks wet with tears, her lips quivering, and her blue eyes too shy to meet his.

It was impossible, he thought, for any woman to look more lovely or appealing, and he felt she was little more than a child.

"Tell me," he said, "why it matters to you what I think and feel about you."

She would have turned her face away again, but his fingers held her chin and made it impossible for her to do so.

She could only look up at him helplessly, thinking that he must see the love in her eyes and know that she was acutely conscious of his lips so near to hers.

"Tell me," the Marquis said again insistently, and it was a command.

Because she was so bemused, so frightened, and her will seemed to have snapped under the strain of his questioning, she told the truth.

"It is . . . because I . . . love you!" she said. "I . . . I know I have . . . no right to do so . . . but I cannot . . . help it."

"Just as I cannot help loving you," the Marquis said, and his lips came down on hers.

For a moment Gilda thought it could not be true and that she had died and was in Heaven.

Then the wonder of the Marquis's kiss and his lips on hers made her feel as if the darkness and fear were all left behind, and he carried her into the sunshine and up into the very heart of the sun.

It was so perfect, so rapturous, that she felt as if they were no longer two human people but one with the angels and with the music of a celestial choir singing all round them.

Then when she felt that no-one could feel such rapture, such joy, such wonder, and still live, the Marquis raised his head, and after an incoherent little sound Gilda said:

"I . . . love you! . . . I love you! I never knew . . . anyone could . . . be so . . . wonderful!"

Then, as if it was too much for her, she hid her face against him and felt the tears running once more down her cheeks.

The Marquis did not speak for a moment. Then he said in a voice that sounded strange:

"Tell me what you felt when I kissed you."

"How can I . . . express it in . . . words?" Gilda asked, and her voice held a rapturous note that no-one had ever heard before.

"I made you happy?" the Marquis said.

"I did not . . . know that a . . . kiss could be . . . like the sunshine . . . the flowers . . . a blessing from God . . ."

The Marquis, listening, knew that she was speaking her thoughts out loud.

"It is the first time you have been kissed?" he asked.

"How could . . . anyone . . . else make me feel . . . like that?" she asked.

The Marquis's arms tightened round her. Then he said:

"That is what I hoped it was, and since you love me, my beautiful one, how soon shall we be married?"

Gilda was very still.

Then, almost as if the glory of the sunshine he had given her with his lips vanished out of sight, she came back to clear, stark reality.

"Oh . . . no!" she said. "I . . . I cannot . . . marry . . . you!"

"Why not?"

Gilda thought wildly before she said:

"For one reason . . . you are too grand . . . too important to marry . . . somebody like . . . m-me."

"That is for me to decide," the Marquis said, "and since, as you are doubtless unaware, this is the first time I have ever asked anybody to marry me, I have no intention of being refused."

"B-but you . . . must be!" Gilda said quickly.

Now she raised her head from his shoulder.

"I . . . I cannot explain . . . I cannot tell you why . . . and it is the most . . . marvellous . . . glorious thing that ever happened to me that you should . . . ask me to be your . . . wife . . . but I have to . . . say 'no.' "

She moved away from him and walked towards the window almost as if she needed the air to go on breathing.

Having reached it, she held on to the window-sill, knowing that in refusing the Marquis she had closed the gates of Heaven against herself and never again would she know the glory and rapture he had given her with his kiss.

When he spoke she started because she had not realised he had followed her to the window and was just behind her.

"I asked you to trust me," he said quietly.

"I . . . do trust you, I would . . . trust you . . . with my . . . life!"

"Then what is the secret you are holding from me?"

Gilda drew in her breath and once again she was tense.

"W-what secret are you . . . talking about?"

"I want you to tell me that," the Marquis said.

Gilda clenched her hands together and tried desperately to think of how she could do what he asked.

As if he realised how difficult her decision was, the Marquis said:

"This morning I went to the War Office and looked up your father's record, a very distinguished record of which any country would be proud."

"I wish Papa . . . could hear you . . . say that," Gilda whispered.

"The records also told me," the Marquis went on, "that your mother is dead and that your father left two daughters."

As he spoke Gilda felt as if the ceiling had suddenly crashed onto her head and the whole room was dark.

She could not speak, for her voice was constricted in her throat. Then the Marquis asked:

"What has happened to Heloise? For I am quite certain that you are Gilda!"

There was a terrifying silence until Gilda asked:

"H-how did you . . . guess?"

He smiled.

"Because you are very different from your sister. Ever since you returned to London after running away from my dinner-party, you have puzzled, intrigued, and surprised me, and I could not understand why you had changed."

Gilda bent her head.

"Heloise . . . died! She came . . . home to . . . stay, and died of an . . . overdose of laudanum . . . so I took her . . . place."

"Why?"

"Because I had . . . no money . . . and if I had . . . stayed on as Heloise told me to . . . do, I would have . . . starved."

As she spoke she thought it sounded a feeble, unconvincing excuse, and it seemed when she spoke of it a very reprehensible way to behave.

The Marquis, however, did not speak, and after a moment she said:

"Now you . . . know why you cannot . . . marry somebody who . . . lied to you . . . and deceived Lady Neyland . . . after she had been so . . . kind to . . . Heloise."

"Heloise was not as kind to her as you have been."

"That is . . . partly because I . . . felt I had to make . . . reparation for my . . . sins."

"I do not think that your sister would have thought of it in quite that way," the Marquis said drily.

"But it was wrong . . . very wrong," Gilda said. "Please . . . please . . . forgive me . . . and let me go home . . . I will never . . . trouble you . . . again."

"To starve?" he enquired.

"I . . . I will manage . . . somehow."

"And you will do that without having any regrets or heart-burnings of what you are giving up?"

Gilda thought wryly of how truly heart-burning it would be to leave him and never see him again.

But regrets were something different.

Aloud she said:

"I will never . . . regret the time I . . . have been here in . . . London . . . and meeting . . . you."

"Does that matter so much?"

"Of course it . . . does. I did not know that . . . anyone like you . . . existed, and when Heloise . . . talked about you I . . . thought I . . . hated you."

"You hated me?" the Marquis echoed in surprise.

285

"I was sure, from what Heloise . . . said, that you had no . . . intention of . . . marrying her, and I thought it was . . . cruel to raise her hopes and prevent her from . . . marrying anybody . . . else."

"Like Sir Humphrey Grange?"

"He is . . . horrible!" Gilda said. "But there . . . must have been . . . other men."

"Not in the same position as I am."

"Your position is . . . unimportant."

"Do you believe that?"

"Of course I believe it! If I were going to . . . marry somebody, it would be . . . because he was . . . a man I loved. Whether he was . . . rich or poor, important or a nobody, is of no real . . . significance."

The thoughts Gilda had had about this before seemed to tumble from her lips without her really considering what she was saying.

Then she turned her back on the Marquis to stare out the window with unseeing eyes before she asked:

"Now that you . . . know the truth . . . what do you want me . . . to do?"

As she spoke she could see the vegetable-patch at home on which she must plant the food she must grow to live on, the rooms inside the house quiet and empty, and if she was afraid or lonely there would be no-one to protect her.

Then the Marquis put his hands on her shoulders and turned her round to face him.

"Shall I tell you what I want you to do?" he asked.

There was an expression in his eyes and a note in his voice which made Gilda feel that once again she was dazzled by a radiant light that came not from the sky but from him.

He did not wait for her answer, but said:

"We are going to be married immediately, my lovely one, and there will be no spies to frighten you, no secrets that you dare not reveal, no starvation or loneliness, only me. Is that what you want?"

"B-but you . . . cannot . . . you . . . must not . . ." Gilda
began.

The Marquis pulled her close against him, and his
lips stopped her from saying any more.

Only when he had given her the sun, the moon, and
the stars and she was no longer alone but a part of him
did they both come back to earth.

"How can you make me feel like this?" the Marquis
asked. "I never thought it was possible that I could love
anybody as I love you."

"It . . . it cannot be . . . true!"

He smiled.

"It will take me a long time to prove it, but first, my
darling, before we plan our wedding I must solve Lord
Hawkesbury's problem and see that the spies of Napoleon Bonaparte are behind bars."

"How can you do that?" Gilda asked.

The Marquis looked down at her face radiant with an
expression he had never seen on any other woman's face.

He knew that her love came not only from her heart
but from her soul and had something spiritual about it,
very different from anything he had known before.

Then because it was impossible when he was touching her to think of anything else, he moved to the mantelpiece to stand with his back to it.

"Now let me consider what you have told me," he
said.

"I have . . . not told you . . . everything."

"No?"

"I am . . . ashamed . . . so desperately ashamed . . . but
you must . . . know."

"Know what?"

Not looking at him, because she felt so humiliated,
Gilda told him the secrets of her sister's jewel-case and
the money that was in Coutts Bank.

The Marquis's lips tightened in a straight line, and
when she had finished speaking Gilda stood looking at
him before she said in a broken little voice:

"Perhaps now . . . you will . . . cease to . . . love me."

The Marquis smiled and held out his arms and she ran towards him like a homing-pigeon.

"I shall have to teach you about love, my precious one," he said. "The real love that you and I have for each other can survive anything, however abominable."

"If you had committed a thousand murders I would still love you!" Gilda said passionately.

The Marquis did not kiss her but put his cheek against hers and said:

"Now we have to think very seriously of everything that could give us a clue, not to the first man who put the information into your reticule, because I know who he is."

"You do?"

"Yes, he works in the Foreign Office," the Marquis replied. "But it is the recipient of this treachery who matters. Describe him once again."

"I . . . I did not get a close look at him," Gilda said with a sigh. "I just turned my head as he said '*Pardon*.' "

The Marquis gave an exclamation.

"As he said—what?"

" '*Pardon*'!" Gilda repeated.

"You are quite certain he said it in French rather than English?"

"I never thought of it before," Gilda replied, "but that is what he said."

"Then I know who he is!"

"You do?"

The Marquis nodded.

"There was only one foreigner at the party last night— the man who accompanied the Princess de Lieven because the Ambassador was otherwise engaged. He is a Russian! Now we know who our enemy is!"

"I am glad . . . so very . . . very glad!" Gilda exclaimed.

"So am I," the Marquis agreed, "for now we can think only about ourselves and our future."

He put both his arms round her and pulled her closer to him and said:

"Where do you want to live after we are married?"

288

"With you!"

The Marquis laughed.

"You may be sure of that, but I was thinking that as you are a country girl you would doubtless be happier in the country than in London."

"To be with you in the country would be the most . . . marvellous thing that could . . . happen to me."

"Then that is where we will be," he promised.

He would have kissed her, but for the moment she resisted.

"There is . . . something I want to . . . ask you."

"What is it?"

"Are you quite . . . quite certain it is really . . . me you want as your wife? I am very . . . unsophisticated and . . . ignorant of your life . . . and the Social World in which you . . . live."

She paused before she went on:

"Supposing when you marry me you find I am only a . . . pale reflection of Heloise . . . and you would have been . . . happier with her?"

Once again the Marquis turned Gilda's face up to his.

"Listen to me," he said, "and it is important that you should know the truth."

"I am . . . listening."

"I would never have married your sister because, although when I first saw her I thought she was the most beautiful person I had ever seen, I soon knew that her beauty was only superficial, and beneath such loveliness she was selfish, avaricious, and, as we both know, treacherous!"

The Marquis paused for a moment, thinking how his instinct was never wrong and he had sensed this about Heloise even though if he had said it aloud nobody would have believed him.

"What I feel about you, my dearest dear, is very different," he went on. "Your face is as beautiful as the flowers and your hair is like the sunshine. What you give me when you speak of your love is divine so that I know it comes from your soul."

Gilda gave a little cry of sheer happiness and the Marquis said:

"That is why we will not speak of the past again. You must forget your sister and make sure that everybody else forgets her too. You are not a reflection of her. She was just a pale, distorted reflection of you."

"You really . . . believe that is . . . true?"

"We will always tell each other the truth," the Marquis said, "and the truth is, my lovely Gilda, that all my life I have looked deep into women's hearts, hoping to find real love, but I never found it until I met you."

Gilda gave a little exclamation of delight and put her arm round his neck to pull his head down to hers.

"Are you . . . sure?"

"Very, very sure."

Her lips were very close to his as she whispered:

"Teach me how not to . . . disappoint you. Teach me how to be . . . everything you want me to be. I have nothing to give you . . . except my love . . . and that is . . . all of me."

"That is all I want," the Marquis said.

Then he was kissing her until once again he carried her up into the Heavens and they found a love which was so perfect that it came not only from their hearts and souls but from God.

THE CALL OF THE
HIGHLANDS

Author's Note

———— ❧ ————

"Marriage by Declaration Before Witnesses," or "Irregular Marriage," was legal in Scotland until the Act was repealed in 1949.

Until the beginning of the Eighteenth Century the Highlands stood a little apart from the rest of Scotland. The sense of isolation was engendered by feudalism, a separate language, and different forms of dress.

During the thirty-five years when not only the kilt, plaid, and pipes were banned, and of course bagpipes, the Highlanders took to carrying sticks as a substitute for the dirk. Then a shorter knife called a *skean dhu* was adopted, small enough to be concealed in a pocket or stuck in the top of a stocking.

The Celtic revival at the beginning of the Nineteenth Century was given impetus by Sir Walter Scott, and when in 1822 King George IV decided to visit his Northern Kingdom he wore the Royal Stewart tartan.

CHAPTER ONE

1803

*L*ord Alistair McDonon was having his breakfast.

That it was nearly noon was not surprising in the Social World in which he lived and excelled.

The night before he had been first at a dinner given by the Prince of Wales at Carlton House, then he had gone on with a number of other Bucks to the latest Dance-Hall, where the fairest and most alluring Cyprians in London paraded themselves.

As if this were not enough, he and his friends had finished up at a very expensive "House of Pleasure" in the Haymarket, where Lord Alistair now regretted that he had drunk too many glasses of French wine.

It was in fact more or less a normal evening.

At the same time, it was taking its toll the following morning, and Lord Alistair waved aside the well-cooked dish of sweetbreads and fresh mushrooms that his valet offered him and instead chose to eat toast and sip brandy.

However he was not thinking of his dry mouth or his aching head, but of the allurements of Lady Beverley.

Beside him on the table was a note, scented with an exotic fragrance, in which she informed him that she wished him to call on her at four o'clock that afternoon.

She wrote in an imperious manner which made it a command rather than a request, but that was understandable for a "Beauty" who had taken the ever-critical *Beau Monde* by storm.

295

The widow of a rich and distinguished land-owner in the North of England, she had come to London a year after his death, discreetly chaperoned by an elderly aunt.

Having both an impeccable reputation and a sufficiency of "blue blood," she was easily accepted by even the most strait-laced hostesses.

A new face was always an excitement in a society which had abounded in beautiful women from the time that the Prince of Wales had been captivated by the alluring actress Mrs. Robinson, and the Social World by Georgiana, Duchess of Devonshire.

Beauty had succeeded Beauty, each in the language of the St. James's Clubs "An Incomparable," and now in almost every gentleman's opinion Olive Beverley eclipsed them all.

She was certainly exquisite, with dark eyes that seemed to hold the same purple lights as those in her jet-black hair, a complexion like magnolias, and features that Lord Byron declared rivalled those of a Greek goddess.

Even the most fastidious Buck laid his heart at her feet, and although Lord Alistair disliked being one of a crowd, he finally succumbed.

Perhaps because he had been more difficult to capture than the rest, Lady Beverley had smiled on him, and finally not only was the door of her house open when he called, but so were her arms.

Despite the fact that Lord Alistair was considered a Beau and somewhat of a Dandy, he was an intelligent man.

He was well aware that his love-affair with Olive Beverley must be kept a secret, particularly from the inveterate gossips.

As the third son of a Scottish Chieftain, there was no chance of his ever succeeding to the Dukedom, and he knew that Olive was setting her sights high.

The Duke of Torchester was squiring her to the Opera, and the Marquis of Harrowby, one of the wealthiest landowners in England, drove her in the Park.

But there was no doubt that when they were alone she found Alistair McDonon irresistible as a lover, and their passion for each other had grown, perhaps because the very secrecy of their meetings added to the excitement.

It was unusual for Olive to send for Lord Alistair in the daytime.

As he took another sip of brandy, he read her letter again, wondering what she had to impart to him.

He had the uncomfortable feeling that it might be to tell him that Torchester of Harrowby had uttered the magic words she was wanting to hear and that she intended to be married.

If he had to lose her it would be upsetting, Lord Alistair thought, and he would certainly miss her while she was on her honeymoon.

But he thought, with a twist of cynicism at the corners of his mouth, that once the first novelty of being either a Duchess or a Marchioness was past, Olive would doubtless once again be eager for his kisses.

"Why do I feel differently with you than with any other man?" she had asked plaintively the night before last.

He had been waiting for her in her bedroom after a dinner at Richmond House when the Marquis had escorted her home and left her at the door, where she allowed him only to kiss her hand.

Lord Alistair had entered the house in Park Street earlier through the garden door, to which he had a key.

The French window in the Drawing-Room had been left ajar, and he had slipped upstairs after the servants had gone to bed, to lie against the lace-edged pillows of her silk-draped bed.

The exotic French perfume that Olive always used scented the air, and he was quite content to wait for her, knowing that when she came they would be fired with a passion which would consume them both.

In fact, when she did arrive it was impossible for her not to fling herself into his arms, and it was a long, long time before there was any need for words. . . .

Only when the candles by the bedside were guttering low and the first soft glow of dawn was creeping up the sky were they able to talk.

"You are very beautiful!" Lord Alistair said.

He held her close against him with one arm and touched the silkiness of her dark hair with his other hand.

He had pulled the pins almost roughly from it so that it had fallen over her naked shoulders, and now he thought it was as soft as her skin, and held him captive more effectively than any chains could have done.

"What was the party like?" he asked.

"Dull!" Olive pouted. "Everybody was very grand and the Duke rather more prosy than usual."

"I am glad I was not invited."

"All I could think of," she went on, "was that I would see you later, but I never knew that time could pass so slowly! I kept looking at the clock and thinking it must have stopped!"

"Harrowby brought you home," Lord Alistair remarked. "Did he come up to scratch?"

"He would have, if I had been a little more encouraging," Olive replied complacently, "but I was afraid if he did so it would delay my being with you."

"I am flattered!"

"Why are you not more jealous?" she asked suddenly, with an angry note in her voice. "Every other man I know, including the Duke and Arthur Harrowby, would be wildly jealous and ready to shoot you dead if they knew where I was at this moment."

Lord Alistair smiled a little mockingly.

"Why should I envy anybody?"

"I love you! I love you, Alistair!" Olive said, turning her face up to his. "Do you realise you have never said that you love me?"

"I should have thought that was obvious without words," Lord Alistair replied evasively.

He knew as he spoke that Olive was disappointed because he had said no more.

But with some peculiar quirk he could not quite explain to himself, he had made it a rule never to tell any woman he loved her until he was certain that the emotion he felt for her was something very different from the burning, fiery passion for which there was another word and which was actually more descriptive.

He knew that not only in this way but in several others he was different from his contemporaries.

It had become the fashion for gentlemen to write poetry, especially in praise of ladies they admired, and those who were able to aspire to verse wrote eloquently and endlessly of their love.

It was now quite usual to speak of "being in love" or "making love" even to Cyprians and "bits o' muslin."

Perhaps it was because Lord Alistair had been well educated that he found it impossible to degrade the English language by using words in such a context, for they meant something very different for him.

Anyway, whatever the reason, he had never yet told any woman that he loved her, and it was inevitable that the omission should be noticed and resented.

"Tell me you love me," Olive pleaded insistently, "and tell me that when I do marry anybody else it will break your heart."

"I am not certain that I have one," Lord Alistair replied. "In fact, quite a number of lovely women have been absolutely certain that it is an organ which when I was created was omitted from my body!"

"Oh, Alistair, how can you be so cruel!" Olive cried. "You are making me think that you are playing with me, and as I love you to distraction, that is something which makes me extremely miserable!"

"I doubt it," Lord Alistair said. "But why are you worrying about words? Actions are far more effective and certainly far more satisfying."

As he spoke, his hand, which had been caressing her hair, encircled the soft pillar of her neck and his lips came down on hers.

For a moment, because she was piqued by his lack of response to her appeal, she resisted him.

Then the fierce possessiveness of his kiss awoke once again the fire within her breast, which had died down, and as the flames leapt higher and higher, matching those leaping within him, it was impossible to think but only to feel a burning, unquenchable desire.

Yesterday Lord Alistair had not seen Olive, but he had known that she was meeting both the Duke and the Marquis sometime during the afternoon and evening, and he was almost certain that she would bestow her hand on one or the other.

The strawberry leaves on a Ducal coronet were very enticing, but the Marquis was very wealthy and of the two was more attractive.

But they were both, Lord Alistair ruminated, puffed up with their own consequence.

Once Olive was the wife of either of them and was gracing the end of his table and wearing the family jewels, she would become only another possession to be prized because it was his and guarded jealously for the same reason.

It struck him that a woman's life when she married was somewhat dismal.

If her husband was important enough, she was just an adjunct to him and was not expected to have any independence in thought or feeling.

He could recall a lovely woman with whom he had had a brief but very satisfying *affaire de coeur* saying:

"The men of the *Beau Monde* are all the same! They desire you in the same way that they desire a valuable painting, a Sèvres vase, or an outstanding piece of horseflesh. But once the treasure is acquired, they are looking round for something new to add to their collection!"

"You underestimate yourself!" Lord Alistair had protested, as was expected of him.

At the same time, he knew she was more or less speaking the truth, but where he was concerned there was no collection to which a lovely woman could be added.

He had enough money to be comfortable and to meet the costs which were quite considerable for a gentleman in the most extravagant and raffish society in the whole of Europe.

He had no Estate whose rents would ensure him a large annual income, but he had no great house to keep up and therefore few expenses other than the clothes he wore, his small household in London, and the two horses which he kept for riding.

Despite this, he enjoyed a life of luxury in the houses of his friends.

Every hostess needed an unattached man, especially one as handsome and distinguished as Lord Alistair, and the invitations poured into his comfortable but comparatively modest flat in Half-Moon Street.

Because of this, he had a real need of the quiet, unassuming secretary he employed for two hours every day to answer his ever-increasing correspondence.

With his secretary to arrange his appointments, his valet to wait on him, and an experienced Chef to cook his meals when he was at home, Lord Alistair's life was one to be envied.

There was not a house in England in which he was not welcome, and the very finest hunters and steeplechasers were at his disposal should he need them.

Perhaps more important, in all the great houses where he was entertained there was always a beautiful woman eager to see that he was not lonely during the night.

"I know you are not a rich man," the Prince of Wales had said to him a few weeks ago, "but dammit, Alistair, I believe you have a better life than I do!"

Lord Alistair had laughed.

"I think you could find a great number of men who would be only too eager to change places with you, Sire."

"Would you?" the Prince had asked pointedly.

Lord Alistair had shaken his head.

"No, Sire, but I know better than most people the many anxieties you have to bear and the difficulties you encounter in your private life."

"That is true, and I consider it extremely unfair," the Prince had exclaimed petulantly. "I envy you, Alistair—do you realise that I envy you?"

Lord Alistair had laughed about the conversation afterwards, but he had known exactly what the Prince meant.

He had thought then that he was extremely lucky in being free, unattached, and certainly not as emotionally unstable as the Prince.

In every love-affair, especially that with Mrs. Fitzherbert, he had indulged in every emotional crisis ever thought up by a playwright.

He had wept, stabbed himself with a knife, and threatened to kill himself if the recipient of his love did not respond.

Lord Alistair, who knew of his secret marriage to Mrs. Fitzherbert, thought that in fact the Prince was deranged to jeopardise his position as heir to the throne should it ever be revealed that he had married a Roman Catholic.

'No woman would ever matter so much to me,' he thought scornfully, 'that I would give up the chance of ruling Britain!'

It was the unrestrained effusions of the Prince of Wales that had made him more determined than ever not to express his feelings unless he believed with his whole heart that they were true.

Even in the greatest throes of passion, some critical faculty of his mind told Lord Alistair that this was an emotion that would eventually fade and die, and not the idealised love which he actually thought was unattainable.

And yet it had inspired great deeds, had been depicted by great artists, and had influenced composers of both music and poetry since the beginning of time.

Love! Love! Love!

Where was it to be found? And was it attainable by an ordinary man like himself?

He doubted it, and yet he refused to accept what he knew was spurious and put it in a shrine which as far as he was concerned would remain empty.

Nevertheless, such ideals were not allowed to interfere with his enjoyment of life, and as he looked once
again at Olive's scented note lying open on the table in
front of him, he thought that if, as he suspected, she
had chosen a husband, he would miss her.

Yet, until the day of her wedding came, he would
make every effort to enjoy the time that intervened
while she bought her trousseau and met her future relatives.

He was quite certain that Olive would not admit
either the Duke or the Marquis to her bedroom until
the ring was on her finger, while for him there was
always the garden door and the unlatched window into
the Drawing-Room.

Lord Alistair's reverie was interrupted by his valet
coming into the Dining-Room, where the Queen Anne
wall-panelling was picked out in white and gold.

It was a small room because Lord Alistair seldom
entertained more than half-a-dozen friends at the same
time, but, like his Sitting-Room which adjoined it, it was
exquisitely decorated.

This had been a present from the very lovely lady with
whom he had been enamoured nearly two years ago.

He had changed flats just as they had become lovers,
and while he could afford to give her little more than
flowers and trifles such as a fan or a little cameo brooch,
she, because her husband was immensely rich, had
expressed her feelings very generously in many different ways.

There were new horses, and very outstanding ones, in
the stables which Lord Alistair rented just off Half-
Moon Street.

There were also canes with gold handles, jewelled and
enamelled snuff-boxes, and paintings that were undis-
guisedly the envy of some of Lord Alistair's friends.

If they suspected who was responsible for them, they
were too tactful to say so.

They merely praised the amazing good taste and
admired the Rubens that hung over the fireplace in the

Sitting-Room and the Fragonard which graced the bed-room.

In the Dining-Room, the painting that drew the attention of those who ate there was a portrait of Lord Alistair himself.

It had been painted when he was a boy, and in it he was wearing the kilt, while behind him was the Castle in which he had been born, and which he had not seen since he was twelve.

Because it was one of the most striking and impressive Castles in Scotland, strangers inevitably stared at the portrait but spoke of the Castle rather than of the boy who stood in front of it.

"I have often heard of Kildonon Castle," they would say, "and it is certainly even more impressive than I thought any building could be."

They would want to say more, but Lord Alistair usually changed the subject.

He was rather sensitive about the fact that he had not been back to his native land for nearly fifteen years.

Lord Alistair's valet, Champkins, put the morning newspaper down beside his Master and picked up the dish of sweetbreads which he had not touched.

"A gentleman to see you, M'Lord!" he said. "I tells him you'll see no-one this early."

"Quite right, Champkins!" Lord Alistair replied. "I have no wish to see anybody at the moment. Tell him to come back tomorrow."

"I tells him that, M'Lord, but he said he'd come all the way from Scotland."

Lord Alistair looked at his valet in astonishment.

"Did you say from Scotland?" he asked.

"Yes, M'Lord, but he don't look Scottish to me, and he speaks English like a native."

"From Scotland!" Lord Alistair said beneath his breath. "No! That is impossible!"

"Shall I tell him to clear off, M'Lord?" Champkins asked.

There was a perceptible pause before Lord Alistair replied:

"No, Champkins. I will see him. Ask him to come in here, and I expect he would like a drink."

"He don't look to me like the drinking sort," Champkins replied with the familiarity of a servant who has looked after his Master for a long time.

"I had better find out what he wants," Lord Alistair said. "Bring him here."

Champkins looked at his Master and Lord Alistair knew he was wondering whether to suggest that he should put on his jacket rather than wear the silk robe he had on at the moment.

He was, in fact, dressed even to his high and intricately tied white cravat, with the exception of his cutaway long-tailed coat.

If there was one thing Lord Alistair thought slovenly it was the type of gentleman who breakfasted before he had dressed and received callers with his night-shirt merely covered by a robe.

Because it was not unusual for Bucks and Beaux, including even the Prince of Wales, to drop in on friends at breakfast-time, he always washed, shaved, and dressed before he saw anybody.

The omission of his coat, which was invariably tight-fitting as the fashion demanded, was the only liberty he allowed himself at breakfast-time.

But without saying what was in his mind Champkins disappeared, and a few minutes later flung open the Dining-Room door to announce in what Lord Alistair knew was his ceremonial voice:

"Mr. Faulkner, M'Lord!"

A middle-aged man with hair grey at the temples came into the room, and for a moment Lord Alistair stared at him. Then he slowly rose to his feet and held out his hand.

"I can hardly believe that it is really Andrew Faulkner!"

"I wondered if you would recognise me, My Lord."

"I feel that is what I should be saying to you," Lord Alistair replied.

"You have certainly grown," Mr. Faulkner remarked, "but I would have recognised you anywhere!"

His eyes rested for a moment on the painting over the mantelpiece, which was behind Lord Alistair's head, then back again to the man who clasped his hand.

"I might even say, without being impertinent, My Lord, that you look exactly as I would have expected you to, only more handsome!"

"Thank you!" Lord Alistair replied. "Sit down, Faulkner. Will you have some wine, or would you prefer coffee?"

"Coffee, if you please," Mr. Faulkner replied.

Lord Alistair nodded his head, and Champkins, who was waiting, immediately withdrew, closing the door behind him.

Mr. Faulkner sat down without hurry on a chair at the table, and Lord Alistair said:

"I presume you are here because you bring me news of my father? I cannot imagine that you have come all this way for just a friendly call."

"No, My Lord. I bring you news which I am afraid will both upset and distress you."

Lord Alistair did not speak. He merely raised his eyebrows; then, as if he felt he needed it, he drank a little more brandy.

Mr. Faulkner appeared to have difficulty in starting.

"It is, My Lord, with very great regret," he said at length, slowly and distinctly, "that I inform you that your elder brother the Marquis of Kildonon and your other brother, Lord Colin, were drowned four days ago in a storm at sea!"

Lord Alistair was as still as if he had turned to stone.

In fact, he just stared for a long time at Mr. Faulkner, as if he felt he could not have heard him a-right.

Then in a voice that did not sound like his own, he said:

"Ian and Colin are both dead?"

"Yes, My Lord."

"How could a thing like that possibly happen?"

"They were out fishing, My Lord, and a sudden storm blew up. One can only assume that the boat was not as sea-worthy as had been believed."

"They were alone?"

"No, there was a fisherman with them, who also died."

Lord Alistair put down his brandy glass and lifted his hand to his forehead.

"I can hardly credit that what you are saying is true."

"The bodies were washed ashore, My Lord. They are being buried today in the Family Cemetery, and a great many of the Clan will be present."

Lord Alistair knew exactly what this meant. The Clansmen would come from miles over the moors as soon as the news had reached them with a summons from the Castle.

Their Pipers would come with them to join with his father's Pipers to play their laments hour after hour on the battlements.

His brothers would be lying in state in the Chief's Room, and they would be carried in procession to the Cemetery, where the Minister would read the last rites as they were lowered into the ground.

As if he waited until the picture of what was happening in Scotland had passed before Lord Alistair's eyes, Mr. Faulkner said quietly:

"His Grace, your father, My Lord, asks you to return immediately!"

Lord Alistair sat upright.

"Return? Why?"

"Because you are now, My Lord, as you must be aware, the new Marquis of Kildonon and hereditary heir to the Chieftain of the Clan."

Lord Alistair gave a little laugh that had no humour in it.

"Not a very appropriate position for somebody who has been exiled from Scotland for fifteen years."

"You are still a Scot, My Lord."

"I am aware of that, but only by blood. My life and all my interests are now very English."

"That I can understand," Mr. Faulkner said, "but your father needs you and so do the McDonons."

"They have managed very competently without me up until now."

"Because your brothers were there, they were assured of continuity when your father died."

There was just an edge on Mr. Faulkner's words, as if he thought it strange that Lord Alistair did not see the point so clearly that there was need to explain.

There was another pause before Lord Alistair asked:

"Are you telling me, Faulkner, that my father wishes me to go back and take up my life with him as if nothing has happened?"

"It is your duty, My Lord."

"Duty! Duty!" Lord Alistair scoffed. "That word covers a multitude of sins and discrepancies. If you look at it honestly, the whole thing is impossible!"

"But why, My Lord? I do not understand."

"Of course you understand, Faulkner!" Lord Alistair contradicted. "When my mother left and took me with her, she made it quite clear that she left my father with his two elder sons, but I belonged to her. I have been brought up the way she wanted and to think the way she thought."

Lord Alistair's voice was sharp as he continued:

"Because you are a friend of the family as well as my father's Comptroller, you know as well as I do that my mother's life was a living hell until she could stand it no longer."

Mr. Faulkner made a little gesture with his hands which was very explicit before he said:

"I am not pretending, My Lord, that your father and mother, while intelligent and interesting people on their own, were together anything but incompatible. But if you will forgive me saying so, even at the time I believed that your place was in Scotland, the home of your forebears, and however Anglicised you may have become, it is still Scottish blood that runs in your veins."

"Pretty words thought up by historians!" Lord Alistair sneered. "What is more important are the thoughts in my mind, the instincts of my body, and the life I have enjoyed since I have been living in the South."

"Your brothers were content."

"Because they never knew any other existence, and doubtless never had the chance of thinking for themselves as long as they were with my father."

Mr. Faulkner did not answer for a moment and Lord Alistair was sure he had scored a point that the older man found impossible to refute.

Then Mr. Faulkner said very quietly:

"There is the Clan."

"The Clan?" Lord Alistair questioned.

"What is left of them. England has neglected, oppressed, and degraded Scotland since the Duke of Cumberland won the Battle of Culloden."

"Who cares today what the Scots think or feel?"

"Perhaps only the Scots themselves," Mr. Faulkner answered, "but nevertheless they are your people, My Lord, and they look to you for leadership in the future."

"Not while they have my father ruling over them with an omnipotence that is not enjoyed by any present-day Monarch!"

"That is true," Mr. Faulkner replied. "In Scotland, especially in the North, the Chieftain is still the leader, the father, and the shepherd of his Clan."

He paused before he said gently:

"Your father is an old man, and the Clan must be assured of a successor when he dies."

"I am sure some of my many relations will be only too willing to play the part."

"Of course," Mr. Faulkner agreed unexpectedly. "Your cousin Euan, whom you will doubtless remember, after the death of your brothers offered to take your place as your father's heir and swore allegiance to him, begging him to appoint him as the next Chieftain."

There was a sudden look of anger in Lord Alistair's eyes.

"I remember Euan well!" he said. "He was always ambitious and eager to push himself forward. What did my father say to him?"

"His Grace heard him out," Mr. Faulkner replied. "Then he said slowly and with great dignity:

" 'I have lost two sons, Euan, which is perhaps the will o' God, but I still have a third, and he is my rightful successor.' "

The way Mr. Faulkner spoke was very impressive, and there was a faint smile on Lord Alistair's lips, despite the frown on his forehead.

"I wish I could have seen my cousin's face," he remarked, "when he received the set-down he undoubtedly deserved."

"He rose to his feet," Mr. Faulkner reported, "and said:

" 'Alistair is now a Sassenach, Your Grace, and I think it unlikely he will return. If he does, you will find him a Dandy and a nincompoop, a man who is interested only in wine and women.' "

The frown deepened between Lord Alistair's eyes and his voice was hard as he asked:

"What did my father reply to that?"

"His Grace did not speak," Mr. Faulkner replied, "but merely walked from the Chief's Room, and when I followed him he told me to leave immediately for London."

There was silence and after a moment Mr. Faulkner finished:

"I came by ship because it was quicker, and I think you would find it more comfortable to travel the same way."

Lord Alistair rose to his feet.

"You are assuming that I will obey my father, but I think both you and he must realise that it is something I have no intention of doing. I may have been only twelve when I left with my mother, but she did not force me to go with her."

"I know that," Mr. Faulkner replied. "Her Grace told me that she would give you the choice."

"It was not difficult for me to make up my mind," Lord Alistair said. "I too had suffered at my father's hands. I disliked him, and I still do."

There was silence for a moment. Then Mr. Faulkner said:

"I hope it does not sound presumptuous, My Lord, when I say that whatever your feelings for him or his for you, he has been generous."

Lord Alistair stiffened, but he knew that Mr. Faulkner was speaking the truth.

When his mother had left Kildonon Castle because, as she said, it was a question of personal survival and she must either leave or die, the Duke had given her an allowance to support herself and her youngest son.

Daughter of the Earl of Harlow, she had gone home, taking Alistair with her, and had sent him first to a famous English Public School and then to Oxford.

He was brought up on the Harlow Estates in Suffolk and whenever he went to London had been able to stay at his grandfather's house in Grosvenor Square.

He had made friends and been accepted with his mother by the highest and most distinguished people in the land.

Because it all had been so new and exciting he had never for one moment missed the great Castle standing in acres of wild moorland or even his elder brothers, who had often bullied him.

When his mother had died three years ago, he had been apprehensive that he might have to change his way of living considerably if his father, who had not communicated with him in any way since he left Scotland, cut off the monies which had been paid to his wife.

It had been a great relief when he had received notice from the Duke's Attorneys that the same allowance that the Duchess had received during her lifetime would be transferred to him.

He had not written to his father personally a letter of thanks, but had asked the Attorneys to convey his gratitude.

Rather sharply, because he was perturbed, Lord Alistair asked:

"Are you saying that if I do not return, Faulkner, as my father orders, he will cut me off with the proverbial shilling?"

He knew as he waited for an answer that Mr. Faulkner was feeling for words. Then he said:

"Knowing His Grace as I do, My Lord, I think if you refuse the responsibility which your father believes is the will of God, then you will cease from that moment to be his son! He will in fact disown you!"

"And put Euan in my place!"

"There are other cousins, My Lord, but there is no doubt that Mr. Euan is the prior claimant."

Lord Alistair faced the fireplace and looked up at the painting above it of the Castle standing high above the sea, the heather-covered moors rising behind it.

As it was depicted with its turrets and towers, it was very impressive and exceedingly beautiful.

At the same time, he was well aware that he would feel dominated and threatened by his father's presence, and there would be also a sense of isolation, living in a world outside what to him was the real world and giving up everything which until now had made his life enjoyable.

Every instinct in his body told him he could not bear it, and yet his brain knew he had no alternative.

He could hardly survive with no money, living off his friends or asking his Harlow relatives to support him.

His mother's father was dead, and his uncle, now the Earl, had a large family of his own and had never been particularly interested in him.

What was more, he was far too proud with what Mr. Faulkner had called his "Scottish blood" to be a scrounger.

He turned from the window to face Mr. Faulkner.

"Very well," he said, "you win! How soon will we have to leave for Scotland?"

There was certainly not the triumph that Lord Alistair had expected to see in Mr. Faulkner's expression. In fact, the older man hesitated, and his eyes seemed apprehensive.

"What is it?" Lord Alistair enquired.

"It had been announced, My Lord," Mr. Faulkner replied, "that your brother the Marquis was to be married to Lady Moraig McNain!"

"Well?"

"His Grace has given his word that Lady Moraig should marry his eldest son to unite their Clans, which, as you are well aware, have been at loggerheads with each other for generations."

There was a silence that seemed to pulsate through the small Dining-Room before Lord Alistair said incredulously:

"Are you telling me that my father will expect me to honour this arrangement?"

"I was afraid this might upset you, My Lord," Mr. Faulkner replied. "But because His Grace considers it a question of honour, he will insist on it!"

CHAPTER TWO

There was a long silence. Then, as if he thought the strain was unbearable, Mr. Faulkner said hastily:

"I hope, My Lord, you will now permit me to leave you, as I have several appointments to keep in London on behalf of His Grace."

Lord Alistair did not reply, and Mr. Faulkner went on:

"I have ascertained that there is a ship leaving Tilbury early tomorrow morning, which will carry us to Aberdeen, where His Grace's yacht will be waiting."

313

Still Lord Alistair was silent, and as if the expression on his face was intimidating, Mr. Faulkner bowed rather nervously and went from the room.

Only when he had gone did Lord Alistair realise that without being aware of it he had clenched his fists tightly in an effort at self-control.

Now he asked himself furiously, in a manner which seemed to burn through his whole body, how he could endure such a future.

It would be hard enough to accept the position as his father's eldest son and prospective Chieftain of the Clan, but to be married to some Scottish woman he had never seen was an humiliation that made him feel that any life, however impoverished, was preferable.

However, he was sure that Mr. Faulkner had not been speaking lightly when he said that if he refused to return to Scotland, his father would disown him.

This would mean that all he would possess in the world would be the few hundred pounds a year that his mother had left him when she died.

While she had been living at home her father had not only provided for her but, as Lord Alistair knew, paid his School and University fees.

This had left the money which came from Scotland free for clothes, entertainments, and anything else he and his mother particularly fancied.

They had gone abroad together while he was still a boy, and when he was grown up he had visited many parts of Europe and enjoyed the experience.

To travel was expensive, and it was possible only because both his grandfathers had been so generous.

The idea of existing in the future without horses, without a comfortable flat like the one in which he now lived, and without the small appendages of wealth which became very precious when one lost them was unthinkable.

And yet, could any money compensate for living in the isolation of the Castle and being married to a woman who was doubtless gauche, plain, and badly educated?

When he thought of the intelligent men in politics and in the Social World whom he called his friends, and of the "Beauties" to whom he had made love, he felt himself shudder.

Then suddenly, almost as if a life-line were thrown to him, an idea came to his mind.

If he was married before he reached Scotland he could not be forced to become the husband of Lady Moraig, and there would be nothing his father could do about it.

It was not the answer to the whole problem, but at least it alleviated some part of the horror of what had been planned for him.

There was almost a smile on Lord Alistair's lips as he realised that if he could persuade Olive to marry him, as he was quite certain she would be only too willing to do now that he was a Marquis, then he could pay back his father in his own coin by being able quite legitimately to defy his orders.

With a spring in his step he walked from the Dining-Room to his bedroom, where Champkins was waiting to help him into his coat.

It had only just arrived from Shultz, his tailor, and it fitted over his shoulders without a wrinkle.

It was in fact so smart that Champkins said with an undoubted note of admiration in his voice:

"This'll be one in the eye for Mr. Brummel, M'Lord, when he sees you!"

"I hope so, Champkins," Lord Alistair replied.

At the same time, he remembered how expensive the coat had been and that he owed Shultz quite a considerable amount of money.

Once again it was being hammered into his brain that as his father's heir he could meet all his bills without any difficulty.

But as a rebel and an outcast there would be every chance of his ending up in the Debtors' Prison.

"Are you going out, M'Lord?" Champkins enquired.

Lord Alistair nodded, and his valet handed him his high-crowned hat, a cane which had his crest on the gold knob, and his gloves.

He knew that in his tight-fitting champagne-coloured pantaloons, with his Hessians shining so brightly that they reflected like mirrors, and the points high above his chin, he looked exceedingly smart as he walked out of the flat and into Half-Moon Street.

Because he had given no orders the night before, his Phaeton, which had recently been delivered from the coach-builders, was not waiting for him.

Instead, Lord Alistair walked slowly towards Piccadilly, enjoying the sunshine because it was tempered with the dust of London, and enjoying the houses rising on each side of him because they were filled with people.

All too clearly he could see in his mind the long stretches of empty moors where only the grouse lived, and he could taste the salt on the sharp wind which would be blowing in from the sea.

As he strolled down Piccadilly, continually meeting acquaintances and being waved to by attractive women in their high-brimmed bonnets driving in open carriages, Lord Alistair was savouring everything he saw.

He felt a deep affection for the pavement under his feet, the trees in Green Park, and the roofs of Devonshire House silhouetted against the sky.

'This is my life. This is where things happen which affect the whole nation,' he thought. 'What shall I think about, talk about, and feel in the emptiness of the Highlands?'

Because it hurt him, he was determined that he would let nobody know yet of his changed circumstances.

Tomorrow he might be the Marquis of Kildonon, but today he was still Lord Alistair McDonon, the most admired, spoilt, pursued young man in the whole of the *Beau Monde*.

He guessed, although Mr. Faulkner had not said so, that one of the appointments his father's Comptroller would keep today would be in Fleet Street to have the news of his brothers' deaths reported in the London newspapers.

Tomorrow *The Times* and *The Morning Post* would undoubtedly headline such a tragedy, but today, Lord Alistair thought, there were still a few hours left in which he could be himself, and not his father's son, to be ordered about as if he were a raw recruit.

Thinking back into the past, he could hear his father's voice echoing through the corridors of the Castle and seeming to fill the big, high-ceilinged rooms.

When His Grace was in a rage it was as if the whole foundation of the Castle were shaken by a tempest, and as he grew older he watched his mother becoming more nervous, her face growing whiter, her eyes more apprehensive day by day.

She undoubtedly had a character and a strong personality of her own, but she was also extremely sensitive.

It had been impossible for her to go on living with a man who was obsessed with his own importance and behaved not only like a King but also like a tyrant.

When much later Lord Alistair was grown up, he realised how brave it had been of his mother to run away, afraid with a fear that was as violent as a dirk-thrust in her heart that she would be stopped and forcibly brought back.

But actually the Duke had been too proud to pursue her, and when he learnt that she had left secretly at dawn with her youngest son, Alistair, he had merely commanded everybody in the Castle never to speak of her and her name never passed his lips.

Only when he learnt that she had died did he assert his authority and insist that because she was the Duchess of Strathdonon, her body was to be brought back to lie with the bodies of previous Duchesses.

The Cemetery which was near to the Castle itself was surrounded by trees and a high wall to prevent the curious from peeping at their betters even though they were dead.

Lord Alistair had refused to meet the older members of the Clan who came to take the Duchess back to her last resting-place.

He had felt resentfully that it was just like his father to claim what he considered was his even after death.

He had therefore contented himself with mourning his mother publicly at a Service of Remembrance which took place in the Harlow family Church.

Now as he turned from Piccadilly into St. James's Street and saw the steps of White's Club just ahead, he knew that this was the place he would miss more than anything else when he was in the North.

The smartest and most exclusive Club in London, it was here that he could meet his friends at any time of the day or night.

At the moment it was filled with congenial souls who smiled at seeing him the moment he appeared.

Half-a-dozen voices called out a greeting as he entered the Coffee-Room, and he seated himself beside one of his closest friends, Lord Worcester, who asked:

"How are you feeling after last night, Alistair? I have a throat like a parrot's cage! It is the last time I shall ever take a drink in a brothel!"

"We were both fools," Lord Alistair agreed, "but the price we were charged for it should have ensured us a good wine."

"I suppose they thought that by that time we would not be very discriminating," Lord Worcester said. "What will you have now?"

A waiter took their orders, and Lord Alistair, sitting back in a comfortable leather armchair, felt as if he must etch the room and the faces of everybody in it firmly on his memory so that when he was in exile it would be a picture to remember.

He thought the same all through the excellent luncheon he and Lord Worcester ate together in the Dining-Room with its red walls, high windows, and gilt-framed paintings.

Then, earlier than Olive was expecting him, he allowed his friend who had an appointment with Harriet Wilson, the famous Courtesan, to drop him off in Park Street.

For the last two hours Lord Alistair had been restless in his anxiety to see Olive and make her agree to marry him at once.

He was quite sure that now that he had a coronet to offer, her love would outweigh every other obstacle and she would consent to come with him to Scotland.

Not perhaps tomorrow, that would be too much to ask, but within a few days.

He had to make her understand that it would be a mistake to antagonise his father more than he would be anyhow by the disruption of his plan.

"He can hardly blame me for already being married at my age," Lord Alistair argued to himself, "and it will be easy to make him believe that the marriage took place before the deaths of my brothers."

He knew he was asking a great deal of Olive.

Most important of all, because he was now in mourning, he would not be able to marry her as she would wish, in St. George's, Hanover Square, with the Prince of Wales present and a large Reception after the ceremony.

Although she was a widow and could not wear white, she would, Lord Alistair thought, in her inimitable way look breathtakingly beautiful.

The fact that she was marrying a future Duke would be accepted by everyone in the Social World as her right and no more than what was expected for her.

It would also be a satisfaction to know he had put Torchester's nose out of joint and also Harrowby's.

He would not only be married to the most beautiful woman he had ever seen, but one who undoubtedly, as she had declared over and over again, loved him with her whole heart.

It was not really surprising, Lord Alistair thought, when they were so well suited to each other, and the fire of their love-making was more intense and more passionate than that which he had known with any other woman.

However, it was not exactly the marriage he had envisaged, and he had an uncomfortable feeling at the back of his mind that he would never be completely confident that Olive would be permanently faithful to him.

Because many married women had been so willing for him to make love to them, Lord Alistair was very cynical about the chance of any woman, if she was beautiful enough, being faithful or loyal to one man for any length of time.

Somewhere, and it was connected with the empty shrine within his heart, there was the idea that he would wish his own wife not only to love him but to be shocked and affronted if any other man tried to touch her.

Then he twisted his lips as he told himself mockingly that it was asking too much.

Only if a woman was plain and boring, as he was sure Lady Moraig would be, was she likely to remain faithful to him alone until death divided them.

Deep in thought, he reached Olive's home without being aware of it, and raised his gloved hand to the shining knocker on the door.

It was opened immediately by a young footman wearing the somewhat flamboyant livery affected by the Beverley family.

Lord Alistair stepped inside before he asked the Butler, who knew him well, and who came hurrying over the marble floor:

"Is Her Ladyship at home, Bateson?"

"She's not back yet, M'Lord. But I understood Her Ladyship was expecting Your Lordship at four o'clock."

"I am early."

The Butler seemed to hesitate for a moment before he said:

"There's a young lady in the Drawing-Room also waiting to see Her Ladyship. She was not expected, so I don't suppose Her Ladyship will keep Your Lordship waiting for long."

"Then I will wait in the Card-Room."

"Yes, of course, M'Lord," the Butler replied, leading the way, "and I'll bring Your Lordship the newspapers."

"Thank you, Bateson."

Lord Alistair walked into an attractive Sitting-Room which rejoiced in the somewhat pretentious name of "Card-Room."

It adjoined the Drawing-Room, and when there were large parties there was room in it for four small baize tables or one large one for those who felt their evening was incomplete without a chance to gamble.

There were no tables now, and Lord Alistair settled himself in a comfortable armchair by the window, hoping that Olive would not be too long and resenting the fact that she had another appointment before he could talk to her about themselves.

Bateson brought him the newspapers, saying:

"I'll tell Her Ladyship you're here as soon as she arrives, M'Lord."

"Wait until her other visitor has left," Lord Alistair replied. "then make sure we are not interrupted. I have a matter of importance to discuss with Her Ladyship."

"Leave it to me, M'Lord."

The Butler went from the room, closing the door behind him.

Lord Alistair made no effort to pick up the newspapers. Instead, he stared ahead with unseeing eyes, wondering how Olive would react to what he had to impart to her.

He could not help feeling sure that she would be radiantly happy at the thought of being his wife, even if it entailed spending some months of the year in Scotland.

'She will sell this place,' Lord Alistair was thinking, 'and will open Kildonon House in Park Lane.'

It had always annoyed him that his father had closed the family Manor in London, which his grandfather had frequently used, and refused to allow either his wife or his sons to stay there.

Every time he passed it driving down Park Lane and saw its windows shuttered and the steps leading up to the door dirty and neglected, he felt irritated.

It was as if the dislike he had always felt for his father and his defiance of him were increased by this monument to his obstinacy and desire for isolation.

"He was born a century too late!" Lord Alistair had always said.

Twenty-five years after the Battle of Culloden, in 1746, the Chieftains had begun to neglect their Clans, and their sons had come South for their education and their amusement.

They had accepted the English as friends, enjoying the delights and entertainments of London as if they had never been defeated and humiliated.

The ancient authority of the Chiefs had been taken from them by the abolition of their heritable jurisdiction, which had given them the power of "pit and gallows" over their people.

The Clansmen had been stripped of the tangible manifestations of their pride, the carrying of arms was forbidden under the penalty of death, and the wearing of the tartan, the kilt, or plaid was an offence which involved transportation.

These cruel laws had later been rescinded, but Lord Alistair knew in his heart that they would never be forgotten.

He remembered reading recently that in Scotland, whenever there was news of a French victory, green firs were planted which symbolised freedom and liberty.

"Oh, God!" he said to himself with a sudden surge of irritation. "Have I got to listen to all that bitterness and fury against the English all over again?"

It had been an integral part of his childhood which he had learnt to forget, but now it seemed to surge up within him like a tidal wave, and he knew that if he was not careful he would be drowned in it.

He heard the sound of voices in the Hall and realised that Olive had returned.

Without thinking about it, he rose to his feet, then remembered with annoyance that she had another caller to see before she was free.

He heard her speaking to Bateson, then there was a click like that of a door opening, and he thought she had come to him first.

Then he realised that the door into the Hall was still shut, but the communicating door between the Drawing-Room and the Card-Room was ajar.

"You wanted to see me?"

It was Olive speaking.

"Y—yes . . . My Lady . . . I am desperately sorry to . . . bother you . . . but I have come to . . . you for help."

The voice that answered Lady Beverley was low and soft and, Lord Alistair thought, very frightened.

"For help?" The question was sharp. "Who are you?"

"My name is Arina Beverley."

There was a moment's pause while Lord Alistair was sure that Olive was looking surprised before she said:

"Do you mean to tell me that you are the daughter of Charles Beverley, my late husband's brother?"

"Y-yes . . . that is right."

"Then why have you come to see me?"

"Because I am desperate . . . absolutely desperate . . . My Lady. Although it may seem an . . . imposition, since we have never met before . . . I have nobody else to turn to . . . and I feel that because Papa was your brother-in-law . . . you would . . . understand."

"Understand what? I do not know what you are trying to say."

To Lord Alistair it seemed as if Arina Beverley drew in her breath.

"You are aware," she began after a little pause, "that my father . . . died two years ago."

"I believe my husband did mention it to me," Olive replied casually, "but as you know, because of your father's disgraceful behaviour in marrying your mother, the Beverley family cut him out of their lives."

"S-Sir Robert came to my . . . f-father's Funeral."

"Which I considered a very generous action on his part. Your father brought disgrace on the family name, and only a good Christian like my husband would have forgiven him after he was dead."

"At the same time," Arina said, "the . . . allowance Papa had always received first from his father . . . then from Sir Robert . . . ceased."

"Did you expect anything else?"

"It would have been . . . Christian to remember that the . . . living still need to be . . . cared for when the dead no longer . . . need help."

"That is not for you to say!" Olive retorted. "Tell me why you are here. I have no time to waste in arguments over your father's behaviour, considering that I never met him, and neither he nor your mother was of the slightest interest to me."

"Please . . . please . . . do not say that!" Arina begged. "I have . . . come to you for . . . help, because . . . my m-mother is . . . desperately ill. My father's death affected her very . . . deeply and now the Doctors say she must have an operation if she is to continue to . . . live."

"That is not my business!"

"My mother's name is Beverley . . . My Lady . . . as yours is . . . and all I am asking is that you will . . . lend me two hundred pounds, which will . . . pay for her to be operated on in a private Nursing-Home by a Specialist in the particular disease from which she . . . suffers."

There was silence, then Arina continued:

"I . . . I will pay it back . . . I swear I will pay it back however . . . long it may take me . . . but every day her operation is delayed . . . my mother grows worse!"

There were tears in the young girl's voice, but Olive's voice was sharp and hard as she replied:

"And how do you expect to repay this sum of two hundred pounds, except perhaps by walking the streets, although I doubt if even there you could raise such a large sum very quickly."

Arina gave a little cry of sheer horror.

"H-how can you . . . think of anything so w-wicked, so degrading?"

"Beggars cannot be choosers! Since that appears to be the only solution to your problem and you are not prepared to raise the money in such a way, I suggest you look elsewhere for help."

"Y-you . . . cannot mean . . . that!"

"I most certainly do mean it! You have no right to come here badgering me to provide money for a woman who should never have tempted my brother-in-law away from his family in the first place, and who is certainly no responsibility of mine."

"Please . . . Your Ladyship . . . please . . . try to understand . . . there is nobody else to whom I can turn for help and I . . . feel sure . . . that if Sir Robert were alive he would have . . . helped Mama."

Arina gave a little sob before she continued:

"When he spoke to me at the Funeral I knew . . . that despite the estrangement between the two brothers over the years . . . Sir Robert was still . . . fond of my f-father."

"If my late husband was a sentimental fool, I am not!" Olive snapped. "Now, as I have nothing further to say on the subject, I suggest you go back to your mother, and if she is ill get her into a Hospital."

"Even if there was a bed available in one of the free Hospitals," Arina replied in a strangled voice, "it would be . . . murder to send my mother into one . . . you have no idea of . . . the dirt . . . the disease which . . . flourishes in them . . . and the incompetence of the Doctors . . ."

"That is not my concern," Olive objected. "Leave now, and do not come back. If your mother dies, it is entirely her own fault, and she has nobody else to blame. I suspect actually she is receiving her just reward for the way she behaved in the past."

"How can you say anything so . . . cruel?" Arina cried. "My mother's only crime was that she loved . . . Papa as

325

he loved her . . . and nothing else in the world . . . mattered to them."

"But now she is finding that money is a necessity!" Olive sneered. "Very well, I hope you find it, but it will not be from me!"

Lord Alistair heard Arina give an exclamation. Then he knew that she was crying.

Olive Beverley must have rung the bell, for he heard the door being opened and she said:

"Show this young woman out and see that she does not come back here again! I am going upstairs to change. Let me know when Lord Alistair arrives."

"But, M'Lady . . ."

As Bateson spoke there was a sudden thump, as if somebody had fallen down, and Lord Alistair heard him give an exclamation.

Without considering that he had been eavesdropping, Lord Alistair opened the communicating door into the Drawing-Room.

Olive had gone, but lying on the floor was a slight figure and Bateson was bending over it with an expression of concern on his face.

As Lord Alistair reached Arina's side, her eye-lids fluttered and she made what sounded like a murmur of apology.

"Brandy!" Lord Alistair said in commanding tones.

Bateson, as if suddenly realising that was the right solution, hurried through the open door into the Hall.

Lord Alistair went down on one knee and thought as he looked down at Arina Beverley that her appearance somehow matched her voice.

She had fair hair and was very slight, and as he saw the hollows in her cheeks and the pallor of her skin, he was sure that she was half-starved and had fainted not only from despair but from lack of food.

As her eyes widened and she stared up at him he saw that they were so large that they seemed to dominate her thin, pointed face.

They were not blue as might have been expected, but the pale green of a woodland stream, and her nose was very strange and, Lord Alistair thought, aristocratic.

Her lips were softly curved, but too thin, again from the first stages of starvation.

"I . . . I am . . . sorry!"

He could barely hear her voice, but somehow she managed to speak.

"It is all right," he said soothingly. "Lie still until the Butler brings you something to drink."

"I . . . I must . . . go."

"In a minute or two."

As he spoke, Bateson came hurrying back with a small glass of brandy on a silver salver.

Lord Alistair took it from him and, putting his arm round Arina, raised her a little from the floor, at the same time holding the glass to her lips.

She sipped, then shuddered as the fiery liquid coursed down her throat.

"No . . . more," she begged.

"Drink a little more," Lord Alistair said firmly.

As if she was too weak to argue, she obeyed him.

She shuddered again, but it was obvious that the darkness which had made her collapse had been swept away, and the colour came back into her cheeks.

"I am . . . sorry for being . . . so . . . foolish," she said in a frightened, hesitating little voice.

"I quite understand," Lord Alistair replied. "You have had a shock, and now I am going to send you back to your mother in a carriage."

"Oh . . . please . . . we cannot . . . afford it," Arina said quickly.

"You will not have to pay anything," he promised. "Let me help you up."

He knew that the brandy had already done its work, and he helped Arina to her feet, realising as he did so how light she was.

While she had seemed very small on the floor because she was so thin, when standing up she was in fact tall enough to be the perfect height for a young woman.

She was still a little unsteady and swayed as she stood, but Lord Alistair gave her his arm and she placed her hand in it.

With her other hand she pressed her plain bonnet firmly on her head and smoothed down her gown, made of a cheap cotton, which had become disarranged by her fall.

"A hackney-carriage!" Lord Alistair said to Bateson.

"Yes, of course, M'Lord."

He gave the order to one of the footmen, who hurried out through the front door into the street.

By the time Lord Alistair and Arina had walked very slowly to the top of the steps, a hackney-carriage had drawn up outside.

Only when they had reached the door of it did Arina take her arm from Lord Alistair's to say:

"Thank you . . . very much . . . you have been . . . very kind."

"I want you to give me your address," Lord Alistair said, "first so that I can tell the cabby where you live, and secondly because later in the day I will send you and your mother some food and wine."

"N-no . . . please . . . you must not . . . trouble yourself."

"It is something I want and intend to do!" Lord Alistair answered firmly. "All you need to tell me is your address."

"It is a lodging-house in Bloomsbury Square . . . it was the only place we could . . . afford . . . but we must leave it . . . tomorrow."

"And the number?"

"Number Twenty-seven . . . and thank you again for being so . . . kind to me."

Arina held out her hand as she spoke, and as it was ungloved, as he took it Lord Alistair felt her fingers were cold and trembled against his.

He gave the address and the fare to the cabman and the hackney-carriage drove off.

As he walked back up the steps he thought he would send Arina not only some food but also a little money, enough at any rate to make sure she would not starve for the next week.

Then he told himself ironically that if he had not decided to obey his father's command, it was something he could not have afforded to do.

He walked in through the front door and said to Bateson as he did so:

"Tell Her Ladyship I am here, and ask her to speak to me as quickly as possible."

"Very good, M'Lord."

Bateson started up the stairs and Lord Alistair walked into the Drawing-Room.

He saw the flowers and thought that what they had cost would have supplied Arina and her mother with quite a number of substantial meals.

Then he told himself that it was ridiculous for him to allow a strange young woman's problems to concern him at this moment when he was so deeply involved in his own.

The thing that really mattered was not whether two unknown women were starving because of some deplorable action in the past, but that Olive would be prepared to marry him by Special Licence.

He knew women well enough to realise that as regards getting married, nobody as distinguished as Olive would wish to be hurried over what to most women was the most important day in their lives.

But where he was concerned, marriage was not only imperative but must be immediate.

To wait longer would be to allow the Duke to suspect that he had married in defiance of his wishes, and that would certainly be the wrong way to start his new life as prospective Chieftain.

No, it was essential that his father should think he was already married when the summons to return to the North had reached him.

Mr. Faulkner was bound to be suspicious since he had not immediately protested that he was already married, but Lord Alistair knew that he had been very fond of his mother and of himself even as a boy, and so could be relied on, he hoped, not to betray him.

The whole plan was beginning to lay itself out in his mind so clearly that he might have been directing a movement of troops rather than of himself and of course Olive.

He had to wait for nearly a quarter-of-an-hour before she came into the Drawing-Room, looking exquisitely beautiful in a gown of glowing pink gauze so transparent that it revealed the exquisite curves of her figure.

It was the fashion among the Ladies of Fashion to dampen their muslins so that they clung closely to their figures, but Olive was skilful enough to choose materials that showed hers without such artificial aids.

As Bateson shut the door behind her, Olive stood for a moment as if to allow Lord Alistair to take in the picture she made.

Then she gave a little cry of delight and ran towards him with a grace worthy of any ballerina on the stage at Covent Garden.

"Alistair!" she exclaimed with delight. "It is so wonderful to see you!"

It flashed through Lord Alistair's mind that her voice when she was speaking to him was very different from the harsh tones in which she had addressed Arina.

Then her red lips were lifted to his, and the seductive expression in her half-closed eyes made it hard for him to think of anything but her loveliness.

"I have something to tell you," he said.

"And I have something to tell you."

"Mine is very important."

"What can be more important than that you are here and, for some reason I do not understand, have not yet kissed me?"

"I want to tell you something first."

"Then tell me, Alistair, and tell me quickly, as I want your kisses and a—great deal more."

The passion in her voice was unmistakable, and Lord Alistair thought it was exactly what he wanted to hear.

Slowly and in a way that was almost dramatic he said:

"My two elder brothers have been drowned, and I am therefore now the Marquis of Kildonon!"

For a moment it seemed that Olive thought she must have misunderstood him. Then as she stiffened, her eyes opening wider to stare at him, Lord Alistair said:

"It is true! And my father has sent for me to go North. So, my sweet, we have to be married immediately before we journey to Kildonon Castle and I present you to my father and the Clan."

He finished speaking, and still Olive seemed tongue-tied, until with a strange little cry that was hard to interpret she asked:

"Is this—true? Really—true?"

"I learnt of it myself only this morning, and it has been a great shock to me. But my first thought was that now we can be married, and I can offer you the strawberry-leaf coronet you have always craved."

To his surprise, Olive, instead of melting into his arms as he had expected, looked away from him before she said:

"I told Arthur Harrowby last night that I would give him his answer this evening. That is why I told you to come here now, so that I could inform you first that I intend to—marry him."

"Now he will be disappointed," Lord Alistair said. "You will marry me and we shall be together as we have always wanted to be."

To his astonishment, Olive walked towards the table on which was a huge bowl of Malmaison carnations.

She put out her hand to touch them, as if to feel they gave her something. Then she said:

"It is too—late!"

"What do you mean—it is too late? If you have not already accepted Harrowby, then all you have to do is tell him that the answer to his question is 'no.' "

Olive did not answer, and Lord Alistair asked:

"Why are you not as pleased as I thought you would be? You have told me often enough how much you love me."

"I do love you, Alistair, but marriage is one thing, love is another."

"I do not understand," Lord Alistair said, and now his eyes were hard.

"I am glad—very glad for your sake that you are now a Marquis and one day will be a Duke," Olive said quickly, still staring at the carnations. "But your Castle is in—Scotland. It is a long—way away."

"There is also a house in London, which I have every intention of reopening."

Olive did not speak, and now he put out his hands and, grasping her shoulders, turned her round to face him.

"What are you thinking? What are you trying to tell me?" he asked harshly. "Are you saying that after all your protestations of love, you would rather marry Harrowby than me?"

"You are hurting me!" Olive complained.

Lord Alistair gave her a little shake.

"Answer me!" he insisted. "I want to know the truth!"

"You are still—hurting me—and it is very cruel and— unkind of you."

Lord Alistair suddenly took his hands away.

"So you have made up your mind," he said harshly. "You will marry Harrowby because he is so rich and because his house and Estates are in the South of England."

"Try to understand," Olive pleaded. "I love you, Alistair, of course I love you, but I should hate having to live in Scotland, where there is nobody to admire me, no Balls, no Opera—and besides, I have always disliked cold weather."

"And the love—the love you have professed so often—does not come into it?"

"I love you, I shall always love you," Olive insisted, "and there is no reason why our relationship should be any—different in the future from what it has been in the past. Arthur is a busy man, and I shall have a lot of time to—myself."

As she spoke Olive stepped towards Lord Alistair, and now her eyes had narrowed again, and as she spoke the last words her lips had an invitation on them.

Lord Alistair drew himself up, his eyes dark as agates.

"I congratulate you, Olive, for what in the past has been a very skilful and professional performance! It certainly convinced me of your sincerity."

His voice was like a whip-lash as he added:

"Let me also congratulate you on becoming the Marchioness of Harrowby, an hereditary Lady of the Bedchamber to the Queen, and undoubtedly a future leader of London Society! What is more, I am sure you will make a great number of credulous fools like myself very, very happy!"

As he finished speaking he took from the pocket of his waistcoat a key, which he threw down on the floor.

"The key into your garden," he added. "I am sure you will need it tonight, and do not forget to leave the window into this room ajar!"

As he finished speaking he turned on his heel. Then as he opened the door, Olive gave a little cry which seemed to be forced from her lips.

"Alistair!" she cried. "Alistair!"

Lord Alistair did not look around, but crossed the Hall, snatching up his hat from a chair.

As a footman opened the front door, he ran down the steps and was striding away down Park Street, saying as he did so, beneath his breath:

"Damn her! Damn her! Damn all women!"

CHAPTER THREE

*L*ord Alistair walked briskly towards Half-Moon Street.

As he nearly reached it, still seething with anger, the sight of a shop which purveyed food made him remember his promise to Arina Beverley.

Because in some obscure way he felt that if he helped her he would be scoring off Olive, he went into Shepherd Market where there were a number of shops patronised by his Chef.

He stopped at a Butcher's shop which was known in that area for the excellence of its meat and ordered a number of different cuts of beef and mutton, besides a chicken.

When the man, knowing who he was, had taken his order respectfully, he asked:

"Anything else I can do for you, M'Lord?"

Lord Alistair hesitated.

It suddenly struck him that if he helped Arina even further, he would be showing up Olive for her meanness and the cruel manner in which she had refused to help a desperate girl who was actually her niece.

The Butcher was waiting, and after a moment Lord Alistair replied:

"Send them round to my flat immediately and put in two pounds of butter and add some fruit and vegetables from the shop next door."

"It'll be a pleasure, M'Lord!"

Lord Alistair walked away, and for the first time since leaving Park Street he felt that the way Olive had behaved to her brother-in-law's child was not the manner in which he would want his wife to speak to anybody, let alone a relative.

Her behaviour had actually been a revelation, for he had never known her to be anything but charming, sweet, and to him passionately loving.

Now he thought that with her social mask off she appeared to be a very unpleasant character, and he blamed himself for not having realised it sooner.

He had in fact, because he was a Celt, always flattered himself that his instinct was infallible and it would be impossible for any man to cheat him or any woman to deceive him.

But he had been deceived by Olive, and he was aware that while she would not marry him, she still desired him as a lover and would make every effort if they met in the future to entice him back to her bed.

Now he understood why even in their wildest transports of desire, some critical faculty had prevented him from thinking that this was real love.

Olive was in reality greedy, avaricious, and ambitious to the point where she would marry the Devil himself if he could give her a coronet, wealth, and a position in Stylish Society.

As Lord Alistair walked up to his Sitting-Room on the First Floor, he saw that Champkins was packing his clothes into a large leather trunk.

Because he had given him no direct order, he asked:

"What are you doing? Who told you to pack for me?"

Champkins looked up from where he knelt beside the trunk.

"That Scottish gentleman returned after you'd left, M'Lord. He wanted to see you important-like and said he'd be back at six-thirty."

Lord Alistair's lips tightened but he did not speak, and Champkins went on:

"He tells me Your Lordship were leaving for Scotland tomorrow morning, an' it's going to take me all night to get all Your Lordship's clothes ready."

Lord Alistair bit back the words of fury that came to his lips.

It was bad enough that he had no alternative to obeying his father's orders, but that Faulkner should be so certain of his compliance made him more incensed than he was already.

Then he asked himself what was the point of kicking against the pricks.

He could stay in London and starve, or he could take his rightful place as the next owner of Kildonon Castle and the hundred thousand acres of Scottish land that went with it.

For the first time since he had heard of his brothers' deaths, Lord Alistair remembered the power his father had in the North, and that his mother had been right when she had said he behaved like a King.

He was indeed "Monarch of all he surveyed," and his people, despite the English laws, looked to him for justice. As far as they were concerned, he, as Chieftain, was the law.

"There are a great many things I shall want to alter," Lord Alistair told himself.

He knew that already in his mind he was accepting his new position, however much his heart rebelled against the penalties that went with it.

He stood in the Sitting-Room, thinking of how much he had enjoyed living here, how comfortable he had been, and how many delightful hours he had spent either with his men-friends or with some beautiful lady.

She would come to him after dark, heavily veiled, but daring enough to risk her reputation and her marriage because she loved him.

For Olive, what he now had to offer was not enough.

It was hard to believe it, and it was still harder to credit that after all her protestations of love, she preferred Harrowby.

"Damn her! I hope she rots in hell!" he exclaimed.

Then he felt it was even more infuriating that she should arouse such uncontrollable emotions in him.

There was a loud knock on the door, and as Champkins ran downstairs to answer it, Lord Alistair realised it was the hamper he had ordered for Arina.

As Champkins came back up the stairs, he met him, saying:

"All right, I know what it is. Go round to the Mews and tell Ben I want my Phaeton brought round immediately."

It was only ten minutes before the Phaeton was at the door.

This was another possession which was not yet paid for, and as he drove off with the hamper at his feet and Ben, his groom, sitting beside him, Lord Alistair thought that he would make sure his father paid for the privilege of having him back.

It would have been an enjoyment for him to drive his two superlative horses if he had not been thinking that he would have to decide whether he would have them sent to Scotland or whether he should sell them before he went.

Although, as he had told Olive, he planned to open Kildonon House in Park Lane, he was aware that he would have to have his father's approval to do so, and he had the uncomfortable feeling that the answer would be a categorical "No!"

"Curse it, I have to have some independence!" he muttered to himself.

He knew as he spoke that it was just bravado.

Once he was back at the Castle, everything would be as it had been in the past, a Kingdom ruled over tyrannically by a Monarch with one idea, and one idea only— his own importance and the greatness of Scotland.

Number 27 Bloomsbury Square was not difficult to find.

The house looked sleazy and greatly in need of paint, while the windows were dirty and so was the doorstep.

Because it looked so unsavoury, Lord Alistair for the moment played with the idea of leaving the hamper for Arina and driving away.

Then he remembered that Olive had treated her as badly as she had treated him, and there was a cynical twist to his lips as he thought that he would let her know in a subtle way how generous he had been.

He knew he had only to tell a few of the gossips in White's that evening that he had learnt of the distressing state in which Olive's sister-in-law and niece were living for it to be a tit-bit which would fly on the air from lip to lip.

Everybody was aware that Sir Robert Beverley had left his wife a comfortable income for life, with doubtless a clause inserted that she lost it if she remarried.

This was so usual amongst the elderly husbands of pretty young wives that it had ceased to cause comment.

At the same time, Olive was at the moment, in the colloquial phrase, "well-heeled," and that she had refused to help her sister-in-law and her niece would certainly be ammunition for the women who were jealous of her and the men whose advances she had spurned.

There was a cruel twist to his lips and a hard expression in his eyes as Lord Alistair climbed down from the Phaeton.

Ben had already rung the bell and lifted down the hamper, and now he took his Master's place with the reins, preparing to walk the horses round and round the Square until they could start off again for home.

A slovenly maid, who looked as if she had been cleaning the soot from the chimney, came to the door.

"I wish to speak to Miss Arina Beverley," Lord Alistair said.

"You'll find 'er on th' third floor, Mister," the maid said, jerking a thumb up towards some narrow stairs that were badly in need of dusting.

"I suspect that is her bedroom," Lord Alistair said. "There must be somewhere else where I can talk to the young lady."

The maid looked at him in surprise. Then, obviously impressed by his magnificent appearance, she said hesitatingly:

"There's th' mistress's Parlour, but 'er be oot at the moment."

"I feel sure she will not mind my using it," Lord Alistair said firmly. "Show me to it."

As if his air of authority left her defenceless and unable to withstand his command, the maid opened a door on the other side of the Hall.

Here there was a small, quite comfortably furnished Sitting-Room, over-cluttered with cheap paintings and the type of china sold by pedlars, but at least it was unoccupied.

"Fetch Miss Arina," Lord Alistair said as he walked in, "and take the hamper I have brought with me upstairs at the same time."

As he spoke he drew half-a-guinea from his waistcoat pocket and put it into the maid's hand.

She stared at it as if she thought she must be in a dream.

Then her face flushed with excitement.

"Yes, Mister, yes, Sir!" she said in a very different tone of voice. "Oi'll fetch th' young lady right away!"

She pulled the door to, and Lord Alistair heard her hurrying up the stairs with the heavy hamper as if she was afraid he might change his mind and demand his money back.

He was thinking that if he did not go to Scotland he would not be able to tip so generously on any future occasion.

Then his thoughts returned to Olive and the knowledge that what he was doing now would undoubtedly damage the picture she had created of her beauty, gaiety, and laughter, and of course her social superiority.

"The Marchioness of Harrowby!"

He spoke the words aloud and heard the sneer in his voice.

Then he told himself that he was wasting his time in letting his thoughts dwell on Olive, when he should be thinking of his own misery on being forced to marry a Scotswoman from a Clan which he could remember as a boy had always been the enemy of the McDonons.

They had fought all through the centuries, warring against each other with raids in which they captured women and cattle.

He could therefore understand his father's desire to end the hatred and the malice that existed between his people and the McNains.

"But not at my expense!" Lord Alistair exclaimed.

As he spoke, the door opened and Arina came in.

She had changed, he noticed, from the cotton gown she had been wearing when he had last seen her into one of white muslin which was limp from many washings.

The result was that it clung to her figure in a manner which Olive and other ladies of the Social World considered fashionable.

It was frayed in places, and, being experienced about women's clothes, Lord Alistair thought that when she had returned to her mother she must have changed out of her respectable gown to save it for better occasions.

She obviously had no idea that he himself would bring the food he had promised her.

She dropped him a small but graceful curtsey before she said:

"How can you be so . . . kind as to bring Mama and me that . . . huge hamper? I do not know . . . how to thank you."

"I always keep my promises," Lord Alistair replied. "I am glad it pleases you."

"P-pleases . . . me?" Arina repeated. "It is like a gift from . . . God . . . and I am sure it will make Mama feel . . . better."

"And you too," Lord Alistair said. "I realise you are very much in need of nourishment."

She smiled and he realised that when she did so her face was very lovely.

"I only took a quick look in the hamper before I came down to thank you," she said, "but already I am feeling very . . . greedy."

Looking at her, Lord Alistair thought that if she were not so thin that her cheek-bones stood out and her chin seemed far too sharp, she might be beautiful.

Then he corrected himself. She was beautiful now.

In fact, as he looked at her now more closely than when he had first seen her lying on the floor, he thought that her looks were quite unusual.

In some way he could not quite define, they were different from those of any other beautiful woman he had known. Yet she could, even in her cheap and frayed gown and with her hair unbound, take her place amongst them.

He had often thought to himself that the women he had known had formed a Picture-Gallery in his mind, which he could walk round, looking at their faces and knowing each particular point of beauty he had memorised about them.

One of his lady-loves had had eyes that always looked like pools of mystery, and it was sad to remember that beautiful though she was, he had found when he knew her well there was no mystery about her at all.

Another had lips that might have been chiselled by a Greek sculptor, and yet another had a nose that he was sure was more alluring than Cleopatra's!

One beautiful woman with whom he had been enamoured for a long time had red hair that echoed the flames she had ignited in him when he touched her.

But the beauty of Arina, he thought, would have been the beauty of somebody very young and Spring-like, if she had not been so thin and her skin pale and lustreless.

Her hair, while it was the colour of sunshine in the early morning, was limp because, like her body, it needed feeding.

Then he realised that because he was staring at her, Arina was looking at him apprehensively.

"Have I . . . said something . . . wrong?" she asked, faltering.

"No, of course not," he replied. "I was thinking about your difficulties and your plea for help from Lady Beverley, which I overheard because I was in the next room."

Arina flushed and looked away from him.

"It was . . . foolish of me to go to her . . . but I did not know . . . what else to do."

"I thought it was very wrong of her not to help you," Lord Alistair said in a sharp voice.

"I had hoped that she . . . would," Arina said simply, "but the . . . Beverley family never forgave Papa and Mama for . . . running away together."

"What did your father do that they considered so disgraceful?" Lord Alistair asked.

Then as an afterthought, before she could reply, he said:

"I suggest you sit down while we talk. After what you have been through, I am sure that you are tired."

"It is . . . kind of you to . . . think about me," Arina said, "but I am not so much tired as . . . anxious about Mama and what to do . . . about her."

As she spoke she sat down in one of the chairs by the hearth-rug, and Lord Alistair sat opposite.

"Tell me first about your father," he suggested.

Arina looked down at her clasped hands before she said:

"It happened a long time ago, but I suppose . . . nobody will ever . . . forgive him."

"What did he do?"

"He was engaged to be married to the daughter of the Duke of Cumbria."

Lord Alistair looked surprised.

He had known that the Beverleys were a respected family in the North, although he had rather suspected that Olive had exaggerated their importance, but he had not supposed that they moved in the same aristocratic circles as he did himself.

"I think," Arina was saying in her soft little voice, "that Lady Mary was more in love with Papa than he was with her, and he was rather pushed into the engagement by his parents and his brother, who were extremely impressed by the Duke."

Lord Alistair thought this explanation was very likely.

"Go on!" he prompted.

As if it encouraged her, she continued:

"Then, two weeks before the marriage was to take place, while the wedding-presents were pouring in, and it had been arranged for the Archbishop of York to marry them, Papa met my mother."

Lord Alistair felt that this was probably something that often happened, but few men would have had the courage to do anything about it.

"Mama said they fell . . . completely and . . . hopelessly in love," Arina went on, "and they both knew it would be impossible to go on living if they could not be together."

"So they ran away!"

"Yes . . . they ran away . . . and were married at Gretna Green, which is not very far from the Beverley Mansion in the North of Yorkshire."

"I can imagine how infuriated both the deserted bride and your father's family must have been."

"They were so angry that my grandfather never spoke to Papa again . . . and I have never seen my uncle until he . . . attended Papa's Funeral."

"I heard you say that to your aunt," Lord Alistair replied, "and also that your father received an allowance from his family."

"I have always . . . understood that it was his . . . mother who arranged that," Arina said, "and although it was very little to live on, we managed and were very . . . very happy . . . until Papa . . . d-died."

"Then the money stopped?"

"Yes."

"There was no reason given?"

"When I wrote to the Lawyers asking why it was . . . delayed, they replied that now that Papa was . . . dead, the Beverley family had no further obligation either to Mama or . . . to me."

Her voice seemed to die away on the words. Then she clasped her hands together as she said:

"We have sold . . . everything that was of any value and . . . if Mama is not operated on soon, the growth that is in her breast will . . . grow larger and she will . . . die! And although I have . . . prayed and prayed there . . . seems to be no way I can . . . raise the money now that Lady Beverley has refused to . . . help us."

The despair and terror in her voice seemed to vibrate through the small room, and after a perceptible pause, almost as if he debated the answer within himself, Lord Alistair said:

"I will give you the two hundred pounds!"

If he had fired a pistol at her, Arina could not have been more astonished.

For a moment she stared at him as if she thought she could not have heard him a-right. Then, without thinking, she said quickly:

"N-no . . . of course not . . . how could I ask you . . . a stranger, to give us . . . so much?"

"Shall I say that it is an act of Christian charity!" Lord Alistair replied, and he could not suppress the mocking note in his voice.

"But you must know . . . it will be a very . . . very long time before I would be . . . able to . . . pay you back. I shall have to find . . . some work that I can do . . . but it may not be . . . easy."

"I am prepared to wait."

"And you will really give it us . . . to save Mama's life? How can I thank you? How can I . . . tell you how wonderful it is for you to . . . answer my prayers?"

Her voice was very moving, and now there were tears in her green eyes, which made them look so beautiful that Lord Alistair found himself staring at her in astonishment.

Then as he did so, an idea came to him that was astounding and at the same time so outrageous that for a moment he found it difficult to grasp.

Yet, when he did so, it seemed as if he too had received the answer to a prayer.

He bent forward in his chair.

"Listen," he said, "I have an idea. If you need my help, I, as it happens, need yours."

"I will certainly help you . . . if I can do so. You know I would do . . . anything after you have been so kind . . . so incredibly . . . kind."

"Very well," he said, "but just answer a question. If your mother goes into a Nursing-Home, where will you go?"

"I thought that if the Doctor would take her, as he said he would, I would try to find a cheap room some-where nearby so that I could be beside her."

Arina paused, then continued:

"But he said that if I could find a little more . . . money, he could give me a room in the Nursing-Home. Although I have not yet suggested it, I thought I might be able to . . . help there in some way . . . perhaps by doing . . . house-work . . . so that I need not be so . . . greatly in his debt."

Lord Alistair had listened attentively, and now he said:

"I have a better suggestion and one which I want you to consider very carefully."

"What . . . is it?"

"I have a part for you to play, almost as if you were on a stage, although you will not be acting in a Theatre."

Arina looked puzzled but she did not speak, and he went on:

"I suggest you leave your mother in the Doctor's hands, and perhaps that would save her from worrying about you while she is ill."

"What do you . . . want me to . . . do?"

"I want you to come with me to Scotland," Lord Alistair replied, "on a visit which will take some little time, but if you will act the part that I require of you, I will pay for your mother's operation."

Arina made a little sound of happiness but did not interrupt, and he went on:

"There will also be enough to ensure that after it is over, she can convalesce in comfortable circumstances, and when you return to her you will both be able to afford to be properly nourished."

"It sounds . . . too wonderful!" Arina whispered. "But suppose I cannot do what you . . . want?"

"It will not be easy," Lord Alistair answered, "but I feel somehow you will be successful in convincing the people you will meet that you are the person you are pretending to be."

Arina looked puzzled before she asked:

"I have to . . . pretend to be . . . somebody else?"

"You will act the part of my wife!"

Lord Alistair spoke the words slowly and distinctly. He saw Arina stiffen and again stare at him as if she could not believe what she had heard.

"Y-your . . . wife?"

Her voice trembled on the words.

"Just as you are in a difficult position, so am I," Lord Alistair said. "What is not yet publicly known is that my elder brothers are dead. I am therefore now the Marquis of Kildonon!"

He paused expecting her to look impressed, but her expression was one of sheer astonishment as he continued:

"My father, the Duke of Strathdonon, has ordered me back to Scotland, and once there he intends me to take up the responsibility that my eldest brother had assumed before he died, and marry the daughter of the neighboring Chieftain, with whom we have always been at war. You may not understand it, but the word of any Chieftain in Scotland is equivalent to a vow made in Church."

"I do . . . understand . . . that," Arina answered.

"You will therefore realise that I would find it almost impossible to refuse to marry this woman whom I have never seen. So, the best way of avoiding a travesty of a marriage would be for me to arrive in Scotland with a wife."

"Yes . . . I can see that is your . . . only way . . . out."

Lord Alistair was aware that Arina was quicker-witted than he had expected, and he said:

"I am supposed to leave tomorrow morning, and once I have reached my father's Castle there will be no escape."

"I . . . I could not go tomorrow morning!"

"No, I quite understand that."

"Besides," Arina went on before he could say any more, "I am not sure I am the . . . right person to do . . . this for you . . . I might . . . fail you . . . and . . . I would not look right."

Lord Alistair smiled.

"Like all women, you are thinking about your clothes," he said. "But I promise you that you will be dressed as would be expected of my wife."

"B-but . . . I could not . . . pay for it."

"I will do that, and if you have any scruples about accepting clothes from me, may I explain that every Theatrical Producer expects to dress his Leading Lady."

He spoke almost jokingly, but Arina did not smile.

"I want to . . . help you," she said, "but I am sure this is not . . . right from your point of view."

"Anything that will save me from having to marry a Scottish woman whom I have never seen will be right for me," Lord Alistair said firmly.

"A-and what . . . happens later?" Arina asked. "I shall have to . . . go back to Mama?"

This again, Lord Alistair thought, was a sensible question.

"We will have to work that out very carefully," he said, "and I was thinking that perhaps when the danger of my having to marry in Scotland was over, you might disappear."

"Yes . . . of course," Arina agreed. "Nobody would be . . . interested in what . . . happened to me anyway."

"You will come South to see your mother," Lord Alistair said slowly, as if he was planning it out for himself. "You will be ill and send for me. After I have joined you in the South, I can inform my father or anybody else who is interested that you have died."

"And they will . . . believe . . . you?"

"We shall have to make sure they do," Lord Alistair said firmly.

There was silence. Then he said:

"If you agree to do this for me, I will give you not the two hundred pounds for which you have asked, but five hundred. This will be deposited in the Bank for your mother to draw on, and after our arrangement has come to an end I will see that you are paid monthly a sufficient amount of money to keep you in more or less the same circumstances as you enjoyed in your father's lifetime."

He was quite certain from what Arina had said that this would not be a great drain on his resources, and it should be easy for him as the Marquis of Kildonon to appropriate such funds from the large allowance he was quite certain his father would allow his heir.

Although he had no idea of the exact extent of his father's fortune, he had always assumed that he was a very wealthy man and that when many Scottish Chieftains had become impoverished after the ruthless repression of the rising of the Young Pretender, the Duke's income came from various other sources that were not affected by the poverty in Scotland.

"You and your mother will be looked after until such time as you are able to marry a rich man," he finished.

"I think that is most unlikely," Arina replied, "since we have always lived very quietly, and our friends, although they are loyal and kind, have mostly been as poor as we were ourselves."

She paused. Then a smile seemed to illuminate her face as she said:

"But we were happy . . . and that was all that . . . mattered."

348

"Of course," Lord Alistair agreed. "But now, Arina, we must return to making plans and do so very quickly. How soon can your mother go into the Nursing-Home?"

"At once . . . if we have . . . the money. That was why I went to see Lady Beverley . . . because every day that Mama is not operated on, the . . . tumour will grow . . . bigger and get . . . worse."

She spoke very quietly, but Lord Alistair heard the terror in her voice.

"Then I suggest you take your mother to the Nursing-Home first thing in the morning," he said, "but do not tell her what you are about to do, as it would worry her. Just say that Lady Beverley has not only lent you the money for the operation but has most kindly arranged for you to stay with friends who live outside of London."

"I am sure Mama will . . . believe that," Arina said, "because she is so weak and ill at the moment that she does not think . . . very clearly."

"Then that makes it all the easier," Lord Alistair agreed. "I suggest that once your mother is in the Nursing-Home, you come back here, where I will collect you and we will buy your 'trousseau' for your journey to Scotland."

Arina did not reply and her eyes dropped before his, and he knew she was embarrassed at the idea of his buying her clothes.

It seemed a little thing when he was also paying for her mother's operation, but it made him understand as no words could have done that she had been properly brought up.

She was not only a Lady by birth but was educated in the conventional manner, which was something he would want in the woman who was pretending to be his wife.

There was a silence before he said:

"I must warn you that we have to guard against something which actually I have only at this moment remembered."

"What is that?"

"In Scotland there is a law known as a 'Marriage by Declaration Before Witnesses.' It means if two people assert in the presence of others, that they are married, then they are in fact legally joined to each other."

Arina started before she said:

"Then what can we do if you present . . . me as your . . . wife and I agree? It might be very . . . difficult for you in the . . . future."

"It will be difficult only if you do not abide by our arrangement," Lord Alistair replied. "That is why I think we should draw up an agreement, which we will both sign, saying that you are acting a part under my instructions and that neither of us will claim later, whatever the circumstances in which we find ourselves, that we have become legally man and wife."

"It sounds, My Lord, as if you suspect that . . . I might not . . . abide by our arrangement," Arina said.

Once again he thought how quick-witted she was in understanding that he was safe-guarding himself against any demands she might make of him in the future.

"I was not thinking of your attitude over this," he said untruthfully, "or my own, but that somebody might want to make trouble once you have left me."

He saw the expression of relief on her face and thought she was very sensitive and he would have to treat her carefully.

Now she said a little hesitatingly:

"I would be very . . . pleased to sign such an agreement as you call it . . . and to assure you . . . My Lord . . . that never in any circumstances . . . would I be so ungrateful as to do . . . anything you did not wish."

"Thank you," Lord Alistair said. "I will bring it back with me tomorrow and make quite certain it is legally phrased."

He rose to his feet as he spoke and Arina rose too.

Then, as if she was suddenly aware of what she had committed herself to, she said:

"You are quite . . . quite certain I can do this for you? You do understand that I know nothing of the . . . Social

World in which you live. I shall . . . make mistakes . . . and perhaps you will be . . . ashamed of me."

"I will see to it that you do not," Lord Alistair assured her, "and if you are grateful to me, I am very grateful to you, Arina. You must know how degrading and humiliating it would be for me to be married in such circumstances."

"Yes . . . of course . . . and I feel Papa would have understood that you would do anything to . . . escape."

"As he escaped," Lord Alistair said with a smile, "and I think it was very brave of him."

"You really . . . think that? You are not . . . appalled and horrified as his family were?"

"No, of course not! I think he did everything possible and it is disgraceful that he should have suffered for so many years for what most people would consider a very romantic and honourable action."

Arina's eyes seemed to hold the light of a thousand candles in them.

"H-how can you be so . . . understanding and . . . so kind?" she asked. "I only wish Papa could hear you say that . . . and when Mama is . . . b-better . . . I will tell her."

"Yes, you must do that," Lord Alistair agreed, "but not at the moment. It would be a mistake for her even to hear my name in case she . . . talks about us."

"She would not do that if I asked her not to," Arina answered, "but because she is ill, it would be best not to worry her."

She looked away in an embarrassed manner as she added:

"I think . . . Mama would . . . disapprove of what I am doing, but as you know . . . there is no other way I can help her . . . and I was desperate until . . . you came."

"You have not told your mother that Lady Beverley refused your request for help?"

"Actually I have not told Mama even that I went to see her. I thought if she said 'yes,' it would be a wonderful surprise, but that if she refused it would be depressing."

"That was sensible of you," Lord Alistair approved, "and it makes it easier for us to do what we have to do."

He smiled at Arina in a way that many women had found irresistible as he said:

"Now go upstairs, give your mother something to eat, and eat sensibly yourself. I have just realised that I forgot the wine I promised you, but perhaps it would be a mistake at the moment, and I will make up for it on our voyage to Scotland."

"Thank you," Arina said, "but we have everything we want, and I hope I can persuade Mama to eat. I know it will give her the strength to go into the Nursing-Home tomorrow."

Lord Alistair drew two notes of fifty pounds each from his pocket and put them down on a table which was laden with potted plants.

"Give this to the Surgeon," he said, "which is half of his fee. The rest I will let you have tomorrow."

He added a number of gold sovereigns, saying as he did so:

"Take your mother to the Nursing-Home in a comfortable carriage and tell it to wait so that it can bring you back here. I will call for you at about noon and pay what you owe the Landlady."

Tears fell from Arina's eyes as she looked at the money. Then she said in a broken little voice:

"I . . . I cannot . . . believe that this is . . . really happening . . . and I am not . . . dreaming."

"I promise you it will not vanish like fairy-gold," Lord Alistair said. "Now do exactly as I say, Arina, and after I have collected you tomorrow, you can leave everything in my hands until you return South to find your mother recovered from her operation, and you can be together with no more desperate problems."

He put his hand on her shoulder.

"Your prayers are answered for the moment," he said, "but you still have to keep on praying."

"I will . . . pray . . . and thank God for . . . you," she said in a strangled voice.

He smiled at her and went from the Sitting-Room, shutting the door to give her time to collect herself and the money from the table before she went upstairs.

Outside, his Phaeton had just completed its fifth turn round the Square.

He climbed into it and took the reins from his groom.

Then as he whipped up the horses and started to drive swiftly back towards Mayfair, he was thinking once again how he could hurt Olive.

He rehearsed the exact words he would utter later in the Club, which would be repeated and repeated as if by a swarm of bees carrying poisonous pollen to every chattering tongue in the *Beau Monde*.

CHAPTER FOUR

M̲r̲. Faulkner had been waiting only twenty minutes when Lord Alistair returned to his flat.

During the last part of his drive he had stopped concentrating on Olive to think of what he should say to his father's Comptroller.

There was a grim expression on his face as he walked up the stairs and into the Sitting-Room. Mr. Faulkner, who had been reading a newspaper, hastily put it down and rose to his feet.

"Good-evening, My Lord."

Lord Alistair walked to his desk and placed on it some letters which he had picked up in the Hall as he entered the building. Then he said in a somewhat aggressive tone:

"I understand that you have told my valet that I shall be leaving with you for Scotland tomorrow morning."

"I am sorry if it was information Your Lordship did not wish me to divulge," Mr. Faulkner replied slowly, "but I understood when I left you this morning that you had agreed to come back to Scotland, which meant we should leave as soon as it is possible."

"I agree with you," Lord Alistair replied, "but actually it is impossible for me to leave tomorrow, and I cannot believe that a delay of twenty-four hours will be of world-shattering importance."

He spoke mockingly and thought Mr. Faulkner looked surprised.

"Sit down, Faulkner," he went on. "I have something to tell you."

Mr. Faulkner did as he was told, and now there was an expression of apprehension in his eyes.

It suddenly struck Lord Alistair that it was strange, considering his father's bullying ways, that Faulkner, who was a very intelligent and well-educated man, should be so devoted to him.

It was something he had never considered before, and because he found it rather touching that after all these years Mr. Faulkner should be so concerned with the McDonon family, his voice softened and he imparted his news in a rather different manner from what he had intended.

"I am afraid," he said, "that what I have to tell you, Faulkner, will come as somewhat of a shock, and it is obviously something which has never crossed your mind, but I am in fact a married man!"

Mr. Faulkner stared and exclaimed:

"Married, My Lord? Your father has no idea of it!"

"Why should he have?" Lord Alistair enquired. "He has not concerned himself with me since I was twelve."

"His Grace, your father, has not only been interested in your well-being but has received reports about you regularly."

Lord Alistair stared at him.

"Are you telling me," he said after a moment, "that my father has spied on me?"

354

Mr. Faulkner looked a little uncomfortable.

"That is a harsh word, My Lord, for what I prefer to think of as a paternal interest on the part of His Grace in his youngest son."

"I can hardly believe it!" Lord Alistair ejaculated, then he laughed. "It is the old story, is it not, Faulkner? The big spider never lets the little spiders go. While I believed I had completely cut myself off from my father, the Clan, and the problems of Scotland, he still has woven his web round me and there is no escape."

He thought that was so true that it was surprising he had not thought of it before.

Of course, the very fact that the Duke had continued to give him an allowance after his mother's death might have alerted him to the idea that his father thought one day he might return to the fold, either willingly or because, as it had turned out, he was obliged to do so.

His thoughts were interrupted by Mr. Faulkner with the question:

"Did Your Lordship really say you are married?"

"Yes, Faulkner, that is what I told you! But the reason my father's spies have not ferreted it out is that it was a secret marriage. Even my valet, who is now packing, on your instructions, has no idea that I have a wife."

"But you will bring her to Scotland with you, My Lord?"

"Naturally! And you now understand why it will be impossible for me to marry Lady Moraig McNain."

For several seconds Mr. Faulkner did not speak, and Lord Alistair said with some satisfaction:

"It will doubtless upset my father's plans for me, but of course there is nothing I can do about it unless I commit bigamy."

He spoke jokingly, but Mr. Faulkner did not smile.

"I will not pretend to you, My Lord, that it is not a shock," he said after a perceptible pause. "But of course the Marchioness of Kildonon will be welcome as your wife and I hope she will acclimatise herself to Scotland and the Castle."

"That remains to be seen," Lord Alistair answered loftily. "But you can understand that because my wife, like my valet, has to pack, it will be impossible for us to leave until the day after tomorrow."

He saw by the expression on Mr. Faulkner's face that he was glad it was to be no later. Then he asked, in a tone of voice which was undoubtedly apprehensive:

"Would it be impertinent to ask Your Lordship why your marriage has had to be a secret?"

Lord Alistair's eyes twinkled.

He knew his father's Comptroller was thinking that perhaps he had married an actress or a woman who was not acceptable to the Social World and was already wondering what the Duke would do about it.

However, Lord Alistair had expected such a question and had already thought of an answer, remembering when he was at Oxford one of his friends saying:

"If you are going to tell a lie, it should always be as near to the truth as possible so that it sounds credible."

It was a piece of advice that Lord Alistair had followed, and he said now:

"My wife is in deep mourning for her father. As she comes from a distinguished and well-known family in Yorkshire, it would be, as you can imagine, almost an insult to the dead that she should marry before the year of mourning is over."

He thought Mr. Faulkner drew a breath of relief before he said:

"Of course I understand, My Lord. That means there should be no publicity about your marriage until some months after you have reached Scotland."

"That was what I thought myself," Lord Alistair replied, "which reminds me—I imagine, while you have been in London, you have notified the newspapers of the deaths of my brothers."

"Yes, My Lord! It will be in *The London Gazette, The Times,* and *The Morning Post* tomorrow morning."

"Then, under the circumstances, the sooner we leave for Scotland the better," Lord Alistair said. "I can assure you that my wife is considering my interests as well as her own in promising she will be ready to sail with such inconvenient haste."

"I am very grateful, My Lord. I shall greatly look forward to meeting Her Ladyship."

As Lord Alistair rose to his feet, Mr. Faulkner said:

"I will go at once to cancel our passages for tomorrow and transfer them to another ship, which I happen to know will be leaving on the tide on Thursday about noon. Will Your Lordship require one or two cabins?"

"Two!" Lord Alistair said quickly. "If the sea is rough, which it invariably is, one has no need of spectators."

Mr. Faulkner hesitated.

"If Her Ladyship is a bad sailor, perhaps Your Lordship would prefer to travel by road. It will of course take a great deal longer, but I have always believed that women are more prone to seasickness than men."

"It is something I have never considered," Lord Alistair replied. "But as the long drive would be tiring and unbearably boring, I am sure my wife would prefer to brave the waves rather than bad roads, broken-down horses at the Posting-Inns, and inevitably the final menace of a Scottish mist."

Mr. Faulkner permitted himself to give a short, dry laugh.

"Your Lordship's eloquence confirms my opinion that the shorter the journey between London and Kildonon Castle, the better for us all."

"Very well, Faulkner, see to it!"

Lord Alistair escorted the elderly man to the door and only when he had left did he remember that he had not offered him a drink.

"I have too much to do!" he excused himself, and went to his desk.

It took him some time to write out first a draft and then the final document that he intended Arina to sign the following morning.

She did not seem the type of woman who would resort to blackmail, but one never knew, and after he had been so disillusioned by Olive he was not prepared to take any chances.

Even to think of how mistaken he had been about Olive's feelings for him brought the frown back between his eyes and set his lips in a tight line.

He was hating her because it was the first time a woman had not been prepared to give him everything he asked of her.

He was sure that the many protestations of love he had received in the past had been sincere, and there were at least half-a-dozen women he could name who, had they been in Olive's shoes, would have been only too eager for him to put a ring on their finger.

He told himself that his feelings were more those of hurt pride than of a broken heart. But that did not make him feel any kinder towards Olive, and when, nearly two hours later and gorgeously arrayed in his evening-clothes, he drove in a hackney-carriage to White's, he was once again plotting how he could hurt her most.

He walked into the Club and immediately met three of his closest friends.

"We wondered if you would be with us tonight, Alistair," one of them remarked. "Come and have a drink. James says he has an almost certain winner for Ascot next week. He will want to tell you about it."

"It is something I am very eager to hear," Lord Alistair replied.

They walked to the bar, but before they reached it they found a number of other cronies drinking champagne and were invited to join them.

They had only just sat down when Lord Alistair, who was facing the door, saw someone come into the room and felt himself stiffen.

It was the Marquis of Harrowby, and he thought he was the last person he wished to meet at this particular moment.

Lord Worcester also saw him and remarked:

"There's Harrowby! Shall I ask him to join us?"

Before Lord Alistair could reply, the Marquis saw Lord Worcester and walked towards him. When he reached the circle of friends, he said:

"Nothing could be better than that you should all be here. You can help me celebrate."

"Help you celebrate what?" Lord Worcester enquired.

"My engagement!" the Marquis replied quietly. "Lady Beverley has accepted me."

There was a moment of silence, which was one of surprise, then a cheer went up. Congratulations were on every man's lips as they lifted their glasses to toast both the Marquis and Olive.

It struck Lord Alistair that this was the one love-affair in which he had been so discreet, at Olive's special request, that it had never crossed any of his friends' minds that he might be upset by the news.

He thought, as he too raised his glass and drank the expected toast, that he had acted his part very skillfully, as he hoped Arina would act hers.

Nevertheless, in all the turmoil and excitement which followed Harrowby's announcement, there was no chance for him to speak in any derogatory way of Olive, and if he had done so it would not have been well received.

'It will keep,' he thought to himself.

He decided too that after all it would be a great mistake for any of his friends to know of Arina's existence.

Only after they had all dined together and the Marquis, having had a great deal to drink, had been pompous and far too long-winded in his conversation, did Lord Alistair think as he drove home that Olive would, in her marriage itself, receive quite sufficient punishment for her behaviour.

Firstly, she would undoubtedly be bored, for the Marquis was a very boring man.

Secondly, Lord Alistair thought, unless he was a very bad judge of character, even her beauty could not arouse the fire and passion which he had found irre-

sistible and which to Olive herself was the very breath of
life.

'She will be bored, bored, bored!' he thought with
satisfaction, and was quite certain that sooner or later
she would use every art and wile in her repertoire to
entice him back to her.

"Shall I see you tomorrow?" Lord Worcester asked
when Lord Alistair said good-night.

He had already received invitations to visit a Dance-
Hall, a House of Pleasure, and to take a pretty ballerina
from Covent Garden out to supper.

"I shall be busy tomorrow," he answered. "And you
will not see me for some months."

"Some months!" Lord Worcester exclaimed. "Why
not?"

"I have to go to Scotland," Lord Alistair replied casually. "You will know the reason when you read your newspapers tomorrow morning."

"What has happened?" Lord Worcester questioned.
"Tell me about it!"

"You will learn soon enough."

"I cannot understand why you are being so mysterious!"

"It will give you something to think about!"

Refusing to say any more, Lord Alistair hurried down
the steps and into the carriage which one of the porters
from the Club procured for him.

As he rode back to his lodgings, he was thinking of
how much there was to do before he could leave for a
new life, which he was quite convinced would be one of
utter misery.

"Dammit," he said aloud. "Why could I not have gone
on as before? I was happy, while now I have to face my
father, the boredom of Scotland, and a pretence marriage."

The idea came to him that the latter, strange as it
might be, might in fact be a saving grace. At least it would
give him something to think about.

It would be amusing to pull the wool over his father's eyes and to circumvent his plans of marrying him to a McNain. He would have to keep very alert to see that neither he nor Arina was caught out.

The whole idea made him think of the pranks he had played as a School-boy and the mischief he and his friends had got up to at Oxford, when they had been pursued by the Proctors and severely reprimanded by their Tutors.

Once again he was up to mischief, although it was certainly more serious than anything in which he had been involved in the past.

There was a faint smile on Lord Alistair's lips as he entered his lodgings. He went up the stairs, thinking that he was earlier than usual and Champkins would be surprised to see him.

However, as he reached the top step, his valet came out of his bedroom to meet him, saying in a low voice:

"There's a lady to see you, M'Lord. She's waiting in the Sitting-Room."

"A lady!" Lord Alistair exclaimed.

It flashed through his mind that it must be Arina and she had come to tell him she had changed her mind. Or perhaps her mother was already dead and there was no reason now for her to need the money so desperately.

Then, as the questions in his mind kept him silent, Champkins added:

"This lady's not been here before, M'Lord. She's heavily veiled. She came in a carriage with two horses and smells of French perfume."

There was no doubt that Champkins was impressed by the visitor and it was quite obviously not Arina.

Lord Alistair did not reply.

He merely slipped his satin-lined cape from his shoulders, handing it with his tall-hat to his valet before he walked to the Sitting-Room and opened the door.

Although it was only dimly lit by a few candles, there was no need for more than one glance at the woman who rose from the sofa as he entered.

For a moment Lord Alistair could hardly believe his eyes. Then as he shut the door behind him he exclaimed: "Olive! What the devil are you doing here?"

She came towards him. Her evening-gown was cut with such a low décolletage and was so transparent that she might as well have been naked.

"How could you leave me so cruelly?" she asked.

She walked forward until she was standing close against him, but Lord Alistair did not put out his arms.

"I have just left your future husband at the Club," he said coldly. "I congratulated him warmly on his engage-ment, and I am quite convinced, Olive, that you have chosen a man to whom you are very well suited."

The way he spoke was insulting, but Olive only gave a little laugh.

"Darling, you are jealous," she said. "And I adore you for it! Oh, Alistair, my sweet, how do you think I could lose you?"

For a moment Lord Alistair thought she had changed her mind and intended to say that she would marry him after all. But as she lifted up her arms and he saw the passion in her eyes and the invitation on her lips, he understood.

"No!" he said sharply, moving away from her.

He walked to his desk and as he did so he wondered if perhaps he had left there the contract he had drawn up earlier in the evening between himself and Arina. Olive would have had no compunction about reading it.

To his relief, he remembered that it was something he had not wished Champkins to see and had therefore locked it in a drawer, and the key was at this moment in his pocket.

He stood looking down at the blotter. Then Olive was beside him, slipping her hand into his.

"Try to understand, darling," she begged. "Marriage is one thing—love is another. That is what all men believe, so why should a woman be different?"

She waited for him to reply and as he did not do so she went on:

"I love you as I have never loved anyone before. My lips yearn for you and my body burns for you. What does it matter what my name is?"

"It matters that you will not do what I have asked you to do," Lord Alistair replied sharply.

Even as he spoke it flashed through his mind that after all she was right. What did it matter to him whether she was married to him or not? What she was offering was something it was unlikely he would ever receive from his wife.

Quite suddenly his attitude to her changed, and he was intelligent enough to realise that he had been right in thinking he was angry with her because she had damaged his pride, but not his heart.

He turned now and there was a smile on his lips and the frown had gone from between his eyes.

"What do you think the noble Marquis would say if he knew where you were at this moment?" he enquired.

"It is something he will never know," Olive replied, "either tonight or in the future."

Now, as if she sensed his change of mood, she moved a little closer and put her arms round his neck.

"Why think about tomorrow or the day after, or the day after that?" she asked. "I am here tonight. No-one will disturb us, and I want you, Alistair. I want you as I have never wanted a man before."

The passion in her words seemed to throb on the very air, and slowly, as if he mocked at himself for giving in to her, Lord Alistair put his arms round her.

Then, as he bent his head and his lips found hers, he kissed her roughly, almost brutally, as if he punished her for the anger she had made him feel.

As she clung to him closer and closer, he felt the fire that she had invoked in him so often before rising to burn through his body, sweeping away everything but his fiery desire for the softness of her, while the exotic fragrance of her perfume seemed to beguile his senses and he could no longer think.

"I want you! I love you! Oh, Alistair, I love you!"

Even while some cynical part of his mind that seemed very far away told him she was lying, automatically he picked her up in his arms and carried her across the room to the sofa.

＊

Lord Alistair, driving his Phaeton, reached 27 Bloomsbury Square at exactly noon the following morning.

He was aware when he left his flat that the pile of luggage in the Hall had grown since he had last seen it, and now there were no fewer than six large leather trunks and the same number of small ones, making a mountain of baggage, which he felt would surprise Mr. Faulkner if no-one else.

He was about to tell Champkins that he had no need of so much when he remembered that he was moving his residence from London to Scotland and it would certainly be some time before he could return to patronise the tailors, who were acknowledged to be better at their trade than any others in the world.

What was more, although he had not told Champkins that they would not be returning to this particular flat, he had the idea that the valet was already aware of it.

Champkins had been with him ever since he had left Oxford, and although at times he had behaved rather like a protective Nanny, he was always loyal and trustworthy.

For the first time Lord Alistair wondered if Champkins would be able to tolerate Scotland any more than he would be able to himself.

He decided that when he returned he would tell Champkins that now he had packed all his clothes, he must arrange to put everything else except small-personal belongings into store.

He knew that this was one of the things that he had meant to plan last night, but Olive had effectively prevented him from thinking of anything but her.

It had been after three o'clock when she had finally left him to enter her carriage, which she had told to

364

return an hour earlier, in the charge of a sleepy coach-man and a footman who was stifling a yawn as he opened the door for her.

"Do you wish me to escort you home?" Lord Alistair had enquired.

"No, of course not," Olive had replied. "I told my lady's-maid, who will tell the household, that I was visiting an aged relation who was having a small birthday-party."

Lord Alistair had laughed.

"Aged relations do not stay up so late!"

"Why should the woman question anything I do? She will be only too delighted to wait on me now that I will be a Marchioness and she will have a far better standing in the servants' hall than she has ever had before."

"Another point for the Marquis," Lord Alistair replied.

He knew it did not even anger him to hear Olive talk in such a manner and he had finally accepted her contention that marriage was one thing and love, as far as she was concerned, was another.

When at about one o'clock Lord Alistair had found that Champkins had retired to his own bedroom, they had moved from the Sitting-Room.

As he held Olive close to him in his own comfortable bed, he had decided, now that he could think clearly, that he was glad she was not going with him to Scotland.

He was well aware how she could complain about the roughness of the sea and the lack of comfort on the ship in which they were obliged to travel.

He was also certain that while she might be impressed by the Castle, she would soon be bored to distraction, even more bored than he would be, and would not hesitate to express her feelings and doubtless show them all too clearly to his father.

He had been so concerned with his own difficulties and so confident that Olive, because she loved him, would solve them for him, that only now did he begin to see all the snags which impetuously he had ignored.

Although she was the most passionate and exciting woman he had ever known, his brain, when not be-fogged by desire, was aware all too clearly of her inces-sant craving for social power and, as her behaviour to Arina had shown, her lamentable lack of human kind-ness.

Only when she had left him and he had gone back to his tumbled bed, which was still redolent with the fra-grance of her hair and her body, did Lord Alistair tell himself that actually he had had a very lucky escape.

No-one knew more than he did how quickly the fires of passion could die down until there was not even a smouldering ember to be ignited into flame.

'Sooner or later that will happen with Olive,' he decided.

Actually, fate had dealt him an ace when Harrowby had circumvented his plan to make Olive his wife.

"It would not have worked," he told himself in more commonplace language, when he woke the next morning.

Driving towards Bloomsbury, he thought that his new method of avoiding his father's command was very much cleverer.

'As soon as her mother is well enough for her to return,' Lord Alistair thought, 'we will think of some plausible story which will set me free.'

What was more, his father would not live forever, and once he was the Duke, he would be able to come South as often as he liked.

He was quite certain that would mean a great number of months of the year when Scotland would have to do without him.

The sunshine seemed brighter than usual and the darkness of yesterday had passed. It seemed almost an omen of goodwill that, as he passed a newspaper-boy shouting at the corner of the street, he heard him call:

"Read of the death of two aristocrats by drowning! Read of the Duke who mourns two of his sons!"

The horses carried him away before the Marquis could hear more, but he knew it must be the report of his brothers' deaths.

He had expected that the news would make head-lines in the papers, and this would mean that now all of his friends would be aware that he was the new Marquis of Kildonon.

'This is how I shall have to think of myself in the future,' he thought, and found it a far more pleasant idea than it had been the day before.

He pulled up his horses outside Number 27 and saw, as he did so, that the door of the lodging-house was open and Arina was standing in the Hall. At her feet was one small and very battered trunk.

She was wearing the same plain cotton dress and untrimmed bonnet she had worn when he had first seen her in Olive's house.

When he stepped down to take her hand in his, he saw that she had been crying. Knowing it was because she had said good-bye to her mother, he did not comment on it but merely said:

"I commend you for being the most punctual woman I have ever known. I am glad you have not kept me wait-ing, as we have a great deal to do."

She gave him what he was certain was a somewhat forced smile, and having paid for her lodgings, he helped her into the Phaeton while Ben attached her small trunk to the back under the seat on which he now rode.

They set off, and the Marquis, as he was now deter-mined to think of himself, asked:

"Your mother is all right?"

"Yes . . . thank you," Arina replied, "and the Surgeon was very pleased that she could come to him so quickly. He was . . . afraid otherwise it might be . . . too late."

Her voice trembled for a second on the last word and the Marquis knew she was fighting to appear calm and self-controlled.

"You must not forget to give me the Surgeon's address so that my secretary can send him the rest of the money."

"I have already written it down for you."

"I can see you are very punctilious, as I am," the Marquis answered. "I find it very irritating when people are careless, forgetful, and slipshod."

"I hope I shall never show any of those . . . faults while I am with . . . you."

The Marquis turned his head to smile at her and realised that despite the fact that her clothes were made of the poorest material and very unfashionable, she looked extremely neat and tidy.

She also had a little of the Spring look he had thought was especially hers when he had first seen her.

She was still pathetically thin, and he could see, as she was looking ahead to where they were going and at the horses' heads bobbing up and down, the sharpness of her chin and the hollows beneath her small cheek-bones.

'She will soon look different when she starts to eat well,' he thought to himself. 'I am sure that because she is worrying about her mother, it will take a little longer than it might do with someone else who had no such anxieties.'

As he drove back into the more popular streets, Arina asked:

"Where are we going?"

"To buy you your trousseau," the Marquis replied.

"You are aware that I shall have no . . . idea what I should . . . choose or what would be . . . correct for me to . . . wear?"

She paused before she added:

"Mama and I have always lived in the country so of course I am in fact nothing but a 'country bumpkin.' "

"That is the last thing you will look when I have finished with you," the Marquis promised. "Leave everything to me."

"I still feel very . . . embarrassed that you should not only . . . choose the right clothes for me but also . . . pay for them."

"Now you are talking like a prim and proper young lady," he replied, "and not like an actress, who would command a very large salary and exceptional benefits at Her Majesty's Theatre in the Haymarket or at Drury Lane."

Arina laughed and it was a very pretty sound.

"You can hardly expect me to aspire to anything so important as either of those Theatres."

"The Theatre in which you will act is very much more impressive, and I shall have plenty of time to tell you all about it while we are at sea."

She drew in her breath.

"Is that how we are travelling to Scotland?"

"Will it upset you?"

"I hope not. But it would be very undignified to be seasick, especially when you are present."

"Why especially me?" the Marquis enquired.

"Because you are so magnificent and I am sure you never suffer from an ordinary cold, seasickness, or tummy-pains like common people."

The Marquis laughed.

"Thank you. That is the most ingenious compliment I have ever received."

"I was only saying what I think," Arina explained. "And I did not mean it . . . rudely."

"It was not rude but delightful," he replied.

As he spoke he pulled up his horses outside a shop which was in a side-road off Bond Street. It was not large and there was nothing frightening about it.

But the Marquis was aware that Arina shrank a little in her seat and there was a worried expression in her eyes.

"Do not be afraid," he said. "I know this dressmaker well. She will be prepared to achieve miracles by providing you with everything you require in record time."

Arina did not answer, but the Marquis felt her fingers tremble in his as he helped her down from the Phaeton.

The shop was small but elegantly decorated. The woman who came towards them as they entered gave an exclamation at the sight of the Marquis and curtseyed.

"It's delightful to see you, My Lord."

Arina thought she was not only exceedingly smart in a grey dress that had an elegance about it, but she was also very attractive, despite the fact that she must be at least thirty years of age.

The Marquis had known *Madame* Celeste, as she called herself, having been born plain Cecily Brown, since he first visited the shop with the lady who had loved him so ardently that she had decorated his flat for him.

"I prefer to have original clothes," she had said, "and that is what I have found at *Madame* Celeste's."

Because after that love-affair was over Lord Alistair had taken several other beautiful women to *Madame* Celeste and advised them as to the gowns which became them most, she had been very grateful.

She had shown her gratitude by spending a quiet few days with him in a comfortable Inn in the wilds of Buckinghamshire.

Being a country girl, she was a good rider, and they had ridden over the meadowlands in the daytime and spent the nights in a low-ceilinged room with a comfortable bed filled with goose-down.

It had been an unusual delight, Lord Alistair had thought afterwards—like picturing the simple wildflowers of Spring, like primroses and daffodils, rather than exotic hot-house carnations and orchids.

He had helped Celeste up to the pinnacle of fame by bringing her many other clients, but this was the first time he had been in the position to buy clothes which he intended to pay for himself.

He told Celeste in a few short words exactly what he required and how quickly, and she flung up her hands in despair.

Then in the practical manner which he advised, she said:

"I will do what is possible, and the rest will have to follow wherever you may be going."

She looked at Arina and smiled.

"I think that almost everything I have at the moment will suit the lovely young lady, and for you, and you only, My Lord, I will commit the unforgivable crime of switching gowns that are nearly finished or half-finished for someone else and starting again for the original purchaser."

"That is what I expected you would say," the Marquis replied with a smile. "We shall also require shoes, underclothes, coats, capes and shawls, gloves, and all the other things which women take for granted but which mount up when you start with absolutely nothing."

Celeste gave a cry of horror.

Then she clapped her hands and ordered her assistant to bring everyone she employed from the work-rooms in the basement and the seamstresses in the attics. There were at least twenty of them.

When she told them what she required, which meant most of them having to work all night, they seemed at first interested and then delighted at the thought of the extra money they would earn.

"It'll cost you a great deal," she said in a low voice to the Marquis while she was waiting for her staff.

"It is of no consequence."

When she raised her eye-brows, he added:

"My circumstances have changed."

"I am glad, very glad, for your sake."

There was no doubt that there was sincerity in Celeste's tone, and the Marquis said:

"You have always been a very good friend, Celeste."

He looked into her eyes and saw that the affection she had had for him was still there.

Then the work-people came crowding into the small Salon and she started to tell them what was wanted.

While Arina was being measured and fitted, amazed by the thousands of different suggestions and entranced by the materials and sketches of the gowns she was shown, the Marquis went with Ben in his Phaeton to collect food.

This he knew Arina would need more urgently than he did, but he had no wish to be hungry either.

A Restaurant in Piccadilly supplied him with everything he asked for and some excellent wine, which he knew Celeste would enjoy as much as he would.

He took it back to the shop and had one of Celeste's assistants arrange it in her office, where there was just room for the three of them to sit round a small table.

Arina was looking very pale and exhausted when the Marquis returned.

But he insisted on her having half a glass of wine, which brought the colour back into her cheeks and, as he was shrewdly aware, gave her an appetite which she might otherwise not have had.

He knew that when people were near to starvation they got to a point when they no longer craved for food and actually found it extremely hard to eat.

It was then that a little wine, though certainly not too much, would stimulate the digestive juices, and once they had started to enjoy their food, it was not difficult to go on eating.

He thought too that because he and Celeste laughed and joked with each other and she teased him, Arina found it easier to relax for the moment and to forget her mother.

So brilliant was Celeste's skill and organisation that by the time they left the shop later that afternoon, Arina was able to take with her two new trunks full of clothes and accessories, with the promise that much more would be ready the next morning before they left for Tilbury.

The remainder would follow them by sea as soon as it was possible to get it completed.

Celeste had sent one of her more intelligent employees to buy Arina the slippers she needed and, on the Marquis's suggestion, a pair of stouter shoes for walking on the moors.

"Will I really be able to do that?" Arina asked.

"If you want to."

"Of course I will want to," she replied.

He was surprised, then thought it was something he might have expected in a girl who had always lived in the country.

He therefore increased the order to two pairs of shoes and suggested that Celeste make her a gown that was not too long, in which it would be easy to walk.

"She cannot be so immodest as to show her ankles, My Lord," Celeste teased.

"But it must certainly not be so long that she trips over it," the Marquis retorted.

Arina gave a little laugh.

"I am glad you did not see me in the countryside where we lived with Papa."

The Marquis did not answer, he only thought that what Miss Arina Beverley could do was very different and would not be tolerated in the presumed Marchioness of Kildonon.

They drove back to the flat.

Now the Marquis remembered that he had to tell Champkins he was married. He was quite sure that his valet would find it hard to believe, but it was essential that if Champkins was suspicious that the marriage was a pretence, he should not voice such ideas in Scotland.

He played with the thought of not taking Champkins with him, but decided it would be intolerable never to have anything but Scottish servants around him.

They would not be trained to the quiet, perfect service that he had found in his grandfather's house or in the great houses of the families whom he had visited without his own valet.

When he helped Arina down from the Phaeton outside his flat in Half-Moon Street, he thought she looked very different from the girl he had picked up at Bloomsbury earlier in the day.

The fashionable pale blue muslin she wore had French ribbons of the same colour crossing her chest and passing under her small breasts, to tie in a sash at her back.

All the gowns the Marquis had bought for her were very high-waisted, as was the fashion which had just arrived from France and which had been set by Josephine Bonaparte, wife of the First Consul.

Over her gown Arina wore a silk shawl patterned in blue, and her bonnet with its fashionably high crown and tipped-up brim was decorated with wild-flowers and tied under her chin with blue ribbon.

It made her look very young and at the same time, the Marquis thought, lovely, despite the fact that she was undoubtedly tired and far too thin.

They went upstairs, and having taken her into the Sitting-Room the Marquis went in search of Champkins, whom he found, as he had expected, still packing but now not in trunks but in wooden cases which were arranged on the floor above.

"I didn't hear you come in, M'Lord," Champkins exclaimed, getting to his feet.

"I have something to tell you."

"Yes, M'Lord?"

"When we leave for Scotland tomorrow morning you and I are taking my wife with us."

Champkins opened his eyes wide and exclaimed:

"Blimey, that's a surprise!"

The Marquis laughed because he could not help it.

"I think it will also be a surprise to quite a number of people in the North. There are reasons, Champkins, for my having such a precipitate marriage, but what is important is that everyone in Scotland must believe it happened at least two months ago."

It was typical of the man, the Marquis thought, that without asking any questions Champkins merely said:

"If that's what you tells I, M'Lord, that's what I believes."

"Thank you, Champkins. I have already told Mr. Faulkner, as I have told His Grace, that the reason for my marriage being kept secret is that my wife is in mourning for her father."

As he spoke the Marquis suddenly remembered it was something he had not told Celeste and therefore Arina's clothes were in every colour of the rainbow. There was no black amongst them.

Quickly, so that he hoped that even Champkins would be deceived, he added:

"Her Ladyship is, however, not wearing black because it was her father's express instruction that no-one should mourn for him. He was, I believe, almost fanatical on the subject and she must naturally obey his wishes. Although deeply distressed at losing him, she wears the gowns she has always worn in the colours that pleased him when he was alive."

"Very sensible, if I may say so, M'Lord," Champkins remarked. "I always thought all that weeping and wailing were nothing more than eye-wash."

"I agree with you," the Marquis said.

Having told Champkins to inform the Chef, when he came in, that there would be two for dinner, he hurried away to warn Arina about the explanation he had just invented.

"It was very stupid of me," he confessed. "I should in fact have dressed you in black, mauve, white, and perhaps gray."

Arina smiled.

She had taken off her bonnet while he was upstairs, and now in her blue dress, her hair arranged by Celeste in a new style, she looked very elegant and very pretty.

"I have been looking at myself in the mirror," she said. "This is by far the loveliest gown I have ever had! And I am so thrilled with the ones that are in pink and green that I could not bear to lose them."

"We will just have to stick to our story that your father disliked mourning."

"It is actually true," Arina replied. "He used to say that it was nonsense that people gave so many flowers when someone died and had never thought to take them a bouquet when they were alive."

Then she added:

"When Papa died, Mama and I could not afford new clothes, so we just trimmed those we had with black ribbon."

"You reassure me that I am not telling a lie," the Marquis said. "It is something I hate doing, and I am sure you do too, so we shall tell as few people as possible. But those which have to pass our lips are of course white lies and therefore are not reprehensible."

He was surprised when Arina, giving a little laugh, asked:

"Are you placating your own conscience or mine?"

Because she had been so quiet and frightened ever since he had known her, he liked the sudden sparkle that seemed to be in her eyes, and he said:

"I think if we are clever we might have quite a lot of fun out of this adventure, which is the way we must think of it."

"Yes, of course. And it is exciting to go adventuring now, after being so worried about Mama, so frightened I would never find the money for her operation."

"You are not to think about it anymore," the Marquis said firmly. "I have not asked you before, but when is your mother going to have her operation?"

"In three days' time," Arina answered. "The Surgeon, who is a very kind man, wants not only first to feed her properly but to give her certain medicines which will make her feel stronger."

When she spoke Arina clasped her hands together, and then she said in a voice that was very moving:

"I am praying, praying all the time that it will be a success. If it is, it will be entirely due to you. I can never, never . . . tell you . . . how grateful I am or how . . . wonderful I think . . . you are."

Chapter Five

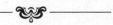

*B*ecause Arina's clothes were packed for travelling the Marquis suggested that they should not change for dinner, which meant that he would not have to change either.

This was a blessing, as he had not yet decided how he should sort out their sleeping arrangements.

They ate a delicious dinner in the small Dining-Room and Arina enjoyed every mouthful she could manage.

All too soon she said with a little sigh:

"I cannot eat any more, but I cannot bear to think of wasting this marvellous food."

"I do not think it will be wasted," the Marquis replied. "At the same time, in Scotland they will be astonished if you do not manage a large breakfast, a large luncheon, and an even larger tea, followed of course by an enormous evening-meal!"

Arina gave a cry of horror and then said, a sparkle in her eyes:

"If I grow fat on so much food you will find it very expensive."

The Marquis laughed.

"Perhaps my money will be expended in a good cause, but I doubt if you will ever be one of the 'fat kine'."

"I hope not," Arina replied. "But I know it shocks you how thin I am now, and *Madame* Celeste was horrified at how my bones stuck through my skin."

It struck the Marquis that although she might be too thin she would be very attractive without any clothes on at all.

Then he told himself that he had no intention of thinking of her as a woman and that he must be very careful not to shock her, since otherwise she would not trust him in the way she did now.

He was experienced enough to know that the way Arina looked at him and what she said about his saving her mother's life were simply the reactions of a child who had been rescued from danger by somebody she not only trusted but respected.

It made him feel old, but he told himself that was what he was in Arina's eyes.

At the same time, from his point of view he knew it was a relief that he was not taking Olive with him to Scotland.

Arina might be afraid that she would shame him or let him down, but Olive's looks and behaviour would undoubtedly have proved an embarrassment.

The Scots would never have understood and would have branded her as a scarlet woman immediately they saw her.

Because he had been convinced that she alone could save him from having to marry the woman of his father's choice, he had not considered until now her impact on the Clan.

Her crimson lips and mascaraed eye-lashes, now that he thought about it, and her rouged cheeks, while the vogue in London, would have horrified the Scots and made them sure that she was a harlot.

'This is exactly what she is!' the Marquis thought with a cynical twist to his lips, 'and Harrowby is welcome to her!'

When he thought of the way she had behaved last night, he knew he had had a very lucky escape and that Olive would be unfaithful both to her husband and to her lovers.

In fact, she was really the last type of woman he desired as his wife.

He thought that nevertheless he would miss her, but not for very long.

None of his love-affairs had ever lasted for any length of time, and as soon as the fires of passion had died down he forgot the woman in question and was ready for somebody new to attract him.

Then the whole game started all over again.

When they had finished dinner the Marquis took Arina into the Sitting-Room and produced the contract he had made out.

She scanned it carefully, reading every word. It stated that he had employed her for the sum of five hundred pounds to act temporarily the part of his wife. When their association was over, she would make no claims on him, but would disappear out of his life and not communicate with him again, unless he desired it.

Finally she read:

> *When we say good-bye, I promise to pay annually the sum of two hundred pounds in half-yearly instalments into Miss Beverley's Bank.*

It was all very clear and concise. When she had finished reading what he had written, Arina said:

"There is no necessity for you to give me so much money after I have left you. I have already said that when Mama is quite well again, I will find some work to do."

"What sort of work?" the Marquis enquired.

"I am not certain," Arina replied, "but I thought I might be able to copy some of the beautiful nightgowns you bought for me yesterday and the . . . other things as well."

She looked away from him and the Marquis knew she thought it immodest to mention the chemises he had given her, which were lace-trimmed and delicately stitched.

"I think you would find that rather hard work and without the security of knowing that you have a regular amount of money coming in," he remarked. "But of course, Arina, as I have said before, sooner or later you will be married properly to somebody who will take care of you and who will also be prepared to provide for your mother."

There was silence for a moment as she thought over what he had said. Then she answered:

"Because you are so kind and thoughtful, may I accept your proposition for the moment with the promise that if I have no . . . further need of your money in the future I can write to you and . . . say so?"

"Of course," the Marquis agreed.

"Shall I sign this document?"

In answer he handed her the big white quill-pen, dipping it first into an ornate gold ink-well.

Her writing was neat and tidy, and when he too had signed the paper the Marquis folded it and said:

"I intend to send this to my Bank. It will be safe there and no prying eyes will see it. At the same time, I will instruct them to pay the rest of the money which is owed to your mother's Surgeon, and three hundred pounds into your Bank, if you will tell me where it is."

Arina hesitated and he said:

"On second thought, I think perhaps it would be a mistake to use a Bank where you are known and which would be aware that you are receiving money from me. It would be better if I open an account in your name at Coutt's and you can draw the money from there whenever you require it."

"Thank you very much," Arina answered. "I am sure what you have thought of is best for both of us."

The Marquis thought she was being very amenable, and because he was sure it would please her, he said:

"I want you now to sit down comfortably while I tell you things about my family which you will be expected to know when you arrive in Scotland. I will also describe my father, whom I suspect you will find as intimidating as I have always done."

Arina crossed the Sitting-Room to settle herself in a large, comfortable armchair in front of the fireplace.

As if he felt restless, the Marquis did not sit down but instead walked about as he started what was really the story of his life.

"My father was brought up by his father to think the world was there for him to walk on," he began. "Most Scottish Chieftains are the same. For centuries they have enjoyed power, and although ostensibly it was taken from them by the British, in the heart of their own Clan they still reign supreme."

He paused for a moment, thinking that was particularly true of his father. Then he went on:

"When my father inherited, he was the most important Chieftain in Scotland, besides being the richest and the greatest land-owner."

"I have heard of him and of your Castle," Arina murmured.

The Marquis was surprised, but he did not say so and continued:

"He revived the old customs, the old ceremonies, and the mystique which surrounded the Chieftains of the Clans. As soon as the ban was lifted on the wearing of the tartan, he put his own servants and all the Clansmen in the vicinity of the Castle into the kilt."

As he spoke the Marquis was thinking of how bitterly the Scots had resented having to give up the clothes that in many ways were a part of their faith.

Because it meant so much to them, they had dipped the traditional cloth of the tartan in vats of mud or dye and sewed the cloth into ludicrous breeches.

In this way they felt that somehow they deceived the British and made the new laws seem foolish.

At first, when the ban on Highland dress was lifted in 1782, it became an affectation of the Anglicised Lairds, the fancy-dress of the Lowlanders, and the uniform of the King's Gaelic soldiers.

But eventually a great number of Clans followed the McDonons, and now more and more Highlanders were looking proud and resplendent in the kilt and the plaid.

The Marquis tried to put this into words so that Arina would understand a little about the land to which he was taking her.

But even as he spoke he knew in reality how little he knew about the Highlands himself, having been away from them for so long.

He suddenly felt absurdly angry that at the age of nearly twenty-seven he should be forced to return like a captured slave to face his father's overbearing domination, which would gradually wear him down until he would surrender not only himself but his independence of thought.

"When you get to Kildonon Castle," he said aloud, "and realise that the whole world revolves in accordance with my father's whim, that even the sun shines and the tides go in and out at his command, you will understand what the place is like far better than I can tell you now."

Only as he finished speaking the words that seemed to ring out because they were spoken with anger and hatred did he realise that Arina was asleep.

Intent on his own thoughts, he had not noticed that she had not interrupted him or asked any questions for a long time.

Now, as he saw that her eyes were closed, he knew she was utterly and completely exhausted by all she had been through.

The emotion of leaving her mother at the Nursing-home had been followed by the long hours of standing as gown after gown was tried on her.

Then had come the ordeal of driving away alone with him.

Perhaps it was his Celt ancestry which had made him aware that she was embarrassed and apprehensive when he had drawn his horses to a standstill outside the building in which his flat was situated.

He had known too that while they had dinner together she was nervous at first and afraid of doing or saying anything of which he would not approve.

When he thought about it, he was sure that it was the first time she had ever dined alone with a man. Perhaps he should have been more understanding and more gentle with her, but he was not quite certain how to do so.

The women with whom he dined alone always made sure that the conversation sparkled with *double extendres* and looked at him in a way which was an incitement to passion.

In fact, the Marquis could not remember when he had had a meal alone with a woman who was not intent on arousing his desire and making herself indispensable to him.

'Arina is only a child,' he thought. 'I shall not only have to teach her what she must do, but protect her from the things that frighten her, and undoubtedly there will be a great many of them.'

Looking down at her as she lay asleep with her head turned against the softness of the silk cushion, she looked very young and very vulnerable.

He saw too that her eye-lashes, which had seemed dark against her pale skin, wore no mascara like Olive's, but were naturally dark but turned to gold as they curled at the tips.

They were in fact the eye-lashes of a very young child, and the Marquis felt that she was not only young and fragile, but like an exquisite piece of Dresden china that might easily be broken if handled roughly.

He opened the door, then picked her up in his arms to carry her to his bedroom.

He had vaguely been wondering how they could sleep apart without Champkins being aware of it, and he knew now that because Arina was asleep there would be no need to involve her in any conspiracy.

He laid her down carefully on the bed that had been turned down for the night.

He thought he should wake her so that she could undress and get into bed, then realised she was so deeply asleep that it would be almost cruel to do so.

Instead he took off her shoes, then skilfully unbuttoned her gown and slipped it off.

He thought with a wry smile that it was the first time he had undressed a woman who was not in the least interested in what he was doing.

He slipped her between the sheets and saw what she had meant when she said that *Madame* Celeste had been shocked at how thin she was. She was indeed far too light for her age and height.

He pulled the bed-clothes up to her chin, and by the rise and fall of her breasts he knew she was so deeply asleep that it would take a great deal more than his gentle movements to wake her.

He stood looking down at her. Then he took one of the pillows from the bed and picked up his night-shirt and robe from the chair on which Champkins had laid them ready for him.

Going to the cupboard, he found, as he expected, two blankets folded and ready in case he should need their extra warmth.

Carrying them all in his arms, he blew out the candles beside the bed, then left the room, closing the door behind him.

The sofa in the Sitting-Room was large and comfortable, and because he too was tired, as thanks to Olive he had slept very little the night before, the Marquis expected to fall asleep immediately, but it was nearly midnight before he did so.

Having been in the Army for two years after leaving Oxford, he had taught himself to wake at any time he wished without the need of being called.

It was something which he had found useful in his Regimental life and later, when, for instance, he wished to go cubbing on his grandfather's Estate, which involved getting up at four o'clock when the servants sometimes overslept.

The Marquis was therefore bathed and half-dressed before Champkins came down from his room on the next floor.

"Good-morning, M'Lord!" he exclaimed. "You're early!"

"I have a few things to tidy up before we leave," the Marquis said, "and as Her Ladyship is still asleep, I had no wish to wake her."

Champkins glanced towards the closed bedroom door.

"Very wise, M'Lord, if I may say so. Her Ladyship may find it hard to sleep when she's tossed about on the waves."

"I hope the sea will be calm at this time of the year," the Marquis replied drily. "And now, Champkins, I want to make sure we have everything with us that is of importance, because I am giving Mr. Groves instructions that everything else must go into store."

Mr. Groves was the secretary, who was expected to arrive at nine o'clock.

Champkins made a grimace.

"Does that mean, M'Lord, that we're not coming back?"

"If we do, it will not be to this flat, but to Kildonon House in Park Lane," the Marquis said in a hard voice.

He spoke with a determination that made Champkins look at him in surprise.

He had suddenly made up his mind that he would fight his father in this matter if in nothing else and would refuse to make his home in Scotland unless he had what at any rate would be a *pied à terre* in London.

He thought perhaps it was the way he had explained things to Arina last night—of which she had heard very little—which had given him a new courage that he should not have lost in the first place.

It was almost as if in telling her about the Scots and how despite the overbearing and cruel domination by the English they had kept their identity and their pride, he had found both those things within himself.

"In fact," he said now, "why should we pay for storage when there is plenty of room at Kildonon House? There will be a caretaker there, and I will tell Mr. Groves to

have everything removed from here and placed in the
Ball-Room until I can arrange them as I wish."

"A good idea, M'Lord," Champkins said cheerfully,
but the Marquis was not listening.

❦

When Mr. Faulkner arrived he brought two large carriages which were more comfortable than hackney-
carriages and which were drawn by two strong horses.

The Marquis, Arina, and Mr. Faulkner were to travel
in the first, and Champkins in the second with all the
baggage.

By the time they left, two more trunks had arrived for
Arina from *Madame* Celeste, along with three leather
hat-boxes containing the bonnets to match the clothes
they had ordered.

"What we have to decide," the Marquis said with a smile
at the mountain of luggage, "is what you will need on the
voyage and what must go down into the hold. I doubt if
any cabin, however large, could accommodate all this."

Because Arina could only look helplessly at her new
pile of possessions, the Marquis was relieved to discover
that Celeste, with her usual common sense, had itemised
the contents of each trunk.

He therefore chose the one which he thought would
be most useful, then opened another to take from it a
long, warm cape which was trimmed with fur.

"It can be very cold at sea," he explained as Arina
looked at it in surprise.

Champkins had seen to his luggage and the Marquis
had contributed at the last moment a certain amount of
food from Shepherd Market and also a few cases of wine.

There was a trunk containing what the Marquis knew
was essential on a journey of this sort—his own linen
sheets, towels, and blankets, besides soft pillows and bedside rugs.

It rather amused him that Arina was astonished that
they should travel in such luxury.

But when she saw her cabin aboard The *Sea Serpent,* which was the ship that sailed regularly from Tilbury to Aberdeen, she understood how the Marquis found its inadequate furnishings extremely uncomfortable.

However, for her it was very exciting not only to be at sea in what seemed a large ship but also to have a cabin to herself.

Because they had been so poor after her father's death, she and her mother when they moved into a tiny cottage had been forced to share a bedroom.

Staying in London, they could hardly afford the cheapest room in a boarding-house, let alone pay for two.

When Champkins had made up Arina's bunk with linen sheets that were too big for it, fluffy white blankets, and comfortable pillows, she thanked him so effusively that he said:

"It's your right, M'Lady, now that you're married to the Master, an' if you'll take my advice you should always see that you has what you're entitled to."

"The difficulty is," Arina replied, "I am not at all certain what that means."

She spoke spontaneously and frankly to Champkins because she already liked him and realised how devoted he was to the Marquis.

In fact, she thought of Champkins as being very like the Nanny she had had until her parents became too poor to afford one and she was old enough to look after herself.

Champkins grinned. Then he said:

"What you have to do, M'Lady, is to stick yer nose in the air, and look down at everybody else as if you was superior to 'em!"

Arina laughed.

"I am quite certain I shall never feel superior to anybody!"

"Just you remember Your Ladyship's as good as what they are, if not better!"

Arina laughed again, and she felt as if Champkins took away some of the apprehension she felt in case she should do something wrong and fail the Marquis by making his relatives suspicious that their marriage was not real.

'He has been so kind to me that it would be unforgivable if I could not help him,' she thought.

She had felt very shy when she had awakened in the morning to find herself in what she knew was the Marquis's bed, and was aware who had put her there and removed her gown.

At first she was so horrified at the thought of what had occurred that she had wanted to run away and hide and never see the Marquis again.

Then she told herself she was being ridiculous.

After all, she was of no importance in his eyes, and it was a very sensible thing to do to take off the expensive gown he had given her, which would certainly have been very creased if she had slept in it all night.

He would have done the same for any woman, old or young, she thought.

She decided that if she appeared shy, embarrassed, or coy about the situation she had caused by going to sleep, it would make her look foolish and the Marquis would doubtless despise her.

Arina wondered how he knew how to remove her gown and undo the buttons at the back of it.

Then, when she had arranged her hair at the dressing-table, she found something which was very surprising.

It was a very masculine dressing-table, very much the same as the one her father had used, but much more luxurious.

The Marquis's brushes, which were of ivory engraved with his crest, stood on top of the low chest-of-drawers on which there was a mirror supported in a way that it could be adjusted to any angle.

Framed in wood, it had three little drawers beneath it.

Arina found it fascinating, and because it was like her father's, without thinking or meaning to pry, she opened the middle drawer.

Inside were a number of loose coins and on top of them a small swan's-down powder-puff.

What she could not have known was that Olive had dropped it by mistake after she had dressed herself the night before and stood in front of the mirror to arrange her hair and repair the ravages of the Marquis's kisses.

She had also powdered her nose, and when she had taken a small box of salve from her reticule to redden her lips, the powder-puff had fallen onto the floor, where Champkins had found it.

It had not surprised him.

It was only another of the things which his Master's "love-birds," as he called them in his mind, left behind. Hair-pins, lip-salves, small bottles of perfume, and even at times articles of clothing, had all been retrieved by Champkins without comment.

He had pushed the powder-puff into the drawer, meaning to mention it to the Marquis later.

Arina stared at it with puzzled eyes.

Then she told herself she was being stupid.

Of course the Marquis, seeing how attractive he was, would have had many women in his life!

Although she was slightly shocked that they should have come to what she realised was a bachelor's flat, she supposed that they had as good an excuse as she had for being there.

Anyway, she told herself, it was none of her business.

However, because for the first time she thought of the Marquis as a man rather than an angel sent from God to save her mother from dying, she could not help being curious.

When she went into the Dining-Room for breakfast she had longed to ask him if he had slept comfortably after giving up his bedroom to her, but she found it impossible to express what she wanted to say.

Instead, she tried to speak to him quite naturally, and not to remember that he had undressed her and put her to bed.

As it happened, the Marquis was so busy with his preparations for leaving that he had almost forgotten what had happened the night before.

Mr. Groves had arrived while they were still having breakfast, and by the time he had been given his instructions, Mr. Faulkner was announced.

All Arina had to do was put on her bonnet and the blue shawl she had worn the day before, and climb into the carriage.

As they drove away from London, her thoughts were only with her mother, and she was praying that she would already be feeling stronger so that there would be less risk when she was ready for her operation.

She had told her mother why she was going away and had promised to write to her every day, although she was not quite certain whether she understood.

"I shall have plenty of time on board ship," she told herself.

The only thing she had asked Champkins to put into a valise was writing-paper.

"I can do better for you than that, M'Lady," Champkins had replied.

Arina had not asked him what he meant at the time, but before he made up the bunk in her cabin, he put a fine leather blotter down on the table and set beside it a small travelling ink-pot and several quill-pens.

"I'll keep them sharpened for you, M'Lady," he promised, and Arina found it hard to tell him how grateful she was.

Only when the ship was actually moving out of the harbour did she feel a sudden tremble of fear at the thought of leaving her mother and everything that was familiar.

She was going to a strange place with a strange man to be with people who, from all she had heard, sounded very frightening—the Duke in particular.

Then she told herself that, as the Marquis had said, it was an adventure, and she would be extremely ungrateful and very foolish if she did not make every effort to enjoy it.

She knew it was something her mother would have felt before she had become so ill.

Her father too had always seemed to make everything they did not only an excitement but also a joyous experience which they would remember and talk about.

Perhaps because he had given up so much when he ran away with her mother, Arina felt he used his imagination as few other grown-up people bothered to do.

It was not only the tales he had told her when she was a little girl of fairies and goblins in the woods, of dragons that lived in the forests, and of nymphs that inhabited the streams.

It was also that his imagination enabled him to live in an enchanted world where stark reality never encroached.

When he told his wife that he loved her and it was difficult to think of anyone else, he spoke the truth. And because she looked at him with starry eyes, their marriage had been an idyllic one.

That they lived in a shabby, dilapidated house and could not afford any luxuries was of no importance!

To them it was a Fairy-Palace; the food they ate was enchanted, and their daughter was not only a gift from God but a fairy-child, looked after and protected by the fairies.

Only after her father had died did she and her mother have to face reality, and it was very frightening.

Arina knew now that her fears were groundless, because her father was still loving and protecting them, wherever he might be now, and had sent the Marquis to rescue them.

She chided herself for ever thinking that they had been forsaken.

"This is a ship like the one in which Odysseus sailed away from Troy or Jason sought the Golden Fleece," she thought as the *Sea Serpent* began to move over the waves, "and the Marquis is a Knight with a sword in his hand, a shield on his arm, ready to destroy any enemies or dragons that may assail us."

She looked up at the sky as she said beneath her breath:

"Wherever we go, whatever we do, we are protected, and I have only to pray to Papa for help for my prayers to be answered."

She smiled as she asked herself:

"How can I have been so foolish as not to have known this before now? It was wrong, very wrong of me to let Mama be so unhappy and grow so ill because she felt we had been forsaken."

She wished she could tell her mother what she had discovered, then she knew she could write it to her. It might be hard to put into words, but her mother would understand.

What she had reasoned out for herself made her feel so happy that when Champkins came to tell her that the Marquis had arranged for them to have something to eat, she went to him with a smile on her lips, her eyes alight with happiness.

It was after one o'clock when they sailed, and because there were no other passengers aboard the *Sea Serpent,* Mr. Faulkner had been able to engage a third cabin, where they could eat on their own.

It was impossible to move the bunks because they were battened down, but all the rest of the furniture had been removed except for a small round table, three chairs, and a side-table from which food could be served.

A steward waited on them, and Arina realised as soon as a rich pâté was offered her that this was the food the Marquis had brought with him.

The pâté was followed by an ox-tongue, well cooked and set in aspic. There was also a salad and a whole leg of pork garnished with apples, if Arina preferred it.

The Marquis was hungry and ate quite a lot of what he referred to as a "light luncheon."

With difficulty Arina prevented herself from commenting that so much food would have sufficed her and her mother for weeks.

She almost felt as if Champkins were beside her, telling her that she must behave as if such a meal were quite ordinary, and far from being impressed by it, she should feel entitled to complain.

Then she gave a little chuckle at her thoughts and the Marquis looked up to ask:

"What is amusing you?"

"Something Champkins said."

"He is certainly a character," the Marquis remarked, "and I am wondering how he will get on at the Castle. With any other man I would be afraid that he might be bullied for being a Sassenach, but I have a feeling that Champkins will hold his own."

"I am sure he will, My Lord," Mr. Faulkner agreed, "and I assure you, we are not such barbarians as you are making us out to be."

The Marquis laughed. Then he said:

"If you are going to be touchy about what I say, I promise you, I shall turn round and go straight back to London. I am well aware that my father will disapprove of my appearance, my conversation, and undoubtedly my thoughts, but he will have to take me as I am, or rather what I have become, living in the South!"

Mr. Faulkner did not reply, but Arina thought she had been right in thinking that the Marquis was a Knight in armour, ready to do battle with whoever opposed him.

The sea was a little choppy but not rough, and Arina stood on deck for a long time after luncheon, watching the coast of England in the distance and looking across the North Sea to where the sky met the waves.

"You look as if you are enjoying yourself," the Marquis said with just a hint of envy in his voice.

"I have suddenly realised how exciting this all is," Arina replied, "and you were right when you said it was an adventure."

"Not a very pleasant one for me."

"But it must be!" Arina insisted. "Adventures even if they are dangerous and uncomfortable are still stimulating, and I am quite certain they open new horizons which we never knew existed before."

She spoke in a rapt little voice that made the Marquis look at her in surprise.

He had expected her to be apprehensive and embarrassed! Instead, he thought, she seemed to glow almost as if she were lit from a light within and to be vibrating to it.

"I am glad you think like that," he said. "I was afraid you would be so unhappy at leaving your mother, as I know you were yesterday morning, that we were in for a very gloomy voyage."

"It would be very selfish of me if I thought only of myself," Arina replied, "and I have read that Knights when they set out to vanquish evil were always inspired by the lady whose favour they carried."

She paused and then said a little shyly:

"As I am the only . . . lady with you at the moment, I am hoping that perhaps in a very . . . small way I can . . . inspire you or at least . . . prevent you from feeling . . . resentful."

She hesitated over the word and the Marquis asked:

"How are you aware that that is what I feel? I do not remember saying so in so many words."

"You may think it very impertinent of me," Arina replied looking away from him, "but when you told me you did not wish to return to Scotland and your father was forcing you to marry a Scottish girl, I could feel how deeply it . . . angered you and how you hated and . . . resented leaving London and all your . . . friends."

As she said the word "friends" she remembered the powder-puff by the mirror on his dressing-table, and thought perhaps that was another reason why the Marquis had no wish to go away.

"What you felt is indeed true," he answered. "I think it was very perceptive of you to be aware of it, and I am sure that you will be able to help me."

"I hope so," Arina said, "but I have not yet been able to tell you how . . . ashamed I am that I fell asleep when you were telling me such interesting things last night."

She looked up at him and added beseechingly:

"Please . . . please . . . do not be offended, but tell me again what you were saying then, and I . . . promise I will not go to . . . sleep."

The Marquis smiled.

"It was understandable. You had had a very long day, and I suspect you had not slept very much the night before."

Arina knew this was true not only because she had been worried at the thought of leaving her mother, but also because her mother needed so much attention. She had risen half-a-dozen times during the hours of darkness to smooth her pillows or give her something to drink.

"It was still very rude of me," she said. "You know if I could help you in any way . . . it would be the most . . . wonderful thing that could ever happen, and it is in fact only if I can do . . . something for you that I shall ever feel out of your . . . debt."

"I have already explained that I am in *your* debt," the Marquis replied, "so I will certainly continue the story I started last night. I think you are intelligent enough to realise that, if we were actually man and wife, you would know a great deal more about me than you know now."

"I would like that . . . I would like it . . . very much."

"Very well," the Marquis agreed, "but as you are tired and beginning to feel a little cold from the wind which is filling the sails, we will go below for your first lesson."

"I have a great deal to learn," Arina admitted, "and it will be very exciting for me . . . but I only hope it will not . . . bore you."

Because she was so eager to help the Marquis, when Champkins came to her cabin to enquire if there was anything she wanted from her trunks which he had not unpacked already, she said to him:

"I . . . I want to ask you something."

"What is it, M'Lady?"

"Because this is all very new to me, if you can think of anything I can do to help His Lordship and make him feel happier, will you be frank and tell me?"

Champkins looked at her for a moment in surprise. Then he said:

"I don't mind telling you, M'Lady, that it took me by surprise when the Master tells me he's married. But now I've seen you, and when Your Ladyship says things like that to me, I thinks that you're just the sort of person who should be with him at this moment."

"Why this moment?" Arina asked.

"Because he's browned off, fed up, and sick of the whole thing," Champkins answered. "He got away from them stuck-up Scots once, and now he's got to go back again, and there's nothing he can do about it."

Arina looked at him wide-eyed.

"I know that because his brothers have died, he is now the Marquis and will one day be Chief of the Clan," she said, "but does he have to go back even if he does not wish to?"

"He's got no choice," Champkins answered. "He's got to go back and get used to stuffing himself with haggis, or whatever it is them Scots stuff themselves with, and enjoy it!"

He did not add that he had heard this by listening at the door when Mr. Faulkner had been telling his Master that he had to return to Scotland.

He had expected it anyway, which was why he had not protested when the Marquis had said they were leaving immediately for Kildonon Castle.

"It will be difficult for him to adjust himself," Arina said as if she was speaking her thoughts aloud.

"'Course it will, M'Lady," Champkins agreed. "What else do you think it would be, giving up his friends, his Clubs, and his lady-loves?"

The last words came out before he could prevent them. Then he said quickly:

"'Scuse me, M'Lady, I shouldn't have said that."

"Why not, when we are speaking frankly?" Arina replied. "Of course I suspected that His Lordship, because he is so handsome, would have lots of lovely ladies in . . . love with him."

"Dozens of 'em!" Champkins said with relish. "They flutters round him like moths round a flame. But he soon gets bored with 'em. Then they comes crying to me: 'When can I see him, Champkins?' 'Please, Champkins, put this note where he can't miss it!' "

Champkins spoke in a mimicking, affected manner which made Arina want to laugh. Then he went on:

"They tips me, an' they tips me well, M'Lady, but there's nothing I can do. Once the Master's bored, he's bored! And your Ladyship can guess as soon as one lady goes out another comes in, just waiting for the opportunity."

"If they are beautiful, why does he grow . . . bored so quickly?" Arina asked.

Champkins scratched his head.

"Can't rightly say, M'Lady. Some of 'em are so beautiful you'd think that would be sufficient for any man. But if you asks me, I think it's 'cause they gets too demanding, they wants too much, and no man likes to think he's shackled to a gold-digger."

There was a humour in his voice that once again made Arina want to laugh.

"Oh, Champkins, you are so funny!" she said. "But I know exactly what you mean."

While she could understand the Marquis's desire for freedom, she thought that her father had been "shackled" to her mother, as he would have put it, and yet they had been blissfully happy for nearly nineteen years.

Then she wondered if theirs was the sort of love the Marquis was looking for, and when he did not find it he grew bored.

Perhaps he was different from her father, but they were both exceedingly handsome, both educated in the same way, and both had been brought up in luxury.

The only difference was that while her father had given up everything for love, the Marquis had been prepared to sacrifice nothing, and that probably meant that he had never loved in the same way as her father had.

'But perhaps he is seeking it,' Arina thought, 'and that will be a quest in which I can help him.'

She was not certain how, but she thought that if he could find the type of love that had made her father so happy, then she would, as she had said to him, be able to feel that she had paid her debt.

"I will pray for him," she decided, "and perhaps Papa will help him just as he helped Mama and me."

Champkins unpacked a very pretty gown of pale green gauze which had a velvet cape edged with maribou to wear over it.

When Arina had dressed herself, she wished there were a large mirror in which she could see her reflection, knowing that the gown was the loveliest she could possibly imagine.

She knew it eclipsed the blue one which she had thought when she put it on must have been fashioned from a piece of the sky.

She found attached to the gown a matching ribbon, the same which decorated the bodice, and which *Madame* Celeste had shown her how to wear in her hair.

"If you have jewels or combs you will not need it," she had said, "but if not, you will find it very effective."

Jewels were something that she was never likely to possess, Arina thought, as she tied the ribbon in her hair with a little bow on the top.

It gave her a mischievous look which was different from the way she had looked before.

She knew also that because the green of the gown reflected the green of her eyes, it made her skin seem very white in contrast.

The evening was warm and delightful as she walked to the cabin where they were to dine.

When she entered it she found the Marquis was waiting for her, and she realised as she glanced at the table that it was laid for only two people.

She felt her heart leap because they were to be alone, and it would certainly be more exciting than if Mr. Faulkner were there.

As if the Marquis knew what she was thinking, he said:

"Faulkner asked to be excused, partly, I think, through tact, and partly because he says he is tired and wishes to retire to his cabin to have a long night's rest."

"I suppose it is rude to say that I am glad," Arina replied, "but I would rather be alone with you, because that makes it so much easier to talk, and perhaps you could go on teaching me."

The Marquis thought that most women wanted to be alone with him for a very different reason.

"I do not want you to become bored with me," he teased.

"I could never be that," Arina answered, "and I promise you that even if I am, I will not fall asleep!"

She paused before she added:

"What I am afraid of is that *you* will grow bored with teaching me."

The way she accentuated the word "you" made the Marquis look at her sharply.

"As you can imagine," he began, "when . . ."

Then he stopped and changed what he had been about to say.

"You have been talking to Champkins."

Arina blushed.

"How did you know?"

"Shall I say I can read your thoughts, and I have a very good idea what Champkins would tell you, which of course is that I am easily bored."

"I am sure it is because you are so . . . intelligent that most people must find it very hard to . . . keep up with you."

Arina thought she had been ingenious in her answer, and the Marquis said with a smile:

"You are not to believe everything that Champkins tells you. He has been with me for so many years that he is inclined to become somewhat familiar."

"I feel he is very much like my Nanny. She was always telling me things 'for my own good'!"

The Marquis laughed.

"I have often thought that myself, and if Champkins were a woman he would undoubtedly be a Nanny who would rule children with a rod of iron one minute, and spoil them the next."

"That is a wonderful description of him, and I think he is a very nice man!"

They talked animatedly while they were served a delicious meal which the Marquis had brought aboard with him, and there was also champagne, which Arina had tasted before but only on very special occasions.

"Papa used to open a bottle at Christmas and on Mama's birthday," she said. "I was allowed a sip when I was small, and half a glassful when I was a little older."

"Now that you are a grown-up young lady, and of course a Marchioness," the Marquis said, "I think you can manage nearly a full glass."

"Suppose I grow unsteady on my feet?"

"Then I will carry you to bed as I did last night."

She blushed as she remembered how he had undressed her, and he thought she looked very attractive.

Then she said in a serious little voice:

"It was . . . very kind of you . . . and I did not thank you this morning because I felt it was . . . something you had already . . . forgotten."

The Marquis looked puzzled.

"Why should you think that?"

"Because I am of no . . . importance, and therefore you would not . . . remember me as you would . . ."

She stopped as if she felt that what she had begun to say was embarrassing, and after a moment the Marquis said:

"Finish the sentence, I am interested."

"It sounds rather impertinent . . . and you might be angry."

"I will not be angry, and nothing we say to each other can be impertinence. If we are to work together on our adventure, it is essential for us both to be frank."

"Well . . . I was thinking . . . but I may be wrong that if you carried a . . . lovely lady to bed . . . like the ones

400

Champkins has told me . . . pursue you all the time . . . you would want to do it because it . . . meant something to . . . you."

The Marquis was surprised at what Arina was thinking, but then he realised it was just the way that somebody very young and innocent would think.

"Perhaps you are right," he said casually, "but what I do remember about putting you to bed is that you are far too light for your height, and if you want to please me, you will eat to fill out the hollows in your cheeks and those which I suspect exist elsewhere in your body."

"I will try . . . I promise I will . . . try," Arina said quite naturally, "and already I feel . . . fatter than I was yesterday."

"That is just your imagination," the Marquis replied. "You have a long way to go yet, and that is why I insist that you have a second helping of pigeon or, if you prefer, the veal, although it has not been cooked as well as I would have wished."

"Please . . . I could not eat any more," Arina pleaded. "I will try to be more . . . amenable tomorrow, but I am used to having just an egg for dinner or making some soup for Mama from the vegetables in the garden, or what was left over, and there was usually very little, from what we had for luncheon."

The way she spoke made the Marquis aware that she was not wishing to sound pathetic but was merely telling him the facts of her past life so that he would understand.

"From all I can remember of my father's Castle," he said, "there was certainly plenty of food, and good food, but not cooked as richly as I have come to prefer."

Thinking back into the past, he went on:

"There is salmon in the river and I hope to catch many of them myself, and lobsters from the sea. There is venison from the moors, and when they have grown larger than they are at the moment, lots of grouse and black cock."

"It sounds very exciting!" Arina exclaimed. "And Champkins says there will be haggis."

"Of course," the Marquis agreed. "Haggis and oat-meal for breakfast. That will fatten you up if nothing else does!"

As he spoke he remembered how there had always been a huge bowl of porridge for breakfast in the great Dining-Hall on the First Floor of the Castle.

He remembered filling his wooden bowl edged with silver, which he had been given when he was christened, and adding salt to it. Then, because his father insisted, he walked round the room while he ate it.

It was a tradition of the ancient Scots that they ate their porridge standing, in case while they were doing so they were attacked by a rival Clan.

The Marquis debated whether he would explain this custom to Arina, then realised it was immaterial because the ladies were allowed to eat their porridge sitting, and therefore it would not concern her.

Aloud he said:

"I wonder how many traditions known to my father and other relatives I have forgotten. If I now show my ignorance, it will not only scandalise them but will give them a weapon to use against me."

There was a little silence. Then Arina said:

"I believe it is a . . . mistake for you to . . . think like that."

The Marquis looked at her sharply.

"What do you mean?"

"You said I was to . . . speak the truth . . . and I think you should not return to your home feeling so . . . hostile. Papa always said . . . you get what you give . . . and I think that is . . . true."

The Marquis did not speak, and she went on:

"We are pretending to be married, and I think it would be . . . wise for you to pretend also to be . . . pleased to see your father again . . . pleased to be home. If they are expecting you to be cross and resentful, it will take them by surprise."

As she finished speaking she looked at the Marquis's expression and said quickly:

"I am sorry . . . but you did tell me I could say . . ."

Her eyes were wide and frightened as her words faded away.

Just for a moment the Marquis felt like telling her it was none of her business and she had no right to preach to him. Then as he realised that what she had said was sensible and what he should have thought out for himself, he said:

"I want you always to tell me what is in your mind, Arina, and I am only surprised that you should have thought it all out so sensibly."

"You . . . you are not . . . angry?"

"No, of course not! You only make me feel I have, been rather stupid."

"You could . . . never be . . . that!"

"I hope you are right, but you have certainly put things into a different perspective from the way I have been thinking so far."

"I know it is difficult for you, very, very difficult," Arina said in a soft voice, "to leave behind in the South everything that . . . matters to . . . you."

She gave a little sigh, as if she was feeling the same. Then she added quickly:

"I feel as if I am being clairvoyant when I tell you that things will not be so bad as you anticipate."

"How do you know that?"

"I cannot explain it, but I think it is because you are so vital, so vibrant, that any opposition which you think you will encounter will disperse when you are there almost as if you were the sun driving away the mist."

She spoke in a dreamy voice which surprised the Marquis and after a moment he said:

"I hope you are right. Anyway, if the mist is there, as I am afraid it may be, I am sure we can disperse it together."

He saw a light come into her eyes at the word "together," and he knew she was thinking that if she could help him it would be very wonderful for her to be able to do so.

He raised his glass.

"To us, Arina!" he said. "Together on a very strange and, I hope, exciting adventure."

CHAPTER SIX

*I*t is wonderful! Beautiful! Just the sort of Castle you should have!"

Arina spoke with such a note of exaltation and excitement in her voice that the Marquis felt himself respond in the same way.

He could not help feeling elated from the moment they had arrived in Aberdeen and transferred from the *Sea Serpent* to the Duke's yacht.

When they arrived he thought that quite unexpectedly he had enjoyed the voyage.

He had anticipated that it would be three days and nights of utter boredom. Instead, he found himself enjoying his conversations with Arina, which often became lectures.

At the same time, he found that she not only asked him extremely intelligent questions but was also prepared to argue with him.

When he questioned her as to how she could have such an astute and at times amazingly logical mind, she answered:

"Papa or Mama used to read aloud every evening, and afterwards Mama and I would start an argument with Papa as to whether the writer had been right or wrong in his assumptions. Usually Papa won the contest, but at the same time it was very exciting and we often became quite aggressive!"

She laughed and added:

"That is something I would not . . . dare to do with you."

Nevertheless, the Marquis found that he had to polish up his brain, and when they reached Aberdeen he had to admit that he had been stimulated and amused instead of being depressed by the voyage.

He would have been less than human if he had not found it gratifying to be greeted by a number of the Clan, all looking magnificent in their kilts, who escorted him and Arina to where the Duke's yacht was waiting beside the Quay.

A Piper played them aboard with "Victory to the McDonons," and when the vessel started to move out to sea they were cheered by a crowd that had accumulated to watch and listen.

If Arina was thrilled at her first sight of the Castle, the Marquis felt a sensation of pride that he had never felt before.

There was no Castle on the whole coast of Scotland that looked as magnificent and enchanting as Kildonon.

Situated high above the bay, with only the gardens between it and the sea, it was silhouetted against the moors which rose high against the sky.

It was not only the Castle itself with its turrets and its spires that was so beautiful, but the Marquis had forgotten how the light in that part of Scotland was lovelier than anywhere else in the world.

It seemed to change every few seconds with the movement of the clouds and the sun, and in the centre of the picture the Castle glowed like a precious jewel.

As the yacht sailed across the smooth water they could see a big company of Clansmen waiting for them on the shore, and as the yacht came alongside the long wooden jetty which was built out into the bay, the swirl of the pipes seemed to fill the air.

The Marquis would never have admitted it, but he found himself wishing at that moment that he were wearing Highland dress, something he had thrown away disdainfully after he had gone South with his mother.

The way he was greeted by the McDonons, the respect with which they approached him, made him once again feel very proud.

As he and Arina were escorted through the gardens to the Castle with two Pipers ahead of them and two following, the Marquis knew he had not only come home but had been accepted as the future Chieftain.

There were flowers in the garden, trees in blossom, and a fountain playing in the centre which threw its water iridescent towards the sun.

There was a great flight of stone steps leading to the balconied terrace, and from there they walked to the front of the Castle so that they could enter by the great wooden iron-studded front door, which had been the entrance since mediaeval times.

Here were more Clansmen, those who were directly connected with the household, and they greeted the Marquis, welcoming him both in English and in Gaelic.

But more eloquent than words were the smiles on their faces and the expressions in their eyes, which proclaimed that they were really pleased to see him.

There was a wide staircase to carry them up to the First Floor, where, as the Marquis knew, there was the Chieftain's Room, in which he was sure his father would be waiting.

There was a wry twist to his lips as he realised that his father was determined from the moment of his arrival to make him aware of his new position and to receive him formally as the prodigal son.

The Major-Domo of the household announced him in stentorian tones:

"The Marquis of Kildonon, Your Grace!"

The Chieftain's Room was so impressive, with the walls hung with the shields and claymores of the past, interspersed with huge portraits of previous Chieftains, that for a moment Arina found it hard to concentrate on the man who was waiting for them.

The Duke was sitting in a high chair that might almost have been a throne at the far end of the room.

She suddenly felt nervous and a little shy as she and the Marquis walked between lines of kilted men standing stiffly at attention.

She was aware too that like those who had greeted the Marquis on the yacht and on the jetty, they regarded her with curiosity.

So far the Marquis had not announced who she was but had merely introduced the Clansmen to her without saying her name.

Now she felt her heart beating quickly, and the only consolation was that she knew she was looking her best.

It was Champkins who had suggested that she wear a gown of deep blue that echoed the colour of the sea, and a bonnet, its pointed brim edged with lace, its crown wreathed with very small pink roses.

The Marquis had looked at her approvingly when she came from her cabin just before they reached Aberdeen.

He had also been aware that it was not only her gown that became her, but that the food she had eaten in the three days they had been at sea had already taken the starved look from her face, the contours of which were already a little fuller.

Now as she moved beside the Marquis she felt that the distance they had to walk in order to reach the Duke seemed interminable.

At last they stopped in front of an old man wearing a huge Cairngorm brooch on his plaid and a large sporran with a top of shining silver on it.

For a moment nobody spoke. Then the Duke, staring at his son from under beetling eye-brows, said in a deep, authoritative voice:

"Welcome home, Alistair. It is good to see you."

He held out his hand and the Marquis grasped it. Then, despite his resolution to do nothing of the sort, in a swift movement his knee touched the ground.

He knew this was an obeisance that his father as Chieftain of the Clan would expect from him, and he had told himself when he thought about it on the voyage that he would be damned if he would humiliate himself. But now it seemed to come naturally to him.

Still with his hand in his father's, he asked:

"How are you, Sir? It has been a long time since we met."

"Too long!" the Duke replied briefly.

Then his eyes, piercing like those of an eagle, turned to stare at Arina.

She knew without his putting it into words what the Duke was asking, and she held her breath because she was frightened.

The Marquis's voice, however, seemed to ring out so that everybody in the room could hear it.

"And now, Father," he said, "may I present to you my wife, who has accompanied me on my voyage here."

"Your wife!"

There was no doubt that the Duke was astonished, but before the Marquis could say any more, he asked sharply:

"You are married? Why did nobody tell me of this?"

"We were married very quietly," the Marquis replied, "for reasons which I will explain to you later."

There was a silence, as if even the Duke found it difficult to know what to say.

Then from the side of the room where she had stood unnoticed came a woman.

With her head held high, she walked to the Duke's side and stood beside his chair, her eyes on the Marquis's face.

She was tall, and handsome in a somewhat masculine manner, with clear-cut features and brown hair with reddish lights in it arranged carelessly under a tartan bonnet which carried on one side of it a brooch which the Marquis recognised as the crest of the McNains.

There was really no need for the Duke to mumble in a very different tone from what he had used before:

"Lady Moraig, you have not met my son Alistair."

"No, but I have been looking forward to it," Lady Moraig said in a clear, unhesitating voice.

She held out her hand, and as the Marquis took it in his, he said a little mockingly:

"It is certainly a new experience to see a McNain in this room!"

"My brother and I thought it was time that we buried those foolish feuds which have kept us busy killing one another for hundreds of years."

"I agree with you," the Marquis replied. "Let me present my wife."

The nod Arina received from Lady Moraig made it very obvious that she was an intruder, and she knew that the Duke was already hostile because she was English.

He had obviously never for one moment envisaged that the Marquis would marry somebody so alien to the Clan and to the great majority of Scots.

But, as if he felt that this was neither the time nor the place for recrimination, the Duke rose slowly and stiffly to his feet.

"There are many of our kinsmen here who wish to meet you, Alistair."

The Marquis nodded his agreement, and the Duke moved forward a few paces with his son beside him, and all those in the room filed slowly along to be introduced and to welcome the Marquis home.

Some shook hands, some merely bowed respectfully, but the Marquis managed to have a friendly word with each man, and indeed there were many whom he remembered from the past.

While this was happening, somebody had fetched a chair for Arina and she sat down, but while another was offered to Lady Moraig, she refused it disdainfully.

Instead, she stood stiff and unsmiling a little distance from Arina, making it very obvious that she had no wish to consort with her.

When the introductions were over, the Duke made a movement as if to leave the Chieftain's Room, and the Marquis looked back and beckoned to Arina.

She jumped up hastily to join him, and as she did so Lady Moraig also approached him.

"What does it feel like to return to the fold after being away for so long?" she asked.

"I will reserve my reply for a little later," the Marquis answered evasively.

The Duke was ahead of them, and as if she refused to acknowledge that Arina was there, Lady Moraig said:

"You know that your father had a plan to unite our Clans in friendship and harmony."

"I understood that you had agreed to marry my brother!"

"Poor Ian," Lady Moraig said in a slightly softer tone, "but we must, you and I, think not only of ourselves but of our people."

"Of course," the Marquis agreed, "and I am looking forward to introducing my wife to the McNains."

His reply swept the smile from Lady Moraig's lips, and her eyes were hard as she glanced for a moment at Arina.

Then as they reached the door, instead of following the Duke, who was leading the way to the Drawing-Room, she walked down the stairs, and Arina could feel her vibrations of anger and frustration almost as if she expressed them in words of violence.

Impulsively she said in a low voice that only the Marquis could hear:

"I am . . . sorry for . . . her."

"I am grateful to you."

Her eyes met his and she knew that although Lady Moraig was not unattractive in her way, she did not compare favourably with the beautiful ladies whom Champkins had described to her as being infatuated with the Marquis.

She thought of the powder-puff by the mirror on his dressing-table, and thought to herself:

'I am sure he loved only really feminine women, which is something Lady Moraig is not.'

There was no chance of having another intimate word with the Marquis before they were in the Drawing-Room, where they were joined by the Duke's close relations.

There were a number of male cousins, and elderly and middle-aged women who Arina learnt lived nearby.

There were also one or two teenagers who stared at the Marquis wide-eyed, the boys appreciating the elegance of his fashionable clothes, the girls obviously thinking him extremely handsome.

The conversation was somewhat stilted and constrained until finally the Duke said in a somewhat ominous voice:

"I want to talk to you alone, Alistair. You had better come into the Library."

"Very well, Father," the Marquis replied, "but first I will take Arina to her bedroom so that she can rest before dinner."

"I imagine you know where you are sleeping," the Duke replied briefly.

"Of course," the Marquis agreed.

When they were in the long passage outside the Drawing-Room, Arina gave a little sigh of relief.

The last hour in the Drawing-Room, when she had been doing her best to circumvent the very curious questions of the female relatives, had been a trial that had exhausted her.

Now, however, the Marquis opened a door in the passage and they walked into a large, attractive room with a big carved four-poster bed and an open fireplace big enough to burn logs.

Arina looked round with interest.

The windows overlooked the garden and the sea beyond, and on the carpet were fur rugs made from the skins of wildcats.

It was an austere room and yet it had a majestic air about it.

The Marquis closed the door. Then he said:

411

"I must congratulate you. You came through what must have been a very trying ordeal with flying colours."

"You really mean that?" Arina asked. "I was so afraid of failing you."

"You saved me!"

"I am well aware that you would not wish to . . . marry Lady Moraig," Arina said in a small voice. "At the same time . . . I think your father . . . hates me!"

"Nevertheless, he believes you to be my wife, and there is nothing he can do about it."

"Lady Moraig was also very . . . angry," Arina went on. "Does this mean that the feud between the Clans will be intensified and you may start . . . fighting all over again?"

She sounded so upset at the prospect that the Marquis laughed.

"Of course not," he said. "We are much more civilised now than we were in the past, and I am quite certain that the elders of both Clans will in time come to respect one another and behave like human beings rather than barbarians!"

"Perhaps it would have been better for . . . everybody if you had . . . married her."

"I would rather die!" the Marquis said sharply. "Or, what would actually have happened—starve!"

He spoke so positively that Arina looked at him, and realising that he was sincere, she said:

"We must be very, very . . . careful not to be found out."

"We will be," the Marquis replied. "Now rest, and be prepared for a very formal dinner. My father dines in state."

As he spoke he went from the room, and as if they had been waiting for him to leave two maids came hurrying in to assist Arina to undress.

As the Marquis came walking back from the river, taking a short-cut towards the Castle, through the heather which was not yet in bud, he thought triumphantly that he had a great deal to boast about.

He had caught no less than four salmon since he had started fishing this morning, and he was delighted to find that he had not lost his skill even though he had not held a fishing-rod in his hand since he was twelve.

Two gillies, laden with the salmon and his rod and gaff, were walking behind him, and he moved quickly ahead of them, eager to get back to boast to Arina of how clever he had been.

'Tomorrow she must come with me,' he decided, 'and I will teach her how to fish. I am sure it is something she will enjoy.'

It was extraordinary, he thought, how Arina had managed to assimilate herself into the life of the Castle in a manner to which nobody could make any objection, not even the Duke, and apparently she was as pleased with Scotland as he was.

He thought now as he walked towards the Castle that whether he wished to admit it or not, it was his home.

Although he had never expected it and in fact had anticipated that he would hate every moment of being back, he had without effort taken up his life where it had left off fifteen years ago.

He had only to hear the Pipers waking him in the morning as they paraded up and down to feel that the years when he had been in the South were fading away like the mist on the moors.

Whatever his brain might say, he was once again a Scot, living on his own land, with his blood quickening to everything that was traditional.

The pipes, the moors, the mist, and the Clansmen greeting him were all so familiar that he could feel his whole being going out to them.

"I came expecting to hate Scotland, and I love it!" the Marquis had admitted to himself last night.

When he slept in the narrow bed in the Dressing-Room which adjoined Arina's he found himself almost ridiculously resenting the fact that he was not sleeping

413

in the great four-poster which for generations had been the bed of the Chieftain's eldest son.

But the greatest change was in his father.

At first on his arrival he had been astonished, for the Duke seemed to have shrunk and become smaller than he remembered.

Then he knew that what had really happened was that he had grown up and he was no longer frightened of his father as he had been when he was a small boy.

What was more, the Duke was now an old man, and although he was still demanding and authoritative, he was quiet and pleasant unless his authority was opposed in any way.

The Marquis had been prepared to fight him, only to find that there was no necessity for it.

"It is a great disappointment to me, Alistair," the Duke had complained, "that you have married a woman from the South, when I planned for you to take your brother's place and marry Moraig McNain."

"So Faulkner told me," the Marquis replied, "but as I am already married, such an idea is impossible."

"Of course," the Duke agreed, "but it is a pity—a great pity!"

To the Marquis's astonishment, he had left it at that, and although it was obvious that he eyed Arina warily, as if she were not trustworthy, he was not rude to her and she took her rightful place in the house.

"Everything has turned out so much better than I had expected," the Marquis told himself.

As a brace of grouse rose almost at his feet and flew away clucking, he began to look forward to the shooting which would begin in August, and he knew that the Keepers' prophecies were for big bags after good hatching.

He had expected to bewail how he was missing Ascot, his friends at White's Club, and the Balls which would be occurring every night in London.

Instead, it all seemed very far away, as if he were living on another planet.

When he rose in the morning he barely gave them a thought, but was intent on thinking of the people he would be meeting and how soon he could get to the river and start fishing.

He also found himself making plans of how he would alter the way things were done, once he was in the position of authority.

He realised that as his father was growing old, the people under him, while loyal and devoted, had grown lax and needed leadership to keep them up to the mark.

"There is a lot that needs to be done here, Champkins," he said as he was dressing.

"I've noticed that, M'Lord," Champkins replied, "but Your Lordship'll sort it all out, as Your Lordship always does."

The Marquis smiled.

Then this morning when he was leaving for the river he said to Champkins:

"You will find my brothers' clothes somewhere in the Castle. I am sure I am about the same size as Lord Colin. Find me his evening-dress, and I might wear the kilt to go fishing tomorrow."

He left the room and did not see Champkins smile, although he would not have been surprised if he had heard him mutter beneath his breath:

"Can't get away from their own blood. It always gets 'em in the end."

Arina, who had been exploring the garden on her own, realised that the shadows were growing longer, and she was sure the Marquis would soon be returning from fishing and would expect her to pour out his tea.

She hurried up the stone steps, thinking that, as she had thought when she had first seen it, the Castle was enchanted.

Everything about it was so beautiful, so exactly what a Castle should be, and she had run out of words to describe it to her mother.

Inside, when she reached the big marble Hall with its dark oak panelling hung with flags captured by the McDonons in battle, she ran up the stairs, hoping there would not be too many people for tea so that she could have the Marquis to herself.

She had learnt that the Castle was always open to any of their relatives or friends, and they would arrive at any hour of the day or night, always to be hospitably welcomed.

She went into a smaller Sitting-Room where tea was arranged on a big round table.

There was nobody there, although as Arina expected the table was loaded with baps, scones, griddle-cakes, shortbread, and ginger-biscuits, besides oatcakes, honey in the comb, and a huge pat of golden butter stamped with the McDonon crest.

She had grown used to the insignia being on anything and everything.

She heard a step behind her and turned to see the Marquis.

She was aware that the sunshine as well as the sea had already tanned his face, and she thought he looked even more handsome than he had in London.

"I was looking for you, Arina," he said. "What do you think? I caught four salmon, one of them over thirteen pounds!"

He spoke in the triumphant tone of a small boy.

"How splendid!" Arina exclaimed. "I am so glad. Can I see them?"

"They will be laid out on marble slabs in the larder downstairs," he answered. "I will show them to you after tea or tomorrow."

"You must be hungry."

She sat down automatically in front of the silver tray on which were a kettle, a tea-pot, and all the other paraphernalia of tea-making, the silver engraved with the McDonon crest.

The Marquis started to spread a griddle-cake thickly with butter, telling her as he did so how he had caught his fish, lost two others, and been broken by one after he had played it for fifteen minutes.

He sounded so enthusiastic about it all that as Arina listened to him she thought it was very different from the rather bored, supercilious manner in which he had talked when they were in London.

Nobody else arrived for tea, and they went on talking for a long time until the Marquis said:

"I had better go have a bath. I believe there are some people coming over for dinner tonight, but I cannot remember who they are."

"There seems to be a party every evening."

"Why not?" the Marquis asked. "There are plenty of servants to wait on them, and the food is good."

"Too good!" Arina laughed. "I am afraid my new gowns are getting very tight round the waist."

"That is what I want to hear," the Marquis said, "and shall I tell you that you look so much better, and it makes you very lovely."

It was a compliment Arina had not expected, and as the colour rose in her face, she looked away from him because she was shy.

"Very lovely!" the Marquis said again.

Then as Arina raised her eyes to his, it was somehow impossible for either of them to look away.

As the Marquis went to his room to change for dinner and Arina went to hers, she could hear him moving about next door and talking to Champkins, and she wished she could join in and be with the Marquis for a little while longer before people arrived for dinner.

She rang for a maid and changed quickly into a beautiful gown which was embroidered and trimmed with lace.

It was a more elaborate one than those which she usually wore, and she hoped that the Marquis would think it attractive.

As she thought of him she realised that it was quiet in the Dressing-Room, and she thought he was either taking a long time over his bath or else he was already dressed and had gone to the Drawing-Room, where they were to meet before dinner.

Because she was eager to see him, she hurried down the passage, only to find disappointingly that the Drawing-Room was empty.

Then she realised there was still half-an-hour before dinner, and she wondered whether the Marquis had gone out onto the terrace on the floor below.

She went downstairs to the stone terrace, but found again disappointingly that there was nobody there.

The sun was sinking behind the moors, its light dazzling and the sea a very deep blue.

Slowly, feeling once again enchanted by the beauty of it all, Arina walked down the stone steps into the garden.

Here the shadows had grown very much longer, the scent of the roses and stocks seemed to have intensified, and the shrubs were bright with blossoms which also scented the air.

She was just about to move towards the lawn when from the shrubs she heard a curious little whine.

She stood listening, and as the curious little whine came again and again, she wondered if it was an animal caught in a trap.

Because she could not bear to think of it suffering, she pushed aside the shrubs to seek for it, and as she did so she felt something hard strike her on the back of the head.

She gave a little cry of pain before there was darkness and she knew no more. . . .

❦

Arina slowly came back to consciousness, aware that her head hurt and it was hard to breathe.

Then she knew there was something thick over her face and she was lying on her back.

Because she was so bemused and for the moment only half-conscious, she made no movement.

Then she heard a man's voice say:

"Oi hopes ye did na bruise her. Her Ladyship said there were ta be na marks on her."

"Oi hit her where Oi were told, on th' back o' th' head," another man replied. "Ye'll see na bruising beneath th' hair."

Arina was puzzled by the voices.

Then as she was able to think more clearly, she was aware that these must be the men who had struck her down, and her intelligence told her that if she moved they might hit her again.

Vaguely, far away in the back of her mind, she recalled her father telling her how after a battle the soldiers who were wounded pretended to be dead when the scavengers came around to steal everything they possessed.

"If a wounded man tries to prevent them from taking his belongings, they kill him!" her father had said. "On one occasion, it was only by playing dead for several hours that I was able to remain alive."

Her mother had given a cry of horror, but now Arina remembered and lay very still.

At the same time, she tried frantically to understand what was happening to her, and she knew that because the men had mentioned "Her Ladyship," her kidnapping must have been on the instigation of Lady Moraig.

But if they were to kidnap her, why did they have to be so brutal?

She could still feel the aching pain at the back of her head, but she was aware that it might in fact have been worse.

Because she had wanted to look her best for the Marquis she had arranged her hair in quite an elaborate *chignon,* and the maid had secured it with hair-pins and also put on the top of it a little rosette of lace to match her gown.

It had looked very pretty, but now Arina knew that if the blow from the club, or whatever it was that had hit her, had not been cushioned by the thickness of her hair, she would not have regained consciousness so quickly.

"How far have we ta take her?" one of the men asked.

"A bit farther," the other replied, "but not too far. She was supposed ta have rowed herself out ta sea."

"That would na seem likely ta me," the other man replied, "considering she's only a wee bit o' a lassie."

"Because Her Ladyship's so good wi' an oar, she expects other women ta be th' same."

The two men laughed somewhat jeeringly, as if they did not appreciate the more Herculean feats of their Mistress.

"She's a pretty wee creature," one of the men remarked.

"A Sassenach!"

"A wooman's a wooman for a' that!" came the answer.

"That's ye're opinion, Jock, but then ye've always been one wi' th' lassies."

The two men talked in a way which told Arina that they were of a rather better class and perhaps were better educated than if they had been the ordinary rough type of Clansmen.

She was sure that if they were carrying out Lady Moraig's instruction to kidnap her and leave her in a boat out at sea, she would have chosen her most intelligent servants for the job.

Then what she had heard made her aware of exactly what was intended.

The Marquis's two brothers had died at sea when they were out fishing, and now it would appear that she also had rowed herself out from the shelter of the bay and had drowned because she had not the strength to row herself back to shore.

'I suppose they will leave me to drift endlessly on the tide,' she thought, then had a different idea of what the men intended to do.

There was only one man rowing, and the splash of the oars seemed to grow slower and slower until finally he stopped rowing, and his accomplice asked:

"D'ye think this is far enough?"

"Oi reckon so, an' there's a nice bit o' wind gettin' up. 'Twill be rough in a short while."

"Naw, wait a wee bit. Supposing she comes round an' struggles?"

"She'll na do that," the other man said, "but if she does, Oi'll gi' her another hit on th' head."

"Ye'll bruise her!"

Arina imagined that the man who had already spoken shrugged his shoulders.

"By th' time her body's washed ashore, they'll na be lookin' for bruises."

With a little gasp Arina suddenly realised what they were about to do. She could almost see it being planned in Lady Moraig's mind.

She had rowed herself from the Castle because it was a calm, pleasant evening, the boat had upset or else the bung had been knocked out of the bottom of it, and she had drowned.

She wondered frantically if after she had been thrown into the water it would be feasible for her to save herself by swimming.

If after leaving her they became aware that she was in fact a strong swimmer, she was afraid that they would return and hit her again, and, rendered unconscious, she would drown.

"What must I do? Oh, Papa, save me as you saved me before!" she prayed silently.

She felt that her father must hear her, and as he had sent the Marquis to save her mother, he would send him now to save her.

But she had the terrifying feeling that the Marquis would not know of her disappearance until it was time for them to go in to dinner, and even then it might be a long time before anybody would suspect that she was in a boat out at sea.

Whenever she had talked to the Marquis about her life in the country, she had told him how she loved riding.

But there had been no reason to explain that unlike most girls of her age, she could swim because there was a large lake near their cottage. From the time she had been very small, she and her father had swum in it whenever the water was warm enough.

Now she was hoping that her evening-gown would not impede the movement of her legs, and what was more important than anything else was to prevent the men from seeing that she could stay alive in the water.

"Let's get on wi' it!" one of the men said suddenly.

"All reet, all reet!" the other replied irritably. "No point in bein' in a hurry."

"Oi want ta be awa' hame," the other said. "Oi want ma dinner, and we've got a lang way ta go."

The way he spoke told Arina that he was not returning along the coast next to the Castle but across the sea to where the mainland jutted out, which she was aware was the land of the McNains.

"First take th' blanket frae her face," ordered the man who was rowing.

Arina stiffened and lay very still.

She felt the thick blanket over her head that had made it hard to breathe being lifted away, and she knew that both the men were staring at her as she lay still at their feet.

"She's still unconscious," one of them said. "Now get into th' other boat, Jock. Then Oi'll chuck the oars overboard an' pull out th' bung."

"She's a pretty wee thing," Jock remarked.

"That's na yer business. Leave the fish ta appreciate her."

Arina was aware that Jock was pulling another boat, which they must have been towing, up to the side of the one they were in.

He climbed into it, and as the man with the oars let them drop into the sea, Arina felt one of them bang against the side of the boat in which she was lying.

Then the oarsman was groping beneath her feet.

He pulled out the bung, and instantly she was aware of the water beginning to seep in.

Then Jock must have assisted him into the other boat.

"Now get us hame," he said roughly, "an' hurry up aboot it. Oi want ma dinner. Let's get on wi' it!"

Arina had the feeling that he might be having a last glance at her, and only when the sound of the four oars in the water moved away and there was silence except for the lap of the waves did she open her eyes.

The water was rising very quickly and now the boat was half-full, but still she did not move, feeling it cold and wet against her body.

When she knew it would soon cover her face, she first raised her head, then cautiously sat up, feeling as if she were in a bath of cold water.

She looked in the direction of the other boat, and seeing that it was now only a pin-point in the distance, she doubted if the men could see her.

Then she looked back towards the Castle, in the direction from which they had come.

With a sinking of her heart she realised that it was much farther away than she had anticipated, and she had been carried out from the shelter of the bay into the open sea.

Nevertheless, she knew it was possible for her to swim to shore if she took it steadily and did not become exhausted or frozen from the cold water.

'Perhaps I will die,' she thought, 'and that would be terrible for Mama.'

She knew it would also upset the Marquis if she drowned, because that would put him under pressure to marry for the Clan's sake, and she was also certain that Lady Moraig wanted him as a man.

'Of course she loves him because he is so handsome,' Arina thought, 'but she is bad and wicked to have attempted to . . . murder me . . . and the Marquis would be unhappy with . . . her.'

Then she knew, and found it incredible and quite extraordinary at such a moment, that she loved the Marquis.

He had saved her mother and now she must save him.

423

It was not only because she could not bear to think of him being married to a woman like Lady Moraig, who was not good enough for him in any way, but also because she wanted to be with him as long as he wanted her.

'I love . . . him! I . . . love him!' she thought.

If she died now, her love would be pointless, because she would have failed to help him as she had promised him she would.

She looked again at the shore and it seemed even farther away than it had a moment before.

She knew this was because the sun had sunk, dusk was falling, and without the light from the moors, the Castle seemed shrouded in mist.

"Help me, Papa, help me!" Arina prayed.

As the water came a little higher in the boat, she climbed out into the sea.

CHAPTER SEVEN

The water was very cold, and as Arina swam and swam she began to feel as if it were impossible to move her legs anymore or bring her hands back to her breast.

She sank lower in the water and felt the sea splash over her mouth and nose.

"I . . . I cannot do . . . it!" she cried. "I . . . can go no farther!"

She tried to see how far it was to the shore, but either her eyes were too weak or it was too dark. As she shut them again she felt that she had miles farther to go before she reached safety, and it was too far.

Then, almost as if she heard her father's voice speaking, she heard the words ring in her ears:

"If you die, the Marquis will have to marry Lady Moraig, and he too will be destroyed!"

Slowly the idea became instilled in her mind, and it was now not only because Lady Moraig would be unattractive to him but also because she was a murderess, and if she murdered once, she could murder again.

"I must . . . save him . . . I must!" Arina told herself.

Again her head was too low in the water and it swelled over her so that she could not breathe.

She felt as if her legs were weighted down with bricks, and her arms were so tired that she could not thrust them forward.

"I love . . . you!" she cried to the Marquis. "But . . . I can no longer . . . help you!"

Then even as she felt herself sinking, her knees grated against something hard and at the same time her head fell forward and her face was buried in sand and sea, and she lapsed into unconsciousness.

Then roughly a voice woke her and she felt herself pulled forward.

Somebody was shouting, a man's voice. She could not understand what he said, but he was shouting and dragging her at the same time, and she thought perhaps Lady Moraig's men were going to try to kill her again.

Then she was turned over on her back and she thought that she must be dying and this was the end.

She felt herself drifting away again into an impenetrable darkness, only to be brought back to life when somebody put an arm under her shoulders and lifted her head.

Even as she was touched she knew who it was, and her heart leapt.

"Arina! Arina!"

She heard him calling her, and because she loved him she turned her face against his shoulder. He was there, he was holding her close, and she was safe!

❧

"Another sip, M'Lady," a voice said in a determined tone.

"No . . . no," Arina said weakly. "It is . . . horrible!"

"It'll warm ye, M'Lady. Ye were cold as an icicle when they brought ye in."

She was not cold now, Arina thought, with a hot-water-bottle at her feet and another at her side. Although they were made of stone, she could feel the warmth seeping through her body, just as the neat whisky someone had made her drink was burning its way down her throat and into her chest.

It was hard to open her eyes, but she managed it, and now she could see the carved wooden canopy of the bed overhead, and on the other side of the room a fire was burning in the big open grate.

She knew where she was, she was alive, she had saved the Marquis, and there was no need to go on fighting anymore.

It had been a long, long swim, but she had managed it.

She shut her eyes again, and as she did so, she heard the Housekeeper say:

"Her Ladyship's asleep, M'Lord, but she's all right. Gawd must have saved her."

"I think she saved herself," the Marquis answered quietly.

Arina wanted to tell him that she had done it for him, but it was impossible to make the effort, and she drifted away again, warm and safe, into a dreamless sleep.

❧

She woke and knew that she had slept for a long time, for the night was past and now it was day.

The curtains were drawn back and the sunshine was coming through the windows.

She stirred, and instantly the Housekeeper, who had looked after her last night, was beside her.

"Are ye awake, M'Lady?"

Arina nodded but it was difficult to find her voice.

"What Your Ladyship wants is sommat to eat," the Housekeeper said briskly, "and ye've had a real good night's rest."

Arina stirred as if she wanted to be certain that her arms and legs, which had felt numb and cold as if they did not belong to her, were still there.

Then as the Housekeeper bustled from the room she lay looking up at the carved canopy on which inevitably was the insignia of the McDonons.

She was thanking God and her father for having brought her to safety.

Then with a little shiver she thought that Lady Moraig might try again, and she thought perhaps she would be wise to leave soon, so that she would not be a trouble and an encumbrance to the Marquis.

He could still pretend that he was married, but she would not be there to be stalked by Lady Moraig as if she were a wild animal, and hated by the Duke because she was English.

'If I leave . . . perhaps I shall . . . never see him again,' she thought.

Then, because she was so weak and because she loved him, tears ran down her cheeks.

❦

Later, after Arina had eaten and slept and eaten again, she felt so much better that she no longer wished to stay in bed.

The Marquis had not come to see her and she suspected that he had gone fishing.

Because she wanted to know for certain, when the Housekeeper came to see how she was, she asked:

"Where is the Marquis?"

"He should be hame soon, M'Lady. He went fishin' this morning while ye were still asleep, but I knows His Lordship'll be coming to see ye as soon as he returns."

The Housekeeper left the room and Arina got out of bed to go to the dressing-table and brush her hair. Then she looked at her face in the mirror.

She had expected to look haggard and strained after what had happened yesterday, making her face lined and ugly.

Instead, her eyes seemed very large and bright, her skin very white, and with her hair falling over her shoulders she would have been insincere if she had not known that she looked attractive.

As if reassured by her reflection, she went back to bed, aware that she felt a little shaky on her legs, and waited.

After a while there was a knock on the door, then without waiting for an answer the Marquis came in.

Her eyes lit up at the sight of him, then she gave a little gasp, for it was the first time she had ever seen him wearing the kilt. She thought that even with the plain sporran and ordinary tweed jacket with leather buttons, he looked magnificent.

He walked to the bedside to take her hand in both of his.

"I do not have to ask if you are feeling better," he said in his deep voice. "I can see that you are."

"Much . . . much better. In fact there is no need for me to be so . . . lazy and . . . stay in bed."

"You must take care of yourself."

She had the strange feeling that while their lips were saying one thing, their eyes said something else.

The Marquis seated himself on the mattress facing her and asked:

"Are you well enough to tell me what happened?"

Arina felt shy. She felt it was somehow embarrassing to tell him that the woman had tried to murder her because she wanted him.

Then, as if the Marquis thought it would make things easier, he said:

"I do not believe for a moment that you rowed yourself out to sea."

"It . . . it was . . . two men," Arina answered. "I went . . . into the garden. I was looking . . . for you."

The Marquis's eyes were on her face, but he did not interrupt.

She went on to tell him how she had thought she heard an animal crying in the shrubs, that she had been hit on the back of the head, and that when she had regained consciousness she was lying in the bottom of a boat.

"Your head is all right now?" the Marquis asked quickly.

"There is only a very slight bruise," Arina answered, "because I had arranged my hair with great care so as to look elegant for . . ."

She stopped, knowing that she had been about to say something too revealing.

It was in fact difficult to speak naturally while the Marquis was still holding her hand in his.

Because he was touching her, she could feel a strange feeling like little shafts of sunshine running up her arms and into her breasts.

She knew it was love and thought that just to look at him made her heart beat so violently that she was afraid he would be aware of it.

She could imagine nothing more humiliating than for the Marquis to know that she had fallen in love with him, when in order to save her mother she was playing the role he had asked of her.

'I must be very, very careful,' Arina thought to herself.

Quickly, her words falling over one another, she told the Marquis what she had heard the men saying while she was lying in the boat.

When she repeated the way in which they had spoken of "Her Ladyship," she knew that he stiffened and his fingers tightened on hers.

Without stopping, she described how they had taken away the bung and rowed off, and when the boat had become nearly full of water and was sinking she had started to swim back towards the Castle.

"How could you swim so far?" the Marquis asked.

"I used to swim in a lake with my father when we lived in the country," Arina replied, "but never such a long distance . . . or in a cold sea."

"It was very, very brave of you, and I know of no other woman who would have been so clever and so courageous."

"I . . . I had to save . . . you," Arina said without thinking.

"Me?" the Marquis questioned. "Or yourself?"

"I do not . . . matter," Arina replied, "but I knew that if I . . . died, your father would force you to . . . marry Lady Moraig . . . and it would make . . . you unhappy."

"Would that have worried you?" the Marquis asked softly.

Arina drew in her breath, feeling a little wildly that she wanted his happiness more than anything else in the world. It was something she could not give him, but she could at least save him from being positively miserable.

She did not answer, and after a moment the Marquis said:

"I want you to tell me, Arina, why you were worried in case I should be unhappy."

"You . . . you have been so . . . kind to me that I want to . . . help you."

"You have helped me already, and when I picked you up off the beach and you turned your head against my shoulder, I felt that you were happy to be with me."

Because his voice was very low and deep, and yet at the same time there was a pleading note in it which she had never heard before, Arina's fingers tightened on his.

"I . . . I thought I was . . . dead," she said in a whisper, "but when you . . . touched me I came . . . alive again."

The Marquis did not answer, and because his silence was rather strange, she looked at him.

Then as their eyes met she felt herself quiver with a feeling she had never known before, which seemed to be rising within her, and making her feel that it was impossible to breathe.

"I may be quite wrong," the Marquis said after a moment, "but I have the feeling, Arina, that you love me."

Because his eyes were holding hers captive, it was impossible not to tell the truth.

"Yes . . . I . . . love you!" Arina whispered. "I love you . . . and I want to . . . help you . . . but I will not be a . . . nuisance, and as . . . soon as you . . . want me to leave, I will do so . . . as I promised . . . without making any . . . fuss."

"That will not be for at least a million years," the Marquis answered quietly.

As he spoke he bent forward and his lips were on hers.

For a moment she could not believe it was happening. Then a rapture seemed to invade her whole body, and it was so vivid, so insistent, that it was like a streak of lightning.

She felt as if the Marquis gave her the sunshine that was outside and carried her high over the moors behind them and into the sky.

He slipped his arm round her to hold her close against him while he kissed her, and she felt that after all she had been through, she was in a Heaven that was Divine, and so utterly and completely wonderful that it would be an agony to leave it.

Then she knew that this was what she had always wanted.

It was the love her mother had had for her father and he for her, and nothing else was of any importance except a love that filled the world, the sky, and the sea, and there was nothing else but love.

The Marquis raised his head and said:

"I love you!"

"H-how can you?" Arina asked. "There are so many beautiful women whom you . . . could love."

"The 'beautiful women,' as you call them," he said with a smile, "are all far away and forgotten, and when I saw you lying on the shore and thought you were dead, I knew that what I felt for you was different from anything I have ever felt before."

"You . . . you love me! You really love . . . me?"

"It will take me a long time, as I have said, at least a million years, to tell you how much."

"I . . . I cannot . . . believe it! You are so magnificent, so kind, so . . . wonderful! I thought you were a messenger from God, sent to save Mama, and not a man who would . . . love me."

The Marquis smiled.

"I am a man, and I find you so alluring, so beautiful, and so very, very exciting, my darling, that I cannot believe I am so fortunate as to find now what I have always been seeking."

He pulled her a little closer as he said:

"Just as you told me we were setting out on an adventure like Odysseus and Jason, like them I have found what I sought."

"Was it . . . love?" Arina asked.

"Love!" the Marquis replied firmly. "Real love, and a love which made you see me as a Knight."

"That is what . . . you have always . . . been."

"That is something you will make me in the future, or rather, a good Chieftain to my Clan."

Arina drew in her breath.

"You mean . . . ?"

"I mean that I am going to stay here," the Marquis interrupted, "and live the life to which I belong and look after my people."

His lips were against the softness of her cheek as he said:

"I think you already know that I cannot do that properly without you to help me."

"Are you sure . . . really sure . . . that you . . . want me?"

"Very, very sure."

Arina drew in her breath. Then she said:

"I have something to tell you . . ."

"And I have a lot to tell you," the Marquis interrupted, "but I know that my father is anxious to see you. Do you think you are well enough to come down to dinner? You can go back to bed immediately afterwards."

"Of course I am well enough," Arina said. "I want to be with . . . you."

The Marquis did not answer. He merely kissed her again.

She could feel his heart beating against hers and that she could excite him seemed the most wonderful thing she could ever imagine.

A knock on the door made the Marquis move away from her, and the Housekeeper came in.

"I am glad you are here, Mrs. McDonon," the Marquis said. "Her Ladyship is coming down to dinner, but I promise we will not keep her up too long."

"She's not to get over-tired, Master Alistair."

The Marquis laughed.

"If she does, you will doubtless scold me as you used to do when I tore my clothes or stole the apples out of your Sitting-Room."

He did not wait for the Housekeeper to reply but went through the communicating door into the Dressing–Room.

"He was always an awful mischievous laddie!" Mrs. McDonon exclaimed.

She talked of the Marquis's escapades when he was young all the time she was helping Arina to dress, and she thought how wonderful it would be if she could ever have a son who, like his father, would be mischievous in the great Castle which was a perfect playground for children.

When she was ready, she realised, because she had been listening to what Mrs. McDonon was saying rather than thinking about herself, that she was wearing a very lovely evening-gown which made her look like a bride.

It was a gown which she had not even seen before, because it had arrived at the last moment just before they left for Tilbury, and she thought perhaps the Marquis might think she was over-dressed.

But when he came through the communicating door she saw by the expression in his eyes and the look on his face what he thought of her.

If she looked smart, so did he, and in his evening-dress with a lace jabot at his neck and the silver buttons on his coat polished until they shone like jewels, he was so magnificent that she felt no man could be so handsome or so overwhelmingly attractive.

His sporran was as elaborate as the one the Duke wore, and the Cairngorm on top of his *skean dhu,* which was worn in his hose, sparkled like a star.

As they walked towards the centre of the Castle the Marquis said:

"I want to tell you how beautiful you are and how much I love you!"

Arina slipped her hand into his.

"I was . . . trying to find words to tell you how handsome you look . . . wearing the kilt."

"It is a good thing that you admire me as much as I admire you," the Marquis smiled, "Otherwise I should be jealous."

Arina gave a little laugh.

"I hope you . . . will be . . . then you will . . . know what I would be . . . feeling."

It was impossible to say any more, for one of the servants approached the Marquis with some letters on a silver salver.

"The post has just arrived, M'Lord."

The Marquis took the letters without much interest, then as they walked into the Drawing-Room to find it empty he opened one quickly and started to read it.

Arina stood in front of the fireplace, thinking how impressive the room was, and yet so different from any Drawing-Room in the South.

The ceiling was very high, the windows set in stone were diamond-paned, and the walls were hung with portraits of previous Chieftains.

Some of the furniture was French and she knew it dated from the time when Mary Queen of Scots had brought the French influence to Scotland.

The Marquis looked up from his letter.

"I have some good news for you, my darling."

"Good news?"

The Marquis glanced down at the letter in his hand.

"When I told my secretary in London to pay the hundred pounds that was owing to your mother's Surgeon, I told him I wished to know immediately the result of the operation, and that the information must come directly to me in case it was bad news."

"Mama is . . . all right?"

"The operation has been completely successful, and your mother is recovering much quicker than the Surgeon dared to hope!"

Arina clasped her hands together. Then she gave a little cry of sheer happiness and flung herself against the Marquis.

"It is all due to . . . you! If you had not given us the money, Mama would have . . . died."

Her voice broke on the words, and there were tears in her eyes, but they were tears of happiness.

The Marquis held her very close against him.

"I am so glad, so very glad, my darling."

"I am sure it was Papa who sent . . . you to us, and now Mama can get . . . well, and perhaps find happiness again."

"We will make her happy," the Marquis promised.

Arina was about to reply when there was a step in the doorway and the Duke came into the Drawing-Room.

Feeling a little embarrassed, she moved away from the Marquis, knowing his father had seen her in his arms.

The Duke joined them at the hearth-rug and Arina curtseyed.

"You are better?" the Duke asked in a more kindly tone than he had used to her before.

"Yes, thank you, Your Grace, much better."

"I understand you were very brave."

He did not wait for Arina to reply but said:

"Outside is the man who found you as you reached the shore. He is an old man, but his eyes were bright enough to see you when you collapsed in the shallow

435

water. You were lying face-down, and if he had not saved you by pulling you up onto dry land, you might have drowned."

Arina gave a little murmur and felt the Marquis's hand touch hers.

"I told Malcolm McDonon to come here so that you could thank him," the Duke said.

"Yes, of course, I would like to do that."

The Duke walked ahead and she and the Marquis followed.

Standing outside the Drawing-Room at the top of the stairs was an old Clansman with a grey beard, nervously twisting his bonnet as he waited for them.

He touched his forehead respectfully as the Duke came up to him.

"I have brought the Marchioness to meet you, Malcolm," the Duke said slowly, "and I have told her it was your quick eyes, which are those of a stalker, that saw her on the beach and saved her life."

The old man murmured something, and the Duke said to Arina:

"He understands if you speak slowly to him, but he himself can speak only the Gaelic."

Arina held out her hand and Malcolm McDonon said in Gaelic:

"I am very glad to have been of service to Your Ladyship."

Arina understood, and without thinking she answered him in his own language:

"Tapadh Leat Tha Ni Glé Thaiwgeal," which meant: "Thank you. I am very grateful."

Only when she had spoken did she see the delight in Malcolm's face and become aware of the astonishment in the Duke's and the Marquis's.

There was a moment's silence, then the Duke gave Malcolm McDonon an envelope which Arina guessed contained money.

He thanked him in Gaelic, and as he walked down the stairs the Duke looked penetratingly at Arina.

"You speak Gaelic?" he asked sharply.

"A . . . little."

"Who taught you?"

She hesitated, then told the truth.

"My mother."

"How can your mother know Gaelic?"

"She . . . she is . . . Scottish."

Arina spoke in a low voice and was obviously embarrassed.

Then the Marquis, as if he could not control his curiosity, enquired:

"Why did you not tell me?"

She looked up at him and answered in a voice he could barely hear:

"I . . . I thought you might be . . . angry."

"Angry? Why should I be angry?"

She did not answer, and after a moment, as if he guessed the answer, he enquired:

"Who is your mother?"

She put out her hands as if she would hold on to him, then dropped them to her sides.

"My . . . mother," she faltered, "is a . . . McNain."

The Marquis seemed unable to speak, and the Duke exclaimed:

"A McNain? Why was I not told? Why have you been so secretive about it?"

As if it was easier to answer him than the Marquis, Arina replied:

"My mother ran away with my father, and because he was English, my grandfather, who was the . . . Chieftain of the McNains, was furious and refused to have anything . . . more to do with . . . her."

The Duke stared at Arina as if he could hardly believe what he was hearing. Then he said:

"Come into the Drawing-Room."

As he spoke, Arina knew he was aware that the servants at the foot of the stairs could hear what they were saying.

The Duke walked ahead, and as Arina followed him obediently, the Marquis took her hand in his, and she knew that he was not angry but supporting and loving her.

She held her head up and, speaking clearly and calmly, gave the Duke the explanation for which he was waiting.

"Although my mother was deeply hurt by her father's anger and his refusal to have anything more to do with her because she had married an Englishman, she and Papa were so happy together that it did not really matter."

"Your grandfather was the Earl of Nain?" the Duke asked sharply.

"Yes, Your Grace, but after she ran away, Mama never used her . . . title."

"He was a good Chieftain," the Duke said, "but he loathed us almost as much as he loathed the English!"

The Marquis laughed.

"That was the attitude of all the McNains, as far back as I can remember. What are you going to do about Lady Moraig?"

The Duke's lips tightened.

"She will be dealt with by the elders of her Clan and sent away."

"Can you arrange that?"

"The Chieftain will do so when I tell him what happened, and the men who carried out her orders will be punished."

The Marquis felt his father had more to say, so he waited.

"Lady Moraig is only a half-sister of the present Earl," the Duke explained, "and they have never cared for each other. But as Chieftain he is eager that there should be peace between our people, and that problem is already solved, Alistair, for you have married a McNain. I am sure also that he would welcome home Arina's mother, his sister, if she will return to her family."

"Do you really mean that?" Arina cried. "I know it would make Mama very happy, for after Papa's death I know she often longed for her own family."

"That is what we will give her as soon as she is well enough to travel," the Marquis said quietly.

Because she felt so happy, Arina forgot that the Duke was there and pressed her cheek against his shoulder.

With a note of laughter in his voice he said:

"You see, Father, after all my misdeeds and the years which as far as you were concerned I spent in the wilderness, I have come back doing the right thing and bringing you what you had not expected—exactly the wife you wanted me to marry."

There was no need for words.

The Duke merely put his hand on his son's shoulder with a gesture that was very eloquent.

Although the dinner had been a long one, as there were quite a number of guests, and the Piper who played round the table at the end of the meal had played two extra tunes which Arina knew were to celebrate her escape from death, she was not tired.

However, she had gone to bed immediately dinner was finished, and Mrs. McDonon had helped her to undress and left a candle alight by the big four-poster bed, and there was a log fire burning in the fireplace.

"There's a chill wind coming frae the sea tonight, M'Lady," she said as she looked out. "Twill be a miracle if ye don't catch cold after all ye've been through."

Arina did not answer but lay back against the pillows, thinking how warm and comfortable she was and so happy that she felt as if little flames from the fire were moving inside her, lighting her whole body.

She was waiting, and it was less than thirty minutes later when the communicating door opened.

The Marquis came into the room, and now he was no longer wearing Highland dress but a long velvet robe which she had never seen before but which she thought became him equally well.

He walked towards the bed and she realised there was a strange light in his eyes that made her feel shy and yet at the same time wildly excited.

She held out her hands towards him.

"I was sure . . . you would come to . . . say good-night," she murmured.

The Marquis sat down as he had earlier in the day, facing her on the mattress.

"Good-night?" he questioned. "I think, darling, you have forgotten something."

She looked puzzled.

"What . . . could I have forgotten . . . except to thank you over and over . . . again?"

"You have thanked me enough already."

"Then what can I have . . . forgotten?"

"That we are married!" the Marquis said in his deep voice.

Arina's eyes dropped before his.

"You said it was only . . . pretence."

"I said that when I was behaving like an Englishman and our contract was English. In Scotland, we have declared ourselves to be man and wife in front of witnesses, and we are legally married by the laws of this country."

Arina felt as if every word he spoke was an exaltation of joy rising up into the sky.

"I have today already written to Edinburgh to register our marriage," he added.

As if she thought it was too wonderful to be true, Arina asked:

"You are . . . sure? Quite sure . . . that is what you want?"

"I am quite sure," the Marquis replied, "and that is what I intend to have! You are mine, Arina, my wife, now and forever, and I will never let you go!"

She thought he would put his arms round her, but instead he waited for a moment. Then he said:

"You know how much I want you, not only with my body but with my mind, my heart, and my soul. But you have been through a terrible experience, and if you wish I will just say good-night to you and leave you to rest."

Arina knew that only a man who was an idealist and the Knight she believed him to be could be so understanding.

Because she could find no words to tell him so, she could only hold out both her arms and pull him towards her. . . .

꧁꧂

A long time later, when the fire was only a golden glow and the flames had died down, the Marquis said:

"I wish there were words in which I could tell you what it means to be here with you in my own home, on my own land, surrounded by the people who love and respect me and whom I will serve as long as I live."

"That is just how I want you to feel," Arina answered.

He drew her closer to him, feeling the softness of her body and knowing that only to touch her was to be aware that he touched the perfection he had always sought in a woman.

"How can I have been so lucky as to have found you?" he asked.

"I am sure you will think it is a . . . strange thing to say, but it was Papa who guided me when I was so . . . desperate and who sent me first to Lady Beverley and in some magical way arranged that you should overhear my conversation with her."

Arina paused. Then she said:

"Only a man with the real instincts of kindness could have helped me as you did."

"It was not only your father but your prayers, my darling, which told me what to do."

As the Marquis spoke he thought it was a strange thing for him to say and to believe.

Yet, he had known ever since his return to the Castle that the supercilious cynicism that had governed the way he thought and talked with his friends at White's and with the women who came and went in his life had vanished.

But now he thought to himself that it was impossible in Scotland to be anything but honest.

He knew that just as Arina had anticipated that the beauty of the Castle and the moors would lift his mind from everything that was small and petty, they had in fact made him bigger in himself than he had ever been in the past.

Now, for the first time, he could understand his father's air of omnipotence and his desire not only for the greatness of the Clan but also for the greatness of Scotland.

He turned his head to look down at Arina and thought in the light of the dying fire that nobody could look more lovely or more spiritual and that she was different from every other woman he had ever known.

He could see her eyes looking at him adoringly, and he told himself he would never fail her and vowed in the future to live up to her ideals.

A falling log made the flames in the fire leap for a moment and illuminate both the Marquis's face and Arina's, and as they looked at each other instinctively their bodies moved closer.

"I love you!" he said.

"I did not know that love could be so wonderful . . . I feel as if we journeyed together through the stars to a Heaven where there is only . . . love."

The way Arina spoke was very moving, and the Marquis's lips touched her cheek before he asked:

"Is that what I made you feel?"

"That, and so much more. But how can I put into words the . . . ecstasy that is . . . God, and yet is me at the same time?"

"My precious little love!" the Marquis exclaimed.

"I have made . . . you happy?"

"So happy that there are no words for what we feel for each other. It is an ecstasy and at the same time very human, because I can touch you and know that you are mine, not only as a woman but part of my very blood."

"Because I am a Scot."

"As I am, and our children will be, and their children after that."

The Marquis paused before he said:

"How could I ever have imagined that I could escape from Scotland and what it means to those who are born here, in whose blood runs an instinct that raises them from human to the Divine?"

"That is . . . what I . . . feel," Arina said breathlessly.

"We feel the same, and we are the same," the Marquis said. "We are one person, my darling."

She put her arm round his neck to draw him closer still, and as she did so she was aware that just as the flames were flickering over the logs, so flames were flickering in them both.

It was ecstatic and at the same time so intense that it was a pain as well as a pleasure.

"I want you!" the Marquis said.

"I love . . . you!" Arina replied. "Oh, darling, please love me . . . please make me . . . yours . . . so that as you say . . . we are one person."

The Marquis's lips came down on hers and she felt his heart beating against her breast.

Then he was carrying her high over the moors and up into the sky, and as he made her his, they reached a special Heaven where there was only the Divine Love, which is Eternal.

ABOUT THE AUTHOR

DAME BARBARA CARTLAND, the world's best known and bestselling author of romantic fiction, is also an historian, playwright, lecturer, political speaker and television personality. She has now written over six hundred and twenty-two books and has the distinction of holding *The Guinness Book of Records* title of the world's bestselling author, having sold over six hundred and fifty million copies of her books all over the world.

Barbara Cartland was invested by Her Majesty The Queen as a Dame of the Order of the British Empire in 1991, is a Dame of Grace of St. John of Jerusalem, and was one of the first women in one thousand years ever to be admitted to the Chapter General. She is President of the Hertfordshire Branch of The Royal College of Midwives, and is President and Founder in 1964 of the National Association for Health.

Miss Cartland lives in England at Camfield Place, Hatfield, Hertfordshire.